Copyright © 2021 Luke R. Harris

All rights reserved

The characters and events portrayed in this book are fictitious. Any similarity to real persons, living or dead, is coincidental and not intended by the author.

No part of this book may be reproduced, or stored in a retrieval system, or transmitted in any form or by any means, electronic, mechanical, photocopying, recording, or otherwise, without express written permission of the publisher.

ISBN: 9798589509427

Cover design by: Luke R. Harris
Library of Congress Control Number: 2018675309
Printed in the United States of America

Dedication for Nightmares by Luke R. Harris

This book is dedicated to the resilient, enduring women who have blessed my life. To my mother, my mother-in-law, my stepmothers, to my sisters, to my daughters, and to my loving wife. All have taught me the strength and power of being steadfast, stoic, and stable in seeking the finish line of life. I am especially grateful to my wife for her never-ending encouragement, and unconditional love to help me to make my dreams a reality. Thanks for my amazing daughters and I dedicate this book to them, to Jasmine, Jacqueline, Jezikah, and Jenevieve.

You will always be in my heart.

<u>The Dream Diaries</u>

Volume One

NightMares

By
Luke R. Harris

Visit https://www.thedreamdiariescom.wixsite.com/website

Table Of Contents

Prologue

Entry #1   Grandma's Old Diary
Entry #2   Death
Entry #3   Denial
Entry #4   Burial
Entry #5   Questions
Entry #6   Last Will & Testament
Entry #7   More Questions
Entry #8   What Am I?
Entry #9   The Raven
Entry #10   My Birthday
Entry #11   Training
Entry #12   Knowledge of Power
Entry #13   Life is a Dream
Entry #14   Only in Dreams
Entry #15   Daydreams
Entry #16   Nightmares
Entry #17   My first Haunt
Entry #18   My first Hunt
Entry #19   The Price of Power
Entry #1   Revolver: What goes around comes around

Prologue

Dear Diary   September 7th

    Michael was supposed to contact me tonight. I stayed up waiting but he never did. I'm worried; I don't like it when he's gone this long on his damned hunting trips. I fell asleep by the phone in the study; I was looking up more information on the meaning of one of my nightmares.

    The strange thing was that I woke up in my bed with mud on my bare feet and blood on my face. Think I must have gone outside in the rain to cry and pray for my husband. That would explain the mud, but the blood I can't explain. I recall most of my dream, yet something doesn't feel right. I don't know how I got hurt.

    In the dream I was in a dark jungle. I couldn't tell if I was searching for someone or if I was being chased. There was a noise from the bushes like the snort of a pig, only it was deeper and hungry. I remember throwing a stick towards the noise and the beast screamed out in agony. I must have hit it and that's when I began to run.

    The beast was chasing me through the thicker parts of the jungle, nearly catching me at times, yet I grew weary of running. I fell to the ground exhausted; the blood curdling roars of the beast conjured up images of the most horrible things. I saw family and friends being torn apart by fear. I witnessed the deaths of my daughter with her husband and children; they were viciously crushed in their car by a drunk driver. I lay there on the jungle floor panicking, not knowing if this was the future I was seeing or just my fears haunting me.

Then the beast had me in its grip. Its head was like a wild boar, but its body was more human than animal. Its rough hands were tightening around my throat. I tried to scream but I was suffocating on the stench of its repulsive breath. I felt my eyes watering and my strength giving out. I couldn't move to save my life and the beast was sucking my breath away. The last thing I remember is the sound of a gunshot or a thunderclap before I ultimately blacked out in terror.

I was screaming for Michael when I woke, it burned my throat every time I screamed. I went to the bathroom to splash some cool water on my face, and then I saw the mirror. I had blood trickling from my eyes like tears and strange bruises on my neck. I searched through my Diary on Dreams or Nightmares for hours after. Nothing in the Diary has given me the answers I sought. I need to know if one can die from dreaming of Death. I need to learn to conquer my fears and control my Nightmares before they destroy me.

Eternally Waiting,

Lucia

Grandma's Old Diary

"The last thing that she would ever do would be to leave me this Diary."

The strange thing about it was every time I filled a page with entries, a new one would appear, yet the book itself never seemed to increase in size. I discovered this because she had left the Diary almost finished, with the exception of the last page.

Grandma wrote: "I am tired of running from... ...*it* every night."

I could only assume what "It" was. By the time we moved in with Grandma Lucia Linda Lamia, she was practically bedridden due to lung cancer. I had been helping her the best I could to be a replacement for her unwanted nurses that would care for her. The doctors gave her six months to live.

Ha, what do they know? Unfortunately, this time they were right. We had been living with Grandma a few months since our parents' death. We had gone to visit Grandma in the hospital, that was when the accident had happened. After their death, after their funeral and after we were allowed to be with Grandma, she needed help to stay alive. And after seeing Grandma in the hospital, all hooked-up to hose to help her breathe, that's when *I* was trying to quit smoking. I figured I'd rather not go out like that. No one should die before their time is up.

I didn't think that this ninety-year-old woman could "run" from anything at all; maybe go on brisk walks, but never run. She stayed in her room for the most part. She hardly ever left. "It" must have been in reference to her cancer, or something else. I decided that I would keep reading the Diary, but I doubted if I'd ever find out what "It" was.

The night before Grandma "Lu-lu" passed away, she invited me into her room. The first thing I noticed was the smell. No, she wasn't dead, yet. It just smelled like a mixture of decaying flowers and cigarette smoke.

I guessed she had let all the "get well soon" bouquets just wither and die. Every time I came to check on her, I could faintly catch the scent of roses and gardenias through the cloud of nicotine in the room.

Oh yeah, she never followed the doctor's order to quit smoking. She said it helped her to think, to calm her nerves. The light from the autumn sunset had already begun to fade outside her windows. Lu-lu was lighting her ancient oil lamp on her nightstand with the embers of her cigarette as I entered.

She didn't like to use electricity on account that "It could jump outta the walls and bite ya in the rear end!"

A fact she so often reminded us of when my brother, my sister and I would come to visit in the summer and whine about her not owning a TV. This was before my parents had died. But this time we were not visiting; we were permanent guests.

My late parents, oddly enough, had no other living relatives. My dad was in foster care most of his life. Mom, well, she was an only child. Doctors told Lu-lu that she shouldn't try having children after a couple of miscarriages. They declared it a miracle when my mom was born. Lu-lu had my mom's picture on almost every wall in her house; this room was no exception.

We were on our way home from seeing Lu-lu in the hospital after she was diagnosed this last spring. That's when my parents died, in the head-on collision with a sports car right outside the hospital's parking lot. We were in the back seats. I didn't want to think about it any more, I was still too angry. Lu-lu said, "It was better to mourn than to seek revenge."

Lu-Lu was the first to speak by inviting me to sit on the bed by her side. She was writing in her diary, a moldy old leather-bound book stained from years of use. It smelled like rotting wood in a deserted garden. I guess she didn't believe in modern pens or pencils either, because she was using a black crow's feather quill and Indian ink from a little jar to make her daily entries. Gently she closed the book as though it was her most prized possession; this made me smirk. Shows what little I knew.

"I want *you* to have it, Bella my child," she lovingly said as she gave me her diary. I pushed it away.

"Why give it to *me*, Lu-lu?" I only asked because she never gave me anything; she thought my mom had spoiled me too much because I was the oldest daughter.

"It *was* to go to your mama next, but now she's home with God," Lu-lu said with her thick Italian accent.

I was mad that she had mentioned Mom.

"What does *God* know about 'home', about *family*, besides ripping 'em apart?!" I barked at her.

Grandma's warm, wrinkled, weathered face grew cold and rigid as she straightened up in her bed.

"Nonabel... ...Lamia... ...Venatora..." She fumed under her breath; her blue eyes turned dark with anger.

I couldn't believe that she had called me by my *full name*; she never did that. Lu-lu always had called us by a different, cute nickname that she had given each of us long ago when we were little kids.

I was "Bella" because she said it meant I was pretty. The twins, Jesse (my annoying younger brother) and Zatie (her name is like 'Katie' but with a 'Z'), Lu-lu usually called them both, "Troublemakers", mostly when they were being bad. When they were good, she called Jesse her "Strong Boy" and

11

Zatie her "Little Angel". I must have really touched a nerve for her to address me this way.

"…blasphemy is not acceptable in my house!" I gasped at her fury; I had no idea she could get so mad.

She continued to rebuke me, "Never, never talk about *him* that way!"

"Sorry, Nana Lu-lu, I won't do it again," her posture relaxed as I apologized for cursing God.

"Now, Nonabel, I want to ask you. What do you think about my book? What is it for?" Her tone was polite as a small trace of a smile that tickled the corners of her mouth.

"It's…… your diary, right?"

"Yes, my Bella, but it does much more. It's a magic book."

"What?" I asked blankly. She must have been kidding.

"No! I am not 'kidding,' this is serious. My book does magic!"

I hated it when she read my mind, especially the weird way she could directly quote my thoughts. That was just *one* of her creepy talents in the arsenal that she would use against us. I had noticed that she could only do it when you were looking directly in her eyes, so I instinctively looked away.

"Look at me when I speak!"

Dang it! She was still doing it. She knew what I was thinking. I decided not to argue with her, either vocally or mentally.

"Yes, Nana Lu-lu." I was careful not to let my thoughts get carried away, again. She eyed me suspiciously before speaking. The "magic" book appeared too heavy for her long, boney fingers to lift. Her inner strength seemed to be the only force driving her to stay alive these days. Lu-lu gleefully unlocked the latch attached to the diary, releasing a faint puff of stale dust. I swear there were cobwebs on the first few pages that floated away as she quickly flipped towards the last third of the book.

Enthusiastically she stopped on a page filled with baby pictures and quickly passed it to me. I sighed and rolled my eyes simultaneously before I reached for the Diary. It was heavy, heavier than I thought possible. My arms strained under the ever-increasing weight the Diary enforced, as though it was siphoning the strength from me. I felt physically faint and weak due to the unwelcome exchange. I let out a pathetic grunt, like it would have helped with lifting.

Lu-lu laughed as she helped me to hold it better. I began to admire her more as the time slowly ticked by. There was something sweet about her when she wanted to be that way. She pointed to an entry that both surprised and horrified me. There was a newspaper clipping that read:

"At 14:02 hours, as a newborn baby girl was being delivered, the doctor discovered that the baby was being strangled to death by her own umbilical cord. Doctor Wilkinson of County Regional Hospital in Corpus Christi, Texas worked as quickly as he could but to no avail. Baby Nonabel Lamia Venatora, daughter of Victor and Victoria Venatora of Corpus Christi, died after several vain attempts to revive her. Dr. Wilkinson was beginning the delivery when complications arose, causing the need for an emergency C-Section.

They discovered that the baby was already purple from strangulation. Yet the strangest thing that was said to have happened after the operation was not just the eerie peace that the deceased baby's mother had on her face as she held the lifeless child in her arms, but as she whispered to her daughter, eyewitnesses say that the baby coughed and breathed with life.

Miraculously, baby Nonabel was alive! Apparently, she was also choking on birth fluids that were blocking her airways. The 'Miracle baby' as she is being called is alive and well with her family."

I was so aside myself that I could barely speak. I never knew about this, but I had to know if it was true.

"How long... was I... um, dead?"

I gulped through my panic. I had died before! The shock was setting in. Grandma obviously knew I was going to freak out, and she warmly hugged me and kissed my cheek.

"You were declared dead at 2:23 pm, and came back at around, oh, 2:50-ish I think. I wrote it down somewhere in here."

While Grandma scanned through the entries adjacent to the news clipping for the correct time, I decided to do the math.

"27 minutes? Wait, I was *DEAD* for 27 minutes?! Grandma, that's impossible!" I could feel my anxiety taking over; I was dead... for 27 minutes... as soon as I was born, I died. This had to be a joke.

"Nope. No, jokes. I'm telling you the truth!" Dang it! Lu-lu had read my thoughts again.

"But how, Grandma, that can't be possible; can it?" I urged her to speak rationally.

"No, nothing is impossible... ...for a *witch*."

"My mom... ...was a *witch*?"

I think my mouth hung open for an unusual amount of time. Grandma Lu-lu must have been off her rocker. She was getting a little kooky in her old age.

"What do you mean? Off my what? Blah! Never mind, go, you think I am crazy. So, go!" She was mad; I never liked hurting her feelings, but I can be a jerk too when I get mad.

"No, Grandma Lu-lu, I'm sorry about what I was saying, or thinking, for that matter. Please, I promise I won't make fun of you," I said as I felt bad for reacting.

She waited, glaring at me. I let her probe my thoughts to prove to her I was being genuine. Her stare intensified, causing the deep blue seas in her eyes to crash against her dark abyssal pupils. I noticed that this was actually happening in her irises, it was happening by magic. Her stare penetrated my mind, it stabbed sharp, cold daggers through the nerves in my brain like a glass of ice water was being poured down the front of my blouse. I shivered with prominent goosebumps up and down my body. She was really trying this time.

"Okay, *STOP!*" I broke out of the trance she had put me under with her stare.

"You know what, my Bella? You are stronger than your mother was. She could never win any of our staring contests," Lu-lu said with admiration.

"Really?" I mused on that for a minute.

"Yes, now shut up, let me explain," Lu-lu opened the

Diary toward the front to reveal a long tri-fold pedigree chart of my ancestors and handed the Diary back to me. I couldn't believe how far back it went, how many people were related to me, connected. She excitedly pointed towards the names of my relatives at random, telling me stories about them and if each was a witch, a wizard, a warlock, an archmage, or whatever weird name she could think up. It was all just a little too much to take in. I could feel my anxiety taking over.

"Wait, Lu-lu, hold up! Are you trying to tell me that *I* am a witch too?!" I asked her but worried to know.

"You could be a witch, my Bella," she shrugged.

"Ugh, that's just great!" I exclaimed in frustration.

"Well, you never know with these things," Lu-lu was calmly trying to reassure me, but I did not want this.

"Come on, Grandma. *I* am a witch?! I have a hard enough time with being an orphan, now I'm a witch?! Ugh! I'm so angry right now!" I threw the book back to her as best as I could and began to leave the room.

"Nonabel, are you mad because it is crazy or is it because deep down you know it's true?!" She exclaimed.

I was nearly out the door when I froze in my tracks because she was right. This was crazy, but I *did* know it was true, somehow. I returned to her side on the bed and apologetically touched her hands. She was trembling with rage from arguing with me. Her pulse was throbbing in her withered hands. Just then, I was aware of the tears streaming down my cheeks because they had landed onto the Diary between us on the bed.

"How can this be true?" I sobbed silently.

Lu-lu touched my face with both hands and raised my lavender eyes to gaze into hers.

"It just is, my Bella," she chuckled and smiled softly. "We cannot change what we are." I had stopped talking by then. I was too lost in thought for words. She just answered my panicked mental questions and let me cry. My anxieties consuming me as I cried.

"Because God made us this way, and yes, I believe in a

Supreme Being," Lu-lu said. This answer shook me out of my stupor.

"But I thought that witches worshiped the Earth or something else and did magic while dancing naked," she laughed at my comments again; well, it was more like she cackled. It was kind of creepy when she laughed like that.

"No, Nonabel; your powers come from within, deep inside your heart. It flows in your blood through your veins," Lu-lu explained.

"Well, why haven't *I* done anything with ma... ... um, it?" I felt silly saying the word 'magic', so I avoided that.

"These things just take time and practice. Don't worry. By tomorrow this will all make sense; I promise. Now go but take the Diary with you. Keep it safe."

"Keep it safe from what, Lu-lu, the Boogieman?" I could tell by the look in her eyes that I should not have joked about that. "Sorry."

"No, something worse; but I dare not speak of... *it* right now. Too dangerous, it's already nightfall and *he* is coming. Oh, I wish I had more time with you, Nonabel."

"More time for what, Lu-lu?"

She took in a jagged breath and shuddered. "Time enough to train you, of course, my Bella."

"Train me?! To do what, use magic?! Okay, whatever, Grandma. I'm done with this non-sense, goodnight," I said due to my overwhelming anxieties.

I pulled my face from out of her hands and escaped from her room of insanity as quickly as I could. The darkness of the hallway of Lu-lu's house enveloped me in pain and grief while I rushed to my room. I faintly heard her calling for me to come back, weeping. I didn't want to, but looking back now, I wish I had.

Once I was in my room, I flung myself headfirst into my pillow. I tried to use it to muffle my screams of frustration. Grandma was crying in her room on the other side of the hall still. I buried my head deeper into my pillow to block out the guilt. It was hopeless, so I put on my headphones and let my radio drown out her ever-painful moans. I was listening to Metallica back in those days. The song was, "Enter Sandman". I knew Mom wouldn't have liked it much. Dad was more of a "rock-stoner guy", so that's where I got my rebellious side from. I think this was one of his CD's from his collection. It seemed old enough because of the frequent times the disc would skip. Some of the songs couldn't even be played due to the scratches. But I didn't care. I just wanted to forget what Lulu had said.

I tried to pull the blanket over my head as well, but it was caught on something heavy. I sat up after I realized that the Diary was on my bed. I pushed it away from me in anger. Magic book, ha! I picked it up begrudgingly. My mother was a witch, yeah, right. What was worse is she said that *I* could be a witch! What were my friends going to say? What about my boyfriend? Derik was not going to like this. It's just that his parents were already so judgmental. They don't like that I stopped going to church. I'm mad at God right now with all that had happened. I did not like going there and pretending to be okay with everything. I had stopped going.

I guess I could kiss Prom goodbye too and not go to that either. If I *was* a witch and something bad were to happen at Prom, I might go 'wicked witch' on everyone at school. That would be a mess.

I just couldn't handle that. It was best not to mention it to anyone. The CD began to skip randomly, so I said 'goodnight' to Metallica and removed my headphones. I tossed the heavy book down onto my bed hard. It bounced open and the pages flopped back and forth until it settled with the middle section exposed.

There was my name again, written within an entry by my grandmother. From the date it looked like I had to be about four or five years old when she wrote it. I read it to myself in a low whisper.

"...she doesn't trust me. Nonabel is the only person in all my travels that I've encountered who can shake off my 'Hypnotic Stare Spell'. I have to really try hard to read her thoughts, she's so strong. It must be her lavender eyes that give her that strength. It is the colour of Nobility, Royalty; very rare. I wish Victoria would allow me to train her in our ways. She is so stubborn sometimes, just like her father. God rest his soul. It's a shame that Nonabel never knew you, Michael. She has your smile, but I'm afraid she has your uncontrollable anger too. Oh, how I miss you Michael."

Grandpa. All I ever heard about my late grandfather Michael was the stories of him being a 'Great White Hunter' in Africa and other exotic places. He would live with the tribesmen and savages, traveling from village to village searching the jungles for deadly wild animals. My dad would tell me these 'bed-time stories' to keep me up at night with bad dreams and also just to make Mom angry. He thought that it was funny, but it scared the life out of me. I was especially scared of the story of Grandpa's Last Hunt. He was in Borneo, I think, tracking a vicious wild boar that had terrorized the villages there for years. They called the beast 'Gor-Nok'; Dad said it meant 'terror' or 'fear', but Grandpa loved challenges like that.

Saving people from monsters was his specialty. Dad said that Grandpa spent weeks in the darkest parts of the jungle, tracking the beast. He lived off bugs and tree bark. Then, at one point his guide and the others had to leave because they were too frightened to get that close to the monster's lair. The guide was the last person to see Grandpa alive, so I guess the rest of the story was what he told the local authorities had happened.

They weren't sure if it was Grandpa's body they found; all his flesh was burned away. They had to identify him using dental records. They did find some of his belongings like his hunting rifle, so I guess they stopped looking for him.

My dad would always fill in the blanks with something elaborate to make Grandpa seem super cool. When I was old enough, Grandma Lu-lu showed me some of his old photos in an album with the newspaper clipping describing his death. He never conquered that terrible beast.

That's when it dawned on me; *this* was the old album Grandma had shown me to tell his stories from all those years ago. I excitedly flipped the pages back a few years. The old pictures and added pieces of clippings would cause the Diary to lay open in those areas that were more adorned. I quickly scanned the articles and then repeated to turn back the years to find Grandpa. His face was smiling back at me when I finally found the pages about his last moments on earth. I studied his photo from his obituary intensely, I *did* have his smile, and thought of how I wish I had known him.

I could tell that Grandma loved Grandpa by that way she swooned over him in her entries. Even though she resented him for his stubbornness by going after that boar alone, she praised him for being brave enough to face his fears. I was starting to cheer up as I continued reading through my family's rich heritage. Lu-lu wrote something here about his death; I eagerly read it aloud:

"Dear Diary   September 9th

Michael was very foolish today; his stubborn pride has cost him his life. If only he had listened to me about my nightmares, my warnings, none of this would have happened. He would have been alive to see the birth of our first granddaughter, Nonabel, who happened to be born today. I should have seen this coming. My only hope lies in obtaining his rifle or any other personal items that he had on him. Then I might be able to ex-tract the past from it to know the truth. No Earthly beast could best my Michael. He could very well be alive seeing how they were too cowardly to search for his real body. Deep down I feel he's alive. If not so, then why hasn't his soul come to me in my dreams, at least to say goodbye? Contact me please, Michael, I'm waiting.

Eternally Yours,
Lucia"

There's so much I never knew, so many questions I would not get answered. How could she have known he was going to die? Could she see the future as well as read minds? What else could she do? What could she possibly be able to 'extract' from his rifle? How could she use it to see the past? Was there a spell in this 'Magic Book' that could do that?

I flew through the pages of the Diary, back and forth, looking for keywords that would stand out. Things like 'Psychic powers,' 'Time traveling,' or 'Seeing the future'. After what seemed like an endless search, I finally found what I was looking for. The page was dedicated entirely to the description of a single spell, that, if performed properly, could allow one to become a 'Seer'. It gave them the power to 'see' whatever they wished, past, present, or future. Pretty cool stuff I'd have to admit. The page was riddled with additions and side notes. It seemed that Grandma wasn't the only one to have used this Diary to study magic.

Was Grandpa a male witch, I mean warlock? Could he do magic too? There were so many notes and additions that he *could* have been a contributor as well. I didn't realize how much of my family history I had just written off as fairytales. How far did this secret go back? Who started all this? Where did they learn these spells? Other questions I'd have to investigate later. Right now, I was going to get some answers. I returned my focus on the spell, noting all its intricate details.

It reminded me of Grandma's recipe for 'Garlic Chicken Lasagna', my favorite. I think that because the first few instructions called for the ingredients garlic and chicken. Except this time the chicken in the spell was to have its head removed, dried in the sun and later ground into a fine powder. As I read, I tried not to let my imagination picture the gruesome details in living color. My stomach wasn't the strongest of the family.

The Seer's Sight

Ingredients Needed
With preparation instructions
Garlic, *best if from a cemetery and plucked before sunset. (100 years old if possible.)* (Note: anything over 25 years will work as well.)
> *Boil in a hot spring or copper cauldron for an hour.*

Chicken heads, *a dozen Roosters caught before they crow seven times at dawn. Remove their heads with bare hands covered in ash from an oak ember. Dry the heads in the sun for three days.*
> *Ground into fine powder with a quartz stone.*

Thorns, *from the fire and Ice rose bush. 2 doz. must be removed with Iron tongs.* (Note: If not done correctly, Sight will fade over time.)
> *Add one every two minutes straight to broth for the last hour.*

Rabbit's foot *must be cut with a golden dagger to prevent tainting the blood.*
> *Add to brew while fresh.*

Cobra's Venom *sucked from one's own hand. Bite must be acquired willingly to ensure the right potency; store venom in a crystal vial to preserve freshness.*
> *Add Last.* (Note: Leave the cobra alive, don't hurt it.)

Mix ingredients in order, do not deviate from the recipe. Potion must be consumed by sunset. Note: if done sooner than sunset, the seer will go blind.
(Note: proceed with extreme caution, once the spell is cast it cannot be reversed or diminished.)

Seer: one who sees things as they truly are, were, or will be. To the seer, time becomes a tangible experience where the seconds slow to feels as minutes, minutes as hours, hours as days, and so forth. The consequences of a day will reveal itself in just a moment allowing the Seer to alter the future or understand the past. Extreme patience is a vitally important virtue that must be possessed before taking on the sight of a seer. (Note: impatience will cause an extreme sense of Paranoia and Doubt in the results of your predictions.)

I really don't know why I had so desperately been searching through a magic book for a 'spell' on time travel. Maybe deep down I hoped that I could find a way to stop what had happened to Mom and Dad. But would I be able to change anything? Well, this spell could help answer that, but it seemed way too complex for me to try right then. Regardless of the consequences, I was hooked; curiosity had baited me into a dangerous trap.

Magic Book or not, I was willing to risk immeasurable anguish in studying from this family diary. I mentally prepared myself for the off chance that I would stumble across an entry about Mom and Dad as I addictively search for more spells. The next spell I stopped at appeared easier, involving much less preparation and no decapitations. It only required that the performer of the spell believe it could work.

Instantaneous Telekinesis

Telekinetic powers for Beginners.
Telekinetic abilities all originate from the same source, The Mind. The power to control, move or manipulate objects with your mind is directly linked to your understanding of the object itself. Discipline your mind to believe that you are stronger than the object. When you understand that it is just a mass of dust and will become dust again one day, you will overpower its will to stay at rest and metaphysically control it. (Note: one should start with small objects then work up to larger things later.)

One must almost convince the objects that it is time
for a change, like water transforms in nature. Water
changes from liquid to solid, from solid to gas, and back
again. Try repeating in your mind these words:
"Ashes to ashes, dust to dust."

It seemed simple enough to try. I mean, if it worked then my grandma wasn't crazy after all. I felt really stupid and childish quoting the words in my head as I half-heartedly pointed my 'telekinetic' aim toward a water glass on my nightstand. Nothing happened except for my stifled laughter as I thought of how Lu-lu might have tried to get me to focus harder.

I straightened up my posture and with a more determined glare I concentrated on the glass of water, all the time whispering: *"Ashes to ashes, dust to dust."* I thought of several things at once: about the weight, size, and shape of the glass cup. *"Ashes to ashes, dust to dust."*

I wondered about how old the water was inside, if it tasted stale and chalky with mineral deposits from Grandma's rusty plumbing. *"Ashes to ashes, dust to dust."* I realized that I *was* stronger than that fragile glass, and I imagined myself violently smashing it against the wall with my bare hands. *"Ashes to ashes, dust to dust."* I watched the cascading shards of glass fly through my room like glistening shrapnel. *"Ashes to ashes, dust to dust."* I could almost feel the thousands of tiny scratches that would burn into my flesh as a result of my anger. *"Ashes to ashes, dust to dust."*

The glass was teetering off the edge of my nightstand before I had noticed that the spell was working. **"Ashes to ashes, dust to dust!"** This time I said it loud enough for everyone in the house to hear if they were awake. I startled myself with the sheer overwhelming strength and confidence that resounded in my voice. A small echo trembled in my room and the glass fell. I saw myself carelessly leaping off my bed to catch it before it shattered on the hardwood floor. I even felt my muscle reacting ever so slightly, wanting to obey my thoughts. But that's what this exercise was about: self-control and mastering the mind.

"Stop!" That was the only thing I could think of. I lowered my left hand which had instinctively flown toward my face to shield my eyes. My right hand, which had been aimed at the glass, was shaking as though it was holding one hundred pounds of invisible sand.

To my utter speechless astonishment, the glass of water came to a stop one inch above the ground and there it waited for my command. With my trembling right hand still extended toward the floating glass, I slowly crouched down to examine it. I had to keep telling it in my mind to *"Stay."* I could feel its natural tendency to obey gravity resisting my commands.

"Stay." The weight on my hand was exhausting. *"Stay."* I bent my head down to the floor and I laid my left hand under the glass, nearly touching it. I curiously watched it float between my two nervous hands for a minute before continuing with this exercise of control.

"Float... ...Up!" I thought to myself while I awkwardly tried to get on my feet from this position. The glass obeyed my command. I gently balanced its weight between my hands, always floating inches away from my skin. Physically it still felt like it weighed the same, even though I was not touching it. The water even swished back and forth as I walked with it back to my bed. All the laws of nature and physics still applied but I had somehow formed an intangible bond between my mind and this helpless glass of water.

I pulled my left hand out from under it, but the glass remained floating in the air under the control of my other hand. I switched hands yet nothing changed; the glass obeyed. I waved and rotated my hands around the glass, and it stayed. I held out my right hand in front of it and said, "Here is the center of your universe, and I command you to revolve around this point. Ashes to ashes, dust to dust."

Slow and steady the glass began to spin, rotating in orbit around my hand like I was its Sun. I could feel my shock and astonishment melt into gleefulness as the glass orbited faster and faster around my hand. The speed had increased such that the water started sloshing out of the glass. The water seemed to be helpless to resist me, as it rotated with the glass in orbit. The drops of water were like a hundred little moons. Each one orbiting my hand. I couldn't help but to laugh at my new toy.

However, toys are only as fun as your imagination and my anxiety allows. It was all fun and games until the pressure of my artificial gravity began to crack and splinter the glass cup. It cracked and broke some more before I frantically leapt to the floor to escape the fragments of glass that were whizzing past my face. The gravitational attraction I had created between the glass and me had failed. It collapsed, crushing the glass until it finally exploded with a loud snap, crackle, and a pop into hundreds of tiny sharp shards. I waited in horror for the barrage of glass daggers to pierce my unprotected back. Nothing happened; I could feel the fading wind that flowed from the epicenter of the explosion yet there was no glass.

I cautiously opened one eye to check and what I saw was so amazing that I had to rub my eyes to be certain it was real. The glass catastrophe was frozen in time and space. A beautiful spherical, glass galaxy hung motionlessly in the middle of my room. It reminded me of a crystal chandelier. I walked around it once incredulously and sat on my bed. Even though this was really cool, it would be a mess to clean up. I knew that once I lost my concentration there would be a ton of glass fragments to clean and I'd never be able to hide this from Lu-lu. I anxiously played with my long jet-black hair as I sat thinking of a way out of this. Oh, how I wished I could fix it, make the glass repair itself. The glass fragments obeyed, and I watched in shock as every little piece of glass recombined to its original state. Then every little water droplet returned to the glass cup that I had bewitched from my nightstand.

I grabbed it quickly from out of the air before anything

else could happen. I took a large swig of the bitter water and set the glass back down on my nightstand. I was pacing back and forth, shaking a little as I muttered frantically to myself in disbelief.

"Did I just do... *magic*?"

I walked over to the glass and took another swig of nasty water. The shock was wearing off and it slowly became excitement.

"I *can* do magic; this is so cool!"

I started walking back for the Diary but abruptly froze in my tracks.

"I can just *tell* the book to come to me, why waste time walking," I said to myself. I raised my hand toward the Diary and saw it jostle in anticipation of my thoughts. It reminded me of a puppy, waiting for me to play 'fetch,' with it; that made me smile.

"Lu-lu's Diary, come to me now!" I commanded.

It rose to the level of my hand, then flung itself furiously towards my chest. It weighed so much; I had forgotten already; I was nearly knocked off my feet.

"I better be more specific with my instructions next time. Ugh! I gotta tell Lu-lu I can move things with my mind!" I stopped myself again as I glimpsed the time on my alarm clock. It was 11:34 pm; Lu-lu was dead asleep by now, so I happily returned to my studies from the Diary. I sat with the book closed in my lap and pondered the possibilities.

"What else can I learn - that is, without waking up the whole house?" I said to myself as I tapped the Diary with my fingernails anxiously. "I got it; I can try flying!"

I quickly sat the magic book down on the bed in front of me, pointed to it and said, "Show me all your spells on flying, floating, and levitation." The Diary swiftly obeyed, opening to a page that resembled a table of contents, yet it was only for the letter 'F'.

"Well, I never thought of asking the Diary if it had a table of contents, but this will do!" I whispered to myself. I ran my index finger slowly down the page, pausing on the more interesting subject headings like "Fat-reducing Potions, faking your Own Death, Fears & Phobias, Fighting Techniques, Fixing broken objects. Floating, Flying..." There it was. I flipped through the Diary to the section on Flying. It included various means of flight, a lot of which I was not interested in. I thoughtfully analyzed each one, considering the small room in which I lived, and the level of danger involved. I chose the method of flight that didn't involve a broom or a flying carpet; I just wanted to fly like a superhero; up, out, and away! Well, maybe I could do without the cape and red boots, but supersonic flight would be really cool.

Flight by Telekinesis

Prerequisite needed is some basic training with telekinesis
As with telekinesis, one must imagine their body as a corruptible object before you can bend it to your will. Fasting for long periods of time, strict diets and rigorous exercise can help perfect your ability to master your body. Total mastery of one's appetites is not entirely required to initiate and sustain self-flight. Simply imagine yourself as the center of the Universe and that all things float away or towards you. Much like "Gravikentics" is the ability to control gravity with one's mind; Aero-telekinesis is controlling one's place in the air around them.

I found it odd that there were no side notes or additions to this spell. Maybe it was simple enough that there was no need, or perhaps Grandma had never tried this one. Either way, I was cautious before trying it. I re-read it through a couple of times to be sure I understood it right.
"Okay, according to this I have to consider myself to be the 'Center of the Universe', yeah, like it could be that easy," I started to laugh at how ridiculous it seemed as I pushed the

book out of my lap and watched it land on the bed four feet below me. That was when I noticed where I was, floating just a few inches below my ceiling. Of course, my natural reaction was to panic, so I lost my concentration and fell spread-eagled onto my bed. Luckily, I hadn't drifted too far or else I would have done a face plant on the hardwood floor.

Unfortunately, the Diary and my face were the major injured parties involved in the collision. My face would heal, just a bruise on my cheek, but I was certain that I had torn a page or two from the open Diary. I lifted my sore face from the damaged pages to watch them organically repair their torn parts.

"Hmph, I guess you are magic," I muttered. I thought it was safer to sit there and just read about spells instead of trying them right away. Also, it happened to be a school night and I would have to explain my injuries to every one of my friends, especially Derik. Being my overprotective boyfriend, Derik would probably stalk the school looking for the 'punk' that did this to me.

I did rather enjoy Lu-lu's Diary; seeing how I could now fly and move things with my mind might make things a little bit more interesting at school. Although it might make thing harder, I still better keep it quiet. Derik was not a big fan of the weirdoes or the goths kids; he was actually a jerk to them. Yeah, it would be better this way, for everyone's sake. I pulled myself up onto my elbows and rested my face in my hands. I could already feel the bruises forming on my cheeks. The Diary was opened to a section about dream interpretation. I continued reading it in hopes that I would be doing a little dreaming myself soon so that I'd forget about the pain that was throbbing in my face.

Dreams

The Places, People, & Things that are made from Dreams.

Throughout time, mankind has never truly comprehended the absolute power that is found in the Dream World. It is a place where your imagination can roam free. Where you can live out your wildest fantasies or come face to face with your nightmares. Those will be discussed later in the section dealing with Nightmares and how to conquer them.

The Daydream is a happy and peaceful place, a sanctuary from the storms of the waking world. In the Daydream we find a person called the Nix of our Daydreams. A Nix is an Astro-projected apparition of your more noble characteristics and your most favorite things zzzz zzzz ZZZZZZZ zzzzzz ZZZZZZZZZZz zzzzzzzzz ZZZZZZZZZZZZZZZZZ zzzzz...

Death

I sat up suddenly; did I fall asleep or was I still sleeping? I couldn't tell. My eyes were so strained from reading the Diary all night that everything in my room was out of focus as I stumbled around to get ready for bed. It was raining outside; the sky was so dark that I couldn't tell the time. My vision blurred painfully when I glanced at my alarm clock. I couldn't recognize the numbers to save my life. Then the lightning flashed outside my opened second-story window. I froze in silent terror as I counted the distance to myself, hoping it was far away from here; "One-Mississip..."

KRRAAAaacckk THUUuuhh-DUHh-DOOooom!! I really hated it when they struck too close. The hairs on my arms stood up on their own and they were accompanied by waves of goosebumps shivering up and down my body. No matter how tough and mature I'd act sometimes, lightning was the *one thing* that could make my bones jump out of my skin. I cautiously walked towards my window to close it before the rain could soak my room. There was another blinding bolt that flashed in the distance, as I frantically slammed my window shut.

I didn't even have time to count the distance before the windowpanes began to vibrate under the power of the rolling thunderclap just outside the house somewhere out in the abandoned wheat field. When Grandpa was alive, he would spend his off-season hunting days pretending to know how to farm. Lightning struck again and I protectively covered my ears from its merciless noise, and sadly enough, I let out a tiny panicked shriek every time it struck. I could barely hear my Grandma calling for me through the roar of the thunder. I probably woke her up. I waited, listening for Lu-lu to call again.

"Nonabel, is that you?"

She sounded so weak and alone that it pained me to the core. I threw on my fluffy gray bathrobe and quietly made my way to Lu-lu's room to check on her. The cold drafty house was relatively quiet, with the exception of the wind blowing in with the bad weather softly moaning outside. It was too dark to see anything as I approached Lu-lu's bedroom. I had to grope in the darkness for her door handle.

I was about to open her door when a noise from the downstairs front room caught my attention. I stealthily snuck down the steep stairwell to the main floor, trying desperately to avoid all the squeaky steps along the way. From about halfway down the stairs I could see the source of the noise. Someone left the front door open and the wind was slapping the screen door against the doorframe. While I was timidly trying to struggle the door free from the wind and rain, I noticed a light coming from the front yard. The light was soft, eerie, and out of place. It was Lu-lu's oil lamp; was she outside in this horrible storm?
I mustered up all the courage I had and walked out in the storm to follow after the light.

"Lu-lu, is that you?!" I yelled as loud as I could, but a deafening thunderclap overhead muffled my screams.

"Nonabel, where are you?"

It was so hard to hear her through the fierce wind and pounding rain. She was wandering to the old barn in the abandoned wheat field. I had to start jogging to catch up to her. I was getting closer to Lu-lu, close enough to discern her frail figure holding the oil lamp in the air. I ran harder to be with her, but the weather was working against me, wind and rain causing me to slip and fall in the mud. The lightning flashed violently across the night sky, illuminating Grandma's soaking wet old body standing in the field, weak and very vulnerable.

Grandma Lu-lu had an unnatural peace about her as she began to dance by herself in the pouring cold rain. She was definitely going to die from something all right: pneumonia for certain. I tried to reason with her.

"Lu-lu, come on back inside, you know you're not supposed to be outta bed in your condition, let alone outside. Now let's go back inside before we *both* get sick... ...or worse, get killed," I cried out.

"There's nothing to be frightened about dear, we are in no danger. Here, take my hand and dance with me," Grandma said as she reached out to me. She was raising her other hand holding her oil lamp high in the rain. She happily swayed back and forth waiting for me, humming an unfamiliar tune to herself. I stared at her incredulously.

"No! I don't want to Lu-lu, I can't, you know how scared I get when there's lightni... AAAHHGGGgg!" The thunderclap right over our heads was horrifying. CAAH-KkkrrRAACKkkk! I really hated it when they were this close.

"Oh, my Bella child, it can't hurt you, there's no need to give in to your fears. Be reasonable, Nonabel, you're much too old to *still* be scared of a little lightning. Ha ha!" BbbAAAaaDDdOOOMmm!

"UUGGHHhh, no! You be reasonable, Grandmother, and return to your nice warm bed inside the house right this instance!" I yelled back.

"Don't you take that tone with me, young lady! You are not quite old enough to be acting like the boss of me either. Now pay attention, I'm trying to help you. This is all for your own good, you know. If you can't face your fears, then you shouldn't have them. It might be too much power for you to control anyhow, seeing that you're new at this," Lu-lu said.

"Ah, Lu-lu, not the magic crap again, I'm too tired and too wet to play this game now. Let's go back inside, I mean it!" I said as my wet hair was whipping me in the face. A frigid wind swept across the field. Rain was drenching us still and Lu-lu took a few steps back, deeper into the field in defiance.

"If you think you can take me, then be my guest. Let's see you try!" She bowed to me mockingly and smiled as she straightened her soaked body against the wind. I approached her cautiously, knowing full well that this could be a trick. The odd silence that crept in between us in the field was a dead give-away that something was coming. The hairs on my arms were standing on their own again. Lu-lu was muttering something to herself.

"Hofu-Lampeggiare!" That was the last thing I heard her whispering before the lightning began again.

KRRAAAaacckk THUUuuhh-DUHh-DOOooom!!

The blinding bolt pummeled the ground just feet between us and I screamed and cried all over again. Grandma was laughing again, this time *at* me.

"Ha ha, ah Nonabel, you'll never be able to control your Nightmare if you cower away every time it's near. Now try again, don't be scared, it's just a tiny shock at first."

"What?!! NO! Grandma, I'm leaving!" I turned on my heels and began my march towards the house; I didn't care any more if the old bat wanted to kill herself or not, I was going to bed. I looked to the house and there she was, furious. I don't know how but she had quickly gotten around me to cover my retreat.

"Old bat, am I?!!" She raised up both hands and screamed to the night sky. "Hofu-Lampeggiare finnito!!"

It was instantaneous, the utter shock and horror flooding through my body when a booming bolt of electricity struck the earth a foot in front of me. I absorbed most of the concussion with my arms, which had instinctively shielded my face once again, yet I had no idea where I was flying to when my body was blown off balance due to the sheer force of the blast. My ears were ringing painfully, and I was temporarily blinded from the point-blank blast of the lightning bolt.

When my eyes regained their sight, I found myself in the mountains where my family would go camping when I was younger. The sun was setting as a fierce storm was approaching the meadow where I was standing. Then I realized that I *was* younger due to my lack in height and the return of my prepubescent body. I was twelve years old again, reliving one of my worst memories.

My family was playing in this very meadow after a nice picnic lunch. I had taken a nap under the old oak tree by the stream. When I woke, they were all gone, Mom, Dad, and the twins, gone. I could feel the panic suffocating me once again. I ran to the stream to splash water on my face so I could wake myself out of this horrible memory, this awful nightmare. Nothing but my cold, wet, prepubescent little girl's face was staring back at me in shock through my reflection in the stream. I ran back and forth in the meadow screaming the names of my family members and sobbing miserably the whole time. It was worse than before because this time I knew that my parents were never coming back, they were dead and buried. Fear and terror were all that filled me, despair was replacing every last ounce of hope in my little heart as reality was sinking in. I was lost. Alone.

It felt like hours had passed by the time the storm got closer. There was thunder and plenty of lightning to go around. I fled from the middle of the meadow because I remembered my folks telling me to not stand out in the open during a storm. I hid under the old oak tree for shelter. It was all in vain seeing how the tree was the tallest thing there. A flash of bright light smashed into the tree, sending debris, and blazing embers everywhere. Lightning kept coming at me as I ran across the meadow. It struck just in front of me like it was trying to flank my escape.

Last time, I was crunched in a ball on the ground crying frantically when my parents found me long after the storm had lifted. I was sobbing so hard that my eyes were sealed shut with tears. All my strength was summoned just to open them again, only to see my grandmother standing in the field of her farm soaking wet from the sleet and rain, still laughing at me. Panic was spilling out of my eyes through my tears as I began to cry. How could she have known about that day? Mom swore that she wouldn't tell anyone about my fears. How dare she use that against me now when I was most vulnerable?

"NO! I'm not playing along with your magical nonsense any more; you don't play fair!" I was shouting by then just so she could hear me over the thunder that was pounding through the valley around the town.

"Fair? Who said anything about this being fair? I call it *training* and if you want it to end then make it stop. Face your fears, Nonabel, and embrace it. Do not give into despair, it only makes it worse!"

"What?!! You want me to get hit?! That's crazy, Lu-lu!" The thunder began to roll as I took a step to leave.

"You *must* let it hit you, embrace fear, let it fill you with its power. It must be allowed to become a part of you. Its power is as the air, in your lungs, the blood in your heart. Get to know what it is, what it can do *through* you, be willing to use it against others, and share your fear with your enemies. Confidence is your greatest ally against it!"

"Against what, Lu-lu?

"Fear!" She raised her hands once more towards the heavens and cackled.

"Lampeggiare de Zeus, haa ha ha!!"

CAAH-KkkrrRAACKkkk BbbAAAaaDdOOoMm!!

The lightning onslaught continued to strike by me bolt

after bolt, paralyzing me with fright. She let it hit me, the lightning filling me with pain and power. I was on the ground, crouched in a ball in the rain and mud; shaking with fear, and pain, because of the fresh memories and the jolts of electricity that were coursing through my veins. I was crying out for my mom and dad, who were not going to save me this time. They were nowhere nearby to come to my rescue, and then I felt nothing except for the pain of loneliness and betrayal. Blackness consumed my mind until all was dark. No more pain, and no more nightmares, but Lu-lu was still screaming for me, calling for help.

"Nonabel, Save Me!!"

The ground was cold when I woke up on my bedroom's hardwood floor curled into a ball, still a little shaken, but alive. The storm was passing, and I wondered if I had dreamt the whole thing. I tried to calm myself as I climbed back into bed.

"Nonabel, *Save Me*!!"

Lu-lu was really in pain now. I shot out of my bed and bolted for the door.

"I'm coming, Lu-lu!" The house was still dark except when the lightning flashed. I had to be careful not to trip and fall in my rush to find her door.

"Hurry, my Bella!" She was panicking, something had her spooked. Jesse and Zatie were standing in the hallway with pained concern on their faces.

"What's the matter?" Zatie worriedly asked.

"Nothing, Zatie, you guys go back to bed."

"Nonabel, hurry, he's coming back!" Lu-lu screamed for help.

"Like hell nothing's happening," Jesse said as he and Zatie followed me to Lu-lu's door. I knocked just to check if she was dreaming; the door was locked. I called to her again. There was a loud crunching and banging noise coming from Grandma's room that ended with a thunderous bang. I thought that she might have fallen trying to reach the door.

KRRAAAaacckk THUUuuhh-dd-DDUHh-DOOooom!!

"Jesse, bust it down!" I ordered my brute of a younger brother.

"Gladly. I'm coming, Granny, hang on!" He slammed full-force into the solid oak door, but he only got bruises as he bounced off of it. "No use, Nona," he whimpered as he rubbed his shoulder sadly. We had to act fast; Lu-lu could be hurt or dying.

"Jesse, go get something to break down the door. Zatie, get the phone, we might need to call for help," I commanded. They left me there instantly, I heard Lu-lu moaning again.

"I'm coming, Lu-lu, don't worry!"

"Sss save mmm me..." she hissed out in pain. There was no more time, she was dying, I had to do something. Magic was the first thought that popped in my head; I could blast the door down with my mind. I hesitated, but I could hear the twins coming back; there was no time to wait. I placed my shaking hands on the door.

"Confidence is the only weapon against Fear. Ashes to ashes, dust to dust. OPEN!!" There was a powerful slamming noise as the heavy door crashed into the bedroom wall, nearly knocking it off its hinges. The twins stared at me astonished before we cautiously entered our grandmother's bedroom.

"I guess all that yoga with Mom really paid off?!" They didn't seem to believe me.

"Lu-lu? Are you all right?" I couldn't see anything or hear her crying any more as I went to light her oil lamp. The igniting phosphorous stung my nostrils as the match sparked to life. I lit the lamp, then turned to see what was wrong with Lu-lu. Zatie was already crying into Jesse's massive shoulder; she must have known what I was not yet willing to accept. Lu-lu was lying peaceful, still, too still; she wasn't breathing.

Her respirator machine must not have been working so I searched the dark room for the source of the malfunction. The room was utterly trashed as though someone was searching for something valuable, but nothing was taken. If a lightning bolt had hit the house, then it would explain the giant hole in Grandma's bedroom where her window used to be. There also were signs of a struggle everywhere; maybe her breathing mask fell off during the fight. The strangest thing was that Grandma was still lying in bed undisturbed, and still under the twenty layers of handmade quilts.

I located the respirator device crushed on the floor like an angry elephant had stamped on it. The oxygen tanks were shattered; that must have been the cause of the explosion. It still didn't explain why her personal belongings were strewn across the room. The lightning flashed again, illuminating the room through the missing part of her wall in a frightening way. I had begun to cry without thinking about it. I knelt by Lu-lu's side and reached for her hand; she was as cold as steel, like ice. I didn't want to accept that she was dead, especially after just learning her secret, my secret. I stood up suddenly, startling the twins.

"What are we going to do?" Zatie was still sobbing.

"I'm going to save her," I raised both my hands in the air, balling them into fists and then slamming them onto Lu-lu's sunken chest. It startled Zatie; she screamed for me to stop.

"Stop it! You're going to hurt her."

"Can't feel pain if you're dead!" She ran out of the room crying. I continued to pound on Lu-lu's frail body, and then proceeded to perform CPR as best as I knew. Her lungs filled like a balloon whenever I breathed for her. There was no change, no pulse, so I kept pounding.

"Shouldn't we call the cops or something?" Jesse asked nervously as he watched me beat on Grandma.

"Yeah, go call 9-1-1, I'll keep trying." Good, maybe I could try a spell while they were gone getting help. He quickly fled the room and I waited until I heard his cumbersomely large feet pounding down the stairs before I tried magic to revive her. I got up off Lu-lu's crumpled body and was pondering what spell could bring her back from the dead. The lightning flashed again, giving me a brilliant idea. I could resuscitate her with electricity. The lightning struck again near the farm. I wasn't as petrified this time; I was more curious.

"What was it that Lu-lu said in my dream?" I wondered to myself. "Lamp, lamper something, ugh, I wish I knew Italian better." The lightning crashed again nearby, bringing with it the memory of Lu-lu trying to help me to face my fears.

"I got it! It was Lamp- Lampeggiare!" Immediately after I spoke the word, a tiny static electric spark arced between my hands, startling me.

"No need to fear what is a part of me. She's right, confidence is the key," I straightened up, clapped my hands together and thought of my dream.

"Lampeggiare!" A powerful miniature bolt of electricity pulsed back and forth between my slowly opening hands. When I felt the charge was too much for my hands to contain, I bent down over Lu-lu and pressed hard on her chest.

"Clear?" I closed my eyes, afraid of what I might see. I could feel her body involuntarily leap a foot up off the bed as the burst of energy transferred into her cold heart. I opened my eyes, expecting to see her smiling back at me. Nothing had happened; she was so still and cold when I touched her neck for a pulse. I thought of trying again but I could hear my siblings approaching frantically.

"What the hell was that?!" Jesse ran to grab my hands as I continued to pound on Grandma; I was crying again, blubbering something incoherent.

"Comm umm um ba-ba backkk!" Jesse bear-hugged me around the waist and pulled me away from the bed. I violently protested against him with all my might; I knew I could save her still.

"Let me go, I can save her, please, Jesse!" He only tightened his massive muscles around my flailing limbs, no doubt to keep me from hurting him more than Grandma. He was whispering in my ear to calm me just like Dad would do whenever I got scared.

"It's over, Nonabel, she's dead. Just let it go." The lamp light that caressed Lu-lu's skin was fading. Her oil lamp was flickering out, and I knew this was a sign that time was running out. I could feel the power to save her, to bring her back pulsating in my veins, but fear of exposing the secret we shared in plain sight of the twins was something I wasn't ready to deal with at this time. Something had to be done before the flame of her life was exhausted completely. I pretended to calm down so that my Neanderthal brother Jesse would loosen his cave-man grip on me enough for me to breathe.

"Thanks... ugh, Zatie, did you call for an ambulance already or not?" I asked.

She was still clenching the phone in her white-knuckled hands. "Yaah hh, yes! They said they're on their way."

Good, maybe I could trick them both to leave again. I thought of the front door, of the old rusted knocker that hung outside. It was my only chance; the flame was getting weaker.

KNOCK, KNOCK, KNOCK!!!

Zatie jumped when I made the knocker slam hard against the door. Maybe I should practice more before trying something else psychically. It was the best distraction I could think of.

"I'll get it; they'll probably need help with the gurney anyways," Jesse was out of the room before I could ask Zatie for a sheet to cover Grandma with. There were just seconds to act, one more chance before the lamp light went out entirely. I clapped my shaking hands together and placed them right over Lu-lu's heart, last chance.

"Lampeggiare!!" I felt a surging bolt of electricity slam into her chest. Her body leapt once more. I checked for her pulse, and she was gone. The last light of the flame flickered out of the lamp forever.

"NO! Lu-lu, stay with me! Come back! Don't you take

her away from me, damn it, you have no right!" I exclaimed my anger at God for taking Grandma from me. I was sobbing once more. I felt a cold breath whispering at my ear, "She's gone." I turned to see who it was.

"Nonabel, uh, here's the sheet," Zatie had tears streaming down her freckled cheeks as she passed me a new white sheet she had found in the hall closet. I couldn't tell if she had witnessed what I was doing or not, but she looked as scared as I did. The thunder rolled outside in the distance again and the sirens were echoing down our street. Jesse was the only one who wasn't crying throughout the whole ordeal.

After the real paramedics took their hand at trying to revive her, Jesse helped them carry her body downstairs. Zatie and I were huddled together in a corner of the room, crying each other into a hysterical frenzy. I recall wanting to watch the weather outside through the torn wall of Lu-lu's room rather than answer any questions. I wondered if it had been some lightning that hit the house; that's when I saw someone or something outside hobbling off into the forest near the edge of the farm. I thought I was going crazy, so I let my hysteria consume me and I resumed crying.

Everyone kept trying to calm me down. I had to tell the police everything that happened, omitting the part about us being witches, of course. The detective heading up the investigation was Derik's dad, Dennis. He was almost going to say that the blast must have been from the lightning, but he could never figure out why all the debris was blown out of the room as though the blast came from Grandma. Was *she* trying to defend herself, but from who or what?

"It must have been from the exploding tanks of oxygen," Detective Bradbury finally put in his report. There were odd signs of a struggle and the only other set of prints in the room was mine. Of course, I was almost accused of the crime, if it had not been for the fact that she died from a heart attack. The detective concluded that the blast must have scared her to death.

We never really got to sleep that night. After they took her away; I had to fill out all kinds of documents and interview with every authority figure in the county until they felt that I could be an adequate guardian of my twin siblings and the sole executor of Grandma's estate until further notice. The estate lawyer finally arrived to deal with everything so we could rest.

The next day we had school; I told the twins they could stay home if they wanted to. Zatie didn't feel like going, but she did not want to be alone either. She was always really sensitive after these kinds of things, anyone would. I wanted to stay with her and keep crying. I would have stayed but I had a quiz in almost every class that day. Jesse was more than happy to ditch for the sake of mourning. I called the Jr. high school to inform them, but the administrator had already heard about Grandma and gave her condolences. Man, news travels fast in a small town.

Derik was waiting for me by my locker, such a good little boyfriend. Well, maybe *little* isn't the correct thing to say. Derik was tall, lean, but muscular. He could have been on any of the various sport teams here at school, he just didn't like sports. Of course, he already knew about Lu-lu, even though I avoided his phone calls all night. I'm sure that his father, *Detective* Bradbury, must have let it slip that 'there was trouble out at old lady Lamia's place again.'

"Your daddy told ya, didn't he?" I regretted starting the day like this, but Derik was always very compassionate whenever I had problems.

"Yeah, he was talkin' 'bout it all through breakfast. You know, he's debatin' on if it was the lightning. You guys should really have a rod mounted to that barn of yours or somethin'," he placed a hefty arm around me and started walking me to class after I acquired the necessary textbooks. "Do ya wanna talk about it?" he finally asked me after a long walk of silence.

"Not really, but I won't get to avoid it either," I stopped and leaned against a locker; I could feel the heartbreak creeping up from my gut. My eyes were welling up. Derik turned to face me, cradling my face with his strong hands. His smile touched every part of his radiant face. His cool blue eyes were exactly like Lu-lu's, piercing me to my already busted heart. It made me sob a little. A lone tear escaped and slowly slid down my cheek. He lovingly wiped it away.

"Sugga, don't cry. You know she's happier now."

"Bb-bah but she was screaming for me when she died, Derik! And I couldn't save her!" Tears and the painfully fresh memories had consumed me; I was a sobbing-wet mess again. Derik pulled me close to him, shielding me from the intrusive eyes of the curious on-lookers that passed us by in the halls of Shadow Peaks High School. Derik hugged me warmly, patting me on the back the whole time. After a few moments, I regained my composure and wiped my sore eyes.

"Nonabel, do ya wanna just ditch school?!" He had his happy-go-lucky look in his eyes. How could I refuse him; reckless carefree fun was exactly what I needed.

"Aw, crap! I got quizzes today. I can't go!"

"Really, what classes?" He didn't look deterred.

"Every class, I really want to, but... you know."
I must have begun to cry because he had my face in between his hands once more, comforting me.

"Wait here, I got an idea!" He left me waiting outside of the principal's office with tears forming puddles in my sore lavender eyes. Derik and the principal embraced like old friends, most likely another one of his father's connections being used as a bargaining chip. He pointed to me over his shoulder with his thumb and they both turned to look at me simultaneously. Judging by his reaction, I would guess that the principal was convinced that I should be allowed to leave. He and Derik shook hands like they had just made a great business deal only they knew about and then he happily walked back out of the office to be with me.

"We got the whole day off! What do you want to do first? Oh, they got the county fair still going, do ya wanna check it out?" He was rubbing his hands gleefully.

"What about my quizzes?" I was still not convinced that we got off that easily. I knew that Lu-lu had just died, but it wasn't like I was going to her funeral.

"All taken care of, darlin', don't sweat it!"

"Okay, but we got to go get the twins first. That wouldn't be fair to them. You're probably right, though; we could all use a little fun right now."

When we got to the house to pick up the twins, they came running out at the sound of Derik's muscle car purring in the gravel driveway. Jesse was leaning against one of the porch columns whittling something out of wood with Dad's old pocketknife. He stopped so he could shun me in a half-mocking way as I walked up to the house with my backpack.

"Tsk, tsk, tsk. You couldn't even stay 'til lunchtime before ditching? You know, I don't think you're going to be a very good guardian," Jesse said as he waved one disapproving finger at me as I got closer.

"That's just it, you don't think!" I flung my backpack into his stomach when he was off guard. "And that's why *I'm* your legal guardian until you turn eighteen, or until they don't feel I can handle it and take you guys away." Jesse hugged me with one arm, sensing that my thoughts were depressing me.

"That's not going to happen, Nona; no one is going to take us anywhere, at least not without a fight," his whispering reassurance made me chuckle. Derik honked his horn a few times and yelled out the window of his car.

"Hey, are we leavin' or what?!" Derik hollered to us. Zatie waved to him in her shy school-girl way. She secretly had a baby-crush on him, but Derik and I could tell. Actually, she liked every one of Derik's friends that had come over since we moved to town.

"Jesse, go get some shoes on, we're going out," I told him as I tossed my back into the house.

"Are you feeling okay? I mean we can all just chill here at the home, if Derik doesn't mind watching TV on a pre-digital dinosaur, that is," Jesse asked. I could tell by Jesse's smile that he wasn't serious, just confused by my choice to leave school early.

"No, we are all going to spend the day at the fair. Try to have some fun. Now go get ready!" I told them. Their innocent faces lit up with excitement as they fumbled over each other to get back in the house to prepare for the day's revelry. I laughed at that some more as I walked back to the car on the driver's side to wait with Derik.

"They seem happy enough," Derik chuckled as he cut the powerfully loud engine of his muscle car.

"Yeah, I hope I'm doing the right thing, letting us ditch and all. I don't want to be a bad example." I said.

"Nonabel, sweetie, you could never be bad. Your heart's in the right place. Let's not worry about anything else, just have a fun time, and go on all the rides 'til we're sick!" He was smiling with his entire face again; I had to kiss him. He was always so positive, I needed that after all that I have been through.

Within minutes the twins were dashing out of the house towards us. Derik started the car and helped me to climb in through his window and I slid past him like a snake to sit in the passenger seat. We opened both doors of his Camaro and pulled our seats forward so that Jesse and Zatie could sit in back.

"Everybody, get strapped in, I'm about to make a jump into light speed!" Derik exclaimed excitedly as he peeled out in the driveway and did a nauseating donut before we tore down the road. Being the son of a small-town police detective meant Derik could almost get away with murder, so speeding and traffic violations were no big deal to him. We had an enjoyable ride to the County Fair Grounds located a couple of towns away. Derik avoided playing his usual mix of hard-core rock n' roll music and opted for easier listening in consideration of our grieving. He would occasionally point out the interesting and historical landmarks along the way, probably to distract us from diving into our despair whenever a sad song would come on. His light-hearted compassion was a welcome necessity. We arrived at the Fair Grounds around noon, and of course Jesse was the first to bring up the topic of food as we got out of the car.

"Nonabel, um, did you happen to pack us a sack lunch or some money, cuz I'm outta pocket change. Grandma was supposed to give us..."

"I know! She was going to give us our allowances today. Just perfect!" I was panicking to myself silently. Derik could sense my anxiety due to his familiarity with my many facial expressions.

"Hey, sugga', I can cover it if you want. I got enough in my bank account," he was reaching for his wallet instinctively.

"No, I don't need your daddy's money!" I felt bad that I barked at him. He went quiet as his smile fled.

"No, I didn't mean it like that; I can take care of this, baby!" I kissed him on the side of his mouth, tenderly. It made him smile a little. I recalled what he just said and went for my purse on my shoulder. I pulled out my tiny black wallet.

"Once she had become bedridden, Lu-lu had me do all the bill paying and the shopping like a grown-up, so she got us a joint bank account," I quickly retrieved my bank card and held it out in front of everyone. Derik and Jesse 'ooohed and awed' jokingly as they eyed the shiny, plastic card.

Zatie clapped enthusiastically at this. "Yea, we're not going to starve!" Then she began to bounce up and down happily. She often acted too childish for her age. I stopped her public display of craziness by dragging her with me to the nearest ATM. I wasn't as shocked as the rest of them when they saw how much I had in my account; I was more annoyed at Lu-lu for tempting my resolve to not do anything foolish with this small fortune. I didn't have a job and was planning on going to college out of state next year after graduation, but now it appeared that it was up to me to be the adult, be the responsible one. I had to take care of them for a while. I sighed heavily at the number of zeroes in the balance.

"Whoa, Nona, is all that for us? I've never seen so many zeroes in all my life," Jesse exclaimed.

"Yeah you have. Remember your last report card?!" Zatie burned him bad and it made her twin brother blush from shame. I would have laughed but I was too angry with Lu-lu to join in.

"Sweetie, are you mad that you're rich?!" Derik was trying to comfort me. I grudgingly pulled out enough money for everyone to eat, play, and have fun while we were there.

"There you go, sugga', was that hard?" Derik said.

"No," I was half-mad, but the fact that we had money was helping me to calm down.

"Now we can all relax, have fun, and enjoy the rest of the day!" Derik was beaming at me again. His gorgeous smile was starting to make me feel better. The twins eagerly snatched their portions of the money I withdrew and began to run towards separate rides. I had to yell pretty loudly for them to hear me calling them back.

"Hey, get back here! We have to decide where we are going to meet up after," I yelled at them. Jesse and Zatie both protested my 'Mom' moment and came back to discuss the plan.

"I think we should just meet back at the car around dinnertime," Derik suggested.

"Good idea, babe," I agreed. "Meet us by his car at 5 pm sharp. And Jesse, don't let Zatie wander."

Zatie got angry at being treated like the helpless little sister. "Aw, Nona I'm not a child, I can handle myself."

"Yes, but Jesse is slightly older, so he is responsible for you," I stated.

"What?! Like by five minutes; still, we were born on the same day," she retorted.

"And I just need to have someone to blame when you get lost." I explained.

Zatie sulked off toward a ride and Jesse chased after her.

"I'll take care of her, Nona, don't worry about us!" Jesse yelled back in his retreat.

We spent the rest of the day walking around and talking mostly. Occasionally Derik would talk me into going on a ride or two, but I insisted on not doing the scarier ones. I just wanted to forget about what had happened last night, forget about magic and nightmares.

I mostly cried on Derik's shoulder the whole day, but he didn't care; he just listened like a good boyfriend should. I didn't know what I would do without him. If he found out about the truth, he would surely break up with me. He was always a big jerk to all the wannabe Goths and wiccan-vegan types. Why wouldn't he just become a complete prick to me? Seeing how I was a *real* witch; I would be the cause of his social destruction or actual. I could never tell him then. Surely Lu-lu never told Grandpa Michael, or did she? Derik never really told me why he hated the weirdos and goths so much. I was pretty sure I would learn why if we ever did break up because of my secret.

Dinner was nice; we ate at a pizza place and everyone seemed to enjoy themselves. I put on my best happy face to not ruin the fun, but Derik always knew when I'm lying. He said that I would blanch, that the color would leave my face, like a reverse blush. I told him that I was just worried about life in general as we drove home with the twins asleep in the back of his car later that afternoon.

When we got to the house, Derik helped me put Jesse on the couch. Then we helped Zatie, in her half-asleep state, to get up to her room. I knew Derik was curious about what had happened, so I let him take a look alone at what was left of Lu-lu's room. He pointed out that he could fix the hole in the wall and offered to help with cleaning up everything.

We hugged and kissed good night on the front porch, and he left me there alone after I reassured him that I was fine. I stayed up watching re-runs and infomercials on Lu-lu's decrepit old junker of a black and white TV she got us after we moved in. Jesse was snoring loud and mumbled something about rabbits all night on the couch. I didn't want to go sleep; I was too tender after all that I had gone through just to have to face my nightmares again. I was getting bored of channel-surfing with the antique remote control. You had to hold the button down for a few seconds before it would respond. I glanced at my mammoth of a brother sawing logs before I tried to practice telekinesis again.

I had not thought about magic all day and it was difficult for me to remember the spell. I got the TV to flip through a few channels before I heard the old rooster crow to announce the coming of dawn and my anxiety melted away with the rising of the sun. It had been a long time since I had watched a sunrise. The distraction was enticing. I made myself a warm bowl of oatmeal with fresh raspberries before I went out to the back porch to greet the sun. The sunrise was glorious! The light played with the colors in the early morning sky like an artist passionately painting for fun and not for a living. The animals were up and scurrying about, foraging in the field for food. The old scarecrow Grandpa made was long since destroyed by the warring crows, rooks and ravens that lived nearby.

This morning was the same as they seemed to peck at it just to make sure that it wasn't going to get up and chase them away. I loved watching the crows or whatever they were. Lulu tried to teach me how to spot the difference. I thought they all looked the same to me. Their feathers were pitch black and there was a slight glint of color that reflected off their wings if you looked at them just right. They seemed so soft and docile; I really wanted to touch one of them.

I never had a pet growing up; Mom didn't like them, mostly because she had lived here on the farm. Mom tried to have our home be the opposite of Grandpa's farmer lifestyle probably because she had to help out all the time. The cawing of the crows pierced through my memories. Several of them were brave enough to get closer to investigate the presence of my pink bunny slippers. I shared some of the berries from my breakfast with them. A few cautious crows got closer, so I tried to coax one to eat from my hand.

It had a long, hard beak that had scratches from skirmishes over food with other birds. The pecking wasn't pleasant, but I endured it as I attempted to touch the bird. Its natural distrust of people caused it to flinch away a little, yet it stayed. I got to caress it a few times before the fighting of its brothers scared it away. When my feathered friend flew off, the rest followed suit and took flight into the warm morning sky. I stood up to follow them as part of me wanted to fly off with them, but my siblings would be waking soon and a teenage girl with bunny slippers flying across the sky might be too much for them to understand. I had to calm myself and decided to just take a walk to the old barn.

The field was damp still from the storm a day ago. Worms and bugs had surfaced to partake of the morning's moisture. This was what I had first thought had attracted the birds. However logical the idea was, I soon discovered what really had them in an uproar. The field was filled with small craters like a gopher or dog had been searching for something to eat. The dirt and plants nearby were partially scorched by a powerful heat source.

Was Zatie out here playing with matches again? There were tiny sparkling crystals erupting from each crater in the field. This must have been what had drawn the birds here. I picked one up to examine it further. I quickly recognized it as quartz from our recent geology lesson in school. Just this stuff was different and was brittle like glass. That's what was odd about it; natural glass can happen due to lightning... Oh no! I wasn't dreaming; it was all real. The argument with Lu-lu right here in the field was real. She was trying to teach me how to use this power. But how could she do that in my dream? Or was I sleepwalking? I kept seeing it happen over and over again in my head. She was *trying* to hit me with lightning. There was a word she had used before she said lightning in Italian or Latin, whatever she was speaking. I grasped for it from my nightmare.

"Hofu…" The word was just a whisper as it escaped my lips, but its power echoed through the field. A deadly chill crept down my spine as the warmth of the dawn retreated from the spell I had uttered. The foraging animals scattered at once at the sound of the word. This made me even more frightened to speak it again. An eerie feeling overtook me as I knelt in the field. Like evil was waiting for me to let down my guard. Goosebumps covered my pale legs down below my shorts to my toes.

Clouds were starting to gather, and a frosty breeze blew through me like the icy breath of death was creeping down my neck. Fear of being caught in a storm was paralyzing me. I was rocking back and forth involuntarily due to the anxiety taking over. I was overwhelmed by the fresh memories of my nightmare. I was worried that I was caught, trapped there again. I was muttering incoherently through fresh tears that spilled from my eyes. *Confidence was the only defense.* I tried to believe her. But what did it do to help her?

"I, uh, I am mmum nna not tuh aah afraid da ya you," I mumbled through my blubbering, hysteria, and chattering teeth. I could feel the ionic rage of static electricity pinpointing me as a target for the first jolt of lightning to strike at in the morning storm. I had to act first, say the word to summon it and end my torture. Lu-lu said I had to embrace it, and let it fill me with its power. The conductive tension was driving me mad as I began to utter the incantation.

"Lampeg…"

"Nonabel, are you okay?" Zatie's honey-sweet voice was at my ear. I looked up at her with astonishment. Why was *she* here in my nightmare? She had been shaking me to help me to wake up. We were on the floor of Lu-lu's room and I had no idea how I got there. I was clenching the old oil lamp with all my might in my hands.

"You were crying for Grandma. You sounded pretty upset," Zatie was concerned for my emotional and mental stability just as I was.

"Where am I, no, why am I in here?" The shock was catching up to me.

"You tell me, Nona. Last thing I remember was dinner at the fair," she was looking confused and frightened. I got up to leave.

"Come on, we got to start cleaning up this mess. I'll go make breakfast," I said in my best grown-up voice.

"Jesse has already made it, he thought that might help." This broke my heart a little; Zatie was tearing up as well. "We just want to help, we love you," she embraced me and began to weep sorrowfully.

"I appreciate that, Zatie, really I do. We'll get through this, you'll see. After the funeral we'll throw a huge party for your birthday and move on with our life. I mean, that's what they would want us to do, right?!"

I was thinking of all of our dearly departed, and I could tell that Zatie agreed with me. She kissed me on the cheek and happily skipped away. I stood for a moment assessing the future and questioning reality. I wasn't sure of my dreams any more, and I was afraid of what I was becoming. I almost struck myself and Zatie with a lightning bolt just then. Poor Zatie would not have survived it and my life would have been over.

No one would ever believe me; this secret could destroy us all. I could not bear losing another loved one, especially at my own hands, particularly because I was a witch. I was too naïve to understand what I was supposed to do with magic. I wished Lu-lu could help me now, but she was dead, and her funeral would be soon.

My best course of action was to bury the Diary with her and forget that I ever learned about what I was or of magic. I'd be better off if my fears and pain were in the coffin with her so I could live a normal life. That way, no one else would get hurt; Derik would never need to know why our future children were levitating or bursting into flames, and we could be happy.

This was why I must forget about what I was and bury my

past with my dead. I could reinvent my life, do what Mom was so desperately trying to do, to protect my innocence. This was what I needed to protect, my loved ones, or I would be the one to destroy the family I had left. I loved my grandmother Lucia, and I would cherish our last moments together even if I was a brat. I hoped that she was in a good place with her husband at her side. I missed you guys, but I was not ready to join you yet. That's why I couldn't be like you, Lu-lu. I had to be me. I was just plain Nonabel, a normal girl, not Nonabel the Witch.

Entry #3

Denial

Derik, and a couple of his friends, came over with tools in hand like he had promised the following Saturday morning. Jesse helped them to rebuild Lu-lu's missing wall while Zatie and I made lunch. She kept looking at me out of the corner of her eye. I could tell she was suspicious of my recent behavior. I was trying hard to pull off my best happy face again, but she wasn't buying it. I had an uncontrollable pout permanently plastered to my face. After learning the family's secret, I started to recognize subtle character traits in each of us that were on the unnatural side.

Zatie, for example, had a strong sense of empathy which helped her to know how people felt. It was almost as annoying as Lu-lu's mind reading. Zatie didn't have to look you in the eye, though. You just had to be with her in the same room. I could tell that she was debating with herself on whether or not to ask me about how I felt. She knew that I hated it being interrogated. It was more annoying than helpful.

The tension in the kitchen was starting to bug me, so I rushed upstairs with lunch for the boys before she could speak. Jesse was picking up the remains of Lu-lu's personal belongings that were scattered across her room, while Derik was replacing the studs and wood slats on the outside of the house on a ladder. The rest of his friends were outside cutting the materials and picking up the debris from the yard around the house.

"Grub's ready, boys!" I exclaimed as I pushed the door open with my hip while carrying two plates of pasta. Derik quickly climbed through the hole in the wall to beat Jesse to the food. They tussled over the bigger plate.

"Hey, let go of my ravioli, Dorik, I mean Derik!"

"Nothin' doing, Jess! Nonabel knows I eat more food than you. Now hands off!" They continued to brawl with one another for the larger portion while I escaped towards the window to survey the progress. Three members of Derik's crew were out in the side yard happily taking their food from my little sister, who was swooning over how gorgeous they all were. The best-looking of the bunch was Derik's cousin, Abraham Johnston, but everyone called him Johnny instead. He was much better-looking than Derik by far.

As fate played it, I met Derik before Johnny at my first school dance when we moved here last spring. I would have dumped Derik in a heartbeat if Johnny ever showed any interest in me. However, Johnny was pure eye-candy, not boyfriend material. He had a new chick hanging all over him every day of the week like girls were going out of style. Derik, on the other hand, was the opposite. During our first few months together, he had told me a little bit of his luck with dating. He could never get just dates, only girlfriends. He usually had one until he smothered her to death with attention.

When Johnny glanced up at me, I waved back at him pleasantly, but I tried desperately to not flirt with him no matter how cute he was. Zatie, on the other hand, enthusiastically embraced him when he came over to get his food.

"Mmm, I think she likes him, don't you?" Derik was at my ear chomping away at his lunch. He shoved an entire piece of ravioli in his mouth before I could reply.

"Uh, yeah, she's quite taken with him, but he's way too old for her, Derik. Make sure he knows that, will ya? I don't want her to get her heart broken by your cousin, the mega-player."

I watched Zatie wearily as she and Johnny continued to flirt with each other. I struggled to mask my jealousy by taking interest in the project.

"So, baby, are we going to be done soon?"

"Well, mmm num, sorry, this is really good stuff. Yeah, we can get done if you and your sister finish with picking up your granny's stuff. Then the boys and I can do the drywall and plastering here inside. Johnny should have the window finished before then if Zatie would just let go of his biceps for two minutes," he pointed down at them with his fork. I turned back to the opening to yell at her in my best Mom voice.

"Zatherine Victoria Venatora, get your paws off that boy so he can finish and drag your scrawny, little hiney up here right this instant!" I maintained a constant glare at her as she pouted away. Johnny and the others had frozen in their tracks, forgetting entirely what they were doing as though I had yelled at each of them individually.

"Whoa, honey, I never knew you could get so angry," Derik had stepped back a few feet from me to be safe from my wrath. I didn't think he was being facetious.

"As for the rest of you hoodlums, get this wall fixed and get on outta here. Seniors shouldn't be picking up on a fresh-man, no matter how cute she is. Now move it!" I screamed at them. They all collided with each other as they scurried off to return to do their jobs. Derik chuckled a little until I focused my glare at him and Jesse. They immediately pretended to be busy with something.

I walked over to the box of broken items that my brother had gathered. It was a shame that so many of her priceless heirlooms were damaged or destroyed in the blast. The funny thing about the mess was that it didn't seem to be because of a bolt of lightning. Could lightning tear pages out of books or open a box to search its contents?

I didn't think so. I still thought that someone had been searching for something Lu-lu had here. But it didn't seem like they found it because nothing was missing, as far as I could tell. That was the part that weirded me out the most; they didn't find what they were looking for. I should know; we had to pack up her stuff and clear it out the other bedroom when we finally could move here. I could just be imagining it, imagining a robbery to rationalize the motives for her death. Not accepting the truth for what it really was seemed to be how I dealt with things. Blaming God for the deaths of my loved ones was the easy way out. The truth is that it was their time to go.

I tried to salvage what I could of Lu-lu's possessions. I decided that I would look in the Diary to find a spell of some sort that could restore stuff to its original state. The repairs to the room went fairly quickly. Derik was really good with tools; he likes that kind of work. He stayed the rest of the day to help me, and his friends took off as soon as the wall was finished. Zatie ran out to the driveway to watch Johnny ride away on his motorcycle.

I think Derik was the only one of his friends that didn't ride a bike. He said that he preferred a steering wheel to handlebars any day. Derik and I were in the seat-swing watching the sunset as they all drove off. I hugged Zatie around the shoulders when she came back to the front porch of the house. Zatie had tears welling up in her eyes.

"Zatie, I know you like him, but he's way too old for ya, kid. He's a senior like yer sister and me," Derik said as gently as he could, gauging her emotions.

"Yeah, honey, Johnny would just break your heart. That's what he does best. There's no real future with a guy like him." I could tell that she was mildly feeling better, but deep down she was still upset that she couldn't be with him. Zatie told us farewell and went up to her room, to sulk no doubt. Derik and I talked for a while about life and the future as the sunset continued on into dusk. It bugged him when I talked of going to school out of state, or about college at all. Probably because he spent too much time on his muscle car and hanging with Johnny and his gang instead of doing his schoolwork. He got angry when I pushed the topic of graduation.

"I'm not the cap and gown type, Bel, you know that!" he said, frustrated.

"But you're smarter than this; I know you can do better," I replied.

"No! I'm not meant for anything more than what I am. I'm good at fixin' cars and that's what I'll do whether you like it or not!" He had a cute, grumpy pout.

"Well, how about doing what your dad does for work, become a cop or something?" I asked.

"No, anything but that. I'd make him so proud; he'd pee his pants! No, I'd never do that," he replied.

"Is this what it is all about? Doing everything you can to not be like your dad?! That's the most absurd thing that I've ever heard!" I responded.

"Yeah, if you have this conversation with him, he'll have you convinced that carrying a gun as part of the job *doesn't* mean you hafta shoot first then ask questions later. But they still do," Derik said as he got up from the swing to pace the porch. He wasn't comfortable with our disagreement.

"Oh right, guns, I'd almost forgotten. Johnny's folks they… they got shot, didn't they?" I replied.

"Yep, so that's why we made a pact never to touch the things. I hafta fake sick or lie about being busy whenever my dad invites me to the range," Derik said.

"Couldn't you just tell him about your deal with Johnny? Wouldn't he understand that?" I asked.

"No, he'd just go off on his theory about the murder and say that Johnny was just like his abusive, murderous father.

You know it was my dad that got Johnny's old man on the most wanted list. Johnny would beat me for talking about it," Derik responded as he sat with me on the porch swing.

"Then don't. I wouldn't want anyone saying crap about my parents either," I said abruptly.

"Sorry, hon, I just forget sometimes," Derik said.

"Well I don't!" I was the angry one now.

"Hey, don't get like that. I didn't mean to get you angry too; I'll just leave before we both say something stupid. I'm sorry," he was up from the seat swing and walking off the porch before I could say a word.

I sat there on the porch, watching Derik drive off angry. I knew he needed time to cool off. I decided to call him later once he and I had calmed down a bit so that I might apologize for being so curt with him. I think I sympathize with Johnny because of our common losses. Derik, on the other hand, had a perfect life. He had the car, the girl of his dreams, and the perfect pair of parents. I never got along well with his folks, maybe because I was too much like Johnny, all chewed up and spat out. Yet somehow, we both ended up walking away from our tragedies unscarred, physically that is.

Next to myself, I'd say Johnny was the best-looking kid at our school. I know that sounds conceited, but it's true. This town's gene pool is kind of shallow. I had been cursed with a flawless complexion and an eerie ability to heal perfectly from an injury without even a trace of a scar to show for it. I noticed it when I was younger, and I tried hard to hide it from my parents. That curse happened again at the time when I would have wanted a memento scar. I think my mom was trying to protect us during the accident because I remember her looking at me right before it happened with pain in her eyes. It seemed like she was regretting something. A scar or something would have been nice, but the curse robbed me of that, leaving me with only a broken heart to show for it. I call it a curse because every year someone is trying to get me to be homecoming queen or beauty queen of something and I don't even try to be pretty. I wish I was ugly just to avoid the attention.

Yet I could never seem to get Johnny to do more than acknowledge my presence whenever I hung out with him. I know I was just setting myself up for a whole lot of heartache especially if Derik knew how I *really* felt about his cousin. I decided to stop moping and finish cleaning Lu-lu's old room and begin moving my stuff into there. I went into the house and found Jesse assuming his usual position: hogging the couch and the remote as he watched wrestling. Jesse had been living and sleeping on the couch since our parents had died end of last spring. I believe that sleeping on the couch was stunting his growth. He would appreciate having his own room for once.

"Hey Jesse, where'd Zatie run off to?" I had to ask him twice before he answered.

"Oh, the crybaby; she's upstairs probably bawling over pretty boy, Johnny."

"You're an insensitive jerk!" I smacked him in the back of his head with one of his schoolbooks. "Your head would be stronger if you would just read one of those once in a while."

"Ow, watch it, you witch!" he said as he rubbed his head. I immediately turned on my heels to face him and I yanked him by the ear.

"Don't ever call me that, understand?!" I whispered to him. He nodded, and I pushed him back on the couch as I walked away.

"Jeez, someone's 'P.M.S.-ing'," I could hear him mumble under his breath as I walked up the stairs to find Zatie. "I heard that!" I yelled back.

I entered my new room and was ambushed by the scent of fresh paint and cleaning chemicals. Zatie was on the floor with a washcloth cleansing the hardwood as she sobbed. I knelt by her, but she didn't cease working. Despite her ability to perceive the emotions of others, Zatie was never very good at hiding her own feelings. She truly wore her heart on her sleeve.

"You know what the hardest part about not parents having is?" she asked.

"What's that, honey?" I asked her as she kept cleaning the floor as she cried.

"Not having someone to tell you if you're doing the job right," she stopped and sobbed quietly to herself.

"Zatie, I totally know how you're feeling, hon. I wish there was someone to tell *me* if I was being a good parent or not." We embraced and cried onto each other's shoulders until they were soaking wet. Jesse walked by and said one word as he saw us there, "Girls." Our sobbing turned to laughter and we finished cleaning the room together with happier spirits.

It was nearly 11:30 at night when we got finished with moving in all Jesse's and my stuff into our new rooms. The new paint and the furnishings I bought to replace Lu-lu's broken things had really helped the feel in the room. It was no longer so dark, gloomy, or outdated. All the doilies and drapes were tossed out and only modern décor was allowed to enter my new haven, according to Zatie the "designer." During that afternoon we went to local All-Mart for some "supplies," as Zatie put it, to help make my new room more "pretty." I had to put my foot down when it came to buying that hideous pink window treatment that she loved so much. I might be a girl, but I don't do pink.

I lied when I said that only modern décor could enter my room, because it didn't feel right not to have something that was Lu-lu's in there. So, to alleviate the bad feeling in my gut, I allowed the Diary and the oil lamp to reside on my nightstand; that was where they belonged. I left the box of Lu-lu's things under my bed until the move was over. I also wanted to wait until Zatie had finished admiring her handiwork before I would try to fix any of it.

We said our good nights and I had Jesse continue his chore of making sure the doors and windows were all locked before he could go to bed. I had to unplug the brand-new, bigger-than-the-couch TV set before he would listen to me. He seemed happier to have his own room. He liked it so much that he decided that a new TV set belonged in his room as well.

After I was sure that they were both asleep I locked my door, pulled out the box of broken heirlooms from under my bed, and took the Diary from off the nightstand. The ancient bindings of the Diary creaked open in an eerie way, causing my skin to be speckled with goosebumps once more.

"I need to look up the purpose of 'goosebumps' sometime, cuz this is starting to get annoying." I whispered to myself as I rubbed my arms. The Diary instinctively flipped open to the section about "Chills, Goosebumps, and E. E. S. P. (Epidermal extra-sensory perception.)" I forgot that the Diary could be a little *too* helpful sometimes. However, I read through the passage with mild curiosity.

Goosebumps

Goosebumps or chills: A. K. A. Epidermal extra sensory perception. It is the body's natural ability to warn us against the presence of the unwanted and the undead. It is a sensation of inward drop in body temperature and the physical presence of "bumps" upon the flesh of the person experiencing it, much like the texture of a skinned goose or chicken. The sensation is one of great importance, it must be developed and trusted if it is to protect one from possible attacks. In some cases, practitioners of magic have developed a heightened sensitivity to even the slightest thought of harm against them made by others. Warning: this sensation can be experienced by practitioners of both light and dark sorcery. Do not think of your victims before you are within striking distance of cursing them, or they will be forewarned.

Maybe it wasn't so annoying after all; I just needed to practice sensing evil more. But where was I going to find evil at this late hour? Before I had realized what I was thinking, the Diary had advanced a few sections to a bleaker, more sinister part of the book. A cold breeze passed through me like before when I was reliving my nightmare. I sighed a raspy breath of frost as I read the title in a terrified whisper. "Demons." My whisper echoed around me in the sanctuary of my new room. No wonder I sensed evil.

Demons

Demons are just one of the many forms of darker magical manifestations available to our arsenal. Demon is a name given to unwanted creatures of untamed demeanor by self-righteous bigots that dare to claim they are more worthy of divine powers than these misunderstood life forms. The Demon can appear in several forms. They can range from titanic forces of nature to ghostly sensations.

To summon a known Demon, one must possess the secret knowledge of their first given name. If you know it, then a protective circle of runes and symbols must be drawn on the floor with either sea salt or white oak ash. (Note: Before you vocalized their name, it would be wise to have a scapegoat or sacrificial victim; it could be human or animal to protect you in case of a mistake in the binding spell.) Once the Demon appears you must bind them to your servitude through a subjection curse.

"Show me the binding curse." The pages flipped again.

Subjection or Binding Curse

First you state the Demon's Full or Secret name. (Note: This will cause them to feel a burning sensation in their inner ears.)

Next state the name of the authority that told you the

Demon's secret name. (Note: Or list the genealogy from which they evolved.)

Then declare that you are their new master and bind them to you by placing consecrated shackles on their wrist or branding them with tongs and a hot poker with your seal of ownership. (Note: State your Full name when declaring ownership.)

After the binding, the Demon might display some reluctance to servitude; but persuasion is easily obtained through corporal punishment or reward.

I don't know why I continued to read about it, about evil, but having a demon to train with seemed like a good idea. The only problem was that I didn't know any demons to summon. Perhaps the trusty Diary could point me in the right direction. Just before I could touch it, the Diary turned its pages back to the section on "Dreams." I was confused by this obvious error, but I decided to review it once more. Shortly into the passage I could see the Diary's reasons for showing this to me.

Dream

The Places, People, & Things that are made from Dreams. Throughout time, mankind has never truly comprehended the absolute power that is found in the Dream World. It is a place where your imagination can roam free. Where you can live out your wildest fantasies or come face to face with your nightmares. Those will be discussed later in the section dealing with Nightmares and how to conquer them. The Daydream is a happy and peaceful place, a sanctuary from the storms of the waking world. In the Daydream we find a person called the Nix of our Daydreams. A Nix is an Astro-projected apparition of your more noble characteristics and your most favorite things...

"That's it! I can summon my Nix to help me train," I

exclaimed rather loudly. "But what is my Nix and what is it called? I guess I could sleep on it and find out tonight." I looked at the time; the hours sure pass while studying magic. I felt the uncontrollable urge to yawn as I flipped through the Diary a little more. I lay back on my pillow and held the massive Diary up with my puny arms. Sleep was overtaking me, and my arms collapsed under the Diary's weight. I was dead asleep before it hit me in the face. I could barely remember if I tried to study again or not.

Everything was so dark and dense as I dreamed. I crawled around the room on the floor, feeling for the light switch or Lu-Lu's oil lamp; just about anything that would make the darkness fade would help. The floor was covered in debris and garbage as far as I could feel, and then I felt it. Lu-lu's dead hand was hanging off the side of her bed even colder than I remembered. I stood up to find the oil lamp on her nightstand. I went to light it but something in the room moved as I did.

The lightning from the storm outside would illuminate the intruder from time to time as I tried to get a good look at it. It was enormous, much bigger than a man, but it was crouching down to avoid hitting its head on the ceiling. It was lumbering around in the room knocking over Lu-lu's furniture. It seemed like it was looking for food, but I didn't want to stay there and find out. I was almost to the door when I remembered that Lu-lu was still there, lying lifelessly in bed. When I turned around to get Lu-lu I found myself mere inches from the beast-man searching the room. It was sniffing the air with its giant snout-like nose. I tried to move away before it could smell me, but just then the room grew brighter. I worried that I had accidentally bumped into the light switch; however, it wasn't me.

Lu-lu was lighting her oil lamp with the box of stick matches from her nightstand. I gasped in fright and confusion. I thought that I was dreaming about her when she was dead; instead, I was dreaming of the moment when she died. This

Monster besides me was the killer and his focus had turned toward the light of the lamp.

"Who's there?! What's going on?" Lu-lu had gotten out of bed and was peering into the darkness by lamp light. The beast was advancing toward her and I was too paralyzed by fear to move. It was getting closer to the light and I half wanted to see what it looked like, but that would mean endangering Grandma. I couldn't live through that again, so I reacted.

A bright bolt of furious electricity snapped from my clenched fists, smashing the monster into the far wall of the room. I moved in between them to protect Lu-lu from the intruder. She touched me on my bare shoulder where the spaghetti straps of my tank-top could never possibly cover; her touch was still so cold that I shook with chills.

"Victoria, is it really you? Have you come back?" Lu-lu was so happy to see me as my mother that I dared not tell her that she was mistaken; besides, I didn't want to lower my guard. The monster was stirring, and I would not let it kill her again, not now that I could save her.

"Yes, Mother, it's me. Victoria. I am here to help." It hurt to lie even if it did make her happy, but my "Mom" impression wasn't good enough. Lu-lu stepped around to face me, illuminating my face with the lamp light. I winced away in shame even though she was smiling at me through tear-filled eyes.

"Victoria was always too afraid to use her gifts; not like you, my Bella child," her tears were welling over at that point with joy. I smiled back as I wiped her tears.

"I'm so sorry, Grandma, sorry that I didn't believe you. Sorry that I couldn't save you," she was wiping my face now as she smiled even greater. The beast was getting to its feet and I blasted it again. Lu-lu cackled with pleasure to see my powers maturing.

"Ha ha, I knew it, I knew it! Your Nightmare Nix is lightning, isn't it?!" She gestured to my hands which were charging up for the next lightning bolt.

"So… our Nixes take the form of our fears?"

"Well, only your Nightmare Nix can use your fears against you. But yes, it can appear as the thing you fear the most. I theorized that yours was lightning because of that day you got lost in the woods. Ha ha, I was right!"

I shot the creature again to ensure its defeat. Grandma laughed happily to herself as she danced around the room. Her giddy mannerism reminded me of Zatie so much.

"But Grandma Lu-lu, isn't *this* a dream? The last thing I remember was studying from the Diary you gave me, the one from the night before *you* died. This can't be real!" I was crying again, and she hugged me.

"In dreams we can go to so many places, my Bella. Some have traveled to the past, why not you. I know you have come from a possible future because I have just given you the Diary before you went to bed. Here, I'll prove that it is not a dream. Read this spell from my book; if you can, then it is not a dream, because we dream with a different part of our minds."

Lu-lu summoned the Diary to me with the power of her mind, making it appear out of thin air, I guess as her way of showing off. I began to read but the monster moved again so I shot it with a devastating bolt from my free hand. Now I was the one showing off. It made her giggle again.

"Lu-lu, we better do something quick because I don't think I can kill it with my little lightning bolts."

"Oh, you're doing fine; just read the spell."

I sighed before reading, but I was soon amazed that I could. It was also remarkable how Lu-lu knew what I was searching for. I read the spell out loud.

"Naming Your Nix

Whether it be the Nix of your Daydream or of your Nightmare; your Nixes need names or else you cannot conquer them. (Refer to the Demon and Nightmares section to understand how to conquer Demonites.) You can give them any name you wish, just be certain to keep them private or else others can control and steal them from you."

"Well, that seems simple enough, hey, I *could* read it! Wait, hey, this is real! Grandma, I can't fight this monster, I don't know enough! I don't know what I'm doing!" I slammed the Diary shut and sent it back to the nightstand just as Lu-lu had done before. That made her chuckle a little to see me move things with my mind.

"Hee he, I knew that you'd be good at this!"

"Grandma, the monster is getting up!"

"Oh, just blast it again while I get ready to trap it." I turned to 'blast it again' only to nearly get crushed by the lunging beast before my hands finally channeled the bolt into our attacker. Light filled the room as the bolt carried the beast back to the other wall. Lu-lu retrieved a few vials of strange potions and powders from her nightstand and began working on her trap.

"We should hurry cuz all my noise is going to wake the others." I vocalized my fears that my siblings would catch us doing witchcraft.

"Nonsense, I have you all hypnotized to sleep until the cock crows. Well, everyone except you, of course; you're too strong for that."

I stood aside waiting to strike the beast again if necessary while Lu-lu worked her magic. She tossed a vial of amber-colored liquid that formed an odd floating circle in the middle of the room just inches above the floor. The liquid swirled to write strange symbols and runes that I recognized from the binding spell for demons I saw in the Diary. She threw a small white bottle with a label stating 'Sea Salt' on it above the amber circle of words. Next, she said something strange; I could only assume that it was in Latin, and then the bottle of salt popped, cascading powder to solidify the words. She pulled me closer so I could get a clean shot if it didn't work, or else she was using me as a shield.

"Grandma, I would prefer not to be a 'scapegoat' and/or 'sacrificial victim', please," I said.

"Oh, wonderful, you've been reading! No, I wouldn't do that to you. Just be ready to zap him if he gets out of the circle. Oh, and cover your ears if he talks. Are you ready?!" She rubbed and stretched her hands before beginning the Binding Curse. Lu-lu took a raspy breath into her cancer-stricken lungs and raised her hands in front of her. With her mastery of telekinetic powers, she clutched the beast-man around the throat. Large, invisible hands prints were pressing deep into its neck; Lu-lu appeared to be enjoying the chance to strike at a foe with such rampant power.

Instinctively the monster woke and struggled to free itself from Lu-lu's invisible death grip. The beast squealed in agony as she lifted it by its throat to hover over the crystal circle of sea salt runes. The whole house shook when Lu-lu dropped the monster in the middle of the circle to crash painfully against the hardwood floor. The salt runes revolved around the tortured beast to form a swirling crystal prison. Every time it tried to exit the circle a white-hot salt rune would burn it.

My soul felt weak when Lu-lu began to chant the Binding Curse; it was the most disturbing sensation. Almost as if a breath of pure evil had filled my lungs to the point of suffocation. I could feel my soul dying.

"Hofu Gor-Nok, the Nix of my Nightmares!"

Every word she spoke flowed from her lips with authority and power. However, each word she said caused the beast great pain; it was trying to cover its ears.

"Thou hast escaped me for the last time!"

The monster's ears were bleeding by now and I felt a great

sense of pity for this wretched creature. There was so much pain and misery happening in the room that I forgot that this beast was my grandma's murderer. As I witnessed her torture of the beast, I unknowingly lowered my guard. I will never make that mistake again. Lu-lu was about to continue with the curse but her Nix smashed its club on the floor, causing a shockwave of fear to radiate around the room.

"Nonabel, no! Move now! You're not strong..."

I moved in front of Lu-lu to protect her, and as I was just about to blast the monster with *my shockwave* of electricity, the cloud of fear had already begun to suffocate me. Terror and panic tore through my nostrils and lungs with the most painful and nauseating sensation. I was twitching and convulsing near the bed as I drowned in my every fear and regret. My mind was coming to a boil, filled with painful images of my loved ones in agony at the hands of the beast. Lu-lu was trying to keep me from slipping into madness but the beast had broken free of the runes. He smashed the runes into tiny glass shards with his club.

"*Suspiritus Draconis!*" Lu-lu screamed as she pulled a strand of bright white smoke from her throat.
Lu-lu suddenly breathed fire like a dragon at the glass shards to protect us. The beast was charging at us now; Grandma Lu-lu stood to face it. I tried to get up to help her, but she psychically pushed me out of the way just before another wave of fear could hit me. The monster was aiming its next attack at me, Lu-lu tried to stop it but she got hit by its club and was thrown against the nearby wall. It was inches from crushing me with its gnarled club before Lu-lu came back to save me.

"No! Not her! *Abracadabra!*" That was what I *thought* she said before I slipped into darkness.

My stomach dropped down into my knees, my eyes were flooding over with tears like I had a chunk of onion stuck in them, and my lungs felt like I was just kicked in the chest by a mule. Even though it was an excruciating experience, I was, for the most part, not dead. If *that* was her version of a teleportation spell, then I'd rather walk home from wherever Lu-lu had sent me. The dark walls around me were narrow, damp, and dirty. I ran my fingers up the muddy walls to find a way out of the terror of being buried alive. There was no ceiling, just open night air, and inches beyond my reach was a patch of grass. My fearful questions were answered as I pulled myself out of the open grave. Lu-lu had made me vanish to the town's cemetery for some strange reason.

I turned to see the name on the tombstone of the grave that I had invaded. It was Michael's; Lu-lu must have thought of him before she did the spell. I couldn't tell if the impact of my landing had caused the crater, but the grave was open when I got there. It was still dark out and rainy, but I didn't really know *when* in time I was since the powers of dreaming had already brought me to the past. Lu-lu *had* said that I time traveled in my dream; maybe this was right after he died. The rain was stopping, and the last few flashes of lightning overhead allowed me to survey the grave. It was definitely empty, and his coffin was missing; I must have gone back a really long time ago. The flash of lightning that struck again revealed the most disturbing part of this nightmare, my parents. There they were, lying peacefully six feet beneath me.

"What the hell is going on here?!" I started to panic and cry as I ran through the forest of tombstones. I must have looked strange to the townsfolk as I wandered the streets in shock and only in my drenched P.J.'s. I had to figure out at what point in time I had arrived. I quickly found a discarded copy of the local paper in a trash can and ripped through it to find the date.

"Oh, thank God, it's yesterday's paper!" I sighed to myself with relief. I frantically looked around to find the nearest person I could.

"Excuse me, sir? Do you know today's date?"

"Why, young lady, are you all right?"

"I'm fine, sir; I'm just late for an appointment."

"Well, it is Sunday, the 2nd of November, ..."

"It's today! Oh, thank you! Thank you, sir." I kissed the elderly man on the cheek and took off in the direction of our farm.

"My condolences, Miss Venatora!" the old man shouted as I turned a corner. That means that it really was today, and sadly Grandma was still dead. Then Grandpa Michael should have been in his grave. But, where was he? Something wasn't right still. My head throbbed with all these questions as I jogged home.

As I neared the farm, I heard the cock crow and immediately after witnessed my siblings waking in their rooms. Soon they would be expecting breakfast, but my bunny slippers could only let me go so fast. I was near the old barn when I paused to take a breath and think before the horror could cloud my thoughts. I saw Zatie turning on the lights in my room, probably looking for me. I needed to get to the house fast, but now I couldn't sneak back into my room. I could fly, but I had not practiced enough to fly fast; I was only able to float. Zatie was coming down the stairs and was *not* going to find me in the kitchen unless I could get from here to there in an instant.

"That's it, if Lu-lu can make me disappear, then so can I." I crossed my fingers and thought hard about the kitchen. I worried more about being caught doing magic than the potential discomfort that the teleportation spell carried with it. "Oh, please let this work! The kitchen, I have to be in the kitchen, now!" I took in a deep breath of cold morning air and concentrated hard on my target.

"ABRACADABRA!" The word echoed throughout the farm as I lost control of my senses and slipped into darkness once more. When I came to, I felt a thick black smoke all around me as I knelt on the cold, hard tiles of the kitchen floor.

Zatie was coughing and complained when she entered the kitchen.

"What are you cooking, burnt garbage?! It smells horrible in here," she was holding her nose and making a disgusted face. I coughed too as I was waving the smoke out of the open window by the sink. I was pretending that I had been washing the skillet that had supposedly burned. I rinsed it off and dried my hands.

"Do you want me to cook? You know I'm better at it than you are." Zatie really was the best cook in the family, and I could take advantage of the diversion to go get changed before she noticed the mud on my clothes.

"Yep, and don't you forget it!" With that said, I rushed off to the shower to wash away my misery and the mistakes of last night. I usually relish my time in the shower, but I couldn't wrap my brain around what had happened last night in the cemetery. I decided to go back to investigate it; however, I needed a good excuse to shake off my suspicious sister.

Luckily, it was Sunday and most God-fearing people in town went to the old church that just happened to be right next door to the cemetery. I rummaged through my closet to find my one and only dress: a lavender sundress with a floral print my mom had thought looked great with my eyes. I finished the ensemble with an old pair of black high-heeled shoes from Mom's collection and my long black raincoat, in anticipation of the storms that seemed to be following me since Lulu died.

"Why are ya wearing black; did someone die?" Jesse said to me as I was heading down the hall towards the stairs. He wasn't very considerate of people's emotions like Zatie was.

"Yeah, our grandmother died. Last week. Don't you remember? Jerk!" I kind of mumbled the last part.

"Oh yeah, I forgot. Sorry. But seriously, where are ya going dressed like *that*?" He asked as he dusted lint off of the shoulder of my jacket. I lied, of course, but Jesse wasn't as hard to deceive as Zatie the empathic freak.

"I need to verify the funeral plans with the caretaker at the cemetery. Lu-lu's viewing is next week, remember?" A sudden panicked look filled his expression and I promptly questioned its meaning.

"Oh, snap! I totally don't have anything black to wear. What am I gonna do, Bel? I don't have any more money; I used up all my allowance at the fair!"

"Don't worry; I'll buy you a suit."

"Ah, could ya make it a leather jacket instead, I..."

"Ah, no! You're getting a suit," I replied.

"Thanks, sis, you're the best!"

Jesse is easy to distract; it is Zatie that I fear might catch on to my secrets. Telling her part of the truth might work, especially if she was distracted or occupied with making breakfast. I ran down the stairs as fast as my high heels could allow and avoided eye contact with Zatie as I searched for Grandma's keys for the old Ford Granada.

"Hey, gorgeous! Where are you off to?"

Must avoid eye-contact; act like I am in a hurry. "I need to see a man about a coffin," I said.

"Oh, that's... nice. Did you want breakfast before you go? I made waffles!" I could feel her trying to probe my feelings, no doubt attempting to catch me in a lie.

"Thanks, sweetie, but I really need to go. Have you seen Grandma's keys?" Crap! I made eye contact; don't get nervous. You are not lying; you really need to talk to someone about the missing coffin from Michael's grave.

"They were hanging up by the door."

"Thanks, I'll be back later; save some?!"

"All right, but they'll be cold!"

"That's how I like 'em." I imitated her tone as I grabbed the keys and closed the door behind me.

Grandma's car was ugly as sin and smelled even worse. It was the most embarrassing car to drive, especially next to Derik's beautiful Camaro. I would have to hide it before he would come over to visit. Perhaps I could trade it in someday, but for now it was sufficient. It didn't take long to drive to the cemetery, but I had to wait through the Sunday service before I could interrogate the priest that doubled as the caretaker with regards to our family plots.

He was a short, balding, old Irishman with a pleasant smile. I weaved through the church crowd to get close enough to catch him before someone else could.

"Miss Venatora! What a surprise to see *you* here!"

"Yes, Father; I am aware of the fact that my family hasn't been in a while." I could feel the blush in my cheeks warming my face in the cold morning air.

"Well, you have been in a bit of a long mourning period since your folks passed on."

"I know, and with Lu-lu passing it doesn't help us with our trust in God but we're getting by."

"My dear, God will always be willing to help you. Now how can *I* help you?" I stopped feeling so pitiful and remembered my reasons for my visit. Michael's grave. Why was it opened, and where was he?

"I was wondering if we could take a look at Lu-lu's plot. I have questions about the viewing next week." We talked casually about life as we arrived in the older part of the cemetery. I was astonished to find my grandfather's grave undisturbed. I quickly asked a few technical questions about the grave-side ceremony and then walked him back to the church.

"Now remember, Miss Venatora, you are always welcome here. Don't be a stranger."

I smiled and shook his friendly hand good-bye.

"I won't, thank you for your help, Father." I looked toward Michael's grave and let my senses search out for anything strange. Nothing, not even goosebumps; it must have been my imagination. I returned home and went through my usual Sunday routine of housework and napping. However, Zatie had beaten me to cleaning, so I went up to my room to do my homework. The Diary was on top of all my schoolbooks when

I got to my room.

I remembered what I was trying to study last night before I fell asleep. I quickly locked my door so I could pretend to be sleeping or studying. I started to rummage through the Diary for a spell to repair damaged things and the Diary found it for me as soon as I had thought it. The opened page was the table of contents for the letter "R".

I looked down the list for anything like the word "repair". Repair, Repentance, Resurrection, Restoration, Revenge... "*Revenge*, what kind of spell is that?"

As usual, the Diary opened to the section. The Revenge Section was chock-full of all kinds of nasty spells to torture and maim one's enemies. I caught myself thinking of using these on a few people, mainly Jesse for being a punk at times. I kept reading on through the day and grew irresistibly tired.

Night had fallen and so had I, into a deep and dreamless sleep. Lightning struck suddenly, waking me in terror that I had shot the bolt off in my sleep. I surveyed my room for signs of damage and was relieved to discover yet another storm brewing outside. My fears of losing control and hurting someone were not too farfetched. As I reached for my new electric lamp that was on my nightstand, I got shocked by a tiny arc of static electricity. This was something that plagued me now that I had become a super-conductor for magical energy. No wonder Lu-lu didn't like to use electricity, and I decided to stop as well. I fumbled through the drawer of my nightstand to find my book of matches. The sweet smell of sulfur burning filled my nostrils as I lit the oil lamp.

I looked around my room again to see what damage my dreaming had caused. It was one of the most terrifying things I had ever done. I walked up to the sleeping body of my sister Zatie that was floating about three feet in the air above what looked to be a circle of sacrificial runes and other offerings. There were fresh blood drops on the floor and I involuntarily let out a gasp when I thought that I might have hurt my baby sister. I put my hands to my mouth to keep myself from waking her. Then I saw the source of the blood; my hands were covered in cuts and scratches.

I found a bloody pocket-knife by the Diary on my bed. The book was opened to one of the darker sections describing sacrifices for enhancing one's own abilities. I began to weep and panic at the thought of what I was doing in my dreams. I had to do something before Zatie could wake up to this nightmare.

"I'm so sorry, sweetie; please forgive me for being what I am," I said to myself as I looked at my slumbering sister. I watched her looking so at peace and I wanted to touch her, but my blood-stained hands shook me out of my daze.

"*Abracadabra!*" I watched Zatie's serene body vanish in a flash of white light followed by pink smoke that was sucked into the miniature black hole that appeared where her heart used to be. In that instant the black hole collapsed, and a tiny pink and red supernova of faint light and warmth rippled out of existence. It was neat to be on the other end of the spell, but I teleport through black smoke, not pink. It must be a Zatie thing to be surrounded by pink. I returned my thoughts to the Diary and my need to repent of this night's mistakes. I called the Diary towards me with my mind and had it float upright before me.

"How do I fix this mess?" Indicating my wounded hands and the remnants of my unknown evil acts in my room. "Show me the 'Restoration Spell'." It instantly obeyed and I scanned the spell quickly to find a way to heal my hands.

"That won't help; I need a spell for healing." The pages of the Diary flew backwards to the letter "H" and stopped on the section on healing.

Healing

First one must rub their hands in hallowed earth either from a church garden or a cemetery.

Next, lay your hands on the inflicted or injured.

Then, while thinking of the victims when they were happy or laughing recite these words:

"What was broken and abused shall again become anew." (Then in Latin say, "Aesculapius Unctura!")

Last, a surge of heat shall escape your hands and fill the victim with the healing power of your own heart.

Warning: one must have love in their heart towards the inflicted person or the injury will be added upon your own flesh seven-fold.

I had to think for a minute about if I loved myself, then I realized that I needed to get some dirt first before attempting the healing spell. I thought of my family's plots at the cemetery and I sighed a breath of regret as I readied myself to teleport with magic.

"I hope it stops raining soon, oh well, here I go again. *Abracadabra!*" I instantly fell feet-first through a vortex of misery to land in a puddle of mud in the dark and dismally drenched cemetery. The wind and rain cleared the smoke away quickly as I got to my feet. I was standing at the edge of an open grave once more. This time it was Lu-lu's in preparation for the funeral in a few days. When I had calmed myself from my momentary panic, I began to rub mud from her grave on my wounds; man, it stung bad. As I was doing this, I noticed something large looming on the other side of the open grave. I waited for the lightning to flash again, but nothing happened.

"*Lampeggiare!*" I shot a small bolt into the sky and got a little flash of light to show me what was going on around me. There was an unoccupied backhoe sitting in the mud, but then I heard a voice.

"Whoa, man, did you see that!"

"Did lightning just hit my tractor? C'mon, let's go check it out," one of the grave workers said to the other one as they exited a pavilion they were setting up nearby.

"No way, man! It might strike again."

"You idiot, lightning doesn't strike twice."

I could hear them getting closer, so I had to do something.

"*Lampeggiare!*" I had the bolt strike the tractor and it made it unexpectedly come to life by magic.

"Holy hoppin' horse crap!"

"Man, see, I told you!"

"Hey, go turn it off before it breaks something out there, will ya?!"

"No way, man! You do it!"

"Fine chicken!" He cautiously got closer and I still needed to heal my hands before I dared to perform another spell to escape being caught. I finished rubbing the mud on my hands and began the spell.

"What was broken and abused shall again become anew, Aesculapius Unctura!" I pressed my agonizing palms together and felt the healing heat flow through them. Unfortunately for me the spell also included tiny glowing special effects that emitted from my hands like fireworks. That was something that the Diary failed to mention. The workers saw this and came close enough to see me. I had to coat my hands again with mud before I could leave so I could heal Zatie just in case I had done something to her while I was sleeping. They got closer.

"Hey you, get outta there! This is private property," he was climbing into the backhoe to turn it off and the other one was coming around it to cut off my escape. It was definitely time to leave. I jumped down into the grave and said the magic words.

"*Lampeggiare! Abracadabra!*" In a blinding flash I was gone, but my theatrics cost me, and I had to suffer through a mild electrocution session on the floor of my bedroom as the smoke cleared. I was getting used to the teleportation but getting shocked will always be annoying. I thought about Zatie and how I should heal her, when without me saying the spell, I teleported into her room. I coughed and fanned the smoke out of my way.

"Well that was convenient, now focus. What was broken and abused shall again become anew, Aesculapius Unctura!" I reached my hands to her chest as if to perform C.P.R. and I got a flash of Lu-lu's death in my mind and how I was too late to save her. My hands instinctively began to arc with electricity, and I had to stop myself from touching her. I took a deep breath and thought of the times when she was happiest. It didn't take long; Zatie was always happy.

"Aesculapius Unctura!" The warm light escaped my hands again and filled her body. A sleepy smile filled her face as she rolled over in her bed. I watched her peacefully and made a resolution to never use magic again, that is once I had destroyed the Diary. I thought of my room and in an instant, I was there; it was a shame that I would have to stop using magic, because I was just getting the hang of it. However, that was the problem; I was becoming addicted and I was afraid that it will take someone else to die before I'd stop.

I found the Diary still floating in midair in my room when the smoke vanished. I grabbed it and thought of the church by the cemetery this time so I could stake out the place before I would visit Lu-lu's grave. Again, with just the mental image of a place and the intent to be there, I was gone. It was a little chilly out and I was only in my P.J.'s, but at least the rain had stopped. The parking lot was empty, and the backhoe was parked by a maintenance shed on the other side of the church near where I had appeared. The workers seemed to have left, most likely scared out of their minds.

I thought of Lu-lu's grave once more and materialized alongside her empty grave. I took one final glance at some of my family's photos with tear-filled eyes and chucked the Diary into the deep muddy pit. I summoned some dirt with my mind from off the pile nearby to bury the Diary for good. This is where it belongs; I'm too unstable and immature to control these powers. I hope she can forgive me.

"I'm sorry, Lu-lu, but I can't do this any more."

I decided to walk home; it was early enough that I'd make it back before the cock would crow. Besides, if I was going to go cold turkey and swear off using magic, then why wait? I just wished that I had dressed warmer.

Entry #4

Burial

I got back to the house well before dawn, so I decided to shower for the second time in so many hours. I was suffering from the cold morning walk and I happily welcomed the scalding hot water. I rinsed rather than wash, I was so tired and miserable. I got out when I heard the pounding at the bathroom door.

"Aw, Nona, I hope that you didn't use up all the hot water. It's my bath day," Jesse whined to me through the door.

"It's that time of the month all ready?" I muttered.

"What? Hurry up already, will ya?"

"Fine, I'm done," I said as I exited the bathroom in my fluffy gray bathrobe and beelined it to my room. I went to my bed and fell right to sleep.

"...think she's sick or something?"

"She is looking kinda pale. Should we wake her?"

I could hear the twins whispering about me in the doorway of my room. I just wanted to sleep, to unplug.

"Guys, I'm fine. Just let me sleep in a little longer," I grumbled through my pillow at them.

"Um, Nona, it's like three in the afternoon. Have you been out drinking and didn't invite me?" Jesse asked half-sarcastically. I knew how much he would have enjoyed watching me get drunk. However, I had to come up with something believable or Zatie, the human lie detector would rat me out. I was studying, that's it.

"I was up studying for a test. Now let me sleep, will ya?!" I flipped my pillow over my ears to ignore any more chatter. Zatie pulled it off of my head immediately and hit me with it.

"Do you mean the Biology mid-term that you were supposed to take today?! I think you missed that one, honey!" She stood up exasperated and waited for a response. I rolled over and looked at her in disbelief.

"What time is it?!" I asked in terror of the answer.

"It's three forty-five in the afternoon, Bel; did you not even go to school? Man, you're a *great* role model." Jesse rolled his eyes and left the room. Zatie stood above me with her hands on her hips and tapping one toe on the hardwood floor. I pushed her out of my way and went for some clothes from my dresser as she began her rant. Zatie doesn't bottle things up like I do.

"Nonabel ...Lamia...Venatora!" Oh no, not the calling me by my whole name thing again. "What is wrong with you, young lady?!" Zatie shouted.

"What are you, my mother or my grandmother? You sound like both. Please, just spare me the lectures, all right?!" I replied as I put on the first thing that I could find which didn't smell horrible.

Zatie was really mad and continued. "Now where do you think you're going? I'm not done talking to you about your behavior, missy!"

I laughed at her and continued my search for cleaner clothes. "Are you practicing being a mom or are you just getting back at me for not helping you with the cleaning yesterday? I told you that I was busy. And now I have to catch my teacher to find out if I can make up the test or not," I said as I got ready to leave.

"Derik already asked for you; in fact, he's downstairs waiting to talk to you," she seemed pleased with herself and the fact that I wasn't perfect. I quickly put my hair up in a messy ponytail and glanced at myself in the mirror before I bolted downstairs to the family room. Derik and Jesse were sharing an extra-large bowl of nachos with jalapeños and were daring each other to eat more than the other one. Derik started to choke when he saw me walking in. Jesse was laughing at his pain, so I slapped him in the back of his head.

"Go get our guest a drink, will ya?! Jerk!" I said to Jesse as I continued, "Hiya, baby! What brings you here?" I tried to act all bubbly like Zatie would if she was being flirtatious. It worked because, for a moment, he did not remember why he came. He stammered for a second as I played with his hair.

"...Uh, I missed you?!" He did not seem so sure of himself, so I decided to kiss him to keep him in confusion.

"Aw, how sweet, thanks, baby!" I said to him as Zatie came in the room and was muttering something under her breath.

"Oh, don't play coy. You suck at it!" Zatie muttered on like that to herself as she began to cook dinner and clean the kitchen.

"So, what do you wanna do, baby?" I was trying to keep up the innocent act, but I saw the light bulb of recollection turning on in his eyes.

"Oh, now I remember; here's your homework and a note from Mr. Peterson about the test."

My plastered smile began to melt as he handed me the papers. "Is it bad, Derik? I'm screwed, aren't I?"

"Nope, I told him about the death in your family and he scheduled a time for you to make it up later." I hugged and kissed him heartily and I swear that I heard Zatie cuss under her breath. I would have to be nicer to her, but later. Now, I just wanted to celebrate with my amazing boyfriend, I made a big scene in the family room by making out with Derik on the couch. Poor Jesse was on the couch gagging in disgust and Zatie was getting flustered in the kitchen by our public display of affection.

"Oh, please; why don't you just get a room!" she finally said as she tossed some dirty dishes into the sink.

"Fine, we're going upstairs. C'mon Derik!"

"Oh, okay?!" He seemed uncomfortable with the whole idea and I only half meant it just to toy with Zatie.

"No, I'm kidding. We're going out instead, get your jacket. I'll be right back; I forgot to put on underwear. How embarrassing, right?" His jaw dropped and Jesse pretended to vomit in his bowl of chips.

"Uh, yeah?! I swear that girl's on crack!" Zatie said as I left the room. I was pleased with my success at yet another attempt to deceive my sister and I chuckled a little to myself as I walked down the hall towards my room. The happiness fled from my soul the instant I entered my room and saw the Diary lying on my nightstand. I gasped and nearly had a heart attack; I covered my own mouth to muffle my scream of panic. Lu-lu must have put it there. With shaking hands, I grabbed it and quickly threw it in my backpack. I quickly changed my clothes and dressed to go out on my date with Derik. That was a good enough cover so I could find a way to destroy that cursed book.

We went for a cruise around town and talked for a while. Derik wanted to apologize for our fight the other day and take me out to some place nice to eat.

"I got a better idea, baby. How about we get it to go, and we have a nice romantic picnic by a fire in the mountains? We could watch the sunset!" I said this to allow me an opportunity to get rid of the Diary more than anything. Derik is a good boyfriend because he's agreeable and easygoing. He'll go for most any idea as long as it requires driving in his muscle car to get there.

"Okay, I've got a blanket in the trunk."

"Oh, lovely, babe! Now let's get some grub, I'm so hungry; I don't think I've eaten anything today."

We went to the nearest place with a drive-thru and I ordered almost one of everything off the menu and Derik got his usual cheeseburger and root-beer. The drive up into the mountains was pleasant; I had forgotten how beautiful the mountains get during the fall. I was so distracted by the scenery that I did not worry about the Diary in my backpack at my feet. Derik noticed it, though, when I got out of the car after we arrived at a cliff-side campsite that overlooked the valley.

"What's in your bag, Bel? It's freakin' heavy."

"Um, it's... a... my homework from today. I was hoping that maybe you could help me with it." I smiled.

"Sure, I mean I think I might know the right answers, but don't trust me cuz I usually sleep in his class." We laughed a little and continued to set up our picnic by campfire. I started to work on the fire and asked Derik to go look for some logs to burn.

"Are you sure you can start a fire, Bel? It's kinda hard even with a lighter," he was mocking me, but I knew that if he was gone, I could attempt to burn the Diary before he'd get back.

"Oh, I can manage it, babe. Just go, will ya?!"
He chuckled and walked away while I pretended to start the fire by rubbing two sticks together. When he had vanished into the tree line, I placed the Diary from my bag onto a small pile of twigs that I gathered with my mind. I looked around one more time before using magic.

"*Suspiritus Draconis!*" I whispered and held my hand out in front of my throat. Instantaneously an infinitesimal strand of white smoke emerged from my mouth like a ghostly dragon. I knew the fire-breathing part was coming next, so I aimed my flammable breath at the Diary. The oil in the leather cover must have been combustible because it flared up and burned really fast. I watched with satisfaction as the ancient pages caught fire and curled into ash then burnt out. By the time Derik got back, the Diary resembled a burnt wad of newspaper. He was impressed by my small fire and he congratulated me.

"Oh wow, Bel! Did you do that by rubbing those sticks together?!" He stood there with his jaw dropped.

"Well, I am pretty hot. It could get hotter. Do you wanna join me?" I bit my lip seductively and he dropped his pile of wood before sitting with me on the picnic blanket. We began kissing and did so on through the night.

When he dropped me off at my house it was after midnight, but I didn't care. I was happy because I finally got rid of that evil book; for once I could probably get a good night's sleep. My elation was momentary when I discovered Zatie watching late-night TV when I came into the house.

"You're late!" She was so angry that she was gritting her teeth as she spoke. I laughed at her attempt to be the adult in the situation. I started to head for the stairs and Zatie began to follow me.

"Hey, I wasn't through talking with you, young lady! Get back here right now!" She was screaming loud.

"No, I am in charge! And what I do is my business! You got me?! Now *you* get off to bed before I ground you. Is that what you wanted to say to me?"

"Yes... Nonabel, I'm just worried. You're not yourself lately, not since Lu-lu... It scares me," She was starting to sob so I hugged her.

"Hey, I'm sorry I yelled like that. Everything is fine, thanks for worrying about me." I said then I kissed her on the forehead and sent her off to bed. She was halfway there when she stopped and pointed to something on the couch.

"Oh, a package came for you today while you were gone. I had to sign for it."

"Thanks, sweetie, I'm sorry that I've been a jerk."

"That's okay, good night!" And she was off to her room. I turned off the TV and grabbed the package from off the couch without the help of magic powers. It was medium-sized and very heavy. It had no return address and it smelt funny, like wet, burnt garbage. I took it up with me to my room and sat on my bed as I opened it. I reached in and pulled out the Diary. My heart stopped and I couldn't breathe; I dropped it in my horror onto the floor. It made the loudest thudding sound and Zatie came rushing in to check on me.

"Are you okay, Nonabel? I heard something fall."

"Sorry, I was trying to kill a spider, I'm okay."

She rolled her eyes and said good night again as she left. When she closed the door, I instinctively teleported there to lock it and again to my bed before the smoke cleared.

"No, I can't do this any more, Lu-lu. Please let it go. I am not a witch! I'm... just... normal." I was sobbing and I just wanted to be free of this nightmare. I grabbed the Diary from off the floor and walked to my desk to pull out the paper-shredder. I tore out page after page and shredded them with delight on through the night until morning. It felt great to toss the giant bag of paper scraps into the trash outside. I went right to work at having a good day and being a better guardian by making breakfast for the twins before they even got up. I even made their lunches and checked their homework by the time they came downstairs.

"Wow, Nona, what got into you?" Jesse couldn't believe that I actually cooked something edible. Zatie was searching my emotions and seemed pleased with my genuine happiness. She sat down next and Jesse to eat.

"How are you feeling today; any better?" She asked as she felt my forehead and cheeks. She tries hard to be a good mother figure. I would have to do something nice for some-day, maybe we would do a girl's night out. She would probably like that. I sat down to join them at the table to eat.

"I'm fine, but just the same I should probably take it easy. Grandma's funeral is tomorrow afternoon and we got a lot of stuff still to do before then."

"Oh, don't forget to buy me my leather jacket!" Jesse said as he walked out the door to catch the bus. Zatie fol-lowed.

"You mean suit!" I yelled after him from the front porch. I went back up to my room in near exhaustion and would have gladly used the teleportation spell to get there if it wasn't for the discomfort it brings. I wearily made it to my room and collapsed on my bed. My face landed on something hard and I sat up quickly, hoping desperately that I was imagining things. I pulled the covers back and found the Diary back to normal.

"Damn it, Lu-lu! I don't want to be a witch any more! Just leave me alone!" I screamed at my empty room as though her spirit was there, haunting me. I began to cry hysterically and shake in fear. There was no hope of being free of this blasted Diary. In my anger I seized it with my mind and flung it to my waiting hands as if to strangle it. I teleported to the roof of the house and flew upward into the morning sky.

My ability to fly was still new to me, but my bitterness gave me greater control of flying and I was gaining speed as I whizzed past clouds and upward. It was amazing to feel so free, but I had to avoid the temptation to enjoy it and just focus on destroying the Diary before it destroyed me.

I soared as high as I dared before I thought I would die from lack of oxygen and held the book above me toward space. I concentrated as best as I could through the pressure and pain in my skull.

"Leave me alone!!!" I pushed as hard as I could with my mind on the Diary. Suddenly a massive shockwave of transparent psychic energy erupted from me and shot the book off into the upper atmosphere. The psychic blast broke the sound barrier and my concentration. I was thrown back down towards the earth below.

I was falling so fast that the heat was scorching my flesh into a boil. I was so weak and tired from casting off the Diary that I could barely stay conscious as I fell to my death. I tried to shield myself from the heat with my mind and the boiling began to cease. However, I stopped watching where I was falling and lost control of my ability to fly. I was fast approaching the farm outside of my house and would surely die on impact. I was so exhausted and overflowed with agony that I dared not think about teleportation or about the word 'Abracadabra' for fear that the pain of disappearing would kill me. Then I was gone, sliding down through the abyss of anguish, and bounced softly on my bed.

"Ow... I'm... dying!" Then I cried myself to sleep.

Hours later, I woke up from having a falling dream where I hit the ground and died. In reality, I had just rolled off of my bed. The impact inflamed my burnt skin and I ached in misery on the floor. I thought of the healing spell and tried it on myself in vain. I forgot the consecrated dirt; and healing Zatie had used up my last bit.

I breathed a painful sigh and thought of Lu-lu's grave. In an agonizing instant I landed in the open pit intended to be her last resting place. I cried out in pain again from the burns and grasped the dirty walls of the grave. With a heap of dirt in both hands I thought of my bed and was there again. Dirt was flung everywhere as I screamed out in pain once more. I rubbed my hands weakly together and with my last amount of strength I recited the spell.

"What... was... broken... and abused... shall again... become anew, *Aesculapius Unctura!*"

The burning agony that coursed through my body changed to comfort and strength. I watched in amazement and exhaustion while my scorched flesh returned to a beautiful creamy-white consistency. Then I passed out for another couple of hours. Zatie had found me on the floor and had called a doctor when she got home from school. I was in bed and awoken by the doctor's medical light probing into my eyes.

"She seems perfectly healthy, my dear," he said.

"I'm fine, just tired that's all," I stated.

"She got home late last night," Zatie said.

"Well, just get some rest and call me if anything changes.

You get better, Miss Venatora," the doctor said as he left my room. Zatie walked him out and Jesse came in to bring me some chicken soup. Being nice wasn't his strong suit, but he vainly attempted at times.

"Here, try some of this; it'll help ya feel better."

"I'm sorry, Jess; I thought I was healthy enough to handle it today. Are you guys mad at me?" I asked him.

"Zatie might be. I just don't want *you* to go dying on me; then I'd hafta take care of her." We laughed at the thought of them alone and I winced a little because I was still sore from my fall. Jesse set the soup on the nightstand and got up to leave but paused at the door.

"Hey, we called Derik; he's..."

I cut him off because I was getting annoyed by being babied. "Aw, please, don't have him come. I'm too tired for house guests."

"No, Nona; he's coming to give us a ride to shop for our black clothing for the funeral tomorrow."

"Oh, well, tell him thanks, will ya?!"

"I will; you rest," he headed for the stairs.

"And don't buy a leather jacket!" I screamed as he closed my door behind him. I sighed in dread and lay back on the pillows. The smell of the soup was intoxicating so I sat back up to eat. I picked up the scalding-hot bowl from off the Diary. I accidentally burned myself on the hot soup when the shock of seeing the Diary again had sunk in. I flung the book across the room in anger with the power of my mind and screamed with frustration.

"Ugh! Please just leave me alone, Lu-lu. I can't take this any more; I never wanted to be a witch. I've done so many wrong things already and I just can't take this any more!" I was crying again uncontrollably to the point of madness. Jesse shouldered the door open as if to save me from a monster and asked me what all the commotion was about.

"I thought I saw a spider; I think I killed it," I said. Jesse sighed and lumbered out of my room, leaving me with the cursed book. I was glaring at the Diary with such dread and fright in my heart.

I couldn't believe Lu-lu was torturing me this way; I thought she loved me. As I thought of her, the Diary opened, and the pages settled on a section about Lu-lu. I painfully sighed and called the Diary to me with my thoughts. It floated softly through the air and settled on my lap. There was a photo of Grandma holding me when I was first born. She seemed so happy and was looking at me with tears in her eyes.

Next to the picture was a note that said my name. I opened it to read who it was from and I gasped in terror when I saw that it was from me. I read it out loud in a frightened whimper.

"Dear Nonabel,

I know this will be really hard for you to understand, but I need you to listen. Grandma Lu-lu can't do this alone and you know it. I'm tired of trying to convince you to do what is right. We need to be on the same page here or else we'll lose. People's lives are on the line here and you can't afford the luxury of being selfish any more. It's time for you to accept what we are, you're a witch and you can't deny it. Nothing's gonna change that fact now so please stop fighting this. Yes, the Diary is dangerous, especially if it falls into the wrong hands. That is why it is imperative that you stop trying to destroy it. You'll need it if you ever want this nightmare to stop. I know this all sounds really crazy; it freaked me out when I first read this but trust me just please keep the Diary safe. You have no idea how much I love and believe in you.

Love,

Nonabel L. Venatara

P.S. Say 'hi' to Grandpa for me."

Now I knew that I was losing it, I was sending notes to myself from the future; Lu-lu must have done this. This was her Diary and it belonged with her in the coffin. I decided that I would bury it with her at the funeral.

"If this thing means so much to you, Grandma, then you can have it back!!" I slammed the book shut and sent it to my nightstand with my mind. I regretted giving into anger and using magic once again. My sorrow and pain consumed every ounce of my energy, I decided to go back to sleep.

I dreamt of nothing; just a blank dark canvas filled my mind. I missed my normal dreams. I missed being happy. The next morning, I woke up before the twins, and I made myself a bowl of cereal while I waited for them to wake. When Zatie came down she was surprised to see me already awake. She gave me a hug and sat down to eat breakfast with me.

"How are you feeling today, sweetie?!" she said with a smile. I started to laugh and cry at the same time as she patted me on the back.

"I'm feeling a lot better, thanks for asking."

"Do you think you're well enough to go through with this today?" She asked me. I could feel her rummaging through my emotions, and I decided to let her do it. I wasn't really sure if she knew that she was doing it. Her ability could just be an automatic reflex that she was not aware of. Jesse came down the stairs dressed to kill in his new black suit. Zatie and I both whistled, and cat-called, mainly to embarrass him; I hate to admit it, but he did look really nice. If only Mom and Dad could see us now.

Of course, it was raining when we got to the cemetery; that's all it did since Lu-lu died, always cloudy, and rainy. She would say it had something to do with *my* powers, but I didn't want to think about that any more. It was time to bury that part of me and all the turmoil that came along with being a witch.

"We'd like to thank you all very much for coming to the viewing of our dear friend Lucia Linda Lamia," Father Patrick O'Leary said as he welcomed us to the funeral from behind the temporary pulpit that was set up under a canopy by Lu-lu's plot in the older part of the cemetery. Grandma's body lay peacefully in a beautiful oak coffin that was left open for the viewing. Lu-lu had most of her arrangements dealt with by her lawyer, a man I rarely saw, but knowing Lu-lu I would probably see him again. The Father went on saying a lot of things about God in Heaven, so I zoned out when he started preaching. After a while he called my name and then I remembered that I had to give the eulogy.

I'd been so busy trying to destroy the Diary that I had forgotten to write anything nice about my late grandmother. Zatie could sense my panic and looked at me with wide eyes as I sheepishly smiled when I got up. I never liked speaking in public because I ended up saying stupid things when I got nervous. However, this time was different because I had something important I needed to say, especially to Lu-lu.

"I barely knew my grandmother before she died, but I knew she loved me and my family. I wish that we had more time together, and I wish that she could have prepared me for the end, but she was taken from me and I want her back. She taught me that life isn't fair, that we need to take what God gave us and run with it. We need to do the best we can with what we have. Everything that I've ever loved has been taken away from me and I have nothing left to give. I've given you all my love, Lu-lu, now take it and run. I'll miss you." I left the pulpit because I had become a blubbering mess.

Zatie met me halfway and hugged me around the shoulders as we sat down. Jesse handed me his handkerchief out of his suit coat pocket. He held my hand while I continued to cry. Father O'Leary said a few more kind words and then invited all those who were present to pay their last respects. It was tradition that the immediate members of the family would be the first to view the deceased, but I was crying so hysterically that Jesse signaled to the priest to allow everyone else to go on ahead of us.

I looked up and watched all of these strangers smiling

and saying goodbye to Lu-lu as they walked by her coffin. I didn't know half of these people, but how much did I really know about my grandmother? Tears were still flowing down my face, tears of pain and regret. It wasn't until I felt the tear drops hitting the Diary, that I remembered I had brought it with me. Now was the time to finally be rid of it and return it to its rightful owner. I stood up suddenly; this startled Zatie and Jesse. We walked up to Lu-lu's open coffin together as a family.

"She's kind of freaky-looking lying like that!" Jesse said in a low whisper, and it made me chuckle a little. Zatie slapped him in the back of the head and told him to 'shhh'. I was holding the Diary on the edge of Lu-lu's coffin and lovingly looked at it as I wiped off my tears from its cover. Zatie could tell that I wanted to be alone and she gave me a kiss on the cheek, then she left. She grabbed Jesse by the elbow, and he followed. I stared at Lu-lu for the longest time; she looked so peaceful. I placed the Diary underneath her hands and leaned in to give her a kiss on the cheek. Lu-lu suddenly grabbed my hand with a cold, dead grip. Sheer terror replaced the tears that were in my eyes as her withered hands pulled me closer to her. I could smell the stench of decay on her breath as she began to speak.

"You little ingrate, the Diary was a gift. Keep it close or I will have to give it to someone else," she whispered in my ear with such disdain in her voice. Lu-lu's vacant eyes were looking in Zatie's direction. My worst nightmares were beginning to unfold as I realized what Grandma was planning.

"No, Lu-lu, you can't; she's just a child!"

"Then keep the Diary," she said with her icy blue eyes penetrating my soul. I could feel Lu-lu intruding into my thoughts; she knew she had me trapped.

"This is madness, Lu-lu, she'll never believe you. Besides, I refuse to teach her, you'll have to..."

"Do it myself?! You're just like your mother. A stubborn pair of mules the both of you."

"Grandma, stop it; this is not who I am! I'm not a witch and I'm not gonna help you; I'm sorry." I had to use telekinesis to help my hand pry Lu-lu's boney dead fingers from my arm. Father O'Leary came up to the coffin and was standing next to me. Lu-lu instantly let go of my hand and returned to her frozen state of death.

"Miss Venatora are you quite all right?" he whispered to me and patted my back.

"I'm fine, father. I just had a really bad year and it's finally starting to hit me. Thank you again for all that you have done. Lu-lu would have loved this." I wiped my tears and returned to my seat next to Zatie and Jesse. Father O'Leary said some final words and a prayer before they closed Lu-lu's coffin and lowered her into the earth. Zatie was getting emotional now, so Jesse walked her back to the car. Everyone else had left but I needed to stay, to watch as they filled her grave with dirt.

I felt nothing, only hollow and empty. I would've liked to mourn her death with loving memories in my heart. Unfortunately for me, I had only been haunted by the memory of how she died and the unforgivable truth that she shared with me that night. It will take me a lifetime to forget what she said and an eternity to forgive her for calling me a witch and tricking me into becoming like her. I no longer felt love towards the only person who really knew me as I am. May you rest in peace, Grandma Lu-lu, and may my secret die with you.

When the workers had finished, I was still frozen in my spot holding a single white rose. My anger and bitterness consumed me, and I thought of sealing her grave with an onslaught of electricity from the heavens. The temptation was so great that I could taste the lust for power causing me to salivate, its power coursing through my veins. As I clutched the rose tighter and tighter in my grip, the thorns pierced my flesh and I reacted. Tiny threads of electricity coursed through my hands, causing the rose to wither and dry up into ash. Jesse came up behind me and told me it was time to go. He put his arm around my shoulders while we walked back to the car.

We had a small 'get together' afterwards back at the house. I was so exhausted and burnt out that I really didn't want visitors. Zatie and Jesse accepted the friendly condolences from the townsfolk and Derik sat with me as I cried more. I just wanted them all to leave.   "Miss Venatora? I'm sorry to do this now but do you remember me? My name is Harold Anderson. I represent your late grandmother's estate."

"Yes, I recall when we met, how can I help you, Mr. Anderson?" I said as I wiped the tears and mascara from under my eyes.

"Could I meet with you next week and talk about her will? I could come by the house if that would be more convenient." He handed me his business card and waited patiently to shake my hand. I took the card, shook his hand, and agreed to the meeting.

"Would Monday be all right?" I said as I looked for his contact info on his business card; there was none.

"Monday would be great; I'll just bring the paperwork and the safety deposit box she left for you. Oh, don't worry about the key; your grandmother left it with us. I truly am sorry for your loss. She was... a great woman," he promptly left and I noticed that only a few people had remained in our family room. When they had left, Zatie and Jesse began cleaning up the house and sent me up to my room. I flung myself on my bed and immediately fell right to sleep.

Finally, I was having a normal dream; at least I thought it was a dream. I was walking through the wheat field at the other end of our farm near the forest. The sun was setting, and the light caused the wheat to glow a beautiful amber color. I heard my mother calling me from the house and I went running to meet her. I must have been reliving something from my childhood. I was excited to see my mother again, so I ran even faster than normal. As I got closer, my mother and I got older. I went from being a little girl to a grown woman and my mother aged until she was incredibly old. That's when I recognized that it wasn't my mother at all; it was Lu-lu. The sun had set entirely, and the storm clouds filled the sky with blackness. Titanic thunder rolled through the valley and there I stood again in the rain as I did in the nightmare I had when Lu-lu died.

She cackled once again and called down her onslaught of lightning from the sky, shattering the earth we stood upon, causing it to all crumble beneath our feet. I began to slip into darkness and worried that I was teleporting again in my sleep. I closed my eyes hard and thought of nothing so as to avoid using magic. The next thing I noticed, I was standing by Lu-lu's open coffin. I saw her body lying there frozen and lifeless. I stepped in closer to see if she was really dead. That was when she opened her eyes and climbed out of the coffin, barely supported by her decaying flesh and bones. I walked backwards through the cemetery; my heart was filled with fear and rage as she began to stalk towards me with an evil grin on her face and a raspy cackle in her throat.

"Where is my magic book, little girl? I want it, give it to me!" Her voice seemed really dry and haggard; it wasn't like Lu-lu it all. It made goosebumps speckle my body and sent an icy shiver down my spine.

"I don't have it, Lu-lu! I got rid of that damn thing and I don't want it any more. Stop haunting me!"

"Don't LIE TO ME, little girl! I want that book!" she growled at me like an angry animal. Why didn't she know where the book was? And why did she keep calling it 'the book'? She nearly always called it her Diary. This couldn't be Lu-lu because I already gave it back to her.

"If you are really Lu-lu, then you would know where the Diary was because I gave it back. But you're not Lu-lu, are you?" This twisted version of my grandmother started to get angry with me and I could sense that it was about to strike at me with great power because my goosebumps were inflamed, alerting me to danger: I prepared myself for an attack.

"You LIE, witch, tell me the truth or I'll have to kill you!" She gripped my neck psychically as she had done to the beast in her room and began to squeeze my throat to the point of suffocation. She made me float closer to her so that she could whisper in my ear.

"Just like I killed your grandmother." I couldn't believe what I had heard; this wasn't Lu-lu at all, it *was* the beast and he was trying to kill me now. I could feel the life draining from me; I had to act quickly.

"Lampeggiare finnito!!" I remembered the first time that Lu-lu showed me this spell as I shot her impostor. Dozens of good-sized bolts sparked from my hands but only a couple of them actually made contact. 'Evil Lu-lu' squealed in pain as it twitched on the ground when it landed about twenty feet away from me. I rubbed my sore neck and throat while I tried to catch my breath again. It was starting to get to its feet, so I readied myself for another ambush of psychic power.

"How dare you hurt an old woman; where are your manners, child? *Lampeggiare de Zeus!*" She cackled into the sky as she shot a barrage of lightning at me. I stuck out my hand in front of me to stop it but that didn't work. I wasn't shocked, though; I actually absorbed it like it was welcomed heat from a fireplace on a cold winter's day. The impact of the force pummeling against my body pushed me back about thirty feet down the row of tombstones.

It felt like I sprained one of my ankles as my feet dug a trench in the mud when I tried to resist. I immediately reacted, sending the harnessed electricity back at her without having to say the spell out loud. It made an even deeper trench when she crash-landed into a line of headstones. Evil Lu-lu lost control of her form and became the boar-beast for a brief moment as it climbed out of the crater. It dusted itself off and returned to the form of Lu-lu. I gasped when I realized that I had just carved a ten-foot deep canyon straight down the middle of my family's plots. Grandpa, Dad, and Mom's coffins lay broken and scattered down the ravine like fallen trees after a storm.

"Oh, crap! What have I done?! Sorry, Mom and Dad." I forgot that Evil Lu-lu was getting ready to strike at me again while I was apologizing. The Gor-Nok dressed in Lu-lu's clothing could sense my dread and regret for my mistakes and took advantage of my moment of weakness. He raised his arms to the sky as a cloud of fear and evil encircled him. It looked like an army of indistinguishable devilish creatures that were made up of ghost-like smoky material dancing around him. It was rather freaky, but then he spoke.

"Yauk Untu He-wanei. En zombia Demoni. Hofu di Morte!" I didn't know what he said exactly, but I know what the spell did. The little ghost demons took possession of the corpse remains of my loved ones, turning them into brain-sucking zombies, I assumed. Normally I wouldn't be afraid of zombies, but I'm a pretty smart girl, and they looked hungry.

"No! That's not fair! Can't you just let them rest in peace? What did they ever do to you?" I cried out.

"No, my dear; there's no rest for the wicked. Not after what they have done to me. Now, bring me the girl!" he shouted to the zombies. I ran through the cemetery in the mud and rain, slipping every time I tried to make a turn. The zombies cheated and traveled through the ground to cut me off. I was trapped, with the Gor-Nok behind me and zombies blocking my escape. I didn't want to hurt my family, even if they were already dead, and the Gor-Nok knew it.

"Dangit, Lu-lu, why didn't you teach me about zombies?" I whispered to myself as I tried to think of something that would work. The zombies got closer and the Gor-Nok, still pretending to be Lu-lu, was cackling wildly as it absorbed my fear.

"Please, guys, you know I'm not the smartest one in the

family. Zatie is so much better at biology than me. It's her brain you want." My pleading was pointless, and my zombie parents reached out to grab me.

"Sorry, guys, but you're not real. Please forgive me... ... *Lampeggiare de Zeus!*"

The zombies and I were bombarded by my barrage of lightning bolts that immediately came to my rescue. I embraced every jolt and surge of electricity with a greater appreciation. The zombies, on the other hand, could only take so much before bursting into flames. When the lightning stopped, I released a powerful shockwave of all the electric energy that I had just bottled up onto the charred skeletal remains of the zombies, scattering their bones in every direction. Evil Lu-lu was slowly applauding.

"So, you're willing to destroy the ones you love over a book. I thought I had you figured out. Oh well, I'll have to do this the hard way," she began to mutter another curse. I was too exhausted to fight with magic any longer; I had to think of some way to trick it, then maybe I could find a way out of this madness.

"Hey, wait. If you really are my grandmother, then you would be able to tell me what she said on the night she died; then I'll give you the Diary," I proposed.

She stopped to listen to my offer. Then she thought about her answer. "I told you that I loved you, Nonabel," she replied.

"Oh, you don't know her at all." I zapped the beast back into the crater with a bolt.

"No, Nonabel! Please stop, I am your grandmother; I am Lucia." I shocked it again as it tried to get out of the hole in the ground.

"You lie!" I cried out as I shot it again. "Besides, she always told us to call her 'Lu-lu'." It changed into the beast every time I shocked it. "And she never called me by my real name." I was crying at this point and getting angrier with every bolt I shot at it. "I was her 'Bella', her beautiful child and you killed her, *YOU MURDERER!!*"

I grabbed 'Evil Lu-lu' psychically around the neck and pulled her out of the hole to rest at my feet as I strangled her. She began to cackle and cough, so I grabbed her with my bare hands to choke the evil out of her without the aid of magic. The boar-beast erupted from the false Lu-lu visage and struck me to the ground.

"I tried to do this the easy way, but you leave me no choice. I'll just have to ask your little brother or sister to give me the spell book. Or better yet, I'll torture them in their dreams until *you* give it to me. What do you think?" He chuckled and pressed me into the mud with his club on my back. The thought of Jesse and Zatie being tormented by Lu-lu's killer both terrified and enraged me, releasing my fury. I shot a massive blast of lightning into the ground that threw us both into the crater.

The Gor-Nok was smashed into the crater wall and I ended up on the floor. He was charging at me now and spouting off what appeared to be spells in some foreign language as he slammed his club on the ground. Each time it did this, a semi-transparent shockwave of tangible fear tore through the ground toward me and I barely rolled out of its path. I looked up to find him standing above me ready to strike me down with a crushing blow.

"Prepare to face your fears, little girl. *Hofu-Lunako!!*" Then he let loose the full power of his fear curse at me. I covered my eyes to shield myself from the blow, then everything went dark like when Lu-lu first teleported me. That was the only way out; Lu-lu had teleported me out of a dream before. Why couldn't I?

His club was mere inches from my face as I thought of my bed and disappeared into the abyss. The Gor-Nok's cries were ringing in my ears as the smoke cleared and I tried to shake off the terrorizing effects of his roar. I sat up in bed dripping with sweat and out of breath. I surveyed my dark room, relieved that I was safe at home again and what I had just experienced was nothing but a nightmare. I wanted to light the oil lamp on the nightstand. I searched in the dark and touched the Diary. I was relieved to discovered that the Diary was safe and sound here waiting for me. I grabbed it immediately and hugged and kissed it lovingly. I opened it to the last entry that Lu-lu wrote. I read the last line out loud to myself.

"I am tired of running from... ...*it* every night."

"Now that I know what 'it' is, how do I destroy it?" Of course, the Diary thought that I was asking it a question and it flipped its pages instinctively to help.

"No, stop! I don't want to learn any more... magic. Just let me write my thoughts in you. You know, like you were a 'normal' diary." It listened and returned to the last page and I found a new entry added under Lu-lu's.

"No, stop! I don't want to learn any more... magic. Just let me write my thoughts in you. You know, like you were a 'normal' diary."

Nanabel

"Okay, that's kinda cool, but you don't have to write *everything* I say. You got me?" The Diary was starting to write what I had just said but then erased it and waited patiently for me to command it again. I told it to erase the last entry I had accidentally written and began a new one. This time I thought of the night that Lu-lu had died and I continued to dictate the events since then to the Diary until it was morning.

Even though I had sworn off using magic, there was nothing wrong with keeping the Diary as a personal journal.

Besides, magic is a hard habit to kick once you get started. I was just going to limit myself to writing in it and avoid studying magic altogether. Then maybe one day I might stop teleporting myself to strange places on accident or I could turn on a light switch without getting shocked any more. Lu-lu was right; the only way for me to keep it safe was by using it. I most definitely didn't want it to end up in the hands of that murderer.

Who knew what he would do once he got it? He was too powerful! I had to remember to look up everything that there was to know about the beast before it came after me again. My biggest fear was that Zatie might go snooping in my room and find the Diary. She loved books, especially old ones. I decided to lock it in the nightstand when I wasn't using it and I began to lock my room whenever I was gone. Everyone thought I was being strange, but I told them to butt out of my business, and they respected my privacy.

I began to enjoy using the Diary as if it was a regular Diary, but I would have to stop myself from doing each new spell that I excitedly came across. I could feel the lust for power rising like a tidal wave each time, but my newfound resolution to be 'magic-free' was stronger. Soon it would all be a bad dream and I would finally be free of my nightmares.

Entry #5

Questions

Dear Diary,

I fell asleep talking to the Diary for so long that I don't even remember when I passed out. So hard to tell what's real any more, everything feels like a dream. By the time I woke up in the middle of the day, I noticed that Zatie had taken the day off to take care of me. And this time I didn't have to fake sick; I really was. Even so, the last few days have drained me so much. I don't remember the last time I slept well.

Nanabel

Besides the fact that Zatie would not let me leave my room, I was too queasy to get out of bed. She really enjoyed playing 'Mom' every once in a while. Later in the afternoon, Derik brought me my homework and notes from our shared classes for me to study. He only stayed for a little while because he was going out with his cousin Johnny to play pool at his uncle's bar. Johnny worked there on the weekends to help out his Uncle Mike sometimes as a bouncer. Derik mainly went there for the free pool and nachos. Johnny would take advantage of his job at the bar to sneak some beers from time to time. He would drink but Derik wasn't much of a drinker.

I felt bad that I wasn't feeling healthy enough to go be with them. Part of me wanted to ask Johnny what it was like for him to cope with so much loss. But I was afraid that the other part of me that was infatuated with him would get the better of me. That was not really fair to Derik, especially after all we had been through. I knew that what I felt for Johnny was just a passing crush and that it would go away the more I avoided him. Just like avoiding magic would cure me of my addiction.

Seeing how I was left alone to my thoughts, I decided to peruse the Diary one more time so that I could figure out everything there is to know about dreams and nightmares. I knew it was cheating but every once in a while, I still used telekinetic powers to do things such as unlocking my nightstand so I could call the Diary to me. I had it float in front of me for fear that the weight would crush my fragile body.

"Show me everything you know about dreams and nightmares!" The Diary quickly obeyed and opened to a familiar section. I reread this section from the beginning because I fell asleep that last time I had started it.

Dreams

The Places, People, & Things that are made from Dreams. Throughout time, mankind has never truly comprehended the absolute power that is found in the Dream World. It is a place where your imagination can roam free. Where you can live out your wildest fantasies or come face to face with your nightmares. Those will be discussed later in the section dealing with Nightmares and how to conquer them. The Daydream is a happy and peaceful place, a sanctuary from the storms of the waking world. In the Daydream we find a person called the Nix of our Daydreams. A Nix is an Astro-projected apparition of your more noble characteristics and your most favorite things or they can embody your carnal desires and darkest fears.

There must be opposition in all things and thus is the nature of your daydreams and your nightmares. One nix cannot live without the other or the price you pay for destroying part of yourself is an eternity of madness. Through time and perfecting of one's skill, the nix will evolve. One must become familiar with both aspects of their personalities to better understand themselves.

Nightmares

The word nightmare is derivative of the words Night and Mara. Mara is the name of an ancient Norse spirit of the northern countries that was believed to torture and smother dreamers to the point of death by sitting on their chest. (See also crib death or sudden infant death syndrome.) It is believed that the pressure of a demon or ghost upon you would induce images and sensation of fear, helplessness, and panic. The Nix of your Nightmares is the most powerful of the nixes. Do not attempt to destroy your nightmare nix; they can only be conquered. Survival is the basic instinct of the nightmare nix and they will do everything in their power to exist, even if it means death to the dreamer.

That was what happened with Lu-lu and the Gor-Nok.
I was getting frustrated with reading the same things over and over again. This didn't tell me very much at all about why Lu-lu's Nightmare Nix was still kicking around still even after she had died. I thought to ask the Diary to search through *her* entries with regards to the Beast. As usual, the Diary humbly obeyed and the pages began to flip, exposing a section towards the back.

Fear

Fear is the uncontrollable and sometimes immobilizing emotion that comes with ignorance of the unknown. Like all things, the power of fear can be used for both good and evil. A little fear can keep us from doing something stupid or dangerous and in that way, it is used for good. A lot of fear, especially if it is used as a weapon, can paralyze, or even drive one's victims to insanity. Fear as a weapon is achieved through a fairly simple curse using one of the seven first spoken languages. Say the word "Fear" followed by a trigger phrase such as (fear) of death, or heights etc.

Just reading about it made my skin crawl. The worst part was that Lu-lu wrote this, that she used this on people. She had done the fear spell on me. I moved from one section to another until night had fallen. Eventually, I got so frustrated with these wild goose chases, and not getting answers that I just went back to sleep. At first, I wasn't certain if I was dreaming or not, as usual. I got out of bed and went to the bathroom for a glass of water. When I turned on the faucet it began to rain in the room and thunder rolled outside in the field. I was so afraid of having that same nightmare where Lu-lu shocked me with electricity that I tried to wake myself up. Slapping myself on the cheek didn't work, I tried splashing water at my face from my glass by my bed. The next thing I knew I was swimming in the creek past the farm in the forest.

When I got to the bank of the river I tried climbing out against the force of the current. The rocks on the shoreline felt like the steps of the front of the house; like before, I was there just by thinking about it. I stood up and opened the front door, and then I nearly had a heart attack when I saw Jesse sitting on the couch watching TV. His expression was stone cold and vacant; he didn't move at all when I walked past him.

I ran up the stairs toward my room, but I never got to the top. The staircase didn't get any longer; I was just not going anywhere. I had to fling myself psychically to the top of the stairs and pull with all my might to resist a near-impassable gravitational force. The house moaned and creaked as though it was coming apart at the seams. The floor of the hallway beneath me snapped in half and I would have fallen through if I wasn't able to grab at Zatie's door handle. I hung there for a minute to assess my situation. The house appeared alive and hungry.

I decided that Zatie's room was my only escape. I tried turning the door handle to open the door, but the handle snapped off in my hands. I fell down to her threshold, I caught hold of it, and pushed the door open with my mind. Something irresistible was pulling me down into the chasm of the house. It took incredible effort both physically and psychically to finally get my body into Zatie's room. Upon entering I noticed immediately that this was not Zatie's bedroom any more. It was my mom's room when she was a teenager. Whatever fear and anxiety that plagued me so far in the dream had since fled and I was left with a feeling of awe and wonderment. Mom was such a hippie; I couldn't count the flowers that were painted on the walls, there were so many.

Before I knew it, I was lost in my survey of her room when suddenly her bedroom window opened. Without thinking about the spell, I teleported to the corner of the room and hid behind the dresser. It was Mom, but she was years younger than the last time I saw her alive. She must've been 16, 17 years old, tops. She seemed very happy and pleased with her ability to sneak back into the house undetected. She wasn't alone, though; a younger version of my dad poked his head in to give her a final 'good night kiss.' He looked like he wanted to come in but suddenly the door handle jiggled, and Mom's look of happiness turned into absolute terror as she nearly slammed the window shut on Dad's fingers. I looked to her bedroom door and I was confused to see an angry yet handsome man in his late forties glaring at Mom.

"Good lord, Dad; you nearly gave me a heart attack!"

Mom said, startled. I had to cover my mouth to keep quiet when I realized that the man in her room was my grandfather.

"You better hope *He* hears your prayers after I'm done with you, young lady!" Michael exclaimed.

"Aw, Dad! Give it a rest; you knew I was gone the whole time. You probably had Mom spying on me."

"I try not to trouble your mother with matters of your discipline; and don't take that disrespectful tone with me. You're still a guest under my roof and you will treat me with respect," he added.

"Even if that respect isn't earned or mutual?!" Mom didn't seem the least bit at all intimidated by Granddad's macho persona.

"And being rebellious doesn't earn it. You were out with that Venatora boy again, weren't you?!" he said. Grandpa Michael appeared to be getting larger every time he spoke, but Mom didn't look as if she was scared by him. She continued to yell at him.

"Why do you care? I can be friends with whomever I want to. He's a good boy, Daddy, just give him a chance!"

"You know why I can't allow you to see him again!" Michael yelled.

"Why, because he's Christian?!" she asked.

"No, because he's not one of us!" he stated.

"I hate you, I hate Mom, and I hate what I am; now leave me alone!" She was starting to cry.

"Do you love him?" he asked.

"What, why?" She was sobbing.

Grandpa let out a huge sigh and appeared to calm down. "Because Love is the only thing worth losing your family for, or your life," he began heading to the door and was fidgeting with the handle as though it was stuck.

"No, Dad, just go to bed; I promise I won't sneak out to-night," she said.

"I left my lamp on in there; will you get it for me?"

"I will, good night, Dad."

"Good night Vicki."

When he left the room, my mom followed him to the door but shut it after him. She whispered something to the door and slid the door handle to the other side, then opened it the other way. Mom opened the door the wrong way and went through. All I could see from my corner of the room was that the door opened up to reveal a new stairwell. I tried to sneak over to get a better look, but Mom soon came down with the oil lamp in her hand.

She was blowing it out when I tripped over a pair of her shoes. I tried to stop myself from hitting the ground, but she had already heard me. She snapped her fingers and the lamp was lit again, but it burned more brightly than I had ever seen it. The light scalded my eyes and penetrated my eyelids when I tried to close them; there was no escaping it. Mom started to panic and screamed at the top of her lungs. Her voice seemed to be enhanced by magic; it was intoxicating and agonizing at the same time. I imagined it was much like a cry of a banshee.

"Daddy! Help me; someone is in my room! Please hurry, Daddy!" Mom's cries for help were ear-piercing. Then all of the sudden, Grandpa Michael appeared out of thin air and took aim with his hunting rifle at me. It was time for me to leave, so I thought of the one place that was far enough away from the house as I had ever dared venture through teleportation. However, Grandpa was a dang good shot, and the bullet followed after me into the vortex.

Fortunately for me, I thought of the graveyard. I knew I could use the hallowed earth to heal my body; because I didn't think that I was going to be quick enough to dodge a bullet. I hadn't found a spell to give me catlike reflexes, yet, so, I decided to let it hit me in the least vital part of my body once I exited the black hole. I felt it crushing the bones in my left shoulder blade and it made me spin a little before hitting the ground. I clawed at the earth around me with my good arm, painfully rubbed my hands together and performed the healing spell on my shoulder.

The whistle of the slight breeze that was passing through the coin-size hole in my shoulder moments before slowly melted away into a warm, calming sensation. I stood up and looked around the cemetery to see if I could find any recognizable landmarks. When I tried to read a nearby tombstone, my eyes went out of focus and my head began to spin. I felt woozy and thought I was going to faint, so I sat down to try to breathe. Lightning flashed, followed by the rolling thunder that echoed through the forest of headstones. I wanted to get back to bed and escape this nightmare, but I had no idea *when* I was or why I was there. I knew teleporting back to the house could risk Granddad shooting at me again, so that option was out. Shocking myself awake with a lightning bolt seemed like a better option, but I had already had that happen in dreams without waking up afterwards. I was starting to panic.

"How do I get out of here? How do I wake up?" The lightning flashed again, and the Diary appeared in front of me out of nowhere. I screeched a little either because, the lightning or because of the sudden appearance of the Diary in my dream. Either way, it took me a few seconds to calm down before I commanded the Diary to show me a way out. It was dark in the cemetery, so it was close to impossible to read anything. In anger I grabbed the Diary with both hands and slammed it shut. Instantly the cemetery vanished from around me and I was safe again in my room. The cock crowed, and I was happy it was morning once more. I wrote my thoughts down in the Diary of last night's adventures.

Dear Diary,

I really need to stop falling asleep while reading the Diary. It only seems to induce nightmares and raise more questions than it answers. I'll have to put it aside for now while I go to the library to search about the Gor-Nok or anything else on Nightmares. I have to know what I am up against if it decides to come back for a rematch. I hope by then I'll be ready to get it out of our lives for good.

Manabel

It totally freaked me out when I woke up later that morning to the sight of Jesse staring at me from the foot of my bed, while eating my breakfast. It was eerie, the way he was studying me, almost as if he was preparing to paint my portrait. It was rather uncomfortable.

"You don't look sick to me. I think you're faking it, but I just don't understand why. I thought you liked school and crap," he said in between bites.

"Jesse, get out of my room and give me another bowl of cereal, jerk!" I presumed that it was his turn to take care of me while Zatie went to school. I was sure that he didn't protest the idea of staying home. Other than him being a little weird at times, I didn't mind having Jesse as a babysitter. He was much easier to persuade to look the other way than Zatie was, and he wouldn't mind at all if I left the house. I went about my affairs like it was any other day. After I had showered, I began to actually feel better. I dressed quickly to get out of the house before Zatie could get home, or Jesse could ask me any questions. I tossed the Diary into my backpack and bolted for the front door before Jesse could react.

"I'm going out. I'll be back later!" I yelled.
"Wha... Where are you going?" Jesse asked.
"The library, c-ya!" I responded as I left.
I had to take the car to avoid suspicion. Plus, I was still trying to *not* use magic as much as possible. It was about a 15-minute drive from the farm to the nearest library in town. I was hopeful that I wouldn't have to travel to the closest major city to find what I was looking for, but I needed to start somewhere. The only positive experience I had there at the

town's library was the friendly and attractive clerk at the desk who helped me find the sections I needed. The downside was that someone had already checked out almost every book on 'dreams and nightmares' in the place.

"Weren't you here yesterday?" the cute clerk asked as he brought me some other reference options to the table I was studying at.

"I doubt it. I was at home sick with the flu." "Well, maybe you have a slightly less attractive twin sister. You wouldn't happen to know if either of you were available for dinner, and a movie tomorrow night, would you?" he flashed a smile as he asked.

"Unfortunately, I'm taken, but my twin sister might be free," I sheepishly replied.

"I'll just give you my number so you could pass it on to her," I sheepishly smiled, and it felt like I blushed as I took his number. I was such a bad girlfriend. I needed to get my life back to normal so that I could enjoy being a monogamist again with Derik. I returned to my search of the library and was only able to find one book that talked about 'lucid dreaming,' something I'd never heard of, but hey, it was a start. I returned home a little before dinnertime with false hope that Jesse had cooked something remotely tasty, but I was disappointed that he didn't. His dinner consisted of sunflower seeds and a cola. Then I realized Zatie wasn't home and school had been out for hours. It was unlike her to be gone without letting me know where she was.

"Hey, Jess. Where's Zatie at? Shouldn't she have made supper by now?" I was mildly concerned about her whereabouts, but way too hungry to sincerely care.

"She's at a friend's house for some sleepover. The number is on the fridge," he pointed to the kitchen without looking and continued to watch TV.

Good, I was glad that she was gone; now I had a chance to search her room for clues that might lead me to that secret doorway. My desire to learn more about Grandpa's hidden room was a welcome distraction from my pointless studies of the Diary. I grabbed some leftovers from the fridge and headed upstairs. Once there, I used my telekinetic powers to open *my* door with my mind as I teleported into Zatie's room. I had to hold firmly onto the plate of food so I wouldn't spill all over her room as I appeared out of the vortex. I almost forgot that I left *my* door open, so I had to concentrate hard to close it from another room. It slammed a little too hard. Jesse would just think that I was mad, so he'd probably leave me alone. I quickly went to work on breaking into the secret door.

First, I tried to slide the handle to the other side like my mom had done in my dream, but it wouldn't budge. I then used my psychic powers to push it into place and only received a mind-splitting headache as a result. Frustrated with my vain efforts, I turned to the Diary for help. I pulled it out of my backpack and sat down in the middle of the room.

"Show me what you know about Grandpa's secret room." The Diary was motionless in my lap. "How do I open a hidden door?" It quivered and flipped open to a section in the front. I had to blow some dust off of it before I could read the page.

Hiding Places

Hiding places can take the form of any mundane object, from a chest to a doorway and so forth. Like a genie's lamp, the hiding place can distort space and time to house a single secret or an entire universe. To properly create one, the object must be consecrated with the ashes of a newborn calf given in sacrifice during the first snow of winter. Then the object must have the unlocking phrase or password engraved into its face with the sacrificial knife. Use the same knife used to sacrifice the calf. With a lock of your hair (also cut with said knife,) paint in blood the same word over the engraving to make it invisible to the naked eye. *Note: The Seer's Sight can be used to locate the unlocking phrase. The sight can help you to reveal the steps to enter the hiding place or and any hidden traps. It would be best to use a poem or a riddle to conceal the unlocking phrase.*

Additional curses and security such as locks, traps, and guardians can be added to ensure the secrecy of the hiding place.

Dear Diary,

In vain I tried for hours to unlock the door. I tried almost every other spell in the Diary from walking through walls to blowing things up, but nothing worked. I guess I am gonna have to swallow my pride and really roll up my sleeves and get my hands dirty if I am ever gonna find out what Grandpa has hidden in that secret room of his. Today I plan on gathering the ingredients I need so that I can have the Seer's Sight. Then maybe I can figure out why I'm having such strange dreams.

Nanabel

I awoke the next morning on the floor of Zatie's room with a sore back from the way I had fallen asleep. I didn't dream, I was so exhausted, and I knew today wasn't a dream because I was able to read the Diary in front of me. Apparently, the last spell it tried to use on the door was a 'deconstruction spell' where you're supposed to rearrange the object like mixing up a jigsaw puzzle; ultimately to conform it to your will.

Obviously, it didn't work the way I wanted it to; otherwise I would have woken up in my granddad's study, instead of staring at a messed up door. I set it back to normal with a 'restoration spell.' I decided I should get back to my room before Zatie came home. I gathered up my books and things, and then tossed them into my backpack and teleported to my room without a second thought.

Upon arriving in my room, I shrieked, being both frightened and appalled by my brother's presence. He was rummaging through my possessions and helping himself to some change from my coin jar on my dresser.

"What the hell do you think you're doing?!"

"Hey, I knocked but you weren't here," Jesse said.

"That doesn't mean that you can just barge in and take whatever you want," I declared.

I was so furious that I almost cursed him with one of those nastier spells I had found before.

"It does if you're not here. Besides, you don't have much change anyways. I'm out of cola. You want something from the store?" Jesse responded.

I grabbed him and screamed for him to leave as I threw him out of my room. I went to bed to get some decent sleep and woke up again once I heard Zatie calling for me from downstairs. She was already home from her sleepover and was complaining about the disgusting state of the house courtesy of Jesse. Of course, he was nowhere to be found and I was still too half-asleep for her questions. When she saw me, her mood changed, and a smile filled her face. Her day off seemed to have done her some good.

"Hey there, sleepy-head! How are you feeling?"

"Better, now that Jesse's gone," I assured her. "He never fed me while you were away."

"Maybe because there's no food in the house," she added. "Well, I didn't know that." I said. Zatie's eyes lit up and she got all excited. I could tell what she was thinking.

"Well then, let's go shopping!" She smiled and clapped a little. Zatie always loved going shopping. This would be perfect; I could buy some of the things I needed for the Seer's Sight potion and pretend I was making Grandma's recipe for 'Garlic Chicken Lasagna'. I told Zatie that would be a good idea and that I would be downstairs as soon as I was ready. When she left, I summoned the Diary to me again with my mind and told it to show me the spell for 'The Seer's Sight.' I scanned through it quickly, so that I could jot down the ingredients.

The Seer's Sight

Ingredients Needed
Garlic, *best if from a cemetery and plucked before sunset...*
Chicken heads, *a dozen Roosters caught before they crow seven times ...*
Thorns, *from the fire and Ice rose bush. 2 doz. must be removed ...*
Rabbit's foot *must be cut with a golden dagger to prevent tainting ...*
Cobra's Venom *sucked from one's own hand. Bite must be acquired ...*

However, it would be next to impossible to find any of these ingredients at a regular grocery store. Not even the almighty 'All-mart' would have things like 'rabbit's feet or chicken heads,' so, we got all the usual things that teenagers like to eat and headed home. Jesse was back before we were and attacked the grocery bags like a savage animal. I let Zatie have kitchen duty while I pretended to go to the restroom. At the top of the stairs, I locked the bathroom door with a nod, then teleported into my room to consult the Diary once again. I double-checked what I had written down for the Seer's Sight ingredients and then teleported to the bathroom. As I left, I made the toilet flush with my mind to complete my diversion and returned to the kitchen. Zatie asked me if I wanted to help her with dinner.

"I'm actually having a little girl problem. You know what I mean? It's that time of the month already." I whispered to my little sister, but Jesse could still hear us.

"That's gross," he mumbled to himself in front of the TV in the family room. Zatie offered me some of her supply, which I politely refused. "Dude, even grosser!" he yelled this time and then dry-heaved to make his point.

"That's okay, sweetie. I'll just head back to the store; I need to get some other things that I forgot," I said as I grabbed my jacket and bolted for the door. I walked to the car in the driveway, got in and drove away. I didn't want to be stuck with this old clunker of a car all night when I could fly or teleport. I drove down the dirt road and thought of the barn behind the house. I concentrated hard on the car.

"I hope this works, Abracadabra!" I said before the car and I fell into the vortex. It felt like I was pulling the car by the steering wheel through mud. However, when we reappeared in front of the barn the car wasn't going slowly at all. I had to act fast so that I wouldn't crash into the barn doors at 25 mile per hour. I forced them to fly open with my telekinetic powers and tried to stop the car before hitting anything inside. The car slid dangerously close to the back wall due to the dry hay and dust on the ground. After I caught my breath, I closed the barn doors psychically and then looked at my list. Getting the garlic from the cemetery seemed like the easiest thing, so I started with that. I appeared on the far side of the Church building to make sure that the cemetery was vacant of *living* people. I also thought it would be prudent to use my goosebumps to sense evil.

After I felt nothing, I teleported to the older part of the graveyard and started to search near the fence line for the garlic. I wasn't sure if I should have old or new garlic, so I returned to the barn. I didn't want to make a mistake with such a difficult potion, so I reappeared in my bedroom to get the Diary and the box of Grandma Lu-lu's things. When I was back in the house, I could hear Zatie telling Jesse that dinner was done. I knew I didn't have much time before she would be expecting me to come home. I went back to the cemetery to obtain the garlic cloves. I fell through the vortex again to arrive in the barn. It was nearly sunset, and it would be getting dark soon, so I took the oil lamp from out of the box and lit its wick with a tiny spark of electricity.

The barn seemed creepier under the eerie glow of the lamp than when it was dark. I rummaged through the box and found a few of the instruments needed to acquire the ingredients, such as a golden dagger that looked like a letter opener rather than a weapon, a quartz stone, and a set of crystal vials, most of the were empty but a few that were filled with strange powders. Fortunately, enough for me, Grandma had the foresight to label these for me. There were vials labeled 'Dust of a dozen Cocks,' and 'Thorns of Fire and Ice.' That left me to find only a rabbit's foot and cobra's venom.

"I could get a cobra from the County's Zoo, but the rabbit is closer than that," I whispered to myself as I thought of Jesse's pet rabbit that Grandma lent him for a school talent show. He never could make that rabbit disappear, but he did get the award for 'School's Funniest Talent,' after he chased the rabbit through the audience.

I grabbed the golden dagger and thought of the hutch behind the house. It startled the animals in the pens and cages to see an amateur witch emerging from a black hole of smoke. The rabbit squealed as I pulled it out of the cage with my ever-increasing power to move objects. Then we returned to the barn and I forced it down on the table near Lu-lu's box of instruments. An invisible hand held its body down but its legs thrashed violently. I was about to chop them off when a rush of pity fell upon me.

"I'm sorry, little bunny. Tell ya what, I'll heal you just as soon as I remove your lucky little feet." Then I grabbed the pile of garlic roots and rubbed the dirt in my hands. Next, with my mind, I suspended the knife to chop its feet. I timidly closed my eyes as the knife worked for me. Afterward, I lay my hands on the bunny's stubby legs and healed them back to their full length through magic. I immediately returned it to the cage and walked by the kitchen window to see what my siblings were doing. Zatie was sitting at the dinner table eating and Jesse was devouring his food on the couch, still watching TV. Zatie had set out a plate for me. I knew that she would be heartbroken if I didn't get back soon.

I decided to fly to the zoo instead of teleporting because I didn't feel I could go that far away successfully. I would have to test my limits later, but now I had to hurry. I shot off like a rocket, into the bright orange sky in the direction of the zoo. When I got close enough to see the zoo workers like tiny ants leaving for their homes. I surveyed the area until I saw the reptile house and I appeared in the hallway within the small building. I was happy that my theory of line of sight teleporting worked. I quickly scanned a map on a near-by wall to locate the cobras. I thought about their habitat and let out a sigh of dread as I dissolved into the vortex and fell among cobras.

Of course, I scared the life out of them by just popping-up in their area. Naturally, they struck at me, but I kept them at bay through the will of my mind. I had to concentrate with great effort as I allowed one of them to bite my hand as I seized it; then I appeared in the barn. My fear of being bitten to death must have given me power enough to get back there safely. I suspended the venom in my veins while I pulled the cobra from off of my wounded hand with my mind and pierced its fangs into the side of the table while I went to work on brewing the potion. Grandma must have been planning for me to do this because she had almost everything prepared. I found the cauldron lying in a corner of the barn with other tools. After I psychically sucked the venom from my hand and spat it directly in as the final ingredient.

I healed my hands as I stirred the potion psychically with the large wooden spoon. I was beginning to feel like a *real* witch. It was almost sunset now, so I took the silver goblet that was with Grandma's things and filled it with the turquoise potion. I went up to the roof of the barn to toast the sunset as I drank the putrid potion down to the final disgusting drop. I think that Lu-lu would have been proud of my conversion. I gagged for a while as I watched the sunset for the last time with normal eyes. I was amazed to see so many different colors in the clouds as the Sun melted into the horizon. The stars popped out like sparkling diamonds in the night sky. I could see the Milky Way clearly in the heavens. With mild effort, I could focus on the planets with crystal clarity. I sat there stunned for the longest time, marveling at the wonders of the universe. I was sure that the potion had worked correctly; that, or I was super wasted - high as a kite!

I popped back into the car inside the barn, then thought of the nearest deserted road by the house before teleporting. My eyes felt ice-cold in my sockets as I saw different roads displayed to my mind's eye. It was as though several roads were displayed just outside the barn. I was overwhelmed by the power of the Seer's Sight. After rubbing my eyes, I picked a street that was around the corner from the farm and was there in an instant.

I felt it was smarter to wait until I was out of the vortex to turn on the car. Back at the house, Zatie was waiting for me. She didn't seem too angry that I was gone so long, because she wanted to talk about the sleepover she was at the other night. I took my plate of food and motioned for her to follow me to her room, Jesse was snoring loudly on the couch. I picked up the remote and turned off the TV with my mind. Zatie didn't notice.

I pretended to be interested in the conversation but really, I was scanning her bedroom with the 'Sight.' It was like washing away the present to see the years that had passed. I watched my mom growing up in this room. She graduated from high school and lived here as she continued to try to live a normal college life, being the daughter of actively practicing witches.

Eventually she married Dad. I witnessed Grandma doting over her and telling her how pretty she looked in Great-Grandma's wedding dress. Grandpa was crying when he hugged her good-bye. The years continued and I saw us playing in there as little kids. I was crying by then, and Zatie stopped talking when she sensed my sadness.

"Nonabel, what's wrong, honey?" Zatie held my hand and I could feel her powers scanning my heart with greater intensity. I pulled my hands away in shock and acted like I needed them to wipe the tears from my sore eyes. Her ability must be focused by touch; I should avoid letting her make contact until I could learn to block her out of my thoughts. I pretended to sob for a second then used my napkin from dinner to blow my nose.

"Nothing's wrong; I was just thinking about Mom. This was her room, you know." I smiled to show that they were happy tears. She hugged me and we cried together. We talked some more until it was late, and I tucked her into bed. I would have to wait until later to search the room properly for Grandpa's secret door.

Dear Diary,

My dream last night was amazing. Thanks to the Seer's Sight, I could explore the full potential of my powers in a safer way than I usually do when I'm awake. I practiced flying to distant lands at super-sonic speeds I mastered teleportation to the point where I can be in two places at once, at least while I was dreaming. Plus, my black puff of smoke that follows me has been reduced to vapors. The vortex is only as strong as I choose. Also, I can use the Seer's Sight to foresee if my dreams will change to nightmares. This will be very useful if I don't want to fight the Gor-Nok just yet.

Nanabel

When I woke this morning, I was casually thinking about what I wanted to do today. Then it hit me like a truck; the power of the Seer's Sight was showing me the entire day within seconds. I witnessed a blur of myself coming in and out of my room in fast forward. I watched me go throughout the house with my mystical X-ray vision. When I use the Seer's Sight, my eyes were watery, and felt as cold as ice in my eye sockets. I scanned the house for my siblings.

Jesse was almost frozen on the couch since that's about

all he does on Sundays anyways. Zatie was cleaning, of course, as we usually do, but I wasn't helping her for some strange reason. I questioned my motives and the 'Sight' answered. Everything around me changed as my spirit seemed to separate from my entranced body, frozen at the edge of my bed, and I was chasing myself through the town. Then I heard a knock at my door. I pulled myself back to the present and joined with my body. Zatie came in timidly with breakfast.

"You feel any better, honey?" Then she sat down next to me on the bed and I began to eat to avoid her scrutiny. She tried to touch my forehead, but I moved to get my glass of orange juice from the nightstand.

"I'm fine; I feel good enough to go to school on Monday. Hey, has Derik called or anything?" I said in between bites.

"Um, not that I know of, but Jesse might know; I'll go check." Then she got up to ask him herself. I used the 'Sight' to watch her through the walls and down the stairs to talk to Jesse. Unfortunately, the 'Sight' is just that, visual with no audio. I would have to look up a spell for super-hearing. I took the time to get ready for whatever it was that I had seen myself doing for the day. Zatie knocked on the bathroom door while I was showering to relay my messages to me. Derik had called. I figured that was where I had gone, or where I was going to go today. This could get confusing.

"Thanks, sweetie, I'll call him later," I said from the shower. I was constantly using the 'Sight' to try to peek at Zatie's room every time I walked by. I knew that I'd need a really good excuse for her to let me be in there alone for a long time. As I got dressed, putting on the exact outfit I had foreseen me wearing, I got a whisper of an idea that could work. *I should redecorate her room* like she had done to mine was what I thought. However, it really did feel like someone had whispered it into my ear, and that was when my goosebumps inflamed. I spun around to see if anyone else was there with me in my room. My eyes iced over with the 'Sight' and I let it go through the different spectral ranges to search for the intruder. Nothing seemed too much out of the ordinary, except my shadow would dance away every time I tried to get a good look at her.

It reminded me of Peter Pan when he was trying to catch his shadow. It was one of Lu-lu's favorite books to read from when we were little. Jesse liked it when she read *Alice in Wonderland* and Zatie insisted that Grandma call it 'Zatie in Wonderland,' because she thought that she looked like Alice. I thought that she was more like the evil Queen of Hearts from the way she would boss us around. Even when she was little, Zatie acted like she was Mom. I was so caught up in reminiscing about our childhood that I was shocked to find myself wading in the midst of the memory playing out in my room. Through the 'Sight', I found myself in my grandmother's room as she was reading us bedtime stories when we were little kids. But now that I had learned the truth about our family, the odd things that happened when I was younger were starting to make sense.

Lu-lu didn't just read the stories to us but made it so we could all share the same vision of them. I know now that she was using magic to conjure up the hallucinations and fantasies; that's why we were so entertained even though she had no television. I was enjoying Grandma's version of a bedtime story when suddenly my mom entered the room and swatted the fantasy away like it was smoke.

She was furious at Lu-lu and began yelling. Unfortunately, she sent us off to bed before she chewed out Lu-lu for using magic, I didn't get to hear the conversation. It didn't matter, because the 'Sight' was only visual. I really needed to find a 'sound spell.' I shook the vision from my eyes and scanned the house for Zatie. She was coming up the stairs with a basket of laundry. I teleported to my bedroom door and opened it before she could; it freaked her out. Or perhaps it was the fact that I still had icy eyes from the 'Sight' that scared her. After we both calmed down from the shock, I offered to help her pick up the fallen laundry.

"Hey, Zatie, I never thanked you properly for painting and decorating in here. Did I?" I asked her.

It didn't take her long to reply. "Nope, but you're welcome all the same."

"So, I was wondering if maybe I could redecorate *your* room for you; you know, like a 'thank you gift' from me to you for all your help. What do ya think?"

"Okay, but I get to pick out the color scheme," she held out her hand to seal the deal with a handshake, but she was most likely trying to perceive my sincerity through her empathic talents.

"Deal, but I want to do it by myself. No interruptions or it will spoil the surprise," I said quickly before she could protest.

"All right, I guess," she wasn't too happy about it, but she was always up for a surprise. I kissed her cheek while she made a list. Jesse tried to yell his grocery demands as I left the house, but I ignored him. I ditched the car in the barn after teleporting it there. Then I popped up to the roof and took off into the sky on a beautiful partly cloudy day. When the All-Mart was in view, I used the 'Sight' to visualize a discrete landing place on, near or in the store that wouldn't attract attention. I teleported to a stall in the women's restroom and flushed the toilet psychically as I left to go shopping.

Last Will & Testament

I called Zatie on my cell from the store when I was ready to select the paints for her room. Mom and Dad had gotten us mobile phones for our sixteenth birthdays. They said that it was 'in case we ever got lost' but I rarely needed it. Grandma had the oldest phone ever, so I avoided phone calls if I could. However, I needed to distance myself from my mind-reading sister long enough to give me time to examine that door in her room. I had the 'Sight' now, so I should be able to find the unlocking word somewhere on the door.

"Hey, Zatie, they don't have fuchsia, but they have passion fruit paint; will that work?" I could tell that she was upset but excited at the same time.

"Wow, you got there fast!" She was getting suspicious of my ability to travel quickly. So I lied.

"It's Sunday, no one's shopping today."

"Oh, you're right; you know I wish you'd have just let me come with you. Passion fruit will be fine. Gosh, the tension is killing me, I just hate surprises!"

"Oh, you'll live. Just stay outta my hair for a couple of hours and you won't regret it. I promise."

I made my purchases of the appropriate painting supplies, a new set of matching bed covers and a retro pink lava lamp. I was planning to bring the room back to its original hippie glory with a 'pink punk-pixie twist,' as Zatie the designer would put it. When I got out of the store, I used the 'Abracadabra' spell to transport myself, and the shopping cart with supplies and all back to the barn. Then I loaded the car with the grocery bags and zapped the empty cart back to the store using the 'Sight' to guide it there safely. I popped into the car and transported the entire boatload into the street down from the farm and drove up the drive. Zatie came running outside to sneak a peek at what I got. I danced my way around her and bolted for the door. She chased me up the stairs of the house and I slammed the door to her room behind me mentally.

Finally, I could get to work on that door, but I realized that in my rush I had forgotten the Diary. I was certain that there was going to be some other catch or trick to getting into the secret room. Maybe Grandpa had booby-trapped it or had something nasty waiting behind the door. I didn't want to take that chance. However, Zatie would be out in the hallway all day and night wearing a groove in the floor with her anxious pacing. I let my eyes ice over to scan the hall through the walls, and sure enough, my sister was beginning her march. I could see past her and into my room.

The Diary was locked in my nightstand, and I could have just as easily appeared there to get it if Zatie wasn't so sensitive to human emotions. I knew I would get caught if I tried to get it myself. I angrily sighed in annoyance and paced a little as I thought of a way to get the Diary from there to here without her knowing.

Then it hit me. No, really; the Diary landed on my head and we both collapsed onto the floor. Zatie was about to enter the room to see what had happened but I slammed the door shut again psychically to stop her. My head was throbbing, and I could feel a lump growing on my scalp.

"Is everything all right in there?" Zatie was jiggling the handle and pushing vainly against the closed door.

"I'm okay, I just dropped something, that's all." I wasn't lying, but I was being vague. Zatie hates that.

"Are you sure I can't help? I really want to!"

"Nope, I got it, just leave me alone, okay!" I said. I could hear her sulking off down the hall and to the stairs. She'd forgive me for being a jerk, someday. I got the painting stuff out of the shopping bags and began to move her furniture to the middle of the room. I picked up the Diary to place it on the dresser.

I was about to close the Diary when the spell on the open page caught my eye. I love how intuitive the Diary can be at times. It was an enchantment for animating inanimate objects. This could be useful since I really didn't want to work on painting the room but work on opening that secret door.

Un-in-animation

Inanimate objects do not move of their own accord to protect themselves from slavery and predators. Please note that some inanimate objects are natural enemies. For example, the Broom and the Mop are enemies and will fight to the death. **Do not animate them at the same time.** This spell is useful for accomplishing the more tedious tasks of household chores. To animate, simply bow or curtsy to the object and say, "Knick Knack Patty Whack, Rackety-Rickety Crack!" The object should bow in turn and ask your bidding through telepathy. You can visualize your desire or tell the object a basic command. **Visualization of the commands will yield the best results.**

I wasn't planning on cleaning until I had finished painting, so a mop and broom wouldn't be necessary. The paint brushes were the first things I animated, and then the paint cans. I told them to paint alternating vertical stripes of passion fruit and maroon six inches wide on every wall and stop when they had finished. I planted myself on the floor in front of the door to work on picking the lock. The description of 'hiding places' that I found in the Diary said that I could spot the 'unlocking phrase' with the power of the 'sight'.

I took a deep breath and allowed my eyes to freeze. I let the 'sight' shift through several different spectrums until I saw something bright red scratched on the header above the door. The 'unlocking phrase' was written backwards and I knew I could use a mirror to read it, but I was way too nervous to see things through a looking glass. I had accidentally seen myself in the mirror once while my eyes were still going through the phases of the Sight; it wasn't pretty. I breathed in a lungful of courage and summoned Zatie's antique vanity closer to me.

I slowly edged over to the vanity to peek into the mirror. I closed my eyes before looking at the reflection and sighed one more breath of dread as I opened them. I saw my shadow dance away again to dodge my gaze and it made me chuckle. Feeling a little braver, I returned to studying the reflection only to be mortified by my own disgusting visage. The irises of my eyes were glowing bright neon blue and the tiny veins around them burnt like lava cracks. My skin had boils at every other pore, and I could see that every nerve in my face was pulsating. My hair was the most terrifying of all; it seemed to be made entirely of tiny long black snakes that slithered in every direction. Naturally, I screamed when I saw the snakes, but I quickly muffled my mouth with my hands to avoid getting caught by my watchful sister.

I looked throughout the house for her and located her in the kitchen making dinner. It was a lovely chicken salad slathered in Caesar dressing. Man, I love Italian food. After I had finished salivating, I carefully positioned the mirror so I could see the 'unlocking phrase' and not my hideous face. I could read it clearly now; it said:

"Along the coast of the gypsies' escape to where we toast to love's first embrace."

"That makes no sense at all, Grandpa!" I exclaimed to myself in exasperation. Suddenly there was a knock at the door. I screamed a little from the shock and peeked through the door with the 'sight' to see Zatie holding my dinner on a serving tray.

"Who are ya talking to, Nonabel?" Then the door handle jiggled.

"Um, no one, honey, I was just talking to myself; it's perfectly natural. Grown-ups do it all the time." I looked around the room quickly to see how the enchanted paintbrushes had done. The room was gorgeous – well, not bad for a novice using magic.

"Nice job, guys!" I whispered to them and they bowed, then collapsed onto the drop cloths on the floor.

"Nonabel, are you sure that you're not talking to someone in there?" Zatie asked again and the door handle turned and jiggled. "Nonabel?" The door handle flipped and twisted again; she was trying to spoil her surprise.

"Hey, stop trying to cheat, I'm not done yet!" I peered through the door again to see her still standing just outside the room waiting patiently with the serving tray in both hands.

"I wasn't going to peek, I just wanted to bring you some dinner; jeez, Nonabel, you're no fun," she replied. I continued to watch her through the door; as she said my name the door handle moved again, but she never touched it. She still had my food in her hands. Was *my* name the 'unlocking phrase'? I had to check, but it would be a little weird if I said my own name while I was *supposed* to be talking to my sister.

"Hey, Zatie, I'm almost done, just leave the salad outside the door and I'll bring the tray down when I'm finished eating. Okay?!" I watched her leave the food and she sulked off down the hall, then down the stairs. She paused a moment in the stairwell with a puzzled look on her face. She scratched her head and I could see her mouth the word 'salad' to herself quizzically; then she shook her head and continued down to the dining room. Oh no, she wondered about how I knew that she had made 'salad' for dinner. Zatie was getting way too suspicious for her own good.

I needed to be careful or I might as well tell her that I was a witch and get it over with. I thought of the tray of food and witnessed it disappear and reappear at my feet. It hardly shifted the plate when I teleported it to my hands next. I was definitely getting better at this stuff. I sat on Zatie's bed and commanded the broom and dustpan to clean while I ate.

The rest of the cleaning and redecorating of Zatie's room went quickly, seeing how I could move the furniture with my mind and eat at the same time. I let the mop have a go at the room when the broom was done, to avoid a strange but potentially cool fight. I tried to see if my name was the key to unlocking Granddad's secrets.

I recited the poem again from memory but questioned how my name was the answer. I sighed and decided that logic didn't have a leg to stand on in the realm of magic.

"Nonabel!" Nothing happened at all, I got angry and left the room, taking the tray with me. I was just about to close the door behind me when Zatie called my name again from the family room to check if I was done. The handle jiggled but only on the inside of her room. With newfound excitement I tried to say my name again but from the outside; it moved again.

I quickly went back in her room and tried to slide the handle to the other side like Mom had done, but it didn't budge. Zatie was coming up the stairs now and she called for me again. I pushed both physically and psychically at the same time when it moved again; yet still nothing. Zatie knocked on the door, so I decided to give it a rest.

"Are you done yet? Are you done yet?" She was annoyed

with me keeping her in suspense. I let her in and sighed, being upset by my crushing failure to get only so close to the secret. She turned on the lights and gasped with genuine amazement as she marveled at my exquisite decorating job. Zatie began to jump up and down enthusiastically like she was on one of those home make-over shows and screamed 'thank-you's' repeatedly.

"This is awesome! You're the best sister ever!"

"I know I am. But hey, it's the least I could do for you being so nice to me when I was sick and upset the last few days." I thought of Grandma Lu-lu and all the pain I had suffered since her passing.

Zatie sensed my grief and hugged me. Shoot, I had left the mop going; I hugged her a little longer while I commanded the mop to stop cleaning. It bowed and fell to the floor; Zatie turned to see what had fallen. I kissed her on the cheek and told her to enjoy her 'new room' as I went down to the kitchen to wash my dishes, hopefully avoiding any of her speculative questions. Jesse was still glued to the couch and I chuckled to myself as I walked by on my way to the kitchen.

"What's so funny? Would you mind sharing with the rest of the class?" he yelled from the other room. I poked my head back into the hall and told him that I found it funny how he still prefers the couch to his own bed, then I went back to washing my dishes.

"Well it's better than being holed-up in my room all night doing strange stuff. I can hear you from down here, you know. It's none of my business but you're weird."

"You're right; it is none of your business. And I want you to try sleeping on your own bed for once."

"What are you, my mother?" he asked.
I smacked him on the back of his head with the closest pillow I could find. "No, but I am your guardian and don't forget it."

"Oh, that reminds me. That lawyer guy called; he's coming over tomorrow with our inheritance. Cha-ching! Bring me tha money, bee-outch."

I whacked him again with the pillow to stop him from doing his ridiculous money-dance of greed he did every time we got our allowances. "Be more respectful than that, jerk! Don't forget that the ones we love had to die for you to get your stupid money! Besides, knowing Granny Lu-lu, you'll hafta wait 'til you are eighteen or something, so don't get your hopes up." I hit him again and went back upstairs to go to bed. Zatie stopped me as I walked by her room; she was holding the Diary on her bed and opening its lock latch. I felt my stomach hit the floor.

"Hey, Nonabel; isn't this the same book you had at the funeral? I thought that you left it in Lu-lu's coffin," she was about to open it, so I slapped it shut.

"Nope, not the same book!" I snatched it quickly out of her hands and retreated to my room before she could reply. I slammed the door shut with my mind and locked the door latch while I was at it. I flung myself on my bed, exasperated by my failure to break into the hidden room. The Diary lay open at my side; usually when it was opened it usually had the right answer.

I was hopeful when I began to read the passage; it was a love letter from Grandma to Grandpa when they were first courting. My preoccupation with breaking down the magic door had distracted me from all my grief and pain I suffered earlier on in the week. I no longer felt like I was mourning their lives; sure, I missed them, but I was happy that they were together, finally. I read the letter with a sudden sense of nostalgia.

To my dearest Michael,   February 18th, 1940

I hope everything is all right; you appeared so angry and frustrated last night. You just didn't seem like yourself. I know that I've only known you for such a short while, but it felt like you were trying to hide something from me the other night. I hope you know that you can tell me anything, I swear there's nothing that would scare me. Especially not after the things I've seen in my life. I want you to know that you can trust me. I've enjoyed every moment we've been able to spend together these last few weeks here in Beirut.

My Aunt and I will be leaving for the Americas soon so I can finish my education, but I would very much like to finish what *we* started the other night. It is so providential that your friend was injured and that my Aunt just happened to know how to cure him. Oh, please tell Harry good luck with his condition, I am so very grieved that he was in such a horrific accident. Therianthropy can be a difficult thing to live with. Please tell him to be careful. I do wish that you would reply to me soon.

With deep affection,

Lucia

The letter was attached to an entry in the Diary written by Lu-lu. Apparently, her aunt didn't want her to date Michael because he wasn't like them. My great-aunt must've been a witch as well. They later met up in Mexico where Grandpa was hunting a monster called Huay Chivo, I think. Now we call it "El Chupacabra," or in English it means goat-sucker; it is a type of vampire animal like a dog or something, I had to look it up to be sure about the translation.

She went with him on the hunt and they got married by an Indian holy man that was a friend of Granddad. They moved back here to Texas to Grandpa's family homestead where he lived with his father. Grandma Lu-lu described her first meeting with Michael's dying father, Dominic Lamia.

Dear Diary,   August 19th, 1941

We got to Texas on his sailboat because Michael

wanted to explore the Caribbean for our honeymoon. I don't like the sea much, so I was glad to be on dry land again. There are things in the ocean that terrify me. Michael was happy to get some fishing in before we got to his Family's farm south of a large mountain called Shadow Peak. We took a carriage from the Gulf of Mexico and traveled that way for part of the day. When we got to the house, we were greeted by the house nurse that took care of his father Dominic.

Michael told me that his father was very old and that he had outlived three wives. Michael was an only child like me. When I first entered the room, I was caught off guard by the smell of death and garlic. The curtains were drawn, and we had to light a lamp to even find him. He was hiding in a far corner like a scared rat. His eyes were blood-shot, and his pupils were dilated, giving him a savage appearance. He was practically naked under his old robe. His skin was blotched with burns and his hair was falling out in patches.

He frightened me. Michael made the introductions and his father snapped at my hand with his sharp teeth. Fortunately for me, Michael was quick enough to move me from danger and calm his father. Later I had to ask my husband what had happened to Dominic that would make him that way. That's when Michael revealed to me *his* secret, his gift and curse that he got from his father. Now I know why he chose me; because I have the power to help them both, hopefully.

Lucia

"Man, you guys are vague, I mean, come on, your Diary doubles as a spell book, Grandma. Why can't you just come out with it? What the hell was he?! Ugh!" I muttered to myself as I closed the Diary and went to bed more confused and angrier than ever. I hoped that the lawyer had better news for me tomorrow or else I was going to drop a magical bomb on that blasted door just so I could get some answers.

Dear Diary,

I had a dream last night that I was with my Grandpa Michael on one of his hunting trips. We were sneaking along a swampy shoreline in the desert and we were trying to catch a giant hippo. I assumed that we were in Africa. We all got ready with our rifles to fire, when suddenly one of the new guys on the expedition got in front of Michael and shot the beast before he could. The shot wasn't very accurate and only grazed the hippo's back. Unfortunately, my Grandpa Michael had shot off at the same time and punctured the young man in the arm. Blood was leaking everywhere, staining the water red.

We took the man to shore so we could stop the bleeding. While everyone was standing over him Grandpa Michael was bandaging his arm. We weren't the only ones hunting that day; a clever crocodile was floating downriver, stalking its prey. Even though my grandpa was a skilled hunter he made a fatal error by leaving a trail of blood. The crocodile followed it straight to the injured man and pulled him back into the river from among us. The rest of us grabbed our rifles to shoot the beast but Grandpa jumped in after him.

It was hard to tell what was happening in the water but after a few minutes of arms, limbs and tails splashing around, Grandpa emerge victorious dragging with him the injured man and the now dead crocodile. While everyone cheered; Grandpa Michael went back to work to save a man's life and that's when I woke up. It was cool to see my grandpa in action.

Nanabel

Today was the first day I had been back to school in a long time. Either it was because I hadn't been here for a while or because of the 'Sight', but I was seeing things at school with a new pair of eyes. It was like I was seeing everyone's aura; the air around them vibrated with colors.

However, if I actually bumped into someone or came in contact with their skin, something entirely different would happen. For a brief second, I could see their past, present or future depending on what I needed to see; it freaked me out. You can understand why I was a little stand-offish when Derik tried to hug and kiss me every time we saw each other in the halls between classes.

"Hey, sugga', how ya feelin'?!" he said as he tried to kiss me. I had to try my best not to let the 'sight' overwhelm me and still kiss him back. I saw flashes of him with his future family; he was laughing at one of his kids during dinnertime. I was glad to see him so happy, but it was hard to tell if I was seeing it from my eyes or if I just couldn't see me in his future. It made me sad to think that I might not be with him then. I had to concentrate hard to not let the 'Sight' get the better of me whenever we would touch as we went through the day.

When I didn't have a class with Derik, I would pretty much keep to myself. Don't get me wrong; I do like using the Sight, but only when I get to choose to use it, not when it happens automatically. For example, it comes in handy when you need to cheat on a test or see what page number you are on in a reading assignment and so forth.

For instance, in English class, we were studying William Shakespeare's *Macbeth* and I had totally forgotten to do the reading. I asked my classmate Cheryl if she had done it; she smiled and said, "Yeah, but it doesn't mean I understand it. That Shakespeare fool was nuts! I don't see why people like him." I agreed and we laughed together.

I touched her hand when she showed me the page number. This time I let the Sight go crazy and it showed me how Cheryl struggled to understand the reading assignment. How she got frustrated with it a few times and threw the book on the floor. I could see the scenes playing out in her imagination whenever she would try to read, and all the characters were played by friends of hers in contemporary clothing. It was interesting to see her imagination at work.

The vision only took a couple seconds, but it felt like I got to be with Cheryl for weeks. Cheryl and I hardly got to hang out at all, but we got to talk a little during classes. If I hadn't met Derik when I first got here, then Cheryl and I would probably be better friends. However, because of how much Derik hovers as a boyfriend, I had to be content with casual acquaintances.

Throughout the rest of the school day I casually would use the 'sight' to aid me safely through the social minefield of Shadow Peaks High. I would let it scan the hallways for the best path of least resistance, allowing me to avoid damaging thoughts that were in the minds of the 'Goths' or, worse, the cheerleaders; ugh. Derik was even harder to elude because of the fact that he pulled some strings to get his locker to be next to mine.

At first it was cute and convenient; however, having the ability to view the hearts and minds of mankind without even trying isn't very convenient at all. I was starting to regret having the Sight because of the darker things I could see. Derik's thoughts betrayed him, but he had a great poker face. He had been worried about me since I'd been 'sick' and wished he could have done more to help. The darker side of him suspected the worst, though. He pondered if I had been cheating on him. No wonder he was so clingy and kissy.

I tried to convince him that I still might be contagious from my imaginary flu. He became resigned to only hugging me and kissing my cheek. It took a lot more concentration to hinder the 'sight' than to activate it. I would have to practice more control when I was around people.

I thought of how I would mentally hold my breath when Zatie had touched me in hopes to keeping her out of my head. By the end of the day I was determined to try to touch Derik's skin without being bombarded by his secrets. I heard him call to me from down the crowded hallway; he was saying goodbye to Johnny and his crew.

Then he ran to pick me up and he twirled me around like he just got released from jail or something. My mind gasped for one last mental breath as my body fought back the nausea. Once I recovered from the spin, he kissed me passionately for a really long time. I had a hard time forbidding my senses from overreacting to the power of the Sight any time I was touched. It was excruciating to resist the energy and emotions that traveled through his warm, moist lips to my frigid mouth. It was all I could do to fight back the anxious power of the Seer's Sight. After we surrendered our embrace, I could feel it had become easier to keep the 'sight' from reacting to him on instinct. It felt nice to finally feel like I could control something.

Derik gave me a good-bye peck on my cheek when he dropped me off at my house. I didn't have to fight the 'sight' any more, yet I could always feel it looming in the back of my head, waiting for me to give in. As I watched him drive away, I took a chance at seeing the moment when the lawyer would arrive. The 'sight' ignited my vision of the front drive. The lawyer drove a new sporty Mercedes Benz; Derik would've drooled all over it. His suit was nice enough for a fancy big city lawyer.

However, when I looked at his face, it would get distorted and blurry like the reception was going bad. I tried to focus harder and that's when his whole frame warped from human to monstrous. In that moment, a crocodile exploded from inside of him and ate his face. I fought back the urge to gag as the real lawyer drove through the vision, running over the crocodile-man. I made a mental note not to touch Mr. Anderson so that I could avoid reliving what I had just seen. I waved to him from the front porch.

Harold Anderson got out of his black sports car and waved back to me as he was finishing a call on his phone and walking to the house at the same time. I left the front door open while I waited for him to walk up our long gravel driveway to the porch. I called into the bowels of the old farmhouse to my siblings. Harold smiled at me when he got to the steps and paused to wipe the perspiration from his forehead.

"It's a scorcher today, isn't it?!" He smiled again. I could tell that he was more nervous about meeting us than we were of him.

"Yeah, it does seem odd weather for autumn. How are you, Mr. Anderson? Did you have a pleasant drive from Austin?" I motioned for him to enter the house.

"Wonderful, I'm just fine, but the traffic was horrible," he held out his hand and I pretended not to see it as I closed the door and dropped my backpack by the coat rack.

"Right, is there somewhere we can discuss the Will?" He peered around our slightly embarrassing mess of a house. I motioned to the dining room table and then I called for the twins again.

"Hey, you guys, the lawyer's here with our money, come get some!" At that moment, I heard a sound like that of thunderous hooves charging towards the stairs. Harold laughed nervously at my comment. I offered him a glass of water and he accepted as the twins fought each other through the dining room door. They were all sitting at the table chatting as I returned with a pitcher of water.

"So, I guess you guys are excited, huh?" Harold said while he fidgeted with his briefcase. The twins muttered something in the affirmative to the middle-aged lawyer, but I just wanted this to be over and done with; I didn't want to think about *why* we were becoming rich.

"Money's well and fine, but I'd rather have my grandmother back," I said while I poured glasses of water for everyone. I could see the guilt settling on everyone's expressions as I sat down and took a sip of the cool water. Mr. Anderson quickly produced copies of Lu-lu's Will and handed them out to each of us. He also noted the date and time on an expensive audio recorder and set it on the table. He then cleared his throat and began to plow through all the legalities and stipulations attached to receiving our inheritance.

"I, Lucia Linda Lamia, declare my granddaughter, Nona-bel Lamia Venatora, as the Executor of my Estate... Of course, you already knew that two months ago, on your birthday, when she told you, right?! He was nervous every time that he had to speak to me directly, but he had a good poker-face, nonetheless.

I let out a sigh and replied from under my breath. "Yes, that was the *only* thing she gave me on my birthday." Lu-lu called me an ingrate for not at least pretending to act glad for the great honor and responsibility of being her heir. Every-one else laughed mildly as I glared at them while I sipped my cool water. Zatie looked confused at my lack of happiness and asked the lawyer what that meant.

"It means that we don't get jack 'til we turn eighteen... or unless Nona mysteriously dies." Jesse kind of mumbled that last part.

"Of course, she would have to die of *natural* causes, he hee! Um, anyways, shall I continue?" Mr. Anderson immedi-ately fell victim to glare of my stunned eyes as I told them that I was not in the mood for jokes. He finished reading Lu-lu's will and explained in 'plain English' most of the legal jargon to Jesse alone but pretended to do it for all of our benefit collect-ively. Jesse was particularly bummed about the fact that over fifty-thousand dollars was going toward his college fund and that the remainder of his inheritance depended on him gradu-ating from school.

Zatie wasn't the least bit upset by the restrictions and declared that she was planning to attend college anyways. She also told Jesse that she would help him with studies from now on. When it came to discussing the 'details' of my inheritance, Mr. Anderson said that it was to be confidential and excused the twins from the dining room.

After I closed the door behind my siblings and returned to my seat, Mr. Anderson produced an ancient envelope from his suit coat pocket. It was stained parchment like a page from the Diary and bore the Lamia family seal of a dragon with feathered wings melted into a spot of black wax. I looked from the seal to the lawyer and wondered about how much he knew of our family secret.

"What's this for, Mr. Anderson?" I already had a pretty good idea, but I still wasn't sure if I could trust him.

"*This* is your grandmother's will. All that nonsense I said to them was just for show. Go on, open it," his demeanor had changed entirely; this wasn't the same nervous man that came to our front door just moments ago. I was the nervous one as the realization that he knew my secret was settling somewhere in my throat. He eyed me with a smirk like he knew what Santa was bringing me for Christmas, and he couldn't keep the secret any longer.

"No, really, what is this, why are you smiling... Ugh, it's stuck Mr. Anderson. That's why you're grinning, isn't it?" I grunted pathetically as I struggled against the adhesive force of the seal. It was definitely magic that kept it sealed and Mr. Anderson knew it.

"Actually, Ms. Venatora, I'm curious to know how you were planning to open the envelope... without using magic." I stared incredulously at his childish grin and began to say that I didn't know what he was talking about when he abruptly cut me off.

"You don't need to play games with me, witch. I know full well the nature of your family's secrets and I hide a few of my own. That's why they chose me. So, go on, open the letter," he responded.

"But I can't. I don't know how to open something like this. Trust me, I've been trying all week." I replied.

"Excuse me?" He asked.

"Never mind. So, how am I supposed to open it with magic, let's say, if I was a... witch?" I asked

"Please stop the charade, Ms. Venatora. I have learned to spot a witch a mile away. Which is good, because if you don't, you're probably under a spell already. Ha ha, know what I mean?!" He laughed.

"No, I wouldn't know, because I'm not one."

"Please spare me; I can spot bad liars too. I know that you're a witch by the way you hold yourself, never touching anyone, never making eye contact for longer than a nanosecond, and unless those are contacts, your eye color, albeit unique, shouldn't change with your moods. However, I knew Lucia's did because of magic."

I looked at him with an untrusting glare and then examined the seal closer. I tried prying it with my mind and got sharp pangs in my brain as a reward. I scanned it with the 'sight' to locate an unlocking phrase like I did with the hidden room and found nothing. The lawyer watched my vain efforts like he was playing the greatest practical joke he had ever done. I gave up and tossed it back.

"I got nothing; can you do... magic?" I was the one smirking now.

"Nope, that's not my area of expertise. Besides, a magic seal of a witch's family crest can only be opened by a member of the family. I could ask one of your siblings to do it for you. I noticed that your sister seemed a bit... different."

"No, that's quite all right. It's just that I've never done... it in front of people, and I don't want the twins to know what I can do."

"So, what can you do, witch? Have you ever seen a letter sealed with wax before?"

"Yeah, Lu-lu did it all the time."

"Yes, but have you seen it done by a witch through magic?"

"Well, if we're talking about Lu-lu, then yes."

"And how did she do it?"

"She breathed on the wax and said... Oh, the dragon! I know how she did it! She always said that it was her Italian garlic breath, but I know better... now."

"Well, let's see it then, witch, open the letter."

I held the letter up in front of my mouth and breathed out a puff of white ghostly smoke upon the seal and whispered, "Suspiritus Draconis."

I hissed a light flame over the seal, and it melted to form my name written in Lu-lu's hand; however, she capitalized the last letter instead of the first. I used the will to wave the smoke away before I handed it to the lawyer.

"Let me read this through before you respond," he said and cleared his throat.

nonabeL Lamia Venatora,
As is customary with our noble family's traditions, I, Lucia Linda Lamia, have chosen the eldest daughter of my only child as my heir. When I am dead and buried it will be your duty to protect our family, our family's secret and the ancient secrets that have been passed down through our bloodline for generations. Guard my Diary with your life. It is yours now, to use and love. All that I have in this life I hereby leave to you, as has been done since the dawn of time. This is not just a one-sided contract, nonabeL; this is a covenant. I give you MY heart anD all my love in Return for a sOlemn pledge that you Will give the Same. ThIs iS A contract to use youR magic Often aS you continUe as the proteCtor Of the Family's secrets and the heir to all of my witchcraft and powers; a contract that you must sign with your blood. Once you choose to follow this path, forever it will be your life. At twenty-six minutes to mid-night tonight, you will receive full access to your potential powers. However, the fullness of said powers can only be acquired through meticulous training and study. Make sure that You FOCUS OR it wilL OverCome and Kill Everyone that you've loveD With all my love,

Lucia

As he finished reading the last lines of the will, Mr. Anderson placed it on the table in front of me.

"Now, then, witch; was there anything I said that confused you?" He asked.

He was so smug; they obviously had a great laugh when they drew this up. I rolled my eyes and sighed in exasperation toward being treated like an idiot.

"Oh, you're not an idiot, Ms. Venatora; just slow, maybe," He replied.

"You read my mind?!" I exclaimed.

"Not exactly, you told me what you were thinking," He said.

"But I didn't, I've been careful about that ever since I found out, or else Zatie would bug me for thinking the way I do," I replied.

"Well, you didn't tell me, but you will; at least she looked like you. Anyways, it doesn't matter now; just look at the will and tell me what you see," he told me.

I scanned through it briefly because I was annoyed, then I began to scrutinize Lu-lu's bad grammar. "Um, to start, she's got letters capitalized when they shouldn't be. But she was born in another country, so, I guess that could explain it," I said.

"Now, just think about it for a second; did she ever do anything that wasn't mysterious or hidden? Just look for the clues," he replied.

I read it again but this time I let the 'Sight' go berserk. I got flashes of when Lu-lu met with Mr. Anderson to draw up this will; he tried to correct the errors, but she stopped him. I looked at it again through different spectrums to isolate the mistakes. Of course, it didn't make sense; it was just a bunch of gibberish. "Yeah, this doesn't mean..." I started saying.

"Anything? Try being her lawyer; it confused me the first

time I read it too. However, codes and ciphers aren't meant to mean anything to everyone else, only to you. Here, it helps if you write it down," he said.

He pulled a blank sheet of paper from his suitcase and gave me his pen before I could ask. I was excited to learn a new secret from Lu-lu, so I quickly jotted the random letters onto the blank page.

All the code looked like this, at first. My name wasn't capitalized correctly; the 'L' was capitalized instead, every time that she addressed me. *nonabeL*. These were the next capital letters out of place: M Y D R O W S I S A R O S U C O F. And finally these were last: M Y F O C U S O R L O C K E D.

"Yeah, this pretty confusing," I said as I passed the page of notes to the lawyer.

"Now, let's see what you came up with!" Mr. Anderson said excitedly as he rubbed his hands together.

"It's a bunch of crazy talk," I exclaimed.

"Probably not; however, I think that you might be right. I'm not saying that I know much about your kind; just the same, I'm curious about what she has left you," he studiously examined the will with the code for a moment. "Aha! I found something. Here. Take a look," he exclaimed.

I took the parchment and scratch paper from him again. He underlined the letters that stood out to him. (MY IS LOCKED)

"That still doesn't make sense," I said.

"Well, my dear that's all I got. Perhaps if you sleep on it, the answers will come. I find the key to every mystery lies in seeing things with new eyes. Oh, speaking of keys, your grandfather left you one for *his* safety deposit box."

He gave me another sealed envelope that I opened with the 'dragon's breath' while Mr. Anderson removed a small metal box from his briefcase. My breath must have been *too* potent because the letter burnt to ash, leaving behind a tiny key.

"I hope that your grandfather didn't have something important to say on that note," he said.

"Me neither," I replied as I fanned the smoke.

He passed the box to me. I was excited as I opened it. My excitement turned to confusion when all I found in the box was another key.

"Not what you hoped for; is it, little witch? Oh well. You should probably be used to it by now."

"This is it?! Gosh, they frustrate me!" I exclaimed.

"I know; I miss them too. Now, Ms. Venatora, if you need me for anything, don't hesitate to call," he said.

"Um, I don't have the number of your office, Mr. Anderson. That card you gave me at the funeral was blank," I explained.

"You won't need it; just call my name and I'll hear you. Know what I mean?" He winked and pointed to his head. "By the way, just call me Harry. Harold is what my mother called me," he added. I walked him out the door and we shook hands as he was getting into his car. He held my hand tight as concentration filled his face. I was worried as to what I might see if I let the Sight react. I mentally held my breath like I had done earlier with my many encounters with Derik today. That practice was helping me to be in charge of the Sight now and I prevented myself from reacting.

"What do you see; do you know what I am?"

"No, I don't want to see it again." I explained.

"You can block it?! I know Lucia couldn't help probing my thoughts. I almost miss it," he responded.

"Harry, we have to talk about what's happening to me; I'm afraid of what I'm becoming," I told him.

"We will, little witch; after you sign that contract. And don't be afraid, you are never alone. Goodbye and good luck," he responded and got in his car.

"Goodbye, Harry." I walked back to the house, pondering the mysteries that clouded my mind. That's when it hit me; Lu-lu wrote about Harry in the Diary. I wanted to just pop into my bedroom and study the Diary all night, but my siblings would be waiting for an explanation of our secret meeting. I vaguely described the ridiculous amounts of money to them and assured them that they would get their shares in due time. Once I felt they were convinced I retired to my room to indulge in my magic Diary.

<u>Entry #7</u>

More Questions

I stayed up late reading in the Diary again, going over the

things that Lu-lu had left me. I read her strange letter dozens of times to figure out the code she wrote, but I didn't come up with much more. Occasionally, I would glance up at the clock on my nightstand to check the time, all the while knowing that something weird was going to happen at 26 minutes to midnight.

Just as a precaution, I decided to teleport to the barn and wait for my 'inheritance' to arrive. I brought the Diary with me to pass the time practicing spells. The curious code left to me by my gifted grandmother gave me a clue. She talked about something called a "focusor" twice; the second time it was backwards. I looked it up in the Diary, and what I learned shocked me, because I never saw Lu-lu performing magic using a focusor before.

A focusor is like a magic wand of sorts. You can basically take any object and use it as a vessel to contain and magnify your powers. Things like amulets, rings even rocks or twigs. As tempting as it seems to have a magic wand, the Diary gave a warning against doing it. It warned that even though the focusor helps you to access your powers quicker, the spell to create an effective focusor required that you surrender a great deal of your magical powers into the host object. The dangerous part is that once you lose your focusor, someone else can use it against you, rendering you powerless.

It appears that Lu-lu had made one for me and locked it away. I studied the witch's contract a few times more and could never bring myself to sign it with my own blood; it was all too creepy. Besides the minor fact that I get queasy at the sight of blood, I was just not certain that hurting myself to prove to my dead grandmother that I was committed was necessary any more. I was a witch, and it was getting harder to hide it from the ones I loved.

I read in the Diary about contracts and covenants and found more reasons for not signing it. These kinds of contracts are irreversible and eternal. Signing something in blood means that you are willing to dedicate every last drop you have to fulfilling your half of the deal. Lu-lu had done it for me. Why couldn't I be willing to do it for her? She sacrificed her life to protect me. Why couldn't I return the favor, and give my life to defend my secret? Fear mainly, not knowing enough about what I was getting caught in; not being able to see what was waiting out there worried me.

The Seer's Sight was very powerful, but at times it was highly flawed. It made possible futures appear distorted and fragmented. It was most effective if I knew what to look for. Asking the Sight the right question was the key to unlocking the mysteries of existence. Wanting to know my future alone was a futile request, because the Sight would show so much of my life too fast that it would be impossible to catch anything of importance. Then, before I knew it, I'd see the grim reaper coming to collect my soul for what I had done to earn an early death, and I don't even know what I did, or would do. Whatever, it was confusing and that was when I wanted to give up. It was nearly time for my "inheritance" to arrive, but I saw nothing coming through the Sight.

I got tired of waiting around, so I decided to not sign the contract and returned to my room. I thought of my bed and began to teleport there but only traveled to the other side of the barn and crashed into a wall. I was too exhausted and bruised to focus on my destination and chose to hobble back home on foot. That night I had a dream; I was at a funeral again. So many members of my immediate family had died before their time that it was hard to tell who this was for. The casket was closed; I didn't remember whose viewing needed that. I felt so small and helpless, almost trapped where I was lying. It frightened me; I wondered for a split second if I was dead. My body lying in a nearby coffin waiting for my deposition. Lu-lu was weeping over the concealed body hidden beneath the black lacquer shell.

I followed the path her tears took to the ground and was led to a black and white photograph of her sweetheart smiling back at me from below. I do have his smile; he would've loved me for sure. Then she walked over and picked me up from my mother. As Lu-lu held me lovingly in her arms, I realized what I was, a newborn fresh from heaven.

If I had only waited one more day in paradise, then I could've welcomed grandpa in at St. Peter's gates. I reached my fragile arms up as high as I could to get Lu-lu's attention, help comfort her in that moment, but I missed her face and hit her necklace instead. She was wearing the old key that her lawyer gave me the other day. She smiled at me for a brief moment, then her face warped into a mask of disgust and anger.

"Sign the contract, you little brat, or I'll pick someone else," she whispered into my baby ears. I got scared and tried to scream for help, not knowing if this was truly my Nana Lu-lu or her killer tormenting me again.

Whichever, I didn't want to be there, she was suffocating me in her attempt to keep me from calling out to my family. My cries merged with the cawing of a lone crow attending nearby. I blacked out as I drowned from the thought of no air and consciously teleported myself to the cemetery. I was in shock from the transition of scenery, but I wasn't starving for oxygen any more. I awoke and found myself kneeling at the graves of my loved ones. I was about to go back to my room to sleep when I noticed something odd. Grandpa Michael's grave had been recently disturbed. I instinctively scanned the area for unseen clues that would shed light on the mysterious activities that happened here. The Sight scorched my eyes and seemed to be operating at half power; the visions were blurry and scattered between the past and present.

Nothing made sense, and I should've been used to disappointments by now, but I wasn't going to give up, and that's when I saw it again. A stranger was at Michael's viewing, dressed like a vagabond and as dark as the night. His skin was like burnt chocolate, his eyes were a swampy green, and his breath was like smoke. He was covered from the sunlight by an eerie omnipresent shadow, so it was hard to discern his face. He waited at a distance until the last of the mourners were gone before he floated across the cemetery to Michael's covered grave. He bent down low and sniffed the air over the grave like he was part animal.

He was muttering something in a strange language and was shaking some kind of savage-looking necklace at the ground. He was casting a spell that was raising his grave and it startled me to see such power that I gasped out loud. He heard me and turned to search for who was there. I couldn't believe that he could see me looking at him across the veil of time as I spied with the eyes of the seer. He sniffed the air again and stalked towards me, so I hid behind a tombstone and he followed.

I knew that I wasn't really there, but I had leaped through time to be with Lu-lu once before, so anything was possible; either way, this was still freaking me out. The stranger sniffed the air again and appeared to have lost my scent. He grabbed at his throat for his primitive charm and shook it again, chanting the words "Dae-tur-natu Hofu Gor-Nok" over and over until his voice changed and so did the rest of him thereafter.

His body trembled and cracked as he doubled in size. He was still very dark, but he lost his chocolate skin in trade for a tough grey-colored hide. His eyes burned a yellow green like cheap fireworks and the smoke from his mouth and nostrils was black, smoggy, and reeked of death. It all happened in a heartbeat and I was facing the murderous monster man-boar once more.

Now that he was the beast his senses were exquisite. He could see and hear things differently, better than when he was human. Unfortunately, he caught my scent again and dropped on all fours. He found my hiding place at lightning speed, sniffing as he ran. The beast encircled my retreat by smashing the tombstones around me with bursts of fear. He couldn't see me and seemed frustrated by my apparent invisibility. However, he was able to smell the stench of fear and dread oozing from my every pore. The Gor-Nok began to mutter a dark curse directed at my position that was powerful enough to reach through the abyss of space and time that I thought was between us. I could feel his potent spell begin to prickle my skin, enraging my defensive goosebumps.

He coughed a lungful of his vile toxic fear gas in my space, and I instinctively began to cough and choke on fear. His magic was starting to penetrate my mind; that's when I found the answer. If he could use magic to attack me while I was having a vision, then I could strike back! Fear of failure was setting in deep and I knew that I wasn't in control of my abilities like before, but I was dying, and no one was going to save me this time.

"Lampeggiare de Zeus!" I screamed as loud as I could through the noxious gas in my throat and only got a whisper.

I created a miniature orb of electricity and watched as it floated across the gap in existence just to be swallowed by the beast. He coughed and chuckled a little in his monstrous voice. "Is that all you got? Ha ha, argh!" His lungs swelled like balloons then blew apart in a giant ball of flames. I feared that the blast would hurt me, so I clawed at the earth and thought of home, hoping for an escape. The force of the explosion was incentive enough to focus all the magical energy I could on getting home. I appeared in my room, yet I missed my bed and crashed onto the floor. Agony coursed all over my nerves, burning as it traveled my body. I took the clumps of hallowed earth I had grabbed when I teleported and rubbed it on my hands and prayed for the healing spell to work. The soothing warmth enveloped me with relaxation as I drifted into unconsciousness.

My alarm clock woke me from a dreamless sleep. I'd rather have some kind of dream than none. A nightmare would be better than nothing. Nothing is never good; I felt so alone without Lu-lu's occasional hauntings. I wanted to find out why I wasn't as good at magic as I was before, but it was a school day and my renewed obsession with the Diary would have to wait. As I gathered my schoolbooks, I secured the Diary and the things that Harry gave me in my nightstand.

When I picked up the letters, I dropped the key that Lulu put in the deposit box. As I touched the key, I got slammed by a vision that was so vivid that I nearly fainted. I saw myself opening the hidden door and a stampede of feral creatures came crashing over me, leaving the house in shambles. Every bone in my body was pulverized by the army of angry hooves marching over me. I had no hallowed earth to heal myself and my last breath had been trampled from me, so it didn't matter. I felt my pain turn into panic as I blacked out and consciously teleported myself to my bed. I felt around the floor for more dirt that had fallen from before and lost my balance. The loud thudding noise caught Zatie's attention as she was leaving for school.

"Nonabel, what happened? You look horrible, sweetheart. Are you sick again?" Zatie asked.

"Yeah, I'm not doing so good." I moaned in pain as she helped me back into bed.

"Do ya need me to stay home?" She was a great babysitter; however, I could get another chance at breaking into Grandpa's study if she didn't stay home.

"Naw, I'm all right. You've done a lot already, and I don't need you to fall behind in your schoolwork. I'll call somebody if I need help," I responded.

"You're sure?" I didn't think she believed me.

"Yeah, thanks." I suppressed a cough and smiled sheepishly as she left. After a little while, I continued my search by crawling on the floor and succeeded in finding some dirt from the graveyard, enough to heal myself again. I went down to the kitchen for breakfast just in case any of my siblings felt the need to hang around.

Later, when I was convinced that no one else was home, I snuck into Zatie's bedroom to discover Grandpa's secret. I wore the key Lu-lu left for me and brought the Diary and the oil lamp as precautions. I inserted the ancient skeleton key into the latch and drew a frightened breath before I said the password. "Lebanon!" I figured it out thanks to Lu-lu's bad grammar in the will.

It worked, the door handle spun entirely, and I slid it to the other side like Grandpa had done in my dream. As I opened the magical door, the hinges creaked like it had been abandoned for years. Dust flooded out from under the door as I cautiously entered the hidden stairwell to his study. I tried to light the lamp with dragon's breath, but I coughed instead, most likely because of the dust. I did manage a tiny bolt of lightning to ignite the wick. I had to find out why my magic is off. Hopefully, the answers could be found here.

The stairwell led up into a space in the attic that didn't exist, I knew, because I had checked. The lamplight gave everything in the study a golden glow like I had discovered a treasure trove in a dragon's cave. From what I knew of my grandfather, I half expected to find a stuffed dragon mounted to the wall; however, he did have quite the collection of big game animals' heads looking down from the twenty-five-foot-tall walls. The study was huge, larger than any room in the house.

Mountains of books covered the floor, books of every kind, not just spell books, surprisingly. All the walls were bookcases that reached almost to the ceiling minus the five feet or so of bare white walls used for displaying Michael's vast collection of taxidermized heads. It was a circular room with no other way in besides the trap door from the stairwell. Lamplight did magical things in this room like nowhere else in the house. I could only see the immediate ten-foot diameter bubble around me when I held still. However, while I was moving, the lamplight appeared to stick to every book that it touched and would retract as I moved away or stood still. The oddly eerie light would magically illuminate the titles of the books as I surveyed the room.

That's when I found Michael's Diary on the desk across the library. My heart was pumping so loud with anticipation of the great mysteries that I was going to discover that I couldn't hear my own thoughts as I read. I read aloud through random entries anxious to learn more of my late grandfather. He traveled the world as a professional wildlife guide and hunter for the wealthy.

However, this was just a cover for his secret agenda to become one of the most powerful creatures alive, a therianthrope or were-creature. I had to look it up in Lu-lu's Diary to get the gist of what it means. Michael wrote several volumes about them, those he found in his travels that were like him: half man and half beast. It was exciting to learn that he was part animal, but he never wrote about one specific kind that he would become. According to his own words, Michael had learned about an old Indian elixir that would make it possible to change into multiple animals, not just the first beast that infected you with its bite. He did speak about his first transformation in his Diary.

Journal entry for: Thursday, October 30th, 1913

Day 5 of the hunt,

We are now so deep into the Uintas that we had to abandon the horses. Our guide, White-snake-feather, says that the grizzly is not too far ahead of us. Hopefully, we have been tracking the right beast, the very one that has been terrorizing the ranchers over the past few months. It was nearly sundown when the beast found us. The hunting party was having dinner when the beast attacked, so rightly we were languid in our vigil to the point that our lookout, Joshua Bannon, was laughing at our stories and forgot his post.

He was the first to go, next was Ephraim Merlatte & Caleb Williams that were the two main ranchers that knew the monster. I was his last victim before White-snake-feather slit the bear's throat. That was the last thing I saw before all went black and the pain began. When I awoke to the singing of the Navajo's holy man Chief Straight-arrow, I knew that White-snake must have saved my life. I asked of the others but knew by the look on his face what White-snake couldn't say. I wanted to know what happened to me. He simply said, "We are trying to remove the demon now. Here, drink this."

I had to stomach the vilest concoction imaginable. My Heart and veins seared with agony, my organs burst and reformed as my bones cracked. Hair grew from every part of my body and I grew to triple my size. There were others now changing in front of me with greater ease and speed. One was half Elk, another half Buffalo, White-Snake was part Eagle, part rattle-snake and part man. The chief remained a man, but I sensed that there was a monster looming inside of him. He gave me another vile to drink, but my massive bear-like hands couldn't manage it on my own so White-snake helped. Instantly, the painful burning returned to my body as I changed back into a man. Thus, began my life as half a man, and half-beast.

Michael Lamia

I studied there all day long, reading everything there was to know about Grandpa, were creatures, and Indian magic. I was writing down the ingredients for the "weremen whiskey", as Michael called it when suddenly I got a flash of Zatie coming home to find the secret door. In a panic I grabbed my Diary and stuff before rushing downstairs to her room. I could hear her calling for me from downstairs as I corrected the doorknob and locked it. She was almost to my room, so I clutched the Diary with all my strength and desperately thought of my bed.

I nearly made it but crashed painfully onto the floor instead of my pillow as Zatie came into my room.

"Oh, are you okay?" She asked.

"Gravity must hate me today," I said.

"I would say so, what were you doing anyways?" Zatie

asked as she helped me back into my bed.

"I wanted my Diary from the nightstand, but I slipped." I wasn't entirely lying to her.

"Well, you get better; I have to study for a quiz. I'll bring you some supper later," she kissed me on the forehead and shook her head disapprovingly, probably because my head was burning with worry.

I woke late at night to the sound of howling, maybe an echo from my dreams. It reminded me of the recipe for the Weremen whiskey potion and sparked my curiosity to taste of that power. It was my current habit to do magic in the barn, especially since Zatie's room was an impenetrable fortress because I made a mess in my rush to leave the study undetected. As a result, she thought that Jesse was in her room, partly because I put that thought into her head when she brought me dinner later. Zatie would, unintentionally, read minds when she conducted her routine interrogations. I was better prepared against her intellectual intrusions thanks to my new-found love for our family heredity. I decided to walk to the barn tonight instead of teleporting to avoid any more injuries. After some time, I began to notice that my powers needed to recharge through sleep, but they were never as strong as they had been when I started.

Most of the ingredients for the potion, oddly enough, were found in Lu-lu's herb garden. The potion only required a few magical techniques; several I was fortunate to already know. However, there was a spell required for binding the chemical elements that I wasn't familiar with called "The Three Circles of Dawn and Dusk." I didn't want to wait three days to feel the pulsating promise of great power again. My addictions to the energy, the adrenaline that magic brings were getting stronger than I could endure. I worried that the Diary would not assist me if I asked because of my selfish lust for power, but I needed to feel special again.

"Show me the spell for the three circles of dawn and dusk, please." The Diary seemed to yawn as it opened; it was probably annoyed with me. After an eternity of slow one-at-a-time page-turning, the Diary arrived at the spell.

The 3 Circles of Dawn & Dusk

The light of the Sun is only available for half of each day in most areas. This spell was discovered as a weapon against nocturnal demons such as nosveratu & ghouls. To create a separate sun, one must gather the four forces of nature: fire, wind, rain, and pain. Note: early witches did not have a word for gravity, so they called it pain instead because of how they felt whenever they would fall.

I went out of the barn and into the field for fear of burning it down when I attempted to conjure a sun. The steps to make a sun were first creating pain, so I punched the wall of the barn and boy did that do the trick. Next was fire and I knew how to do that with the dragon's breath spell. What I didn't know was that the fire would remain in a ball of flame floating directly over my throbbing hand. Then was wind; I didn't know that spell so I just blew out a lungful of air and hoped that I wouldn't extinguish the fire.

It stayed above my palm and began to swirl with the wind which revolved around a tiny gravity well. Last was the rain, and it would rain whenever I did a lightning bolt from a storm cloud. I shot a bolt into the sky and it attracted thunderclouds. Shortly after the clouds came in, the rainfall followed. When the first drop hit the fireball, the fire went out and the gravity well collapsed.

I was so disappointed that it didn't work I stared open-mouthed at the spot over my hand where my flame had been. A split-second later I was blinded by a flash of light, brighter than I had ever seen. When the scalding pain had ebbed from my eyes, I was happy to see the warm glow of my golf-ball-size sun floating in my hand. I was so elated that my powers worked enough to get this spell to stick. 'Sticky' is a good way to describe how the tiny sun would react whenever I moved my hand.

It was magnetically attracted to the pain in my palm. Having use of my powers again was a welcomed distraction from the pain I had felt with my loss of Lu-lu, and the newly formed cut on my knuckles. As soon as I acknowledged that the pain was subsiding, so did the strength of my new toy. The sunshine was flickering, and it was starting to collapse, so I whacked my hand against the barn again like it was a faulty flashlight.

Immediately the sun was recharged but would wane whenever I let myself lose focus on the pain. The adrenaline from the magic rush was such a diversion that I almost forgot why I made my little sun. I carefully carried it back into the barn to finish the Weremen's whiskey. I reread the spell to be certain that my makeshift sun would work. I commanded the sun to rise and set by the power of telekinesis, all the time saying, "Ashes to ashes, dust to dust"; to myself in case my powers weren't working. After each cycle of the sun, the potion would change colors and thickness.

When it was done, I set it on the old workbench so I could finish reading the steps to the potion. Next it said that I needed to insert hair, skin, bone, and blood samples of the animal I desired to become. I started to fantasize about the different powers I could have by changing into any one of my favorite animals. The thought of being powerful again was intoxicating, and exciting. It was so exciting that my goosebumps inflamed, tickling me all over. At least that's what I thought until I heard a very loud noise slam against the barn doors.

That's when I changed my mind about the goosebumps reacting to excitement and prepared for danger. There was a little wind still brewing about outside from the storm I conjured but I couldn't sense anything else. I snuck to the crack in between the doors to get a better look. I would have used the Seer's Sight, but everything had been off with my magic, so I decided to use my own eyes instead. I couldn't move fast enough to avoid the blast of pure fear as the Gor-Nok blew the doors off their hinges with his awful powers.

"Give me the book, little girl!" he squealed in his horrible pig's voice. The Diary was on the workbench alongside the Weremen's whiskey, neither of which I wanted him to have. I could feel one last trick up my sleeves and decided to try it before he could notice them on the table next to him. I thought of Michael's secret room with all my heart.

"Abracadabra!"

"No! Now you die, witch!" The Gor-Nok smacked me in the chest with his massive club for making them disappear. The blow from his club sent me through the air on a collision course with the nearest barn wall. Luckily, my head knocked a few boards loose enough for me to crawl through before the Gor-Nok could strike again. He trashed my escape hatch with a blast of fear, knocking me down in the field. Now I wished that I had signed the contract when *Harry* gave it to me; I wished *Harry* was there.

"Darn it, *Harry*, why didn't you give me your number? Now how am I supposed to call you with a blank business card?" I muttered to myself as I crawled to safety in the woods.

"There is no point in hiding, girl; I'll tear this place apart until I find you." I snaked behind a rock as he sent shockwave after shockwave of fear into the woods after me. A lucky shot pummeled my hiding spot, forcing me to leave. He charged in after me, knocking down every tree in his way. I couldn't run any more, nor did I think that I had enough power left to teleport myself out of danger. I shot a lame-looking lightning bolt at him that barely did more than tickle. He laughed at my embarrassing assault.

"Is that all you got?!" He slammed his club into the ground, sending a fear-sawblade made of his transparent demons crashing into my back as I tried to run away. He chuckled as he stood over me gloating. He relished in my agony as his invisible demons tore my sanity to shreds. Paranoia had succeeded in paralyzing me completely as the Gor-Nok laughed at my defeat. I was going limp and numb from the pain and convulsions as he prepared to crush me with his gnarled club. Somewhere Death was smiling.

Harry, why did you lie to me? The Gor-Nok was laughing louder, so loud in fact that I could barely hear the deep growling that came from behind me in the woods. I couldn't begin to describe what Harry had become. He wasn't like the werewolves I had seen in all those bad late-night movies Jesse watches. Harry had long boney fingers, with razor sharp black nails like needles. His long arms and broad shoulders were strapped with slender yet powerful muscles that made fighting the beast look easy. The Gor-Nok tried to run away but Harry was so fast it was like he split in half to cut-off his enemy's escape.

Harry growled horribly and bared spiny teeth in a wicked smile. The Gor-Nok smashed the ground again near Harry but he leaped into an attack, dodging the shockwave of fear demons. Harry crouched over the Gor-Nok's head and shoulders, biting and clawing at his tough hide until the Gor-Nok was able to throw him through a nearby tree.

"I will kill you next time, witch, this I swear!"

"Not if my friend kills you first. Go get 'em, Harry!" I yelled as the coward fled for his life. Harry seemed a little dazed from getting hit by a tree and was lumbering around lost and confused. When I called to him, he didn't even recognize me, almost as if he wasn't himself at all. That's when I sensed danger and took caution as I approached him. He was hurt bad; I could tell by his low whimper. He almost bit my hand off, though, when I tried to touch him. Harry growled and began to bark aggressively as he stalked me back into the woods.

His blood-red eyes glowed bright with hunger as he crouched down before his attack. I was powerless and pitiful as I sobbed and pleaded for mercy.

"Harry, stop! This isn't funny," I said.

"Oh, I think it's terribly funny," he replied.

I was shocked to hear his voice so clearly as he growled, still a werewolf ready to kill me. "Harry, change back already. I'm done with the whole wolf thing," I responded.

"Wolf? I don't turn into a wolf, I'm a crocodile." The wolfman bared his teeth once more before he lunged at me through the air. I covered my face and prayed for a miracle. The next thing I noticed was the sound of the wolfman yelping in pain. The real Harry Anderson was holding the wolfman by its tail as it struggled to catch me. The werewolf turned its attack towards Harry, who wasn't the least bit afraid. Harry grabbed the wolfman by its neck and slammed him into a boulder, crushing it with the werewolf's body.

"If that's not you, Harry, then who is it?" I asked.

"I'm not sure, but there's a way to find out. Get the Diary, Lucia has a spell for unmasking my kind," he said.

"Yeah, about that, my magic isn't working any more. I was going to ask you how come?" I replied.

"Did you sign the contract?" Harry asked me.

"Um, no, I get sick at the sight of blood." I said.

"She told me that you were stubborn, I knew I should have made you sign it in my presence," he reached into his suit coat pocket and produced another copy of the contract. I automatically gulped at the thought of signing it with my blood.

"Uh, Harry, I don't suppose that you would happen to have a knife or a needle, would you?" I asked timidly.

"No, I don't usually make it a practice to do business in the woods. However, we do have an unconscious werewolf handy. Here, give me your hand."

I cringed, swallowed, and closed my eyes all at the same time that I timidly held my arm out to him. Harry used one of the wolfman's claws to make a pinprick in my palm. He then gave me that same claw to sign the contract. Again, I cringed to see my blood, but at least Harry was happy about it.

"So, do I get my powers back now?" I asked.

"Unfortunately, no, you're going to have to wait until the witching hour, which is later on tonight," he was disappointed with me, but I was glad that he was on my side.

"Well, I guess we'll have to do this without magic, like normal people. Now Miss Venatora, give me a hand with this guy. We need to get him into the light to identify him."

I helped Harry the best I could, but my strength was nearly gone, and I could barely stand by myself, let alone drag a six-hundred-pound monster out of the forest. Dawn was approaching, causing the sky to turn a light purple. We laid the were-beast in the wheat field just outside the barn.

"So, what are you gonna do, check his wallet?"

"Well, seeing how he doesn't have any pockets, I doubt that he brought it with him," he said jokingly. I was glad that Harry was in a good mood and not still bitter with me because I didn't sign the contract. He went quickly to work trying to identify our new ally. Harry knelt down on the beast's arms as he examined his face. It reminded me of a surgeon performing an autopsy of a murder victim. Harry seemed to know what he was doing and soon concluded. He stood up, wiped his hands on his pants, folded his arms across his chest and nodded his head up and down.

"Harry, do you know what it is?" I asked.

He didn't answer right away but continued to nod his head. "I will tell you what he isn't; he's not a werewolf, that's for sure. Wolves have more hair; this guy is practically hairless. In a few minutes, when the sun rises, he should change back to his human self. The curse only works at night," he explained.

"I wondered about that; so, you become a monster every night?" I asked him.

"Only if I want to; at first you have no choice unless you learn to conquer it or if you have help."

"Like Lu-lu, like the potion she would make for Michael?" I replied.

165

"Yeah, it's nasty stuff. I did not want to take it, but I had to; it was the only thing that kept me from becoming 'it' every night." He shuddered a little at his memories.

"Does it hurt; you know, when you change?"

"Like you can't imagine, kid, now be quiet, the sun's nearly up," he said. I stared with great anxiety and anticipation at the were-beast's face, hoping it would reveal the face of a new friend, a friend who saved me from the Gor-Nok. As the sunlight caressed his ghastly features, I expected to see some marvelous display of magic only to be disappointed once again.

"What, that's it, nothing?!" I exclaimed. I looked at Harry incredulously, hoping for answers but saw that he was in shock as well.

"I can't believe this; do you know who this is?!"

"No, should I?" I responded.

"My dear little witch, this is your great-grandfather, Dominic Lamia. I bet your grandmother told you all about him." Harry began to chuckle to himself until he noticed that I didn't know what he was talking about.

"Well, it's a long story, longer than I want to get into; but I will try to summarize it. Your great-grandfather Dominic wasn't like Michael or me; his body couldn't take the transformation. He couldn't be half and half like we could. It had to be all or nothing, and your grandmother made sure of that. She cursed him to roam these... aw, shoot, he's waking up!"

Harry tried to keep my ravenous great-grandfather at bay while I made my escape, but Dominic was too fast for him. I knew for certain I wasn't going to get very far but I had to try. At the moment that I could feel my strength giving out, Dominic at my heels. Harry tackled him from out of nowhere and wrestled him to the ground. He was amazing; this timid lawyer that came to meet me the other day was now wrestling a monster in my backyard, displaying inhuman strength and speed.

"That's impossible! How're you doing this, Harry? The

sun's up; you can't access your abilities, can you?"

"Sorry, I'm a little busy right now! I have to stop your great-granddad from killing you first," he said as he fought back Dominic's razor-sharp claws. After a brief tussle, Dominic gave up and became very tired and docile. Harry was petting him like he was an oversized dog and whispering in his ear to calm him. I was too frightened to move, let alone look him in the eye.

He was frightening, one of the most terrifying things that I had seen in my life. Yet he was family, and I couldn't help but feel sorry for him. I sometimes feel so sorry for me for being caught up in this nonsense of magic and monsters. Once Harry was sure that great-granddad was no threat to me, he beckoned me to come meet him.

"Now come closer, but not too fast because he will bite you if you come off as too aggressive," Harry said.

"Nut-uh, I ain't gettin' anywhere near that thing, family or not!" I exclaimed as I crab-crawled backwards a few more feet to be safe.

"Don't be ridiculous, Miss Venatora, it's bad manners to be rude to one's elders," he held out his hand. I gulped and cringed as I came closer to give him mine, keeping my eyes closed the entire time.

"Now, let him smell you. He needs to know that you're related to him." The beast moved forward to smell my hand and fear made me want to leave but Harry was too strong for me to get away.

I hated being small and fragile sometimes. Great-Granddad sniffed curiously around my hand and up my arm with his wet, cold nose. My goosebumps were freaking out but mainly because his nose tickled so bad. Before I knew it, he was sniffing up my chest to my neck and licked my face like a puppy.

It made me giggle a little, but I was so grossed out that I tried not to laugh. It did make me smile to know that Dominic wasn't afraid of me any more.

"All right, ha ha, Harry, get him off of me!" I said. Harry was chuckling too as he pulled Dominic back and continued to pet him. Dominic whimpered and looked confused as I smiled at him. Harry seemed to understand him and tried to keep him calm.

"He recognizes your smile, but he doesn't know who you are. Dominic, this is Michael's grand baby. Ha, yes, I know that she is not a baby anymore."

"How do you know what he's thinking?"

"Oh, my kind can hear thoughts. I only vocalize my side of the conversation for your benefit, little witch."

"Do you only hear were-people's thoughts, or can you hear other people too?" I hoped that didn't sound rude or racist.

"No, my little witch, you're not being rude or prejudiced by asking nor am I when I address you by your proper label. You're a witch by definition and design; what else can I call you? Albeit 'were-person' may be a little too vague and incorrect; I prefer the label 'were-croc,' for it is what I am," he explained.

"But, Harry, you didn't answer my question; aw wait a second. You read my mind, didn't you?!"

"Correction, I *heard* your thoughts because they were about me or for me to hear; however, reading your mind is different, more invasive like Lucia could do." *Or your younger sister for that matter; let's see if you can do it too, little witch.*

"Harry, Zatie can but I can't, I mean, I haven't done that, not that I know of at least. Hey, did I just hear what you thought?!" I replied.

"Ha, I knew it, but now the question is who gave you that power; Michael or Lucia?" Harry replied.

"Well, how do we find out?" I asked him.

"Have you ever lied to Lucia or your sister, or put a thought into someone's head and got them to believe it?" Harry asked me.

"Yeah, like all the time; but then that would mean..." I

shared.

"That you get the power from Lucia, I know. However, there's another way to test it for certain. I'm going to think of two separate things in different ways, meaning one thought is about you and the other isn't. Now let's see what you can really do!" Harry had a strange *Focus* on his face like he was trying to smile and frown at the same *Time, Focus and Time*; why did those two words stand out in my mind? I didn't think that my powers were working enough to get into his head.

But they are; you're just not focusing enough, like the time we met in my office.

"Harry, I only heard the last part about meeting you before at your office, which I've never done. But you're wrong, I was focusing enough; I just can't use my powers like before," I replied.

"No, the test worked, you're just not working. Not until tonight at least. Don't worry, your powers are coming back. However, being able to hear the one thought that was about you and not very much of the other means that you're part were-beast too and best take caution not to be bit by a rabid animal until after you're able to make the transition potion," he responded.

"Don't worry, I'll be careful." I assured him.

"And I'll be listening in case you need help again. Oh, don't be scared of Dominic, he's out here in the woods to protect your family; it's his job."

With that said, Harry patted Great-Granddad on the head and walked towards the woods. Dominic gave me one last lick on the cheek before dashing off to follow Harry. *Thank you, Harry*; I wished that I got to say that before they left.

Later that morning, I actually got ready for the day and made breakfast for my siblings before I walked the long way to school, making certain to pass by the cemetery. I never heard much about Dominic before, not even from Lu-lu while I was growing up; Mom would avoid any questions on family history and now I know why. I visited the family plots to check on how they were doing, just to see if the Gor-Nok was disturbing them or not. I also decided that it was probably a good idea to have some spare 'hallowed earth' at home just in case of emergency. I had brought a used jam jar from the pantry with me to the graveyard. I knew that someone like me should probably stay clear of scary stuff like graves and dead people, but I guess that I hoped my loved ones would be waiting there for me to tell me that they were proud of me for signing the contract.

When I got there, everything was fine. There were even some fresh flowers by Lu-lu and Michael's graves; most likely left by *Harry; thanks again.* Mom and Dad's headstones were shiny from the morning's dew. I wondered what Mom would say about me becoming a witch full-time. All I knew was that I was never alone thanks to my new were-beast bodyguards.

School was okay, all except for Derik. He wasn't his usual smothering-boyfriend-self. He was treating me like I was fragile or broken whenever I saw him. In my absence, he began hanging out with his cousin Johnny more these days. This meant more bitter-sweet moments of torturing myself every time I tried to exist around Johnny. I mean, I should have been trying to keep Derik from running off to play grease-monkey rather than crushing on his cousin.

Johnny, I was glad he couldn't read my mind; boy, that would be embarrassing. The rest of the day, I went about repairing the damage of my off-and-on attendance of my social life. I gathered the missing homework and returned home going the long way again to clear my head.

Derik had offered to drive me home, but I told him that I was going to say 'hi' to my family in the cemetery before going home. *That's a little morbid and weird, but maybe she still needs space?* He thought, at least it sounded like his voice in my head, but I knew that he loved me anyway, so it didn't matter what he thought.

It was nice to know what people were thinking about me, thanks to Michael's gifts. I continued to practice that when I got home to the twins. Jesse was worried that I would find out that he took the suit back to the store and got a leather jacket instead.

"Hey, I don't care what you do with the suit now; the funeral's over," I said to him as I came into the house. Jesse tried to hide the look of embarrassment on his face as he hid the jacket under a couch cushion. Zatie, on the other hand, was trying to figure out what I was talking about and wondered if I had truly lost my mind all at the same time; she was quite complicated.

"Yeah, I'm okay, thanks for asking," I said as I patted her on the head and went to my room to sleep.

When I got to my room, I had almost forgotten what a slob I was when I was sick or practiced magic. I put my schoolbooks down and I attempted to move things with my mind. It was slow going, much like trying to drive down the freeway in first gear. Yet I was able to do things a little bit with magic. I started to worry again that I wouldn't get my powers back, but then I remembered that Harry said they would come back tonight.

Perhaps there was some kind of enchantment placed on the contract that would rid me of my magical abilities until I signed it. It made sense because Lu-lu was always testing peoples' loyalty. That was what all this had been, one of Lu-lu's sick, twisted tests to see if I was going to join her or abandon her.

After a while I gave up doing everything with magic and finished cleaning my room with my bare hands. It felt nice to use my own elbow grease for once but felt like I was running a little low. I glanced at my alarm clock just to see how long I had been working. Time flies when you have to do everything by hand. I decided it was getting late and I did not want to frustrate myself with trying magic any more until my powers returned, so, I went to sleep.

Entry #8

What Am I?

My alarm clock was blaring in my ears like a warning siren. It took a couple swats at the nightstand to shut it off. My eyes were sore and burning as I squinted in the dark to see the time. It was 11:30; I must have missed dinner. It was unlike Zatie to not call me down for meals. I decided to listen to my body for once and get some food. I could hear the wind blowing outside as I went down to the kitchen. I watched the storm through the kitchen window as I made myself a sandwich.

At first, I couldn't tell if I was hungry and salivating over the food, or if the storm was provoking my lust for power. Either way I was outside eating my sandwich in almost tornado like weather as though it was a sunny day in the park.

Storms did not frighten me anymore; I had new fears and more terrifying nightmares than being struck by lightning. Getting shocked isn't that bad; it actually kind of tickles. It's like getting a really deep tissue massage from one of those vibrating chairs you find at the mall. I really didn't mind it; I actually miss using magic to conjure electricity. And that was probably why I went outside: in the hopes that I would get shocked and feel powerful again since my powers were not working.

Before I knew it, I had wandered out toward the barn. There was a light coming from one of the windows; it was the oil lamp. I could've sworn I left that on the nightstand, but there it was in the barn burning bright. I opened the doors with my mind because of the food and drink I had in my hands. Lu-lu was happy to see me using magic despite her curse with the contract.

"Ha ha, I knew my curse wouldn't work on you! You're just too damn strong and stubborn for that. Come here and give me a hug." Lu-lu stood there with open arms by the oil lamp near my workbench in the barn.

Of course, I was hesitant; wouldn't you be after the last attempt to deceive me? However, my goosebumps didn't react, nor was I scared to see the ghost of my dead grandmother hanging out in the barn in the middle of a storm. I was more startled than scared; I just didn't expect to see her; it had been so long.

"Lu-lu? Is that you? Because if it's not, I got no problem frying your ass!" Lu-lu didn't like cussing, so I was testing to see if it was really her.

"Did you kiss your mother with that mouth? I should slap you for your disrespect. Now get over here and give me a hug, but don't kiss me with that potty mouth. Totally inappropriate!" We laughed as we hugged, even though I should not have been able to hug her.

"But, Lu-lu, you're dead! I shouldn't be able to touch a ghost. How is this possible?" I asked. I was already crying both from shock and grief.

"It's all right, my Bella child, the lamplight makes it so you can see and touch me. But why are you crying, did you miss me?" My sobbing was stopping but I did not want to stop hugging her for fear that she should disappear when I *did* let go.

"Oh, don't worry, I'm not going anywhere. At least not right now, we have business to attend to," she picked up the lamp and motioned to the field outside. I followed her out to where she began to burn a circle in the ground, placing me in the middle. She was chanting and dancing as she was burning the circle. The storm above me began to part like the eye of a hurricane. I watched my grandma with delight as she finished pouring the liquid fire from the oil lamp. Then she handed the lit lamp to me. She stood inside the circle with me and held my hands around the lamp.

"Now, my Bella, blow out the oil lamp to finish the summoning spell," Lu-lu said, holding it with me.

"But won't you disappear? No, I'm not gonna do it. Not now that I have you back; I won't let you go again." I began to cry again, and Lu-lu wiped my tears.

"I promise that I'll never leave you, not again. Now blow it out and stop being so stubborn," Lu-lu said. I didn't want her to go but I didn't want her to be mad at me either. I drew in a frightened breath and made a wish as I blew out the wick of the oil lamp. As the light faded, so did Lu-lu into the darkness. The flaming circle extinguished as well, and I was left alone in the smoke and rain. Once again, I began to cry when I realized that her promise to be with me was too good to be true. I started to walk back toward the house, but the circle of smoke was like an invisible barrier preventing me from leaving.

The smoke began to gather into four different pillars, one in each direction. Slowly they began to take shape and the one directly in my path to the house slightly resembled my grandmother. Before too long they were more solid and had more distinguishable facial features. As they were finished solidifying, I could recognize the faces of my parents and grandparents. I was so overjoyed from seeing my mom and dad that I began to cry yet again. I wanted to touch them but Lu-lu stopped me.

"I'm sorry, my child, but your parents have been dead far too long. The magic won't work the same," Lu-lu did appear to be more substantial and alive than they.

"Why are you guys here, what do you want?"

"It's time for you to receive your birthright as was

175

promised in the contract. We're giving you your powers back, cry-baby!" She motioned for me to stand in the center again and she began to chant a phrase in Latin or Italian, I couldn't tell. The others began to chant as well; it was weird to hear my dad and mom perform magic. After a few times of them singing the spell in harmony, my body began the float three feet off the ground.

Great waves of energy were crashing against me from each of them in turn. Each wave felt different; Grandma's wave was cold as ice, my mom's wave felt like fire, my dad's wave was like leaves and grass clippings, and Granddad's was like a gale force wind in a wild sea. They didn't say much except for the chant and as each person took turns blasting me with their powers, I could see them start to fade and disappear, until Lu-lu was all that remained. After she had blasted me with her last wave of energy I collapsed to the ground and was crying from the pain.

"Come back, why can't they come back?" I cried.

"In time, child, you'll see them again. Now I have one last gift to bestow upon you. When it is done, I will be gone forever. I cannot help you any longer, they won't allow it. I'm sorry, but this is the only way."

"No, don't go, I can't survive it, not again!" I was sobbing again.

"I have to do this, it's the only way or else he'll win. Do you want him to win?" Lu-lu asked.

"No, but I don't want to lose you guys." I cried.

"Then let me do this and say goodbye," she said.

I was crying too much to protest any more, to fight against the spell. Lu-lu hugged me and we began to spin and float in the air as I had done before. I saw that the stars and the Moon flew past us in the sky in retreat as the sun rose. A beam of light from the sun broke through the storm clouds and pierced Lu-lu's back, filling me with her energy and powers. I could feel her soul seeping into mine. I saw her life from start to finish in the blink of an eye. I endured the agony of her death one thousand times and had the image of her murderer's smile engraved on my heart. And then there was nothing, no more pain and no more death. Lu-lu was gone and I was alone to drown in an ocean of tears shed over the ones I loved and lost.

I awoke to the most mind-numbing headache. My eyes felt like they were bleeding, and my lungs felt deflated. My entire body was like a giant bruise and my bones ached as though they were shattered. My mouth was so dry that my tongue was stuck to the tissue on the roof. I needed something to drink, so I reached around for my nightstand, but I couldn't find it. I tried to open my eyes, but they hurt so badly; and my room was too bright to see anything straight. I continued to blindly search the room for something to drink when a pair of hands grabbed mine and held them tight. It was my sister Zatie; I could tell by her perfume.

"Wa, wa-water-," was all I was able to cough out. Zatie quickly helped me to take a drink. It felt amazing to be able to quench the thirst and to breathe again.

"Thanks, honey, I needed that." I tried to get out of bed but Zatie stopped me before I could.

"Nonabel, don't get up. The doctor says you're not ready yet. I mean, you're lucky to be alive."

"What are you talking about, where am I?"

"Jesse and I brought you to the hospital because we found you unconscious in the field after the storm. What in the world were you doing out there?! The doctor says you got struck by lightning. Are you nuts or on drugs because I want an explanation for your crazy behavior?" Zatie questioned me.

"How long was I out? How long was I unconscious?" I asked.

"You were out for three days in a coma! Derik, Jesse, and I've been taking turns staying with you. You had us all worried sick." Zatie replied.

"When can I go home? I don't like hospitals."

"I'll go tell the doctor that you're awake and we'll find out. I'm sorry, I got angry; just don't scare us like that anymore, honey," Zatie hugged me and left the room. Shortly a man came into the room dressed in a doctor's robe and holding a chart.

My eyes were still a little blurry and I didn't recognize the man. He started to speak to me with the strangest voice. He was African or something, but he spoke English with a French accent. He asked me how I was and introduced himself as a doctor and said a last name that I could never pronounce for the life of me. He began to check my vitals and probe my face everywhere with lights and scopes. When he was done, he said as far as I could understand that he was going to give me a sedative to help me sleep.

"No, I don't want to sleep any more, I just want to go home!" I screamed. He wouldn't let me get up and fought with me to inject my arm with the drug. As I touched his bare arms my eyes were inflamed with the Seer's Sight and his false visage melted away to reveal my enemy trying to kill me. I had to get him out of there, away from all those people, away from my sister. I thought of teleporting us to the forest outside my house; hoping that he wouldn't want to face my were-beast bodyguards that would be waiting for us there. In that instant, we were submerged into my dark vortex, struggling to overpower one another.

We came out on the other side near the river in the woods. I landed on top of the Gor-Nok in his human form and smashed his head against a rock. He dropped the syringe on the riverbank, and I scrambled to get to it first. He was in too much pain to go after it, so I smashed it with my foot. He was beginning to get up and was choking on the dark residue of the vortex. I guess he wasn't holding his breath when we went under. The dark water of the vortex only *felt* like water, but it was still breathable. I took advantage of his moment of weakness and began to strangle him with my mind. I lifted him up into the air and relished in his misery as I continued to strangle the life out of him. It felt absolutely exhilarating to have my powers again. I was elated to watch my enemy suffer in my hands. Then he began to laugh, so I closed tighter on his throat, yet he still laughed psychotically.

"You can't kill me, witchling, ha ha, gahg..."

"I can sure try." I increased my psychic grip around his neck. I began to charge up a bolt of electricity between my hands.

"You can't kill what is already dead," he said.

"If that's true then you wouldn't be afraid of death. But I know you are because you're trembling."

"I've met death and, gagh, I shook his hand; gagh, I am not afraid of him!" The Gor-Nok was getting angry because he knew I was right. I knew he was afraid of me, of death. It felt good to be able to read his thoughts to see his fears and turn them against him.

"Okay, if you're not afraid of death then let's invite him to play," I blew out a loud whistle. "Oh, Dominic; come here, boy!" I whistled again for my great- granddad to appear and in seconds I could hear his footfalls charging from the woods toward us. I smiled at the Gor-Nok and projected a thought of my great-grandfather beating him up from the other night.

"No, not him again, gagh, I'm not strong enough."

"Then I suggest you run, coward!" I blasted him with my bolt of lightning and teleported back to the hospital before Dominic could arrive to finish the job.

I used the Seer's Sight to locate Zatie and the real doctor before I left the vortex and I decided to teleport into the nearby ladies' room instead of my hospital bed because they had already seen that I was gone. When I exited the vortex there was hardly any smoke at all. I was happy to have my powers again and I could tell that I was getting stronger now that I was losing my fears of them. The doctor took his turn examining me and after a little mental manipulation, I had him convinced that I was healthy enough to go home.

"Well, you look fine to me, I think it's time you went

back home, Ms. Venatora," the doctor said.

"Are you sure? I mean, she's been sleepwalking like this ever since our grandmother passed away. Isn't there some kind of medication you can give her?" Zatie wasn't convinced of my miraculous recovery, so I gave her a little push as well.

"I'm fine, the doctor says so. Now let's go home." With the help of my increased abilities I was able to get everyone to see things my way. Zatie was no longer a threat to my secret. In fact, it was actually kind of fun to mess with her using magic. Several times as we drove home, I put the thought in her head that a stray dog or cat was trying to cross the road in front of us, and she would swerve to avoid them. I couldn't help but laugh at her and she would chastise me for thinking that it was funny. When we got home Derik and Jesse were on the couch waiting for me.

Of course, Derik treated me as fragile glass if he heard that I was sick and he didn't want to hug me as tightly as he usually would. I mentally convinced him that I was fine just so he would hold me a little bit longer. My excursions with magic led to my neglecting our relationship. It was pushing him away and I had missed him. I put the notion into Jesse's head that Zatie had food in the kitchen, so he left the couch. Derik and I sat on the couch while Zatie and Jesse were arguing about the absence of food in the kitchen.

The Seer's Sight showed me that Derik was going to leave to take care of some errands for his mom. I didn't want him to go but I knew that I had other things to do as well. He told me he had to leave and promised that we would hang out again when I was feeling better.

I wanted to practice my powers of mental manipulation and probed his thoughts once more. I confirmed that he was in fact going on errands for his mom, so I let him go. We kissed goodbye on the front porch, and I watched him drive away into the sunset. I went back into the house to use the Seer's Sight to foretell what the rest of my day held for me, but the twins were arguing so loud that I couldn't hear my own thoughts. I projected the thought out loud for them to be quiet and immediately they stopped fighting. They both wondered what had happened and I couldn't help but laugh at them.

"Hey, guys, stop fighting and make me some dinner, I'm starving!" I pushed the thought of Grandma's garlic chicken lasagna into both their heads at once and waited to hear them began to cook. I laughed again to myself as I began to realize the positive aspects of being a full witch.

I turned on the TV with my mind and used it as a cover while I allowed my thoughts to be clouded with the visions of the day through the Seer's sight. I saw my family having a pleasant dinner, mostly because I controlled their thoughts to keep them from squabbling with each other. Later, I saw myself using my new abilities to hypnotize Zatie into a deep sleep as I 'tucked her into bed.' Then I was able to access Grandpa's library undetected.

I saw myself spending the rest of the night studying there and falling asleep. I decided that I should buy or create a cot of some kind for all the long nights I would undoubtedly be spending in the study researching ways to destroy the Gor-Nok. Once I had decided that I should buy a cot, I saw myself waiting until the twins were asleep before teleporting to the store to buy it. I began to understand how the Seer's Sight worked based on my intentions. If I just let the visions play out in my head, then they would show me one possible reality.

However, if I decided to change my mind on how I would act in that reality then the vision would change to show me the end results based on my choice. It was a very complicated and powerful gift that I knew I needed to perfect and understand. I got up from the couch, shut off the TV with only my desire, and sat down in the dining room to wait for dinner.

A couple seconds later, Zatie walked into the family room to announce that dinner was ready, but she couldn't find me. I subliminally suggested for her to check the dining room and to bring me a cola while she was at it.

"Oh, there you are. And I'll be right back with your drink, diet, right? No ice?" I answered her questions internally to test her abilities, not thinking of anything but the ice in the glass. She seemed to act more like Lucia than Michael when it came to reading thoughts.

As I had foreseen dinner was pleasant mainly because I wanted it that way. I caused the twins to separately be consumed in their thoughts about what they would do if they had all their monetary inheritance. I didn't need psychic powers to know what Zatie was going to do with her share. Most of the time, Zatie is an open book, mainly because she was always reading other people.

Jesse, on the other hand, imagined himself surrounded by wealth and power. I really should not have been surprised since he is one of the laziest people I know. Perhaps making him wait until after he had finished college would give him time to grow up. I know that the responsibility I had been given helped me to grow up just a little.

We were done with dinner around 8:00 that night and I would usually let them stay up till 10:00 studying or relaxing. Of course, you know who would be studying and who would be relaxing. I sat with Jesse to watch some TV and to mess with his head a little bit. As he was flipping through channels, I would make them skip ahead or back until he thought that the TV was broken.

He gave up on fixing it and went to bed early with only minor persuasion on my part. Later I went to Zatie's room to convince her to go to bed by repeating the same thought that she was sleepy over, and over again until she passed out while she was telling me about her homework. Once she was asleep, I thought of the lamp appearing out of my vortex and it did so. Immediately, I went to work in Grandpa's study by locating the Diary and the were-men whiskey that were waiting for me on the desk. I reread the guidelines about becoming a therianthrope. I found them in a letter from Michael giving instructions to Lu-lu. He wrote of the missing ingredients and methods that the Native Shamans would use for the "bitten," he had needed it to help Dominic.

Dearest Lucia,

After days of tracking, even as a part animal from time to time; I finally found White-Snake Feather hiding in a cave. He seemed disappointed that I sought him out. He told me that he cannot give me what I sought. I asked him what he thought I wanted. He said one word: Power. He warned against it, knowing how to trade totems is more than men should have. I told him that I needed that formula to save my father and that, if I had to, I would beat the secrets out of him. We fought for days; I was not able to keep him on the ground when he took flight. I had to shoot him down, at which point he accepted to teach me the formula. I told him that if I had this, then I could finally sleep at night; that you would no longer be in danger. I am sending this letter on ahead as I shall tarry with my brother-in-arms to learn more of totems. White-snake Feather has much to teach us of my people. Lucia, my love, please use this to save Dom.

Michael Lamia

Weremen Whiskey

White-Snake Feather's Formula can cure or curse.

Note: Caution taking on multiple totems. Be one not all.

I had to look this up in the Diary, when White-Snake Feather spoke of "totems," he meant the creature that would share your spirit. ... A Totem is a spirit animal of sorts, kind of like a dream guide. Michael wrote of being multiple animals at different times, not at once. Such a transformation would shatter ones very soul creating a veritable monster. Few have tried and lived.

It still didn't stop him from trying, and he achieved it! The potion made it possible to go through the initial change quicker, with less pain. Michael and Lu-lu improved it for more experienced therians to change into whatever animal you had tissue samples of to add to the vile concoction.

I'd forgotten that I needed to find a host animal that I could add to the potion. Often when I had fantasized about having this power, I thought it would be cool if I could turn into a bird like a hawk or a raven. I thought of the aviary at the state zoo and I had confidence that I could make it there, and before I was done thinking about it, I *was* there, no more smoke, and that motion-sickness from teleporting was gone. I was enjoying having my full powers.

The aviary was a large glass dome filled with moonlight and humidity like a hot summer afternoon at my old home in the south. They kept most of the tropical birds in this area, but the crows, ravens, and rooks were kept in the surrounding hallways just outside of the dome. There was an ornithologist's office at the very end of a long hallway lined with different glass aviary cells filled with different birds. I had to come here with Zatie for a school project she was doing; this was one of my favorite areas. As I thought of that fond memory, my Sight went active, allowing me to revisit that event. I was so innocent then, no loss, no pain. I shook away the tragic thoughts and remembered my mission.

I was like a kid in a candy shop, drooling over the possibilities. However, I had to stick to just one, for now. I didn't know which one to pick, which one was strongest, which would give me the most power; I needed more info, so naturally I appeared in the ornithologist's office at the end of the hall to get it. I was greeted by the startled screams of the ornithologist still working late in her office. Darn it, should've used the Sight before just showing up! The power made me too confident and reckless; as I contemplated what to do, she was still screaming and started throwing books in my direction.

I stopped them with my mind and her with my sheer will and anger. "Oh, shut up and sleep!" I think that's what I said, but it sounded like Latin. I wondered about what I had said as her limp body slumped to the floor. I took her seat and pushed her snoring body aside to make room in her cluttered closet of an office. After what seemed like an eternity of reading to the annoying sound of sawing logs, I finally found my choice.

I chose the rook, mostly because it looked the most like me and the strange legends surrounding them as being birds of death and misery. Much like death and misery had surrounded me lately. There was also an entire rookery that lived in the woods by the barn, it should be easier to catch them there than steal from here. I raised the snoring doctor from off of her cold office floor and set her in her chair without even glancing at her as I continued reading about my new obsession. I snapped at her with my fingers and slapped her gently across both cheeks to wake her. She was in a haze as I said my parting words.

"Hey, sleepy-head, I'm going to borrow this, but you're not gonna recall a dang thing about tonight, are ya?!" And with that last hypnotizing thought I sank rapidly into my vortex and arrived at the barn.

As I began to study in privacy about the rook (*Corvus frugilegus*), I summoned my magical tools, the Diary, the Lamp, and the small caldron of weremen's whiskey from Michael's study. The rook is heavily weighed down by myth and symbolism. It is bird of death and misery, much like the raven. A new rookery near your house was considered unlucky. I thought of the crows, rooks, and other birds that pestered Granddad's old creepy scarecrow in the back of the house by the fields.

In that instant, I heard the caws of the birds and instinctively appeared at the scarecrow, starling the different feuding flocks as I landed on a helpless bird. I tried to grab the injured bird and the others all swooped into protect it. I got my hands around its wounded body and the others poked and pecked at my hands until they bled. Wow, did that sting, like nothing I had ever endured!

I got pissed, screamed at the birds and they tried to flutter off, but I stopped them with sheer will and rage. I would have enjoyed the spectacle of slow-motion birds swimming through the air, but the stinging pain burned through my nerves attacking my mind, causing me to panic as I remembered Harry's warning not to get bit. *Sorry, Harry, I messed up.* My mind raced, aided by the Seer's Sight to recall any time, ever, that I had been bitten or scratched by an animal; never!

My blood was boiling over as adrenaline was crashing through my veins; I knew I didn't have much time before I turned. I vanished into my void taking the murder of crows and other birds with me to the barn. I bounced onto the floor near the workbench with my captive feathered followers crashing everywhere. The sudden impact dazed some of the birds, but others were trying to escape; this could not happen. I needed them for my potion,

I didn't exactly know which ones had bit me, so I tossed them all into the pot. Their cawing was drowned out by the boiling poison. Their cries of pain were pale compared to the terror that was tearing through my soul as I endured the first stages of the therianthrope transfiguration. As my new form started tearing through my flesh with new black talons, I began to black out, hoping Harry might hear my caws.

Flying felt so good again, I forgot the joys of self-sustained flight. The wind rushing through my flaxen hair and plumes. The world was small below, the city lights like tiny stars in the night sky above.

Nonabel, take another sip little witch. You're not out of this yet. Dom, it is going to be a long night, please keep watch over us. Circle the barn, keep us safe. The Other One might attack her while she is weak. Protect the family, she needs you!

Harry, are you with me? I feel you here in my dreams, is this a dream?! My head is spinning.

I'm here; drink the rest of it. You foolish girl! Why?!! I warned you, but you did it anyways. God, what bit you?! Damnit, we're in for a rough night. Shoo, you blasted buzzards, get away from her!! What did you do to yourself, child?

Harry was in my thoughts as I flew through the night and dreamt of power and freedom. My mind was everywhere, I could see my body as if I were looking from a distance, and all at once I could see from several different spots of my body. My hands, my hair, my flesh had dozens of tiny dark eyes all sending visuals to my brain. My fingertips were a collage of claws and beaks all at once, then pulsed and reverted back to my fingernails. *I am pretty sure something went wrong.*

Oh, my dear; something went terribly wrong. I've never seen anything such as this. Lucia would know how to fix you. Here, Nonabel, drink this one. We're almost out of this, just stomach all of this last glass and we'll be done.

Harry, that's enough! I thought.

"Get out of my head, Harry!" I screamed and kind of cawed at the same time as the last of the primal surges finished their course through my body.

"Well, aren't you a sight for sore eyes?! It's good to have you back to your, well, normal-looking self," *how do you feel? Was it worth the pain?! You are such a fool.* He thought out loud. *Harry, I can hear your voice just fine, your thoughts don't need to be as loud.* "Man, whiskey is right! I've got the worst hangover," I exclaimed.

"Good, perhaps you are done being stupid," *You're like a dang trust-fund kid needing me to bail you out after a night of boozing. Grow up, will ya!*

"All right, Harry! Can we be done with the double conversations?" *Does it ever turn off?*

Nope, not while we are around one another. I could leave if you'd like.

"No, I don't want to be alone. I really messed up, Harry. They all came at me at once. I didn't know what to do!" I exclaimed.

Well, the worst is over for now, "Sorry, I'll try to vocalize my thoughts of you, bad habit. How do you feel now?" he asked.

"My head is pounding; my vision is blurry. It's like I have eyes in the back of my head. Is that normal?"

"Not really, you are the first half-and-half I've ever met. Frankly, I didn't know what was going to happen if you were to turn by accident." *Being a witch and all. What the Devil bit you? You're a mess!* "Sorry. Did you catch the animal that did this?!" Harry asked.

Did what? "Yeah, I put it into the potion," I said.

"What, the birds?!" Harry asked.

"Yes, the birds!" I exclaimed.

ALL OF THEM?!?! "Oh, dear God! What have you done?" Harry was freaking out.

I finally got a clear vision of the scene; my sight was focusing through my natural eyes; the scene was grossly unnatural. Fragments of crows, rooks, and ravens were scattered, splattered, and shattered, shredded flesh from bone and swimming telekinetically in the air above the cauldron. All still somehow living, twitching, and writhing through it all. All my doing, all my fault, all me.

"What have I done?!! *What AM I!*" I was screaming, screeching, cawing mostly, and crying hysterically again. Harry held me, trying to calm my storm, yet I scared him. I wanted to vanish, but he held me there; I was tethered there with him. *What am I becoming?*

I didn't remember drifting to sleep; I wanted to fly away, but my wings were broken. *The transformation has phases; howbeit, you are normalizing quite quickly, for a witch.*

Harry, you're in my thoughts again.

Am I? It seemed like that was where you needed me. I can leave if that is what you desire?

"Let's use our words, Harry. My head is throbbing that's all," I responded.

"As you wish, Ms. Venatora. Apart from the 'throbbing,' how do you feel? Do you feel human again?" he asked out loud.

"No, my flesh feels raw, bleeding. Am I hurt, cut still? Please look, I can't see clear enough yet."

"Well, you should, - eventually heal faster as a were-rook, I guess that's what you are now. However, you don't seem complete."

"Oh, yeah, I know a spell for fast healing. I need your help, though," I replied.

"All right, it's been a while since I've seen magic up close. What can I do to help?" Harry asked.

"I need you to get my jar of dirt," I said.

"Excuse me?!" he asked, for clarification.

"It's in my room, I have it for emergencies," I said.

"Your jar... of dirt."

"Yeah, ha. Don't make fun, it's hallowed ground, I can't do it without it. Now go!" I said, pointing back toward the farmhouse.

Harry laughed as he sprinted from the barn towards the house.

Oh, Harry my jar is under my bed. I tried placing the mental image in his mind of my small jar of hallowed earth that was wedged between my nightstand and my bed post. As I waited, I tried to stand by holding onto the workbench, nearly tipping it. I pulled myself up to witness the tragic horrors my powers had reaped. Dozens of half-living helpless bird fragments floated like the first glass of water I crushed with my mind. I could feel their pain, all at once. I reached out for one.

"Don't!" Harry suddenly returned with my jar of dirt. "We don't know what you did to them, what they could do to you. Let's fix you first, then maybe them."

I called the jar of hallowed ground toward the work-bench. Harry was slightly startled; it was cute.

"When was your last time... to see magic, I mean?" I was worried about my thoughts.

"It's been ages, but you're not my first witch." "There's others, besides Lu...?" I asked.

"Lucia. Yes. Well, how does the dirt work?"

"Give me a moment." I scooped out a huge helping; I knew it was going to take a lot to recover from this.

"Now, fair warning! I usually pass out after I finish glowing," I explained as I rubbed dirt everywhere.

"Glowing?!" Harry asked incredulously.

"Yeah, it's super warm, like the Sun is hugging you. You should try it sometime!" I suggested.

"Okay, what should I do now?" he asked.

"Stand back but be ready to catch me when I fall." "As you wish," Harry replied.

I took the handful of dirt and I rubbed every inch that screamed and ached in agony. Harry seemed a little uncomfortable watching what he was hoping would be a magical demonstration of, well, magic, but instead he was visually assaulted by the awkward display of me touching myself. Not very attractive.

I wouldn't say that, Ms. Venatora.

"Harry, thoughts!" I screamed at him.

"I'm just saying, it's not that you're *not* attractive!" he stated.

"Harry, enough!" I replied.

"Sorry," he said quietly.

"Thank you, now please. No THINKING. I need to concentrate." I was so not thinking about healing. What was that healing spell again? I heard the pages of the Diary turning for me.

"Are you doing that?!" Harry inquired, pointing at the Diary as it finished turning pages to the correct spell.

"Yes, now quiet." I summoned the Diary to me.

Show-off. Harry thought.

Yes, quiet please. I re-read the healing spell because I had forgotten the pronunciation of the healing phrase in Latin.

...Then, while thinking of the victims when they were happy or laughing recite these words:

"What was broken and abused shall again become anew." (Then in Latin say, "Aesculapius Unctura!")

Last, a surge of heat shall escape your hands and fill the victim with the healing power of your own heart.

Warning: one must have love in their heart towards the inflicted person or the injury will be added upon your own flesh seven-fold.

I can't recall ever seeing you happy.

Harry, STOP!

"Now your thoughts are engraved in the Diary!" I screamed at him as I closed the Diary. I'll have to erase the side-comments later.

"Sorry," he said as he imitated the action of locking his lips with an imaginary key.

I closed my eyes, I had to laser-focus to block him out and think past the pain toward happiness and healing. I remembered hugging my mom.

She did have magical hugs.

HARRY! I couldn't stay annoyed; thoughts of Mom were vivid and powerful. The warmth began to swell in my heart. I could feel my incomplete flesh restoring, returning, *turning...* wait, what?!

Turning, you're turning, Nonabel. You're becoming the birds!

I opened my eyes, to see what he was squawking about. To see through the eyes of all those reviving rooks and ravens as they revolved around me was riveting. My flesh would blacken and grow feathers and scales as each new bird bonded with my flesh. Flaxen feathered wings would flap from under my hair as the transition settled from a flock of birds to my dark hair and pale skin again.

"Here, use this to cover up," Harry handed me an old flannel blanket that had been in the barn for who-knows-how-long.

"Wait, what?! Where are my clothes, Harry?!"

"It's an occupational hazard of becoming a were-beast, we tend to tear our clothes to shreds when we transform. I carry a back-up overnight bag in my car."

"Ugh, turn around, Harry, I don't want you to peek. I need the Diary for a spell I saw once. Can you please hand it here?" The Diary knew what spell I wanted and had flipped to the section before Harry could fetch it from the workbench.

"Restoration Spell, huh? Sounds like something to fix furniture... or..."

"Clothes, I'm going to fix my clothes," I called the Diary from his hands by sounding a quick whistle, like I would a trained pup; the Diary obeyed. After a short time scanning the spell, it was coming back to me. I had used it to fix Zatie's door, clothes should be simple.

"Nonabel, couldn't I watch, I mean the magical bit; of course, not the getting dressed part?!"

"Of course that's what you meant to say, *Harry*." I chuckled, annoyed, and began to chant the restoration spell to my tattered clothes. I added an extra display of flying articles of clothing for Harry's benefit.

I appreciate that, it's not every day that I get to witness a magical wardrobe malfunction.

"Well, my dear; now that you're all put back together, I shall have my leave," he took my hand, kissed it gently and sprinted out of the barn.

That's it, you're just going to leave me?! I thought.

Some of us have day-jobs; lawyer, remember. Not only your guardian angel.

But what if I have another lapse in judgement?

Don't worry your pretty little head, songbird; I'm never too

192

far away. Dominic, all is well! Good night, old friend.

Thanks, Harry, I thought as I gathered my things and vanished from the barn to my room.

Dear Diary,

I had a dream last night that I was flying; not psychically, but on a thousand wings. I was a flock of birds, or a 'Murder' of crows. Murder was right, I damn near killed all of them, but now we are one. I tried merging the Murder into one massive form, to become me again. I did different phases with mild success. The Dreamscape was definitely a safer place to practice transforming. Traditional therianthropes change between a man and were-beast form, but rarely into the full totem host creature completely. Only few had achieved this level like White-Snake Feather and the skin-walkers of his tribe. The whiskey helped Grandpa be other animals, but my half-therian, half-witch blood adds other options. Dominic is stuck between man and totem to avoid a painful death. It prolongs his condition so I might find him a cure. I need to study up on dreams again, turn my dreamscape into my magical "proving-grounds." Then maybe I'll stop waking in weird places.

Nanabel

Zatie was growing more suspicious of my abilities; she believed my lies less and less. I kept having to come up with reasons to be in her room or explain myself to Jesse whenever he would catch me leaving. I think that he was secretly jealous of all the 'laundry,' I had done for Zatie as an excuse to be in her room.

Zatie was exposed to more magic as I made her 'sleep' or 'forget' just so I could access the Library more to learn about Michael and the Gor-Nok. I most likely would either have to tie Zatie down with some form of magical bonds, or drug her so I could get into the Library on a nightly basis. I just felt bad poisoning her with potions; what if I was causing her permanent damage? I couldn't chance it. There was so much more at stake and so many things I had to learn that lay in the Library.

That was the real treasure; the Library. The Diary was like an index of the entire Library, only a sample. If the Gor-Nok got in there, we were done for. I tested the security of the Library by teleporting myself into the study once; it was not pleasant. I was in the dark vortex of teleportation, I could see the exit-point, and as I tried to emerge, thousands of dark, clawed hands clambered at my legs, clawing me, clutching me, and dragging me down to the depths of the crushing abyss.

I always retreated to my entry-point before I drowned in darkness between dimensions. I could teleport objects like the lamp and the Diary in and out at will, just not anyone sentient. I found that I could teleport if the door was open, but it would have been dangerous and stupid to leave it open; when it was closed, the defensive properties of the hiding place spell governed a space that did not exist in the real world.

The Raven

The nights of burning the midnight oil, studying all hours in the Library for answers, began to blur together. I found that the passing of time in the Library was very different than what was happening out in reality. Hours outside equaled days in the Library. Sometimes I would need a break from my renewed thirst for knowledge and power to simply get some much-needed fresh air.

I enjoyed an occasional night flight as either the entire murder of crows or just as one solitary bird. The rest of my body would rest in a trance-like state of dreams and shared senses with the lone crow.

I got so good at the transition that my little crow and I no longer needed to bond physically just as long as we were connected psychically. One night as I studied in the Library, I had decided to send one lone bird to hunt outside. I had fallen asleep at the desk while holding the oil lamp. I was reading in the Diary about demonic possession, hoping to understand how the Gor-Nok could haunt my grandmother's dreams. I'm pretty sure this is why I had this dream.

I woke up in a cage as one solitary bird. I was still in the library, and I saw someone carrying the lamp, and I feared someone had somehow broken in. I attempted to scream, but all that came out was cawing. The figure with the lamp came closer, and the lamp illuminated their face to reveal my grandfather's smile. He opened the cage and lovingly set me free. I landed on the desk to take a gander at what he was writing. He was researching a monster that had been terrorizing the small villages in Borneo. I couldn't believe what I was seeing.

This was the moment where Grandpa was planning his own death, unintentionally of course, but, doing it nonetheless. I would have to put a stop to it; well, at least try to. I knew that I couldn't reveal myself in my human form. The last time that he saw me in the house, he shot me, so that was not an option. I was limited to the powers I possessed as a solitary bird. I cawed at him to draw his attention.

"Not now, Twilight," he dismissed me with a scowl. "I am very busy," he said. I shot from my perch onto his notepad, and he swatted at me. I hopped up to dodge his hand and landed back on his notes. I gripped the page with my claws and tore it from the rest of the book. I flew around the room towards one of the bookshelves near the ceiling, hoping to escape my grandfather, forgetting that he not only was a great hunter, but a powerful therianthrope.

His neck elongated as he became a monstrous giraffe; then he snatched me in his mouth as though I was a fallen leaf. Before I knew it, he turned back into his human form and snatched the paper from my claws.

"Bad, Twilight," he scolded me and grabbed me by my claws. I tried to escape his grasp, but he threw my helpless body down the stairwell and out the door.

"Go cool off, Twilight," he muttered, slamming the door in my beak. I fluttered, flapped, and clawed at the door to no avail. I flew around the vacant room and spotted the open window. This was no longer my mother's childhood room, no more painted flowers, just white sheets over old furniture and boxes of forgotten memories. I took flight into the night sky and flew over the town trying to gain perspective.

Was I dreaming, had I travel through a forgotten memory of my grandfather? He thought that I was his pet bird; maybe I had absorbed that bird's memories when I absorbed all those birds. Who truly knows how these things work? I attempted to teleport, I even tried to change to a human, only to have searing pain course through my tiny bird-body. I must have been dreaming.

I just needed to get my bearings on when I was and find a way home. I soared past the town cemetery, thinking that it may give me some dates as a point of reference. I glided to my family's plots, only to see that they were missing headstones. This was the past!

Or maybe a memory from the bird. I knew that falling had always helped me to wake, still hoped this was a dream. I flew as high as I dared not knowing my feathered lungs' limitations. I stalled, pulled my wings in close to my body and dropped like the stone to the earth after David killed Goliath. I spun into a barrel roll and lost focus on the ground as everything around me got nauseatingly blurry.

As I blacked out from the fall, my tiny body flopped onto the Library's hardwood floor next to my resting human form on the cot. I regained consciousness in my own skin and found my little bird twitching on the floor. I psychically pulled the bird back into my hand and marveled at the soothing sensation of being united with my newly named, nightly lookout, 'Twilight.' I watched her little body swim through the flesh of my arm, up my neck and emerge restored as it flapped its way out of my black mess of bed-hair. Twilight landed on the perch on Michael's desk; we were grateful to be whole again. The two of us were close but we rarely needed to bond. My siblings even began to accept the Raven as part of my life.

I left Twilight in her cage one night and returned to my room for a normal night's rest. I was restless, it was almost painful to be apart like that. In reality, she was right across the hall, but in the really real world of magic and monsters, she was dimensions of space and oceans of time away from me. I thought of her cold and alone; I had taken the lamp back to my nightstand, leaving her in the darkness of the hiding place. My thoughts of her isolation consumed my dreams until I bonded with her mentally, became her, small and trapped in the cage.

I tried to get out and thought of the cage opening and it did so. I had my powers this time! I had to be certain it was not a dream, so I leapt from the cage and transformed mid-fight. No pain, just seamless transfiguration back into my human body. I kept spare clothes in the Library, as suggested by my mentor Harry. I think he would find this combination of magic and mutation fascinating.

I resolved to call upon Harry to aid in my studies of my grandfather and the Gor-Nok in the morning. I had to exit the study through Zatie's room carefully without being detected. I quietly and quickly shut and sealed the door before teleporting back into my room only to startle poor Twilight who was perched on my headboard of my bed. I psychically pinched her beak shut to muffle her caws as I re-absorbed her into my flesh once more. I had inadvertently discovered how to swap bodies with my tiny bird-self.

Dear Diary,
Note to self, discovered a new way to teleport that seems to bend even the rules of magic and mutations. Harry might want to witness it.

I discovered that I can teleport into the library, despite all the magical security features in place; if I leave one of my broken bird-fragments of myself (or Totems as White-feather called them) in the old bird cage by the desk. I can go on through my day without the broken pieces of myself and I had done so without getting into a lot of pain or trouble magically speaking. It kinda feels like I'm starving, or really thirsty when my totem is missing. After a few days, depressing thoughts come crawling into my mind. I know Zatie would say some melo-dramatic heart-broken poetry quote about loss and anguish, ugh.

Nanabel

I had another dream that I was powerless, but I got to have a moment with my grandfather. I also got to see when my grandfather made the mistake of going to hunt that monster in Borneo. I squawked in a panic as I saw my grandfather's fare-well kiss on Lu-lu's indignant cheek as the memory slipped away.

Tonight, I tried to induce that dream again hoping to get more details because his notes on the Gor-Nok from his jour-nals were lost; some of his other tools and equipment got lost when he went to hunt my enemy. I held the lamp as I did last time to induce these dreams.

It sort of worked this time and I ended up arriving after Michael's funeral seeing his smile again in the memorial photograph from before. The funeral was closed casket be-cause of how burnt and charred the remains of Grandfather's body were. All they had to identify him with were his den-tures. I watched as everyone departed the funeral, this time as a bird.

I saw my mother passing my small infant body to Lu-Lu. I recalled this moment from an earlier dream. Lu-lu was tell-ing me to keep the Diary safe. I tried using my powers, maybe to move objects with my mind while reliving this memory, but it hurt to think the incantation; I maybe had to say it aloud. However, as I began to articulate it with cawing, Lu-lu heard me and turned to scowl at me as she was trying to hush my newborn self in her arms.

I flew away to avoid dealing with an angry version of my grandmother. I perched in a nearby tree to continue my recon mission and waited until the funeral was over. I lost track of the time and kind of dozed off while I sat waiting. There was a loud commotion nearby that startled me. I flew in closer and saw the Gor-Nok wounded on the ground, gagging on his own vile fear toxin. I remembered this instant; he was weak, and I could use this moment to my advantage.

I saw the Gor-Nok transform back into its human form and begin attempting to do something magically to Michael's coffin. He called it up out of the ground and as it rose up, the ground beneath it built a staircase of mud and earth revealing where the Gor-Nok had been hiding all this time. He staggered into the opening and I tried to fly in after him; before I could sneak into the pit, the Gor-Nok sensed me watching him and stopped me mid-flight with some primitive chant. As I lay on the ground helpless, suffering from the fear toxins in my tiny bird lungs, the Gor-Nok reached down to crush me in his human hands.

He held me in his clutches and began to squeeze. I felt my bones crack and my life drain in his grip; I knew my death was coming. I did not know if I had any more tricks left up my sleeve; magic in this form, seemed to escape me. Escape would be nice, but all I had left was fear, pain, anguish, misery, intense terror, knowing I was about to die.

I didn't know what else to do, none of my other tricks would work. I thought, maybe if I could just turn back into my human form, I may have more access to my powers. I thought about each limb carefully as the Gor-Nok succeeded in crushing my wings, my feathers in his grip, and next my ribs and legs.

The pain seared through my limbs and I could feel them getting weaker just as he got stronger. What is the power of fear? Fear seemed to unlock the very essence of his transformation. I could sense it in his heart and his mind as he watched my helpless tiny feathered body in his grasp as I tried to resist his grip. As my body writhed and wriggled, then slithered in and out of his hand, I caught glimpses of my new form. I kind of was not a bird nor was I human; I was some type of mixture, a harpy.

My body was so seriously in pain and terror that I changed all of that into rage and used my new hand talons to slash at the Gor-Nok. I gripped some soil from the cemetery, leapt up in the air as a I flapped my wings and tossed some dirt into the Gor-Nok's eyes to distract him. I flapped away for some cover and rubbed the dirt in my claws. I tried my best to recite the spell in my mind, for all that came out of my mouth was screeching, hissing, and cawing. The healing spell began to do its best to repair and strengthen my new form as I tried to take flight. The Gor-Nok recovered his vision and managed to hit me with his club smashing me into the tombstones below.

I could hear his hooves thundering towards me as I regained consciousness. I snaked and slithered my way through the maze of tombstones for cover. My magic wasn't full strength in this form; I would need to practice later to know how to execute simple spells. Various species and creatures emerged from my body as I attempted to change and transport myself across space and time, across dreams and nightmares. I didn't know when I was in space and time, so I couldn't call for Harry or Dominic to save me. Also, I was nowhere near the farm, so calling for help wasn't going to work.

I had to figure out how to fight him on my own with my limited powers. The Gor-Nok roared and began sending shockwaves of fear demons tearing through the tombstones. I kept as low as I could to evade the shockwaves and the crumbling gravestones as I slithered to safety in the woods near the cemetery. As I was dodging and weaving shockwaves, I would pluck some feathers painfully from my body and left what I could behind as evidence to try to throw off the Gor-Nok.

I retreated into the woods and reverted into a simple crow, then flew as far away as I could. The Gor-Nok cried out in anger and defeat as he realized I was nowhere to be found. I didn't think that this version of the Gor-Nok had made the connection between me and my were-rook; that we were the same person. Falling from a stall at full speed could bring me back from my dream, "time travels" as I was calling them for lack of a better phrase; it would work before, why not now?

As I flew through the woods and rose to the skyline, I was met with a group of other birds and was surrounded in their cluster. It clouded my path with feathers and blackness as I suffocated and panicked, then lost consciousness in the cloud.

I emerged from the vortex of darkness and feathers into my cage in the Library not just as one bird but my entire murder, crammed together in the cage. I could feel the outer bodies of the birds being smothered and crushed against the wires of the cage. I felt wires snapping and stabbing into birds. Beaks and talons, clawing and pecking at each other each. We were panicking in terror and claustrophobia as we all tried to destroy one another to survive; one of us had to survive.

I was so numb to the pain of tearing myself apart in self-loathing that the sweet release from this cage was worth more than the terror and torture I was causing myself. I could register their pain; I could fill each and every one of them. I suffered through their sorrow and misery as they tore themselves and each other apart to escape. There were more than one hundred of us trapped in that small cage and more kept emerging from the vortex, from its center.

Realizing that I was in the study, in the Library, in the cage, appearing through Twilight's body; I knew that there was a version of myself, at least one spare bird still in my bedroom, also writhing in pain.

I latched onto that thought, ignoring all the anguish, and slipped back through the vortex. I was taking as many of my fallen friends with me as I quickly fled to the exit-point, where I was gasping for air and sanity. I emerged as blackness and feathers as we tore apart poor Twilight. I was thrashing in pain on my bed, then on my floor. My mangled form somewhat resembled the harpy as I caught myself in the mirror.

Memories and flashes of the terrible nightmare encounter with the Gor-Nok caused me to relive that recent traumatic event. I twitched and trembled on the floor as I passed through the motions of the fear toxins still present in me. My body regained some of its strength and composure.

As I crawled around on the floor looking for my jar of hallowed dirt, I noticed I was bleeding from nearly every inch of my body. I was covered with scratches, puncture wounds, and claw marks from attacking myself to escape the cage. I finally found some dirt under my bed, rubbed it together in my hands and applied the warm healing glow to my tattered body.

After causing myself so much pain, I resolved to call Harry to help me investigate this mystery.

I love a good mystery; how can I help?!

"Oh, hi, Harry, are you nearby?" I said to myself.

KNOCK-KNOCK; there was a tap at the front door with the knocker. I went downstairs, talking to Harry as if he could hear me.

"Of course, it's you, Harry. Were you in...?"

"The neighborhood, yes. I decided to stay close enough to spring into action *if you ever called.*"

"Is that disdain I detect in your voice, Harry?"

"Yes, I am *a little* upset that you haven't called on me again." *However, I forgive you, little witch.* "How can I help?" He smiled.

"Nonabel, was that the door? I was getting a ride to... Oh, it's Mr. Anderson! What brings you by this fine evening?" Zatie was suspicious.

Quick Harry, think of something! I thought to him.

I still don't know exactly why... He was confused as I interrupted his thoughts.

Just come up with something quick or Zatie will start prying.

"I... uh, forgot to have your older sister sign some of the Estate papers. I shouldn't be here too long."

Nice one! I thought to him.

Thanks, but seriously, why am I here? Harry asked in his mind.

I'll have to show you later. "That's right, I got a voicemail from you about it; Zatie, could you give us a second?" I shoved her back into the house before she could answer. *That was close.*

I know, so why am I here? Harry thought.

Wait, Harry, where is your car?! Ugh did you...?! I asked him in my mind.

"Run, yes!" *Oh, I see how that would be problematic.* He finally got it.

Stop the think-talk for a second, Harry, I have to probe your mind for your car's location. I thought.

"You're doing what now?!" Harry asked.

In an instant I caused his fancy-pants car to drop into the front drive of the farmhouse. It set off his car-alarm and startled Harry.

"Ha-ha! You didn't see that coming, did you, Harry?" I asked.

You enjoyed that too much! "I hope nothing is broken," Harry went to his car to inspect it and shut off the alarm. He opened the car door still in shock.

Harry, while you are there, you should grab some fake documents in case we have an audience, I thought.

What am I doing here, Nonabel?! "Here's those papers!" He smiled and waved a handful of papers.

I wanted to show you some of Michael's hunting plans in the study, but Zatie lives in the room where the secret door is hidden, so, we'll have to wait. I thought as he showed me the documents.

I'll pretend to drive off as though our business has concluded, then summon me to return, Harry thought.

Sounds like a plan, thanks Harry, I thought back.

"Well, that's that! Hope you have a lovely evening, Ms. Venatora," Harry got back into his car and returned to a nearby apartment he had for emergencies.

Let me know when the coast is clear, Nonabel, and I'll sprint back, he thought as he got to his apartment.

Think my name when you're outside, don't knock, Jesse is sleeping on the couch, I thought back to him.

Will do, Nonabel, he replied to my mind.

Zatie's friend Autumn came by to pick her up for another sleepover a few minutes later. *I think Zatie does it to avoid my drama.*

I don't blame her, little witch, you are kind of dramatic. Harry's voice was in my head.

Harry! Privacy! I screamed the thought at him.

Well, you weren't thinking of me, but don't keep thinking thoughts to me, he replied.

Oh, nice to know, and FYI, the coast is clear, Harry, come on back! I thought back.

I'll be there in two shakes of a croc's tail.

Very 'pun-y', Harry, I thought.

I heard a loud thud in the backyard and let the Seer's Sight scan the property for intruders. I could see through the walls of the old farmhouse and spotted Harry near the back-field, waving at me.

Hope you have an empty stomach, Harry, I thought to him as I waved out of my window.

Why, what would I need...? he was thinking.

In that instant I opened a vortex under him and met him in the dark abyss to help him get to the exit-point. I swam up to Harry as he panicked for non-existent air. I smiled at him and took his hand. We swam to the exit-point and emerged from the black puddle in the middle of the Library out of the remains of Twilight's body.

"Please, never do that to me again!" Harry screamed in-between dry-heave coughs. I chuckled as I lit the oil lamp on the desk with my breath. Harry began to regain his professional composure as he stood up to admire the floor to ceiling bookshelves full of magical lore.

"Impressive, isn't it?!" It felt nice to have a friend to share this with.

"Thank you, for sharing this with me. Michael was very private about his study. Also, thank you for considering me your *friend*," he smiled.

"Harry, of course you are my friend. Now here's why you are here." We went over Grandpa's notes, records, charts, and journals for what seemed like days, searching for clues on how to stop the beast. I was hoping that Harry could shed some light on Michael's reason to go hunt the Gor-Nok. Harry mostly shared his stories of learning to hunt with Michael; I really enjoyed the tale of his first hunt when he got attacked by the crocodile.

"Oh, no, not that one! Why do you like that one?" he asked me with a bashful grin.

"Because it shows that you are vulnerable, that there's a real person under all that bravado. It's cute!" I was hitting on his chest, in a second-grade, schoolgirl fashion, forgetting myself, my misery, my boundaries, and embracing my weakness as I kissed Harry on the edge of his mouth. I immediately recoiled in shame.

"Don't," he breathed out.

"I'm sorry, Harry, I was weak," I said embarrassed.

"Don't be. We are instinctual, carnal. And weak due to the therian animal attraction," he stated.

"That's it! I need to find it's weakness, what is it's source of power," I responded excitedly.

"Who, the Gor-Nok?! He's a were-beast of sorts," Harry said as he looked over more notes.

"Yeah, but he does magic like me. Like me? Harry, he's just like me! Both witch and were-beast, he's not a demon at all! I've been going about this all wrong!" I said as I was pacing the room.

"Well, I wouldn't rule out all the possibilities; that thing is pretty evil," he replied.

"I know what I've gotta do, Harry," I said.

"What's that little witch?!" Harry asked.

"I've gotta go to the scene of the crime, to the place where Grandpa died," I responded.

"I'll get us accommodations and a guide to the area

where…," he was saying as he got up to leave.

"No, Harry, I need you here to watch over the twins in case he returns," I said as I blocked the door.

"I agree, plus I can make up some elaborate excuse for your absence," he said as he smiled.

"I've got that one covered, I'm going on a college campus trip on the East Coast. I need to pick one anyways," I responded.

"Harvard, Lucia had it picked… No, you are right, you are perfectly capable of deciding that alone,"

"Focus, Harry, we need to narrow down which tribe had hired Grandpa," I reminded him of the mission.

We spent the remainder of the evening gathering intel on Granddad's last expedition. Harry confirmed that Michael was commissioned by a village of warriors of the Dayak people. Harry loved studying other cultures, especially useless facts. However, there were a few things that he shared that were helpful, such as the fact that the people of Borneo speak around 170 languages. I redirected my studies to learning spells that could help me solve this mystery.

When the search was over and Harry had drifted off, I called it a night. I helped Harry to teleport back out of the farmhouse and near the woods.

"Nonabel?" asked Harry. "Does that ever get easy?" he coughed out more dark water.

"Nope, I'm just used to it now," I replied.

"Are you sure that you don't want me to go with you on this trip? You know, as muscle," he smiled.

"I need you to keep an eye on my family while I'm gone," I assured him. He smiled and waved before he left. I continued to learn a couple more spells, potions, and things to take with me as I prepared for the trip to go to Borneo.

The Gift of Ancient Tongues potion

Xenolalia or speaking in multiple tongues is a phenomenon where people speak words that are seemingly in languages unknown to the speaker.

Ingredients required and preparation instructions:
Mistletoe, best if from an Oak tree from which an innocent lover was hung. (Note: anything else will cause mouth-sores.)

Boil in a hot spring or copper cauldron for an hour.
Mocking-jay tongues, *a dozen birds are needed. Remove their heads with bare hands covered in ash from an oak ember.* (Note: To save time, burn the branch from the same oak tree.)
Dry the tongues in moonlight for a week and keep them out of the sun.

Ground into fine powder with a quartz stone.
Wax, *from a deaf man's ear. must be removed with Dragon's Breath.* (Note: If not done correctly, you will lose your own hearing. Magic requires sacrifices, & mistakes will cost just as much.)
Toad's tongues *must cut with a golden dagger to prevent tainting the blood.*

Add to brew while fresh.
Spit from a Liar's tongue, *given in anger from the accused; store spit in a crystal vial to preserve freshness.*
Tongue of a dead man. Soaked in a thousand tears (Note: Saliva from an ancestor works as well.)
Mix ingredients in order, do not deviate from the recipe. Potion must be consumed by sunset.
(Note: I left the ingredients in the potions & powder pantry of the study.)
You are very welcome,

Nanabel

That spell was just as complicated as the Seer's Sight; it's almost as if someone thought it would be hilarious to watch me gather all of these ingredients. I am glad that some future version of myself was helping me, or maybe I was spellcasting in my sleep again.

Anyways, I was glad for any help, even if it seemed *too* convenient or extremely odd. I used the Sight to scan the Library for the pantry mentioned. I saw a ghostly apparition of me pulling on a book from the Potions shelf to reveal a secret doorway into a small kitchenette hidden from me this entire time.

I watched the past version of myself making the potion and spending lots of time working in here. I have no idea when I would have done this, but I trusted the vision and sensed no evil or ill will. I gathered the ingredients for the final brew and got to work.

The potion was going to take some time to brew. Over the next few days, I jotted down a few spells to use on the expedition, just in case I ran into trouble. I didn't really think about if I would be able to use them or even see them later. I thought to tattoo some keywords of the enchantments on my arms to kind of remember what to do and what to say for different spells.

I finalized my *real* travel plans and fake ones with Harry's help. Looking between maps and on the laptop, Harry added, "Oh, also there's the Miri Marriot, executive suite is a good place to stay"

He continued, "I had a colleague that stayed there on *their* trip to Borneo and he said it was superb." I just nodded, not really paying attention. I was mindlessly listening as I was flipping between pages and sections in the Diary. I didn't really care for fancy hotels, just reaching Borneo safely. I would probably end up in the first cheap hotel I would find.

Harry was still talking. "Oh, or the Hotel Le Derby Alma in Paris; the Presidential suite this is the best one so far I believe," he marked it on the map with a big star. "So, I've marked the major hotels...," his voice started to fade out.

I was lost in my own thoughts and not too worried about his. I would be flying to travel, I wasn't prepared to teleport to somewhere I couldn't see, and I would try to contact Harry occasionally to check on things at home. I wasn't sure how wide the cellphone range would be way up high. I thought about what it would be like flying up that high; would I feel light-headed, queasy, bloated? I had never been afraid of heights. I was getting pretty good at flight as a bird.

"What do you think?" Harry asked.

"Hmm?" I didn't realize he was still talking.

He sighed. "Could you at least pretend to be interested in this?" He glared as I nodded my head.

"Sorry. What were you saying before?" I asked. I came out of my study-daze.

"What do you think about the Gor-Nok?" He queried.

I frowned. "In what sense?"

He pointed to the Diary and asked, "Your grandmother believed he was her nightmare correct?"

I nodded and said, "Well, you've witnessed him before and fought him."

"I don't think it's likely that *I* would be able to see him, if he was just a nightmare," he continued.

I added. "In fact, I've seen him and fought him, as both the monster and a man."

"I've never seen him as a man," Harry stated.

I pretended to be more interested now and I pointed out, "He has also mastered therianthrope skills just as I have."

"Well, I wouldn't say that *you* have 'mastered', managed is more accurate!" Harry interjected.

"I fear he has many powers beyond what we have come to understand," I stated, "It's difficult to understand *what* he is." I took a second to process this. I had never thought too much about what he was, just that he needed to be stopped. I guess I never really thought before acting. Harry was still calculating.

"I just always thought he was a beast," I said sheepishly. Harry nodded, taking in my small, feeble feedback.

"It's so peculiar to think about. What is he? I must admit I don't think I can prepare you enough for what you'll find in

Borneo," Harry said worriedly. I just nodded. I felt like a bobble-head. It was a lot to take in.

In truth, I wasn't prepared for what I'd find in Borneo, probably more questions. The Diary and everything I had learned still left me with questions. Questions of *how* my grandfather died hunting down the beast that was terrorizing a village in Borneo; and *how* my grandmother had reoccurring nightmares about this supposed beast. I just had to find out what exactly *he* was.

As a precaution, I locked the Diary and the oil lamp in the Library, just in case. I started a regular 'journey journal' to document my travels and to jot down notes; that way, my spells wouldn't fall into the wrong hands. I discovered, quite by accident, like most of my magical lessons, that I could use the vortex as a 'Hiding Place' of sorts. I used it to store things, like my bag of back-up clothes; so I could cover up after every transformation.

I decided to fly to Borneo, mostly by taking turns telekinetically and as one or all of my murder of crows. I had my fake luggage and travel plans in hand as I hugged the twins good-bye. Zatie, of course, was the only heartbroken of the two. Harry had come by the house with his fancy car to make it seem like I was going to the airport. He tried to talk me into changing my flight plans.

"Nonabel, you really should reconsider a safer, more traditional means of air transport," he said.

"Thanks, but no. I've already made my decision," I reminded him. We stopped by his apartment parking lot and stepped out of the car. I scanned the area for prying eyes.

"Well, looks like the coast is clear, I'm off!" I said.

"Please contact me if you need anything," he said.

"Thanks again for keeping an eye on things, I'll check in soon, somehow," I launched off the ground, feeling the anxiety of the trip melting away with the exhilaration that followed.

The wind roared in my ears as I gained momentum, until I finally broke through the clouds. My clothes clung to me because of the moisture, but I hardly noticed. I almost forgot about my fears of the journey as I spun through the sky, hollering like an idiot. I must've seemed ridiculous, with my hair whipping in my face, and prancing through the clouds. I rolled up my sleeve, glancing at the spells I jotted down on my forearms, while I glided across the clouds.

Ok, Nonabel, I thought to myself. *You had your fun. Time to put on your big girl pants and figure out where you're going.* Reluctantly, I paused in the sky, and pulled the map from jacket my pocket. I glanced over it, mostly using the Seer's Sight to help. After sufficiently analyzing my route, I tucked the map back into my pocket, and continued my flight. A few hours passed with seemingly smooth cruising. Key word: seemingly. Psychic flight was physically easy to handle at slower speeds, but higher speeds required forming a psychic barrier around me to prevent the need for a helmet to protect my face. I didn't notice the mental strain that psychically flying had on me, until it was almost too late.

The Sun had ducked down beneath the clouds and my eyes began to droop. I quickly cast a spell to keep me awake for a little longer. At least until I found a place to stop and rest. I yawned, rubbing at my eyes. I pulled my jacket around me tighter. *I probably could've chosen a better outfit for flying.* I scolded myself, looking at my list of spells on my arms for something to warm me up. Suddenly, I felt all of my remaining energy drain from me entirely and everything turned dark.

When I woke again, I was no longer floating across the clouds, I was falling to my doom. My stomach immediately felt like it fell out of me, as panic took its place. Was I dreaming or was this real? I wasn't willing to test it by continuing to fall. With all my strength I launched back up into the air so I could orient myself. Once I had managed to right myself, I looked around the horizon.

What happened? Where was I? I shook my head. *You're a witch, Nonabel. Figure it out!* I caught myself having very loud, mental discussions that normally, I wouldn't, with others around who could hear, mostly Zatie, and now Harry. Harry instantly tried to call my cellphone; I guess that I was low enough to be in range.

"Hello Harry, yeah, I didn't mean to contact you." "Well, I thought that I heard your voice in my head and I saw a vision of you falling. I have never seen anything like that!" he added excitedly.

"Yeah, um, I *was* falling... asleep. Then actually falling, but I'm fine now," I reluctantly replied.

"That's it! I'm calling in for an extraction. There'll be a jet there in an hour. Tell me your location."

"Whoa, Harry, call off the rescue for now, I'm fine! I'll check in at a hotel and I'll call you later," I hung up without saying good-bye. Mostly because I was embarrassed and pissed at the same time. Using the Seer Sight, I found that I was less than a hundred miles outside of Brazil.

Maybe it would be best if I took a break from mentally flying for now. I split myself into a hundred black shards that all sprouted wings and feathers; we all swooped down towards the jungle valley below.
The lush, lucid landscape swiftly transformed into colorful, cultivated city streets as I neared the coast. We approached the more densely populated towns and started seeing billboards that read 'Rio de Janeiro,' I knew that I was close.

We landed on a rooftop in the city, and I mostly merged together, leaving some of the flock to scavenge and scout around. I reached into the vortex and pulled-out my bag to call Harry. "Harry, hi. I'm in Rio," I said.

"Which Rio? Rio Grande, Rio de Janeiro?"

"That one!" I responded.

"Wow, you're making great time! I take it that you need a room for the night?" Harry asked.

"Yes, please. I'm exhausted, and..."

"Starving, I know just the place. Call you back when it's done," he said.

I joined the rest of the crows and scavenged for scraps to

tide me over. The crows found some bugs and grubs to feast on. They loved it, but I tried to not enjoy it too much, even though our collective consciousness was telling my brain that this was delicious.

Harry called me back with the address and confirmation info for the hotel. I decided to walk there, maybe try hailing a taxi if I felt brave enough to attempt using the gift of tongues to speak Portuguese. I pieced myself back together by summoning the rest of the crows. Once I felt complete, I summoned the first cab out of the alleyway. The cab driver was a friendly old Brazilian man with a big mustache. He even got out to hold open my door for me.

"Boa noite, Jovem! Para onde gostaria ir?" is what I heard him say. What I understood, inside me, spoken by a still, small echo; almost like a whisper was: *'Good evening, young lady! Where would you like to go?'* I replied that I was fine and politely asked him to drive me to the hotel that Harry had booked for me.

I heard all of that in English, but the echo in my mind was in Brazilian Portuguese, and I understood it; so weird. However, it worked; I was grateful because the driver promptly confirmed the address and conducted us through the streets of Rio. We had a few minutes of chit-chat, which I still understood in the same manner. I appreciated this new ability of the gift of tongues; it truly was a gift.

After a pleasant journey through the gorgeous city, we arrived at my humble rest stop for the night. Ugh, thanks *Harry*, for the 5-star hotel! Not what I had in mind. Harry called my cellphone as I got out of the cab and I thanked the driver.

"What *did* you have in mind, Nonabel?" he asked.

"Wait, did you hear my mental exasperation just now?!" I asked Harry.

"Yes, however, I cannot seem to broadcast back to you

with such strength and clarity. That must be the witch in you, not the were-rook," he responded.

"Interesting, back on topic. Why such a nice hotel?" I inquired.

"Resort, actually. All-inclusive. Don't worry that pretty little head of yours; I took care of it, it's on me"

"It's not about the money, Lucia already surprised me with that gift. I just don't need the luxury," I replied.

"Well, it's booked. No refunds. Enjoy!"

"Ugh!" I sighed.

He hung up on me and started thinking as loud as he could, *'I'm not listening, blah blah blah.'*

You're annoying, Harry! I thought-screamed.

I reluctantly checked in and had to stifle any mental eye-rolling as I was both impressed and annoyed by the accommodations. At night, mostly when I sleep, I would send out Twilight to enjoy the nightlife and to aid in dream-stimulation. Otherwise I would have an anxiety induced nightmare. I'd often let Twilight's independent instincts guide her as she flew, like having a car in cruise-control or a plane on auto-pilot. However, the beach and the coastline were gorgeous that night, so I took control of the flight.

My dream of flight-seeing the beach and the bay was so tranquil, like the calm before the storm. My anxiety over where this journey would take me was creeping into my dreams, filling them with blackness. As I slept, I dreamt of the void between nightmares and the unknown destinations found in the dark abyss of the vortex of teleportation. An infinite starlit sky of exit-points appeared before me as the stars at night, each inciting me to visit a new world of possibilities.

I think I was sleep-teleporting again, and the temptation to just exit this void and kick in my enemy's front door was too powerful. I was glad my anxiety and fears gave me boundaries to avoid crossing, they safeguarded me from mistakes I couldn't afford to make any more. I called on all my strength to wake.

Morning greeted me with the happy cawing of Twilight at the open patio door, inviting me to enjoy the new day. After I left a few messages with Zatie and Harry, I went to check out of the resort before I made my journey across the Atlantic Ocean towards South Africa; maybe Madagascar might be nice. Harry had questioned my flight path, suggesting a shorter route, but this one gave me more opportunities to rest on dry land and do a little sight-seeing. I would stop when I got tired again.

I spent the night as the flock, and we took turns sleeping or hunting in the jungle of Madagascar. I wanted to stop here to see the chameleons: Derik said they were his favorite animal in the entire world. I wondered if it would be his totem - that is, if he were like me. Ugh, he wouldn't believe half the things happening in my life. We were worlds apart now in so many ways. He was so understanding and easygoing; I really don't deserve him. That and I having an unfaithful, wild heart was why I would probably lose him. As if all the secrets weren't enough, I kissed Harry; oh God. I was so embarrassed, especially since he could hear my thoughts of him, ugh! I took out my frustration during the hunt as I caught a beautiful specimen, for research and to carry on Michael's collection of creatures in the Library.

After I rested for the night, I planned the next leg of the journey. I flew over the Indian Ocean then to Malaysia; and finally I arrived in Borneo. In the morning I pretended to arrive with the other tourists. I got a ride to the area of the island where Michael visited.

I found the Dayak village that had hired my granddad, and I talked with the locals. I was hoping to talk to a witch doctor or a medicine woman, but with my luck I met the village idiot. After a few glasses of some vile drink at the local watering-hole, he told me a couple stories about the legends of the Gor-Nok.

He shared stories about the Great White Hunter, meaning my grandfather and of his duel to the death with the Beast. Stories about the origin of the Gor-Nok revealed that he was a practicing witch doctor that created potions and messed with chemicals, mixed rituals, and had familiar spirits. "And then there was a tale of when he was sent to fight a monstrous animal, this giant wild boar that was attacking people and destroying the villages and junk," the village idiot shared.

"The Gor-Nok went on this quest and promised to go do this thing and the chief of the tribe said, you know, '*I'll give you riches, and power; and I'll give you one of my daughters for a bride and set you up,*' he continued.

"They had a huge party and everything's cool. And the Gor-Nok was starting to think this was going to be awesome! *All I gotta do is like poison this animal or something and this works.* While they're having a party later, the giant boar monster attacks and every one of the villagers flee. So he's angry and mad and he just goes at the monster; he takes some potion or something that was supposed to give him courage or strength or whatever he did, and he went to attack it and it overpowered him and beat into him; and he being kind of magically inclined and part of this whole world and witches and monsters didn't know that he was also a monster," he said.

"Therianthrope," I interjected. I had what I needed to know and decided to leave the idiot to his drinks. The Gor-Nok probably knew of skin-walkers or spirits that could pretend to be animals. But he did not know he was going to be one. I only believed part of that story. Later that night, the owner of the inn directed me to the village wiseman. His story was much better.

Long ago in their village there was a beautiful woman who was the daughter of the king. To protect the people from his enemy, the king sold his daughter into slavery. She became the queen for the enemy and bore him a son; she hated the child and she cursed him. She died after childbirth and the child was seen as an abomination because he did not look like a baby but more like a pig than human. The wicked king kept the child as a prisoner and would torture him whenever it seemed fit. As the child grew, he became more like a man and was not seen as an abomination, for he was an obedient son. He gained the wicked King's favor, for he was a mighty hunter and conquered the white boar.

It was a ferocious battle and the boy almost lost his life, but he was good at playing dead and killed the boar after it had bitten him. The bite never healed, and the infections spread like wildfire through the body and consumed the soul. They could do nothing to save him, not even end his life. And after that he was no longer a man and became an animal, living alone in the jungle. Later the hunters came across footprints of the man that changed into boar hooves. They tracked the beast to a cave where they found many skulls of men. They hurried back to the village to warn them but were overtaken by the beast. Only one man got away and lived long enough to tell us of the boar that walked like a man: the monster known as the Gor-Nok.

I was able to arrange an interview with that man just to find him near the end of life, lying in his deathbed. I wanted to ask him for details, but he was so feeble, and I worried about the strain the repressed memory would have on him if he talked about it. Maybe if he could just think about it, I could use the Seer's Sight to peer into his memory. While I was there, the village idiot arrived at the elderly man's home to visit. It was his grandfather, that explained why he embellished the stories of the Gor-Nok.

I told him that his grandfather had information that would help me find out what happened to my granddad. He woke up his grandfather, rather rudely and kind of yelled at him to talk to me.

"Aren't you being a little too loud?" I asked, "he doesn't seem that well."

"Oh, he's just super-old. If you're not loud, he doesn't

listen," he responded. I conducted my interview as gently as I could, despite his grandson yelling at him. When we got to the part of the encounter with the beast the old man's heart stopped. Perhaps having to relive the memories had caused it. I gave my condolences and stepped outside. I felt it insensitive to pry any further.

Later that evening the old man's family hosted a somber funeral where they burned his body. I asked the grandson for the reason. He replied that it was their way. Afterwards, he told me that he knew the place where my grandfather had died, and in the morning, he could show me the way. I met with the young man to go to the place where the hunt ended, only to have him tell me that no one goes there because of the scary stories surrounding that place. He said that Death lives there; I would live a happier life if I just went home. I was tired of people getting in my way, so I used my powers of persuasion to hypnotize him into pointing out the way.

I saw the vision of the place in my mind and released him. Before he could wake, I dissolved into my cloud of crows and we took flight. We flew up the dark mountain to a cave where the beast would hide, but, as I had suspected, it wasn't there.

I needed to know for myself if the monster was real or just a nightmare. I found the dried skeletal remains of what I thought was my granddad. I wanted to believe it, but I wanted to touch his belongings to know if it really was him. I transformed back into my human form and manifested my clothes from the vortex all in one swoop. I touched his old rifle and saw his last moments.

Journey Journal,

In Borneo finally, I discovered the cave where they hunted the beast. I found him... Michael. I know now that this is him; I confirmed it by use of the Seer's Sight. I touched the trigger of his rifle still clutched in his withered hand. His last remaining moments fired off in my mind's eye as the vision played out all around and through me. I felt it all; the hurt, the loss, the terror of his worst fears consuming his soul as he lost his mind to the madness.

His form shifting between his totems, the spirits of wild beasts filled his aura. Blackness swirled around him, reminding me of my crows. A name on his lips, 'Victoria' and such regret in his heart. And his killer laughed as my grandpa died all over again in my arms.

Nanabel

My Birthday

I had to find a way to save him. Why else would I be both blessed and cursed with these gifts and responsibility if I was not meant to save Michael?!

HARRY!! I know that you can hear me! Damnit, find a way to answer, I need your help... ...he's DEeaaADDdd! I was crying so miserably now. The phone was useless, I was too remote. I knew it was useless for me to expect someone like Harry to be able to reply telepathically. He was not like me, a witch like me could respond. Zatie.

If I chose to go down this path, there was no turning back. I desperately needed the Diary and it was so far from me. There were spells for restoring things, and I had seen a whole section on time travel in the Diary. Hell, whole volumes were in the Library; if I could get back there and consult their wisdom, then I could calm my rage and anguish. It felt rash and as though I was acting against my better judgement, but I had to try. I reached out to Zatie with my mind. I used the Sight and every trick I could to call to her; I even planted the thought in her mind that her phone was ringing. She answered!

"Nonabel?! Is that you? Your voice is all echo-y." *Ha-ha,*

I'm glad to hear you too, honey! Listen, I'm in a bad spot, I thought to her.

"I'd say, the phone isn't even showing you on the caller-ID," Zatie said as she looked at her phone.

Don't worry about that Zatie. Hey, did I leave my Diary on my nightstand in my room perchance?

"Uh, let me go check. Nope. Nothing."

Damnit!

"Hey watch the language!" Zatie chastised me.

Sorry, it's just that I really need some information that is contained in Lu-Lu's Diary. Here, go back into your room again. I thought to her.

"My room, how did you know that I was...?"

Don't worry, just go.

"Okay, bossy. I'm here, now what?"

Watch, just watch.

I slammed her door shut, witnessing her shock and amazement through the Sight. "Oh, dear God! Nonabel, this isn't funny! Are you and Jess playing a joke?! I'll get you later, Jesse!" Zatie declared.

I know it's not funny, honey; nor are we playing a joke on you, sweetie. Zatie, I haven't been entirely honest about things in my life since Lu-Lu's passing.

"Wha-what do ya mean Nona?!" she asked.

Hell, there's no real easy way to say this so I'll just come clean. I am a witch, like my mother, and my grandmother before me, I thought to her.

"Wait, what? Now I know that this is a prank. Jesse, enough already, open the door!" Zatie called out.

Fine, I'll prove it, hang up the phone; just turn it off. I watched her do it through the Sight.

Now say my name, backwards! I said in her head. She screamed like a banshee and cried a little. She looked at the phone again. *Still not convinced?!* I flung her phone from her

222

hand and it bounced off the wall, then onto the floor. She screamed out again.

I am doing this, because I can, because I am a witch. DO YOU BELIEVE ME YET?!!

Zatie was sobbing on the floor, I had crushed her little heart with my revelation of the truth and... my lie.

I understand if you don't trust me from this moment on. I hated Lu-lu for so long for telling me the truth. I know how you feel, I thought to her.

"Nona, how?! I don't understand!" she cried.

I'll show you how; do you believe me?

"Yes, I'll try, somehow," she chuckled a little. "How can I begin to believe in something impossible?"

It may seem like the world is backward and flipped upside-down. I made her furniture float to the ceiling, leaving her clinging desperately to the hardwood floor.

But we may have to go backwards to set things right, I thought to her as I let all her stuff crash to the floor again, startling her, and she covered her face with her arms and curled into a fetal pose to protect herself.

Calm down, I can fix it. She opened her eyes to a perfectly restored room. *Oh, I folded your clothes too, you're welcome.*

"Thank you, I guess" she stood up to look around.

Go to the door... Please.

"Okay, can I leave now?" she asked.

Not yet, I need you to say my name but backwards. "Excuse me?! What would that even sound like, and why?" she asked.

Just say it. It's actually the name of the country where Lu-lu met Grandpa.

"Lebanon?!" The doorknob jiggled, turned, and slid across the wooden panels of the door to the opposite side. *Did it move on its own?!*

"Uh-huh..." *Don't worry, I'm going to be with you every step of the way. Now go in,* I told her.

"Nona, what is this place?"

It's a hiding place, created by Lu-lu for Grandpa Michael and her to practice their powers. I've been calling it the Study or the Library. You'll see what I mean when you go in and up the stairs.

"Stairs?! It's so dark, I can't see any..."

I thought of the lamp; now that the door was opened, I could have access to my toys inside. I remembered the spell Mom had done to light the lamp, I looked it up in the Diary to save me from having to do the Dragon's Breath every time. *Incedium ex lucerna.*

"What did you say?"

Nothing, nevermind. Wait, could she hear me thinking of the spell?

"Oh, there's a light! Is that Grandma's old lamp?" she started to question so many things in her mind, but we needed to focus on the task at hand.

Yes, and yes, it's magical too. Now go find the Diary, it should be on the desk by the lamp.

I only had enough light cast for her to see where she was going to illuminate the Diary.

"Wow, it's so messy in here. Do you live up here, Nona?" Zatie asked.

Ok, sweetie, I need you to focus please. Open the Diary, I thought to her.

"Okay, now what? Whoa?!"

I started to flip through the pages with my mind, mostly to mess with her, but partially to speed up the process. I found the section on time travel and used the Sight to scan the pages.

"Wow, time travel?! For reals, is this legit?!" She was a little too excited about all this.

You ask me that, now?! Zatie, I need you to understand some very important adult stuff right now. Ok?! I thought to her.

"Okay," she responded.

This is not a game. Magic is not a game! People we love have died to defend this Diary, this room, this way of life. I can fully explain it all when I get back; just let me focus, please, I thought to her.

I scanned down the sections of the table of contents. I found the page number for 'how to design a device to travel through time.' I flipped the pages again, this startled Zatie and she screeched a little.

"Ahwck! Wait, no! I was reading that," she said.

Don't, I don't have time right now to explain.

I read through her eyes in the section on Devices. "If I'm reading this right, then the plans are found in another book," she said.

Watch-out, incoming! I called the book from off the shelf like a pet bird. Zatie had to duck out of the way as it landed on top of the Diary. "The Tinkering of Nikola Tes... Hey!" Zatie was reading again.

*I said **DON'T**.* I found what I needed, tore the pages from the book psychically, and sent the book back to the bookcase. Before Zatie could read any more, I teleported the pages to me, and started to push her body out of the Library.

I want you to promise me that you will stay out of here and forget what you saw. Or else.

"Or else what?!" she demanded.

I'll make you forget, forget, forget, forget, forget.

I left that last word stuck on repeat; okay, I was trying to hypnotize her. With that, I pushed her away from the door and slammed it shut in her face.

I pulled the pages through the vortex and got to work on creating the time-travel device.

The Nevergator

In our pursuits to master our own destiny we come across rare objects that can alter reality and turn back time itself. In order to prevent one from altering the future by changing events in the past; a sacrifice must be offered of one's own life, more specifically, Time for Time.

The spell requires a sacrifice of one year from your life each time it is used and an additional amount equal to the quantity of time through which one travels. If one were to go back in time just one day, the sacrifice would be one year and a day from off of the end of one's life. Thus, one year to even access the power, plus the amount of time traveled. The spell needs a compass, a pocket watch, and an empty box. Put the three together by bending the box with one's mind through telekinesis. Inside the box will be a new device, orb shaped with several different instrumental gauges called "the Nevergator." **To operate, the Nevergator needs to know the date, time, and place where you want to go, and it will take you there: but it has to be within one's own lifespan.** Chant the words: Space, Time and Thought (note: in any of the 7 first languages.) as you chart a course on the device to activate.

As I read the instructions, I found a caution written in my own handwriting, that said, "... every time it was used. I warned me that I could screw with time itself, I could wipe myself from existence."

The spell wasn't as complicated as I had feared. Plus, I found the things that I needed right there in the cave with Michael's old hunting gear. I hastily threw the compass and the pocket watch into a small cigar box after I had dumped out the bugs and junk. I slammed the lid of the box and crushed it all with my mind. I could feel the tiny gears and sprockets warp and crack under my mental strain. I think that I overdid it though, because the whole thing shattered and fell to pieces on the cave floor. I tried the to catch the pieces with my open hands only to make it worse. The broken pieces were everywhere. I was kneeling on the floor sobbing, because I had messed it up somehow.

A few seconds later I heard the tinkling of the tiny gears clinging back together as time was reversing the damage. As the watch and compass were nearly merged into a new device, the wooden cigar box reformed itself around the new shiny object. I sighed in relief as I looked inside the box to find a new hand-held device of curious workmanship; it was unlike anything I had ever seen; the Nevergator. I reached for it in the box, and at once noticed that the device was somehow magnetically attracted to me. I stopped myself from grabbing it.

Was I ready for this? Was I really going back so long ago? I didn't know *when* I was going; I did not know the exact date when the event took place. I looked around at his discarded items for clues. I tried the Sight on the rifle again to see farther back before the incident. My Sight engaged as the scene of carnage played out before me. The guide and the other village warriors were being attacked by the beast after they had gone deeper into the cave. I stopped the vision and reversed it farther back.

The hunting party, led by Grandpa Michael, stopped to rest in a clearing on the trail below the cave of the beast. I spied my granddad writing in a journal. He was writing about the expedition so far. I was waiting for him to write the date, but he was deep in thought.

I tried to probe his mind for the date. He sensed my presence somehow and turned to see who was behind him as he drew a pistol. He sniffed the air much like the Gor-Nok did. I had been seen before in dreams and visions by others. And let's not forget that Michael had shot me once during a dream.

I retreated back into the jungle as the crows to gain more eyes on this scene. He could not sense me any longer because I stopped invading his mind. I'll just let this moment play out; *be patient, we'll kill this beast on the morrow*, I heard in my head as he wrote the date.

My birthday, like I had suspected. I finished reviewing the visions from the remains I found of the victims of the hunting party. He killed them with their fears, shockwave after terrifying wave until their hearts stopped. I witnessed more of Michael's last stand before the remaining few fled the scene in terror. He was all alone, I needed to see it for myself.

All the remains belonged to others in the hunting party, but Michael's body wasn't here, and it was certainly not at home. That monster had taken his place somehow. The Gor-Nok was using Michaels grave as a doorway or a hiding place. I suspected that Grandpa's body was missing still. *Where are you, Grandpa?*

The time had come to find out; I called the Nevergator from the box to me. I caught it in my left hand and witnessed the chain twist itself around and through my wrist as the Nevergator activated.

The device had become white-hot and fused itself in the back of my hand. My heart was pounding so hard in my head and the echoes of future memories resounded in my mind. I was too weak to resist the power of the Seer's Sight and the compulsive way it wants to show me everything. I ached from the loss of a future I might never enjoy because of what I was about to do to save Michael. My sacrifice was these distant familiar years of living and dying all at once. Love, life, and loss; so very much loss. I must make it stop; I must make the monster suffer for my loss.

I turned the gears of the Nevergator to the appropriate date and my guess of the approximate time of the fight between Michael and the Gor-Nok. Light began to pulsate through my veins of my arm, brighter near my hand, with the Nevergator being the brightest light. I thought of the place and the time of the event much like with the teleportation spell, all the while chanting the keywords of the spell.

"Spatium, Temporis, Cogitari!" I hoped that thinking of that space and time would help. The burning light from the Nevergator seared my flesh with blistering pain. I slapped down onto the light with my other hand. I was expecting to black out as normal, yet this time, all was white, just light.

It felt electrifying and exhilarating all at once. It was a sensation of pure energy; I was pure energy! I knew I was speeding through space at the speed of light, even though I didn't see any black void with speckled stars. It was breathtaking to feel so much pure power pulsating through me, pushing me down through time.

Lightning, I felt like lightning when I finally arrived, as I struck the ground. My impact caused a momentary displacement of time, slowing it down, then speeding it up. Michael and the Gor-Nok were paused in their titanic clash as I landed in between them. Time stopped, then an explosive shockwave emitted from me, knocking them both off of their feet and out of their animal forms, turning them into mere mortals to bow beneath me at my immortal feet as I descended as an angel of death.

I was pulsating with adrenaline and power, lightning pouring from my limbs, lifting me in the air. The two clumsy combatants were clamoring to their feet. I shot lightning, striking the Gor-Nok in his human form before he could transform. Michael couldn't believe what he was seeing; *an angel* was the thought I heard. I didn't turn to see him; I kept my focus on the Gor-Nok.

My adrenaline overdose was wearing off, transforming me back from pure energy to my normal teenage girl form. Michael lurched towards me to put a hand on my shoulder. Not looking away from my enemy, I activated the lightning surge from my hands and told Michael to *stay back* with my mind.

"Victoria?!" he asked as he turned my shoulder and my focus toward him. I smiled a little and instantly felt my elation change to dread when my goosebumps warned me of an attack. He saw it too.

"Victoria, look out!" A sawblade of fear demons came tearing through my spot. I pushed Michael out of the way with my mind, as I burst into a cloud of feathers and talons to evade the shockwave.

The Gor-Nok was changing back into the boar-beast as he charged towards us. Michael called out to the wild beast of the jungle to his aid. His cries seized mental control of my crows, commanding us to lead the attack. We pecked and slashed as the Gor-Nok swung his club in vain.

Other beasts arrived at our aid; Michael pounced onto an unsuspecting lion. *Michael?! What are you doing?! Help me?!* I thought to him in my panic.

"I'm out of supplies, Vicki. Keep him distracted while I restock!" he exclaimed as he retrieved his 'supplies' and simultaneously healed the beast with the speed of a surgeon. I admit, I was awe-struck to watch him in action. He did this to a few more animals in less than a minute. The herd of wild beasts was not so well received by the Gor-Nok. He pummeled the larger ones left and right. Only a few of us smaller creatures could sneak through his blows.

Their cries of agony filled the air as the Gor-Nok's club crushed their bones. He laughed and gained strength from our pain. Several of my birds were damaged and needed healing. I gathered myself into my harpy form as I attacked the Gor-Nok's neck and face with my talons. He squealed with pain and coughed up some of his fear toxins from the depths of his evil soul at me. I couldn't breathe; my body defensively reacted and shattered into hundreds of feathered shards; each bird retreating in a panic.

Michael mixed one of his species samples with one of the dozen tiny vials of weremen's whiskey that he had in his jacket, spun three times, and downed the potent potion. I was confused as to why he did it that way, that's not what I read in *Lucia's recipe.*

Lucy's version requires too much magic and not enough moxi! Michael thought-shouted at me as he transformed into a were-rhino. He was massive, and every bit as big as the Gor-Nok. They tore through the clearing toward one another. I regained my composure as a were-crow, mostly for strength, and to conceal my identity from Michael.

Michael noticed that I was not Victoria. *You fight differently. Your magic is raw, undisciplined. My Vicky is too calculated and strategic. Not visceral and emotional like you, Angel.* Mom, she could always beat me at a game of chess then I would get mad and toss the board. I got distracted by my trip down memory-lane and almost got hit by the Gor-Nok's club. I blasted him with a ball of lightning at close range, knocking him away from Michael and myself.

Victoria's therian-totem is a black cat. What are you? A harpy? You remind me of my pet raven, Twilight. Are you her, Twilight sent to save me?! Did Lucy send you?! He was petting my harpy head lovingly.

"I was sent by those that love you." **NOW FOCUS!!** I thought that last bit too loud; even the Gor-Nok heard me. I shot lightning bolts at him when he was about to strike Michael.

"Focus on the fight, Michael!" I shouted.

That's what's different, my focusor, Vicky had to use my focusor to channel her magic during a fight. Michael was thinking to me as he tried to guess my identity.

"Michael, the monster, look out!" I screeched that last part like Mom did from that dream. I had learned to weaponize the banshee's cry to create a vicious shockwave like his fear demons. It was one of my new spell-tattoos that were written on my arms. It was an effective spell because it disorientated your victims.

"Nice one, Angel! It'll take the beast a bit to come back for more."

Quiet, Michael! I hissed as I thought to him. We stood at the edge of the clearing looking into the dark jungle where the beast had fled for cover.

I shifted my Sight through different phases, but he was hiding too well. *I am not seeing him, I am going in.* I thought to Michael. I extracted one of my long wing feathers and created a black sword.

"Hey, that's one of White Snake-feather's tricks! It's

sharp, but not too strong," Michael said as I handed it to him and made my own talons grow ten times longer. I put one to my mouth and shushed him.

"I'm going in. Watch my back," I whispered.

"Angel, no! That's what he wants," he replied.

It's a trap! he thought to me.

Then let's smoke him out! I shifted from my harpy, were-crow form back into my human self, all the while changing my black feathers into new black clothes to cover my nakedness. Mostly because my next spell didn't play well with feathers.

Michael was amazed. "That's a new trick, Lucy taught me to use the restoration..." he said, but I interrupted him. *Quiet!* I shushed him again. He shifted back into an old man and restored his clothes to him.

You can think it to me if it's important. Otherwise, quiet! I thought to him. He looked embarrassed, even as macho as he was.

I was just going to say, I mean think, was that old White Snake-Feather and I would just go without...

Yes, quiet! He was as annoying as Jesse and talked as much as Zatie.

I put a finger to my lips. I drew out the Dragon's breath and blew fire at the dried brush around the jungle.

"Now that I've seen; that's Lucy's trick. Now I really must know. Who are you?"

Quiet!

"But I can't keep calling you Angel," he replied.

No, Angel is just fine. I sprouted only my wings and lifted off of the ground with their power; then hovered there to fan the flames. The smoke intensified as I caused it to move into the jungle.

Michael, be ready! I sense something coming, something big, I thought to him.

"Oh, I'm ready with something big," Michael instantly tore through his human form to transform into his first totem, the old grizzly bear. Small animals began to flee the jungle followed by something thunderous.

Ready! I thought to him. From the fire emerged an enormous elephant.

Oooh, I need that one, he thought and chased after it. I turned to tell him to stay and wait with me, but before I could speak...

"**Hhhh**eraAa**AAw**wghh!!!" The Gor-Nok was glowing with green flames as he leapt down on top of me out of the jungle like some sort of apex predator. He seized upon me, scorching my feathers and skin; I screamed for help,

"MICHAEL!! Please help me!! It burns!"

"I'm coming for you, Angel!" Michael cried as he downed the vial and changed forms from a were-bear to a were-elephant in full sprint, thundering across the ground. I desperately needed to escape; I didn't dare try teleporting while I was back in the past. I had no idea what teleporting might do to the Nevergator. I couldn't risk being stuck here forever. I decided to separate into the flock; he crushed several pounds of me, but most of me was able to get to safety as Michael plowed into him with his tusks. They pummeled each other with fierce primal power, more than I had ever accessed through *my* totem.

Now, don't doddle; help me finish this Monster! Michael thought as he was strangling the beast with his trunk. I looked at one of the spells I had written on my forearms, a spell to give me the *talons of death. It mostly caused incurable wounds to my victims.*

Well, do it and make him one of your victims, he thought. After I gathered back into my human form, I reread the spell for the talons. I changed into my were-crow, gaining strength from my totem host animal.

"Makucha ya kifo! Aaawwgh!" *Goodness that kills! Why does it hurt so much when I do magic as my were-totem?* I thought to Michael.

That's because you're new at this, Angel. But this one can do magic in his were-form, and that takes years as both. Michael was lecturing me on magic while still battling the beast.

Mazoezi... hufanya... kamili... Practice makes perfect; that's what we both heard in our minds. Fear prickled my feathered skin as I caught the vision of this moment in my mind.

"Michael, get away from him NOW!" I cried.

The Gor-Nok caught us in a moment of despair and gained strength from this enough to strike. He had coughed out his fear toxins into Michael's elephant face. While Michael was staggering back for clean air, the Gor-Nok tackled him against some rocks. Michael was getting torn apart both mentally and physically. I could hear his thoughts of pain and feel every ounce of it all at once.

Michael, you have to change back to a man, the body will heal, and the mind will be clear of fear. I thought that warning to him, hoping that the beast wouldn't hear the thought or understand it. It heard me, chuckled, and readied its club to strike Michael when he was back to being a man. The blow was swift and smashed into the rocks that were below Michael, kicking up dust and debris. When the dust cloud had cleared, the Gor-Nok couldn't find Michael; he was gone.

I pulled Michael from the vortex and gave him my last vial. "What animal is in this?" Michael asked me.

"Chameleon, now hide!" I said as I took flight towards the Gor-Nok, evading his shockwaves and evil sawblades made of fear demons to get closer.

I had so many spells going at once; Seer's Sight, the werecrow, talons of death, telekinesis, teleporting objects to heave at him, lightning, ball lightning, anything I could throw at him. It was exhausting and he was younger, in his prime, vastly more powerful.

Yes, more powerful than you, I heard his whispers at my ears as I flew closer. He was getting into my head, whispering at my ear. That's when I saw it, I caught a glimpse of one of his tiny fear demons clinging to my mess of feathers and hair by my shoulder, whispering fears of failures into my ear. I knew that shocking myself with lightning had saved me from his demons before, plus it was time to face him as a witch, with greater access to my gifts.

I called down a load of lightning to strike all around and through me, hoping to hit the Gor-Nok and myself. It worked! The little fear minion fizzled and popped off of my shoulder. I rode the lightning down to the earth, crashing into the Gor-Nok.

I appeared before my enemy, in most of my awesome glory. As a witch, now I could whip out spells without too much of a thought, and with greater intensity. I had some fun new magic tools at my disposal, like my new talons of death. The Gor-Nok chuckled when he saw me extend my shiny black claws. I guess that it must be funny-looking to see a young girl with razor sharp claws.

"No, no, it not dat, girl. It be your accent. It all wrong. Try like dis," he laughed.

"MAKUCHA YA KIFO!"

His battle cry echoed through the valley. Instantly my goose-bumps enraged as I watched spikes, spines and talons erupt from his massive arms and hands.

I had to move quickly; I saw him backhand me in the face, crushing my skull. I trusted the Sight and used it to help me dodge and weave to evade his earth-shattering blows.

He was wrong about me; I was more powerful than he. I got stronger through struggle, not from others' fears and failures. From not accepting my failures as final, but learning what I was meant to know from defeat, loss, and pain. I was a survivor, I was NEVER going to quit! He was still trying to listen to my thoughts, I projected the battles from before where I had battled him. It distracted him and I slashed at him with the talons of death, cutting his face. The beast squealed in anguish and grabbed at it.

"Oh, that got him good, Angel!" Michael cheered me on from the sidelines.

"Are you going to get into this fight already?!" I screamed at him.

In a second Angel, I'm just lining up the shot.

BA-ddooOOooomm!! The shot echoed all around us, and the beast instinctively reached for his shoulder to stop the painful wound. I took advantage of this instant to strike. I slapped my clawed hands together and chanted the spell to turn my talons into a sword.

"Naakaiiłizhinii-nineez-Ga-gih-At'a'-bigaan!!" I swung my black sword against him, chopping his ribs.

That really pissed him off good, Michael thought.

The Gor-Nok used his free hand to swing at my feather-sword, shattering it. The searing raw pain screamed through my hands as the sword was a part of me. He swung, knocking me a few yards away with his club. He raised both his spiked hands above his head to slam down on me, but Michael took his next shot across his stomach. ***BA-ddooOOooomm!!*** The beast groaned and turned his attention towards Michael, now hiding in the tree line, sniping him.

The Gor-Nok shredded the tree line with psychic saw-blades of fear one after another, tearing up the jungle. I sprouted wings to fly away from the Gor-Nok. He sent a saw-blade at me as I was only a few yards away. The little demons took hold of my wings and started tearing out my feathers as I flew higher. I cried out in agony and tried to change into the murder of crows to escape. They still clung to each of us, biting, clawing, tearing us to shreds and feathers. I gathered myself together, struggled through the pain and desperation as the fear demons were tearing through my flesh to get to my soul. I was pretty sure that I was falling by now, my mind was overflowing with fear.

I couldn't remember the words for my spells, I forgot how to conjure lightning, to teleport, move things with my mind, all lost, except for what I had written down. written... down... I had written something, on my arms. I could barely read it through the transparent fear demons tearing at my skin. "Attornitrus... Applausi!" I choked out as the fear demons were crushing my windpipe. Nothing, I had forgotten that this was one of those spells that required a bit more than vocalizing or thinking about it.

I needed to stretch a small lightning bolt in between my two hands like I was pulling taffy. Then just as the lightning strand was going to snap, you must smash both of your hands together to create a concussion blast, with an extra shocking bit of lightning to be really scary and just plain mean.

I needed to be scary, to be mean now; I mustered the strength through the flesh searing pain to perform the spell's actions with my weakening hands. I got the tiny bolt to start but it electrocuted one of the demons instead. After a few more interrupted attempts I finally executed the spell and all of the remaining fear demons with it. I landed in the trees near the clearing, hitting tree limbs and snagging on vines all the way down. I was stopped a few feet from the jungle floor by the vines. I took a minute to breathe out a sigh of relief.

I scanned the area for Michael or the beast; I thought it was best to avoid thinking the monster's name. I might have been unconsciously projecting my attack plans and allowing it untethered access to my thoughts.

I agree, Angel, we should avoid attracting attention. Michael thought to me.

Michael, wait. How can you send thoughts to me if you don't know my name? Harry said I have to speak-think the name of the person for the message to get across. I pushed the thought at him.

Oh, taking therian lesson from a lawyer are you little witch? Yes, If I knew your name, that would help our conversations to be... more private. Michael broadcast.

Michael, you were almost right when you called me Victoria. I was reluctant to finish this thought. *Michael, I am Victoria's baby...*

Nonna-belle, Grandma's beauty. I had a dream of Lucia and a baby, that is what she called the child. It's a pretty name, but it sounds...

Like an old lady's name, yes. Mom told me. I could feel him clearer now, feel his emotions in my heart.

His joy, sadness, and sorrow. So much sorrow from lost time, due to pride and arguments.

Now you're using the witch's skills, Nonna. You got that prying skill from Lucy, he thought back. That made me chuckle through my tears.

Michael, are you safe? I thought as I grew my talons to help cut through the vines.

Yes, Nonna, the other one is trying to track me. However, it is difficult to track a tracker.

Michael, why are you tracking him, wasn't he just there? I thought back to him.

Nonna, he's tracking you now, you reek of fear; I think he can smell it, like a dog, he thought. I looked around my vicinity with the Seer's Sight for trouble. I shifted through different spectrums until I found a set of eyes that could see scent as separate colors. If an object was moving or sweating, it would give off color like a heat wave.

Oh, yeah, Michael, I can see that now, I'm bright yellow with fear! I can see the fragrance flowing in the air. I spoke-thought to him.

Look, Nonna, do you see it all flowing to the same point? Is it gathering together?

Yes, Michael, it's leading down to a path in the jungle. I projected the scene to him.

Nonna, don't go down there; let it come to you. It can't resist the smell. Now that it can't hear us, we might be ...

...able to trap it. Michael, I see what you are thinking, I'll let it take the bait.

Nonna, pretend like you are hurt.

I am hurt! The Gor-Nok's little fear demons tore my feathers out! I could hear the small creatures of the jungle scurrying away as the Gor-Nok got closer. I thought of the trick I had done with the mop and broom.

I whispered an enchantment to the listening trees and

bowed to them. I began to work on my wounds, wincing a little too much.

Nonna, that's working, it is almost to you! Be ready. Michael thought to me. I slowly loosened the earth around the trees with my thoughts and continued to stitch up my wounds, whimpering in pain. I could hear the Gor-Nok coming closer, killing the grass with its every step. I couldn't see it; I was blind with my back turned away, working on my injuries. It was ready to pounce; I could see its intentions and I let the fear of getting caught off guard frighten me, filling my pores with the stench of fear and dread.

Michael, I think it likes to play with its prey. It gains strength from fear. Michael, are you there? Michael?!

Nothing, no thoughts, no animal noises, no sounds of any kind, apart from the beating of my terrified heart; pounding in my skull. I saw him pounding my skull! All of my senses went crazy; my goosebumps freaked out, making my skin crawl as the Sight took over, showing the Gor-Nok pounding my skull with his club. *Hold still,* I thought to myself, as I held the vision in my mind. I held my breath waiting for death. He was relishing in my fear; the tension in the air was as thick as the humidity.

He leapt from the darkness of the jungle brush, shouting his war-cry, swinging his club high above him, exposing his under-belly to a swift, decisive blow. I ignited a bolt in my hands, turned to face him in his mid-air assault, and slapped my palms together thinking of the thunderclap spell. It caught him off guard and the shockwave flung him towards the trees. He hung oddly from just below the branch of a tree. Something invisible was strangling him.

Michael, you're the chameleon, that's amazing!

Nonna-Belle I've got the beast. Oh yeah, the lizard, right. It's not too powerful, as physical prowess is concerned, but effective for stealth recon or rescue missions. That is once you get the double vision of its separate eyes figured out, he thought.

Right, do you have any bright ideas to effectively kill this monster?! I thought back.

I don't know, I figured strangulation was effective enough, he thought to me.

Nope, I've done it psychically and physically, but it didn't kill it, I thought to Michael.

While we were going over a list of possible death-strokes, the Gor-Nok took advantage of our lack of focus, pulled a small dagger from its voodoo shrunken-skull thing, and slashed wildly at Michael's invisible tail. I was worried about striking Michael if I shot a bolt of lightning at them. The Gor-Nok slashed through Michael's tail, so I teleported him away from the battle.

The Gor-Nok leapt down and swung his fist at me, hitting me in the head. I fell to the ground, nearly blacking out. Warm liquid slid down my forehead over my eyes; I knew I was bleeding bad. I was out of hallowed dirt and running out of options. As he swung towards me with his club, I changed into the flock of birds and quickly gathered myself behind him. I was barely human again when I retaliated.

I threw small javelin-size lightning bolts and he threw a translucent saw blade of fear demons at me. As it got closer a few of the demons jumped at me, fighting to enclose me with fear. I charged my body with electricity, killing all of them, and the rest of the fear-blade hit me in the head. It knocked me into the jungle, so I hid behind a tree. The Gor-Nok could smell me now that I was in pain, then he knocked the tree down on my leg. He was about to jump onto my leg. Little fear demons were frantically throwing rocks at me as I lay helpless.

Michael had turned into a lion then heroically jumped at the Gor-Nok. The beast caught Michael by the throat and began beating on him. While they were fighting, I transformed into a bunch of birds and started pecking the Gor-Nok. He grabbed some of me and crushed some of my birds. Grandpa bit him and ripped off one of his fingers. He screamed as he pounded on Michael. I quickly teleported him away as the Gor-Nok hit a rock in half. I charged up lightning in my hands, and he bashed me with his club.

He pounded on me as I brought a bunch of trees to life to attack him. He swung his fearblades, slicing off their limbs. I ran from the scene to regroup with Michael in the clearing. I left some of the animated trees to occupy the Gor-Nok as I took to the air to scan for Michael.

I am here, Angel, he thought to me. I could hear the fatigue in his inner voice. I opened my black wings and walked down from the sky to where Michael was quenching his thirst by a stream.

"We can't keep going like this, I'm running out of tricks, and we're both badly hurt," I said as I examined his wounds. He brushed my hair from my face to see me better. I smiled as he smiled.

"Oh Nonna, I'm so sorry I wasn't there for you and your mother today," he sobbed, and we smiled together. "I'm guessing that you were born today, I can feel it. I always know when I am forgetting something special. I never make it back, do I, my bella child? That's why you..."

But I interrupted, "You're here now. I need more hallowed earth for the healing spell," I said, then Michael pointed to a barren area on the other side of the river.

"That's an Elephants' Graveyard, it's hallowed to the animals," he replied.

"Okay, Gramps, hang tight. I'll be right back. Hide if it comes back," I told him.

"I'm ready, I'm not afraid of death, I fear losing you, losing my family now that I have you," he said.

"Don't talk like that, we'll be back home soon," I hugged, him then I ran across the water with my telekinesis. It made him chuckle.

I entered the graveyard full of discarded bones to find the hallowed earth for the healing spell. I was so exhausted, and hot, unbearably hot. It was getting hard to breathe as I scraped at the dry parched soil with my talons. I was fighting back the tears, the worry of failure, my doubts, and my fears. I pushed through the despair and dried crust to the raw earth with buried bones. I thought that it was odd that a spell to heal came from a place of death and decay. I gathered a handful of dirt to heal Michael and shook off a bit of shivers as my goosebumps were alerting me to dangers.

Michael, I'm flying to you, hang tight! I flew up out of the boneyard in case the Gor-Nok was nearby. I swooped down towards Michael when the coast was clear. I was letting my fears get the best of me.

"Everything will be fine, my Angel. Tell Lucy that I fought gallantly," he was sounding defeated.

"You'll tell her yourself. After I heal you, we're getting out of here with or without that beast's head for your wall," I rubbed the hallowed dirt in my own hurting hands and placed them on Michael's heart and arm.

"Think happy thoughts, Aesculapius Unctura!" The warmth began to swell and surge in my palms and I shared with Michael some of my fondest memories. Thoughts of all the lost time that he could have shared with us. Family outings, birthdays, and holiday visits to Lu-lu's house. All the happy times, blocking out the dark times and death.

As the healing began, I got caught up in the moment, thinking of memories of Michael happy. Mostly from family photos, but then I recalled the time he shot me in my dream. BA-ddooOOooomm!! The shot echoed from my memory, then all around us, and through me. I felt something snap and pop; then a splatter of crimson drops appeared on Grandpa's smiling face as it was fading into shock and terror. Michael had instinctively reached for my shoulder to stop the bleeding. Somewhere, Death was laughing.

Michael was pushing down on top of me, trying to keep me from Death's door. The Gor-Nok's club smashed into him, sending him flying backwards into the river. I could feel him drowning, choking on blood. Or was I confusing his pain with mine, his mind with mine. I thought of his body teleporting to the elephant's graveyard. The Gor-Nok knelt over my battered body, relishing in my defeat. He was whispering to me in Swahilli or something, but he knew that I understood.

Much of his incoherent ramblings were boasting of his power and victory over the white devils, but then he mentioned the hallowed dirt. He wanted to know what I was planning. I don't know if I was whispering or thinking it, but I said *healing*. I thought of healing Michael and how great it would have been if he was at full strength, restored to his glorious, monstrous self. The Gor-Nok asked me to show him the spell.

"Come closer," I said, then I whispered in his ear, "Fulgur orbis," A blinding white blast of light exploded from his ear. He had flown a few feet from my body because of the blast. I was starting to black out from blood loss, so I fumbled around for the remaining dirt. As I was healing myself, I could see the Gor-Nok picking himself up from off the ground, coddling his head in his hands. No doubt he was suffering from shell shock.

He could hear me thinking of him and he turned his rage towards me and began to charge at me. I was still healing; my hands were busy. If only Michael could heal too. Out of nowhere, Michael as the great grizzly came rushing to sideswiped the Gor-Nok, smashing him into the nearby boulders. Michael came bounding quickly to my side to check on me. He seemed healthy and happy, good as new.

Better than new, Angel; whatever you did to me worked, I'm as healthy as a horse; I mean a bear.

"But how?! I asked him. "I didn't think that I got to finish the spell."

"Nonna-belle, can you stand, can you fight?"

"I believe so, I might have a few more tricks up my sleeves!" I rubbed my hands over my magical tattoos on my forearms.

"Oh, I recognize that one, 'Artis Locis' is what Lucy would say to get me to do the dishes," Michael said, pointing to one of my tattoos.

243

"Yeah, it can be used to switch places with someone if you are touching them," I knew that I might need it for a quick get-a-way, short-distant teleportation trick, when the right opportunity presented itself.

The Gor-Nok was stirring; he was trying to get up. Michael had really rung his bell with the last blow.

"Dear God, why won't you die, you bastard?!" Michael screamed as he charged in to attack. As Michael got close enough to slash at the boar-beast, the Gor-Nok spun, jumped, and smashed down hard onto Michael's neck. I teleported Michael out of harm's way and back at my side before the Gor-Nok could strike again.

"Are you okay, Grandpa?!" I asked.

"Yeah, watch out for his agility," he gasped.

"Rest here, I'm taking this to higher grounds," I let a swarm of feathered friends escape through my black hair and we took flight to the sky. I changed into the harpy. I psychically raised the earth from underneath the Gor-Nok, lifting him and the ground he stood on high into the air to meet his death, to meet with me.

I was strong again, more confident, more powerful than before, and his fear was feeding my confidence. The Gor-Nok was scared, not knowing how to hang on to the rising earth beneath him. After a few hundred feet, I made the patch of earth he was clinging to vanish from under him, teleporting the ground he was recently standing on to the vortex, sending him into a free-fall. I made the earth and rocks appear over him as he fell so that it would bury him once it and him impacted into the fast-approaching ground below. I was above the patch of dirt pushing it down faster with my telekinetic powers. I was happy that I was going to bury the Gor-Nok alive.

The earth and rocks shattered a lot sooner than I thought, because we were not quite to the ground yet. When the dust and dirt cleared, I was startled by an onslaught of the Gor-Nok's fearblades bursting through it all to strike me. He caught a hold of one of my wings to slow his fall. We spun frantically out of control in the air. He was about to stab me in the back with his skull dagger, however, Michael was able to get a shot in through all my spinning feathers and shot his hand, knocking him from me. The Gor-Nok collided with the rocks in the boneyard and I landed into the river. Michael helped me to drag my soaking-wet bruised body out of the water and let me catch my breath on the river's edge.

I was coughing up water; at least I thought that it was water until fear demons were spewing from my mouth. Michael viciously screamed at the beast and readied his rifle for the next shot. I got a flash of the next few minutes with the Sight; it was really difficult to work out through all the fear and panic clouding my mind. I teleported Michael to be shielded behind me. Better me than him. Michael grabbed my arm and whispered in my ear, "Artis Locis," teleporting me through him, switching places instantly. Then he was seemingly sliced in half from out of nowhere by the fearblade of demons. And the Gor-Nok laughed.

Michael had willingly stepped in the way to absorb a fatal blow of fear intended for me. His mangled body lay as though dead and the Gor-Nok chanted at the ground to summon tree roots to seize at my arms while I was distracted, mourning my grandfather. I tried to use my talons to get free.

The Gor-Nok took my clawed hand and snapped off one of my talons then plunged it into Michael's back. I screeched like a banshee at him, but he backhanded me in the face. The monster grabbed the rifle from off the riverbank to fire at Michael's head. I begged him to spare him and choose me. He changed his mind at the last second and took aim at me instead. I had seen my death, in that instant I first used the Seer's Sight, I knew... this was not that day.

I blasted the murderous monster with the full-force blow of lightning from my heart. He was thrown a hundred feet away, back deep into the Elephant's Graveyard. I crawled to Michael's side as he lay dying. I tried to heal him, but it wasn't helping. I had no choice but to seek help elsewhere.

Torturous Training

I screamed 'Abracadabra!' so loud that the ground beneath us shook as we slipped into the vortex. I was floating unconsciously as we teleported. Teleporting with Michael's dying corpse. Not knowing what to expect inside the darkness. Not knowing if I would be able to reach the other side. Not knowing if I would be able to break the barrier between space and time. Not knowing if I would be able to drag his body through the dark waters of the abyss. I would rather face the unknown darkness of the abyss, searching for a beacon of light in the hopes that on the other side was our home, than to remain where I was to fight a monster that would end up killing us both.

I took the chance and slipped into the vortex with Michael's cold body. Dragging his body through the dark water was harder than anything I had ever had to do in my journey this far. He weighed a ton outside of the vortex, being large and mostly made of muscle. But now that he was deadweight and I was so exhausted; this was going to be an arduous journey.

The demons that live in the bottom of the abyss can only be described as lost souls thrusted into outer darkness. Like a lake full of bottom feeding fish or in a pond full of sharks. I was the fresh meat. Fresh meat dragging bloody chum along with me trying to attract the attention of the deadly pool of hungry sharks.

I haven't spent too much time studying the intricate details of the vortex and the powers of teleportation. From what little time I have spent in here, I had only made a few observations. I spent that time actually using the vortex, not taking notes. Most of my trips through the abyss passed quickly and effortlessly. Not a whole lot of sightseeing was happening during the quick little in and out trips.

I avoided teleporting since I was so far away from my home, lost out of time itself. I had never traveled farther than a couple of miles through the vortex and now I am crossing literally through the Earth to the other side dragging my grandfather's dying body with me.

Just as I feared, my strength would wane, and Michael's limp body would sink to the bottom-feeding abyss monsters. That was when they would try to take their shot at grasping, or clawing, or biting at our ankles. Every time they would target him, they would pull me farther down as well; removing more and more of what little strength I had. I didn't know if I could use any other powers or magic tricks while in the vortex. I was taking a huge risk just using the vortex while I was an entity lost out of sync with time, in a place that I shouldn't be.

Most of what I do with magic violates all my understanding of the laws of physics and ethics. I was already breaking so many rules by going back in time. I didn't want to risk completely tearing apart the fabric of space, time, and the reality I was currently living in. I thought that perhaps doing something less invasive in the dark water to defend myself could be helpful.

I risked extending my talons of death to see if those would at all be effective on the dark abyss demons. The magic worked at quarter-speed though, it was so slow and arduous. The agony was flowing up-and-down my nerves; tearing my muscles apart in my hands, wrists and forearms as the talons extended so very slowly in the darkness.

When the claws felt as though they were fully retracted, I could endure the pain no longer. I used them as well as I could muster to scare off any would-be predator that wanted to make Michael their prey. I felt so out of breath. Not that you really would breathe in the vortex, but the idea of drowning always creeps in when you spend too much time in between worlds in the dark water. It felt like water, everything looked like water, came out wet like water. It seemed to obey most of the laws of physics for water. Let's just say it was like water for the sake of argument.

If that's the case, then using electricity is out of the question. Using fire or the dragon's breath is out of the question. Using the banshee's cry might be pointless, but it was worth a try. I screamed as loud as I could, but everything seemed so muffled and useless. The rippling echo-wave of my cries began to grow and reverberate from me towards the abyss like sonar or a depth charge. As it got stronger, the bigger the wave would grow. The stronger and more intense it became; it scattered the monsters below. However, my sense of breathlessness and exhaustion would increase tenfold every time I did the banshee's cry.

Slowly, but surely, I was making progress, and this gave me hope that helped give me strength to endure to the end. Just knowing that I had some weapons I could use to defend myself and Michael in this unknown frontier was all the glimmer of hope I needed. That glimmer, that small spark, that tiny dot of light kept growing stronger, larger, and brighter. And as I got closer, I could see the exit-point, the threshold between these two worlds. I didn't know what would be on the other side. I didn't know what the farm was like 18-ish years ago. I didn't know what Grandma Lucia was like; all I knew is that she was not expecting me to pop-up on her doorstep on today of all days, my birthday. I tried not to get lost in thoughts of past birthdays and family memories. Memories are so clear now that I'm outside of time, lost in thoughts.

Your thoughts affect the destination in the journey as you travel through the abyss of the vortex. You have to focus as much as you can, both conscious and unconscious thoughts on getting to that tiny speck of light on the other side. After what seemed like an eternity of struggle, toil, and anguish; I was getting closer. I was suffering due to the blindness in the dark abyss. I was clinging desperately to Michael's dead-weight and trying hopelessly, helplessly to defend him; I could see the exit-point.

In my anguish, I pushed on ahead, pushed to power on; ignoring any other thoughts, sounds or feelings. Ignoring my exhaustion, my hunger, and my thirst. Denying the pain of every aching joint, bone or muscles tearing at the raw expose nerves. Ignoring the blood seeping from my body, attracting enemies all around me. All of it had to be pushed from my mind so I could focus on reaching the light. I got to the exit-point, it took every ounce of psychic ability to push us through the threshold, shattering it like ice in a frozen lake, bursting through the border of reality and the spaces in between.

As we appeared out the vortex, we were both tumbling and crumbling in a pile, a heap of failing exhaustion over top of each other. I gasped for actual air and coughed out a lung-full of dark water. I grabbed at Michael's wound and used all my remaining strength to pull the broken Talon from his back. I tossed it hatefully aside then rolled over the seemingly dead body of my grandfather while in the side yard of the farm near the driveway.

Lucia was driving back to the farmhouse from her visit to see her new grandchild. She was talking on the phone with Victoria, discussing possible baby girl names.

"I was thinking something Italian, more ancestral but pretty. What do you think, Mom?" Victoria asked.

"Belle, that is pretty, well, it means 'beauty' in Italian," Lucia said mindlessly as she drove.

"Grandma's beautiful baby girl," Victoria was gushing over her new baby in her arms.

"Nonna belle neonata," Lucia recited vacantly.

"Wait, what was that one?! Say it slower, Grandma. You're auto-translating again," Victoria said.

"Sorry, it's a nervous reflex. I'm tired and stressed. I just need something to take my mind off worrying about your father, that's all," Lucia said.

"He hasn't called, yet?" Victoria replied.

"No. I'll call Harry. He'll know what's going on," Lucia said as she worried about what was wrong.

"I know you miss Dad; I miss him too," Victoria said as she tried to comfort her.

"I'm sorry that he wasn't home yet, for this day. I wish he could have been here to meet her," Lucia said as she continued driving.

"He would have loved it! He'll meet her, I know it. Now, what was that name you said before, just say it slower so I can write it down," Victoria said.

"Nonna, Belle...?" Lucia repeated questioningly. "Yes, that's pretty! Nonabel. What do you think, my beauty?!" Victoria was talking to the baby as if she could understand, "Oh, she smiled! That settles it. Nonabel Lamia Venatora," she continued.

"If you like it, knock yourself out. Oh, hang on, Harry's calling," Lucia said.

"Love, ya Grandma," Victoria said.

"Yeah, yeah, I'm not quite used to that name yet, all right, bye honey," Lucia switched the call on her phone using magic.

"Lucia, something went wrong; we need to talk..." Harry said urgently.

I was weeping so bad I could not tell if my tears had soaked Michael and me or if it was the residual wetness of dark water from the abyss that had made us so wet. I was still in the mindset of a Banshee in anguish and as I cried out like the mother of all banshee, like La Llorona, calling to the heavens for help. They answered, darkening the storm clouds. They gathered in a circle to mirror my rage, my pain, my power.

I could feel the lightning building up ionic energy in the sky, waiting for me to command the strike as I began to administer breaths to Michael. Trying to get him to breathe again. I pulled a lightning bolt from the sky into my hands to start his dying heart. I checked his breathing, his pulse; nothing. His body was getting colder and as I wept, so did the sky.

I can imagine what this all may have looked like to any normal person who might happen to be driving by the farm at this moment. To catch a glimpse of some dark creature crouched over an elderly man performing an archaic form of cardio-pulmonary resuscitation. I must've looked so terrify-ing to Grandma Lucia's eyes as she pulled into the driveway in the pouring rain to see us like that.

"NOooo! Not my Michael?! No!" She was sobbing on her knees in the rain as soon as she fell out of the vehicle. She was in such pain, but I had to keep trying. I caught another bolt to surge his heart.

"Wait, no. Stop this!!" Lucia reached out her hand and seized upon my neck with her mind.

"UkkKKgh, Lu-lu, trust me! I have to finish this, gacCchh, Please!" I coughed out. She wasn't letting go of me, and I was all charged up with electricity. So, I activated a thunderclap. Lucia saw it coming and teleported. She had to release her grip upon my throat though, and I continued performing CPR on Michael. I was letting the Seer's Sight aid me to anticipate her next moves. Lucia appeared in the house and was getting something from the Library.

I continued to perform CPR. I knew that I had to hurry. I was just finishing administering another shock to Michael's heart when Lucia had returned, this time armed with a small sword.

"Stay away from my Husband, witch!" Lucia's eyes were red, raw with hurt and hate. She was thinking of ways to kill me, maim me, how she would torture me.

"Lucia, I can save him, let me help!" I begged.

"You have done enough, you murdered him!" The storm reacted to Lucia's rage. I was panicking for a new reason now, she misunderstood what I'm doing.

"Get away from him NOW!!" Lucia demanded.

"You don't understand, there's not much time. I must finish this, please," I said in vain to plead with her.

"No! I'm finishing this, by ending you!" Lucia said as she unsheathed the short sword and power surged from it. The storm was drawn to it, even the lightning was attracted to it. I was being pulled towards it magnetically. It helped her to focus energy, channel all of her emotions, her hurt, her rage into one soundless blast of energy. I was so lost in carefully studying this new power that I totally forgot to brace myself for the impact of the blast. I was knocked a few yards away near the old fields by the woods before I heard the sonic boom of the energy bolt. I was not here to fight an old woman.

"Old, am I?!" Lucia cackled at me as she sent another blast at me. I deflected it with a thunder-clap, hoping that it would work.

Lucia and I were equally matched as opponents, we could foresee each other's moves and intentions. Both of us have the gift of foresight from the Seer's Sight. At times it was as though I was fighting an older version of myself. I admit that Lucia was much more skilled at sorcery and the use of magic for both defense and offense to the point that she was almost mean with both. Sometimes she got to the level of seeing my moves before I could, and she had planned counter-attacks using my own attacks against me.

It was as bad as playing a grandmaster in chess playing someone who just learned what chess was that morning. It was as bad as a 12-year-old playing racquetball with her 67-year-old grandfather. The grandfather can send the ball all over the room making a little kid chase after it until they pass out from exhaustion while they stand there in one spot. That's pretty much what it looked like as Lucia mopped the farm with me.

In her rage, Lucia did not care for property nor nostalgia; nothing was sacred. We put holes through the farm, through the barn, and through the house. We even damaged her car; I think she dropped it on me once, it's hard to recall. I let myself use teleportation more often now that I had been through the syrup slow dark abyss once before since I time-traveled. Plus, the abyss gave me a safe place to retreat and a place to hide, to recoup while I recovered. It gave me a way to rest while she was planning her next attack and trying to guess where I would come out on the other side. I snuck back up from the abyss to snag Michael from his own shadow.

Lucia sensed it and tried to hang on to him, but I zapped her with lightning from behind while she was distracted. I was able to pop us over to the cemetery and get some hallowed earth to heal his and my wounds. The healing wasn't working for him, so I frantically resumed CPR, aided by my lightning. However, this had attracted Lucia's attention. I checked Michael's pulse, it was weak, but it worked, his heart was beating again!

As I was there at the cemetery in an open grave with Michael, Lucia had appeared. She had snatched him from my arms through teleportation and started burying me by collapsing the walls of the grave with her mind. I decided to play dead, just let the darkness overtake me. I thought of it just as the darkness had consumed me and I found myself in the abyss of the vortex again.

I had dived into the vanishing point and had no thought of where to go. So, I just wandered aimlessly in the vortex trying to think of someplace where I can escape to that would be safe enough to keep me from fighting with her. Since she was in the graveyard and I had not thought of an exit-point yet, she couldn't anticipate my moves unless she was in the abyss with me. That was when my goosebumps went off and I saw something break through the ice, the barrier between the two worlds; it was Lucia.

I knew I needed to study this place more, I knew little to nothing about it and that gave me a vantage point, an idea. It was a gamble and I had prayed now that I had a way into the Study, even if she didn't like it. Even if she had put up the defenses already, I knew that I could break in. I thought of my bird Twilight. Before I left the vortex, I screamed a shock-wave banshee cry in Lucia's direction as a diversion. Knowing that my misdirection wouldn't hurt her, but distract her, as a way to protect my escape.

I felt myself fluttering through thousands of wings, thousands of feathers spilling out into the cage in the Study. I opened the cage with my mind, and we poured out to fill the darkness of the Library, then I gathered together into one form. I was barely whole; birds were still merging with my hair as I began pulling books from the shelves with my mind.

I released various different sections of birds out of me to find some more specific spells to help defend against Lucia's coming onslaught. I didn't have much time; I had made the mistake too often of thinking her name. I found one spell on defense. It was the spell that she had used to lock up the Library and keep people from teleporting into here. I had summoned the necessary runes, potions, and powders; then got to work quickly through using a cauldron in the middle of the room.

Throwing things together, I ignited a fire all while keeping an eye on the vortex. I had sent one of my birds into the abyss to be a lookout. I had barely enough time to finish the ritual before the bird came back out of the vortex cawing, "She's coming! She's coming! Look out! Look out!"

When the 'lock-out spell' was complete the walls of the Library creaked and tightened. Things became straighter, shelves that were sagging regained their strength. The gaps between the floorboards tightened. The door to the Library slammed shut, and I could hear Lucia pounding on it from the other side.

I had probably a few seconds left before she'd figure out how to get in. I summoned more books, I separated myself into more birds and had each of my little crows all reading books. I was over-loading on knowledge, and it still wasn't enough to stop this; I needed more. I slammed my fists on the books in my frustrations and made the words on the page bleed.

I looked at the palms of my hands in amazement to see that I had unconsciously learned a spell to literally absorb knowledge by touching the pages. It was so exhilarating, so powerful, and intoxicating.

I slammed my palms down onto the opened books in front of me and sucked the words right off the pages and watched the dark words travel onto my pale skin. I was lost and distracted by all the new things I was learning that I had completely ignored my goosebumps.

There was no sound but a flash of blinding white light that felt so peaceful. It felt like I was still dreaming as I woke to a dark room. I could hear voices talking behind my back and there was something in the room with us, growling. I could hear chains, clinking metal, clanking chains dragging on the floor. Lucia was whispering to someone, but they were not here. Sometimes she'd give the growling creature commands to 'sit, lay down,' as she patted it on the head and told him it was a good boy.

Lucia was talking to someone still on the antique phone, saying that she doesn't know who this person was, who I am.

"Yes, I've got Michael stabilized, but just barely and he's not going to make it," Lucia said frustrated.

"Why can't you heal him?" I heard the voice ask.

"I need to go try some other techniques," I didn't hear what Lucia had requested of Harry, but she had made the mistake of saying his name.

"No, just come see what you can get out of this person. Call me when you're finished. I'll be gathering ingredients to undo whatever curse this witch has done."

Lucia left the room door open and I could see the light from the oil lamp in the next room. I knew now that she was somewhere in or near the Study. I fought to release myself from these bands, but the ropes tightened and burned every time that I would move or struggle.

I tried to teleport but couldn't fully phase out of this world into the world underneath because she has tethered me to this room. I tried to use the Seer's Sight to see how I was bound.

Lucia had kept everything in darkness and blocked my view. I attempted to change into a bunch of crows, but the ropes would burn my feathers. I tried electricity and instead of the electric current burning the rope it burned me. It just seemed that everything that I was going to try was going to burn me. And the monster dog or whatever was in the room; this creature in the room with me would get restless when I would hurt myself.

At one point the creature became curious enough and came in close to investigate. It sniffed at my hands and my face; I had no idea what this thing was. I didn't know if it was some kind of hellish, nightmare creature that Lucia had at her disposal. I had just kept thinking in my mind for it to *go away, leave me alone.* And I cried. Sometime had passed, I had lost track of my concept of time; but I heard voices outside of the room. Lucia was talking to Harry.

They had agreed on something and came into the room with the oil lamp being the only source of light. My eyes were so sore and sensitive. I had used every spectrum phase of the Seer's Sight that my eyes were glowing, burning a bright lavender. I must've looked so deranged, wild, and feral. I was wet from my tears.

Lucia had examined my bindings; she looked at the ropes to see if I had figured out how to escape and noticed my burns. She cackled and laughed at my futile attempts to escape and then she backhanded me across the face with a fist full of ball-lightning as part of her hand. I think that she had cracked my cheekbone.

Lucia looked at me and Harry and asked him, "Could you please find out what she's done to Michael?" "But she's just a girl! There's no way she could've done this to him," Harry said. Lucia grabbed his face. He said "No! I'm not doing it Lucia!" She held the lamp up to his eye level and swung it slightly and commanded him with an inner thought and actual voice that reverberated in the room. "Do it!" she said, "Do it! You know what to do."

Lucia left the room and the lamp with us. Harry seemed angry, he seemed mad that she was making him do this. He seemed like he didn't want to do this.

I told him out loud, "I know you don't wanna do this Harry!"

He shouted, "Quiet! You don't know me! You don't know what I want. Don't know what I can do!"

I could sense his intentions, I said, "Stop!! We don't have to become the monsters."

"I have no choice," against his will Harry changed forms to become the were-croc. I was already in so much pain; I was so sore, exhausted, hungry, starving, thirsty, tired, and tortured. What more could Harry do? I had to reach him; I knew Lucia had him hypnotized. He felt like he couldn't stop hurting me; I had to try something.

I kept saying, in my mind, *Harry, you're stronger than this! You're stronger than her! I forgive you; I believe in you, I love you. You're my friend. Remember me Harry! I need a friend.*

The whole time I was trying to hypnotize him; speaking to his mind, my words were the only sound I could hear. I saw him repeatedly hit, scratch, punch, and tail-whip me. The more I spoke, the more he lost his strength and the will to torture a friend. Until finally he changed back into himself and left the room.

He said to Lucia, "She should be ready to talk." Lucia doubted him and said, "I'll be the judge of that!"

Lucia cracked her knuckles, then stretched her palms and fingers like a great musician or a composer about to conduct a beautiful symphony. She called to her various instruments of all different shapes, sizes, designs, and elements. She seemed like she had done this before.

My mind was wandering a little bit in my fatigue to pages from the Diary, to journal entries of Lucia's misadventures. I had thought of times where she would have used these torture techniques to extract information from her enemies. In all reality, I really didn't know what kind of a person Lucia actually was. She had been nice to me before because I was family, she was at least her level of such niceness. I could have changed all of it with ending my enemy. But I failed and caused her loss. All that pain and loss turning her into a torturing, vindictive person.

Letting my mind wander seemed to be the only way to ignore the pain, but Lucia had ways around that. She had some corkscrew-shaped metal object that she plunged into my forearm. It was wrapping itself around my bones and Lucia had ignited the metal by chanting something in Latin. I was too incoherent to understand.

There really is no way to describe what burning from within feels like or smells like. I really wouldn't wish it upon my worst enemies. I believe this is the part where I would begin to beg for death. The only thing that had kept me alive was knowing that I could save Michael. That was the only thought I could focus on. I fixated on that thought. I was so fixated on that thought that I couldn't even hear what Lucia was saying with her mouth. She tried using the lamp light to hypnotize me. I kept repeating the thought in my mind, *I can save, Michael, I can save Michael.*

Then I remembered that she could hear thoughts like Zatie, and I can hear her thoughts if we allow others in. The thoughts become clearer when you begin the thought by announcing the person's name. So, I started thinking, "Lucia, I can save Michael. Lucia, let me save Michael. Lucia, I am here to help; please let me save Michael."

She was getting extremely frustrated with my apparent inability to talk or be hypnotized; so, she lashed out irrationally by whacking me in the side of the face with her oil lamp. The glass shattered on impact and cut my head. The magical oil flowed over my hair and face, then the flicker of the flame ignited all of it.

Lucia sobbed as I wailed in searing pain and flames. This is how, this is how it's going to end. Before I blacked out, I thought I heard her say, "No, you can't save him. You can't save Michael."

Something ice cold and wet splashed all over my face and body. I expected to feel the severe burn of my flesh aching and reacting to cold water only to look down to see my creamy white skin restored. I was no longer burned! At this point I'm not even certain if I ever was burned or if this had all been a bad dream.

Lucia, Grandma Lu-Lu was known for pulling people into her dreams to torture them with greater power. I could be chained to a bed somewhere unconscious. She had slapped me across the face and told me to wake up. She asked me what I was searching for in the Library.

"Why did you have all the books open? Why are there words missing? Are you here to steal from me? Are you here to steal our secrets? What are you looking for, witch?!"

I tried to tell her, "I was trying... to find... answers. I'm here to help."

She said, "You've helped enough!"

I said, "I was looking for a spell..."

Lucia interrupted me, "Yeah, I can tell you're looking for a spell! It's written all over your arms. These are all offensive, aggressive, vicious, evil spells; only a dark sorceress would use."

"I was helping Michael... we were fighting... a monster. We were losing... so I thought of Home."

She asked, "Whose home? This is my home! Michael's home!"

"This is my home too, Lucia," I muttered.

Lucia grabbed my face and held it up to the light to examine it with her fully restored oil lamp. The light pierced my eyes, even as I shut my eyelids; I could still see the light. Lucia looked into my eyes as she opened them. Lucia looked at them searching for something. I knew she was probing me for the truth. I knew it was time to let her in.

I let her see everything; every memory I ever had. Every

thought of growing up here in this place; all the visits, the time we were being babysat by grandma, so Mom and Dad could pursue their schooling and career.

All the summers we spent with her; the summers she was not supposed to be teaching us how to use our powers. The afternoons we spent frolicking through the woods with her and the other creatures of the forest; fully using our imaginations as raw wild magical creatures.

I showed her all the laughter, all the happiness, all the good family memories. Always sharing my name; starting it as a whisper, echoing it through time and eternity. Pouring these memories, pouring out my soul into her soul and heart. Begging her, pleading with her to remember who I am.

Lucia let go of her grip psychically, spiritually, and physically and fell to the floor gasping. She was crying in her astonishment; still waning with emotional sickness from the images that still flooded her mind. She pleaded with me, "Please stop! This cannot be. She's just a baby. I just saw her. There is no way..."

"...that I am her? That I am Nonabel."

Lucia teleported from the room leaving me in complete darkness by taking the lamp with her. I wasn't asleep but I didn't know if I was awake. I couldn't tell whether it was a dream, or what was real. Shapes and ghostly images danced around in front of my eyes in the darkness. It seemed as though I had my face sticking through the ice barrier of the abyss, admiring the dark creatures that lived along its ocean bed of the void between worlds.

I remember reading about this phenomenon called 'pareidolia', I think that's what it's called, what one experiences when they stare into darkness. We start seeing heat vapors, wind, moisture over our eyes; whatever you want to call it, but we start imagining things that aren't there and our brains start to daydream looking at a blank dark canvas.

I saw something dark moving in the water, coming towards me. It had long spiny claws, it was hairless. It had long and lengthy legs and a slender body. And it licked my face, then started panting. My panic turned into laughter in my insanity. This creature reminded me of Dominic.

When I thought his name, Dominic began to wag his tail and pant in excitement. I thought that this may be an opportunity for us both to be free. I believe this room is where Lucia has kept Dominic. To keep him from harming anyone, to keep him out of the way, to hide her and Michael's shame. Their failures of not figuring out how to fix his condition, to change him back, to heal him.

I wonder what it was that she has planned for me and Michael when she fails with us. Was she going to lock us in between worlds and not deal with her feelings or mistakes? I don't like to run away from my mistakes. I don't like to hide from them; I don't want to fear. I'm not ashamed of fear or mistakes. Hard work builds up who we are, our character, our integrity. Especially the way in which we face our mistakes. Come in head-on to conquer them. Not locked away and forgotten.

I thought out loud so to speak, projecting thoughts to Dominic. I asked if he wanted to go outside to play. I thought it in my mind, a bunch of images of us playing fetch outside. I projected the memory of our first meeting; or now my first meeting with him. I projected that I was Michael's grandbaby. I showed him my smile and Michael's smile. I showed him our time together; Michael and I working together to fight the Gor-Nok.

Dominic seemed excited and I asked him if he knew how to get out; how to break our chains. He did not, he whimpered in defeat. He thought of Lucia, of her shackling the collar around his neck, locking it with the magical key. A key! I had seen a key, and Lucia used to have it around her neck. Michael used to have a key around as well that they gave me when we signed the contract.

I was trying to remember what I did with that key; did I bring back with me? Where would I have put that key. My key should be in the future somewhere. Zatie may be able to find it at some future date. But in all my studies and all the power I have gained, all the experience that I had been through, and in all the battles I fought and lost; I could not see a way that Zatie would have a chance to even begin to come rescue me.

So, all those avenues are dead-ends. Endless powers and possibilities and I had to be so far away. I needed something else that I could use, so I scanned in the dark. As I tried to think about escape my hands would instantly tug my restraints. Wrist would twist the bones causing the bindings to burn against my skin.

This burning would put off light. The light which gave me a little glimmer of what the room looks like. I tried to use the Seer's Sight, switched through phases of the visual spectrum. I came across a form of night-vision. Dominic was glowing funny, but I could see his smiling face, his tail wagging, his tongue hanging out, and his eyes all filled with excitement.

I agitated the bands again to increase the light in the night-vision; to get a better look at the room. This was a torture chamber! All the walls were covered in weapons! Weapons of every kind. Knives, swords, daggers, spears, shields, whips, flails, arrows, and chains. One sword I recognized; it was the Roman short sword that Lucia had used against me in our battle outside.

I reached out with my mind to try to get something to come off the wall. I was so weak, so exhausted from the pain in my soul. The torture of my mind and body in ways I had never imagined. I was still waning, still weak.

All I needed was a spark, a glimmer of hope in darkness, one shining beacon. A possibility for escape from all of this pain. If I can just concentrate, use it to focus. By-pass the power, the spell she had on me. And maybe, just maybe I could use it to overpower her. I tried to shake the room, to shake the chair, tried to shake the bands. I tried to shake the swords and try to convince Dominic to reach it. She kept him on a short leash.

I have to focus, channel and fight through the pain. Fight through the spells. One thought, focus on one thing. Focus, focus, focus, focus, focus, focus, oh yeah! That's hers! That's her focusor, a magic wand of sorts; that's her talisman, her amulet. Imbued with their power. I could see it now with the Sight. I had activated a vision, showing me the memory of when she had consecrated this weapon for him. His family heirloom, it was Michael's. I had better not think about Lucia. It's his family heirloom, me, and Michael's family. Michael's focusor, she had made this for him. This is the one he was talking about that belonged to Victoria; that's when it moved. When I thought of her name.

I thought of my mother; I felt her name, I thought her name, I screamed her name like a banshee now through all the pain, and the sword flew to me, nearly stabbing me in between my legs. I took my bound hands and began to rub ropes on the blade. The blade was sharp and imbued with power and would heat up as two spells were battling against each other for dominance.

The binds were still clinging to me, not letting go of their power. Scorching and searing my flesh but they were loose. The sword was succeeding, it was saving me. Michael's focusor made for him, given to Victoria, that answers to her name, was now serving me.

Lucia had heard me think her name one too many times and was coming to check on me. I had already freed myself and freed Dominic. I used the sword to blast away the wall of this dark room to create chaos and an escape for myself and my hairless friend.

I didn't care who was on the other side of the walls. I didn't worry about what was happening in the Library or what was reality; I had power again. I scanned the room with the Seer's Sight, looking through every spectrum for evidence of Lucia. I found her body; I could see it with x-ray vision under the rubble and debris of fallen books and shattered bookcases.

I moved the fallen books with my mind and began the work of restoring the wall all at once while I called Lucia's body into the air and I woke her with a psychic slap across her face.

Harry was in the room attending to Michael. He was about the shift forms when I told Dominic to attack. Harry backed off, I told Dominic to sit, and told him that he was a good boy. The Sword was ignited as I held it to Lucia's throat; with my other arm extended holding her in the air by her neck.

"Now, you listen to me! I tried to be nice. I tried to beg. I tried telling you the truth, but now I have to show you what you do not want to see!" I opened the vision of our last moments right before the Gor-Nok stabbed Michael in the back with my claw that he ripped from my hand.

Lucia tried to look away, she tried to hide her eyes. "No! Don't shut your eyes!" I screamed like a banshee at her to listen, to look, to understand.

"I was forced to hurt the ones I love. I was forced to come back here; crawl through space and time to see you today. I need your help! I was forced to learn magic. I was forced to grow up. I was forced to protect my family when you left me. You left me! I was abandoned to my own devices. To my own understanding. Why don't you understand who I am?! Your beautiful baby girl. Lucia, all I want is for you to believe me. I came all this way across time to try to undo the horrible things I did. The way my family members end up. Every one of them is gone. My fault. It's all my fault," I cried out most of that. Then I completely ran out of energy as I released them from my hypnotic vision filling their minds. I collapsed.

I dreamt that I had heard a lullaby that I used to sing

when I was very little. I couldn't see my body when I reached to touch my hands and face. I felt spongy, transparent, and ghost-like. I shifted through the different visual spectrums until I could finally see myself clearly but everything else would totally go glass-like and transparent.

I switched back to see with normal eyes and accepted that I may only be me seeing this through the Sight. I may not even be here in this memory. Grandma Lu-lu was visiting my mother and her new baby Nonabel.

Lu-lu was enjoying a moment with her granddaughter, studying her face, and studying her eyes. Accepting the truth, realizing that all I had told her and shared with her were not lies. Realizing that I have lived this child's life; that so many things of this child's life was predetermined, pre-destined to happen; whether we liked it or not, and no matter what we did to change it.

I moved in closer to take a look at baby 'Belle' as Lucia and baby Nonabel stared into each other's eyes. I was barely getting a glimpse of baby me when she suddenly turned her tiny face towards me. Lu-Lu looked at me and motioned for me to back up. I didn't understand if I was just seeing this through the Sight or if Lu-Lu was sharing the vision. How could I also be there? I had many dreams since learning magic where the bounds of reality, space, and time didn't matter. I have so many things to learn still, and I need so much help.

I looked around the room to see my mother and father were taking advantage of a visiting family member, caring for their new baby by sleeping. They were resting on the couch and the hospital bed. I studied my parents and enjoyed watching them while they slept peacefully. I got a flash of their funeral, they look just as peaceful. I got a flash of the accident; remembering Mom looking so terrified and panicked. Mom had looked back at us from the front of the vehicle where she sat. In the front seat, my dad tried to do what he could to avoid what was coming. I saw my mom's eyes clash with power and change color; that brightened color indicates that she used magic to protect us, shield us, against the crash and she mouthed, "I love you."

I sat in the corner of the room sobbing, trying to keep quiet, then Lu-lu shushed me. I was disturbing baby Nonabel and caused her to fuss a little. With a wave of her hand, Lucia had teleported me back to the Study. When I arrived, I saw Michael's body lying on a cot; they were doing their best to sustain him.

A while later, after her visit at the hospital with my mother and her new grandbaby, Lucia came home. She was humming to the same lullaby. I asked her why Michael was not healing. She said, "I believe I know the answer, but I don't like what it means," she took my hand and as she held my hand, it changed from being transparent and ghost-like into flesh and bones again at her touch.

Lucia examined my pinky-nail saying that it was broken. I knew what she was thinking, and I recoiled my hand back in embarrassment. I had done it; it was me that had stabbed Michael. Lucia grabbed my face; I was crying again, and she looked deep into my eyes trying to hypnotize me.

Saying over and over again, "This was not your fault, you had no choice. This was not your fault, not your fault," she had let go of my face.

"It was that monster's fault," I said as I went to try to tele-port, but I couldn't phase between two worlds.

Lucia asked, "Where do you think you're going?" "The monster is weak! I can finish him! I can end this! I can make up for my mistakes! I can avenge Michael!" I said as I kept trying to teleport in vain.

Lucia said, "No you can't. Not now that I've removed your powers."

"What!? Why would you do that to me!? I can end this! I know how to stop it!" I screamed.

"Sweetheart, you and Michael at full strength, with all these weapons at your disposal still could not defeat it! You would lose and I can't bear the thought of losing another family member. I can't bear the thought of losing *you* now that I have you. I love you, my bella child. I'm so sorry I didn't believe you before," Lucia said as she was tearing up.

"Fine, I'll deal with him later. What can we do for Michael now?" I said as I came back to his cot.

"I found fragments of your claw in his wound that were becoming cancerous. Until I saw your vision of his final moments, I didn't understand what it was.

"The talons of death. I've killed him, haven't I?" I was sobbing again.

"It's not your fault," she tried to comfort me.

"I am ready to do what I must do. We need to release Michael," Lucia said as we hugged and cried. We unconsciously shared more memories as we embraced. Happy times, happy tears. I asked her as we ended our hug, "How do we help him?"

"When we do this, Michael will wake from his coma; but he won't have much time in this life. I'll have to say goodbye for good," she said decidedly.

I started crying again, "No! There's got to be another way?!"

She lifted my chin and said, "There's no other way, what's done is done. I can't have you going back to face it; I can't have you stomping all through time causing more trouble. I bound you here to this place, I removed your powers. You can only do magic if I allow it. You'll get it all back when... I die. I know now I don't have much time either. The end has come sooner than I had expected. Come, we have much to do."

I returned with the claw from the yard. Lucia had allowed me to teleport and scan the battle scene for my discarded talon. I was embarrassed; I was so ashamed of what I had done with this weapon, this part of me made to destroy my enemies, not hurt my family. I threw it down at Lucia's operating table and retreated to my corner then hid in the darkness, nuzzling with Dominic. I was as hideous as he looked on the outside, just that is how I felt on the inside.

Lucia said, "I believe you got your lack of emotional control from both me and your grandfather. Neither one of us in the family can control ourselves."

I said "Well, there is another... person. I'm not gonna talk too much about the future, or our family because I don't wanna mess anything up any more than I already have. But I learned to block out a lot of things and thoughts by having her around. I miss her so much."

I started to sob and weep again. Lucia came to coddle me and held my head in her arms. She lifted up my chin, smiled lovingly at me, then slapped me in the face. "That's the Lu-Lu I know; the Lu-Lu I love," I said.

"I love you too. Now let's get to work," she explained to me that we needed to reattach my claw to restore me to my rightful frame. Her theory was that by restoring my wounded claw that the fragments that were broken off in Michael that were causing a cancerous and incurable disease would allow him to finally die. The talon's full power activates by stopping his heart ending his life.

I recoiled from Lu-Lu. I refused to help. "No, there's got to be something else we haven't tried?!"

"You're just being scared and selfish," she said as she pulled at my hand.

"You, you are the coward, you're giving up!" I screamed at her. She rebuked me and reminded me that I wanted forgiveness. I wanted to atone for my mistakes, this is how I do it. Restoring things back to its starting position.

"Fear can keep us from making mistakes," she said as she granted me access to my powers; I called the talon back to me and watched it turn into a crow mid-flight. The crow entered back into my heart and found its way back to my hand restoring my fingernail. The black veins in Michael's body were retreating. Combining together to form a solid mass of feathers.

Black feathers came out of his wounded back and into my body.

"We are going to talk about what you've been doing, young lady," Lucia said in astonishment. When I felt that I was whole and every ounce of dark evil cancerous pain had been removed from him, that his soul may be released from pain and anguish; I told Lucia it was done, we have only seconds.

Michael was moaning and moving. He smiled when he saw her and called her name, "Lucy is this Heaven?" Grandpa thought he had died and gone to heaven.

Lucia asked, "Why would you think such a silly thing, Michael?"

He replied, "Don't you see the angel in the room?" Lu-Lu had to check still, she had to test the validity of my story and she asked him, "Michael, what Angel do you see?"

"I see my daughter's daughter with all her beauty just as her mother and her mother before her. She's her grandma's beauty, she's every bit as pretty as you were the day that I met you in Lebanon along the Gypsy Trail. The day I fell in love with you, Lucy," he replied.

Lucia was sobbing now her eyes were overflowing with sorrow.

"She is who she says she is. I know you have doubts, Lucy. Don't be mad at us. We fought a good fight, but this fight is now yours; and it's always been hers to finish. Help her, guide my sweet angel. I will always be with you," he said before he kissed her.

Lu-Lu sobbed as they kissed one more time before he died in her arms. We cried for hours it seemed. Harry came to the house to help us move the body. Michael weighed a ton even with our magic his weight was still impressive. Harry handled him like a ragdoll as though he was nothing. Harry somberly, humbly carried Michael out to Grandpa's favorite spot on the farm where he would watch the ducks across the pond near the woods. Lu-Lu crafted a casket of stone and raised the earth with her mind. I watched her power in amazement. I stood by Dominic; he had somehow known that his son was dead. I told him he was in a better place and I swore I heard Dominic's voice speak to me telling me, *there's no place better than with family*.

I hugged him. Calmly, Harry put Michael's body in the casket. We all took turns having a silent moment with Michael at our private service.

"Shouldn't Victoria be here? To say good-bye?" I asked. Lucia felt it was best to not interrupt Victoria's recovery with this tragedy. So, Lucia and Harry plotted to have a fake body brought to the cemetery after being shipped back from Borneo. Pretending they had found his body in the coming weeks. I got to spend my graveside minutes alone, mostly crying. I gave Michael a kiss and swore on his grave that I would avenge his death and destroy his killer with my last breath.

Knowledge of Power

Harry began making arrangements to have Michael's 're-mains' brought back from Borneo to have a public viewing. Lucia thought it would be best to wait a while after my recent birth, before announcing the death of her husband. She wanted to give Victoria time with baby me before breaking the bad news and breaking her heart.

Lucia was getting my new bedroom set up in one of the many hidden rooms of the Study. She had lots of questions and naturally that's why she set me up to sleep in the 'interrogation room,' as I called it. Lucia had been keeping Dominic in there during the day and would let him out at night while Michael was gone.

I told her it would be fine if Dominic stayed with me; he and I are already friends. Dominic yelped, and thought to my mind the word, "Family."

"Yes, Dominic, I meant family," I said as I petted him. "You can understand him? Then that means...?"

"I'm like Michael just as I am a witch like you."

"I saw the crow, is that your totem and your Nix?" Lucia asked. "Yup, I'm going with a theme."

"I'm confused, how do you separate your totem from your flesh? Michael and I studied therianthropy syndromes for years to find a cure for Dominic, for all of them. We could never succeed in separating the host from the totem once the bond was formed."

"Yeah, I screwed-up when I was following the steps to the spell and became *several* birds instead of one," I blushed as I admitted to my mistake.

"Wait, what?! How did you even survive that process?" Lucia argued.

"I almost didn't, if it weren't for Harry."

"My Harry? Our Harry? He doesn't know magic, he's like a bull in a china shop. I hardly let him in here, let alone in the house," Lucia replied.

"He's a quick study, and a good ally. I'm glad he's around," I responded.

"You met him before coming here?" she asked.

"Oh, yeah. He introduced himself after the funeral," I accidentally said too much.

"After *my* Funeral?! Then that would mean, that Victoria…" she was saying.

I interrupted her train of thought, "She kinda swears-off magic for some reason and…"

"Didn't sign the contract, right, you did," she said.

"Yes, I am the heiress. But I don't want to discuss details of future events," I said sternly.

"Fair enough, but I have so many questions." Lucia wanted to know how I can be back in time, "Are you a dream-walker? Or have you mastered the astral plane projection spell?!"

I said, "No, I'm here… because of the Nevergator. I created one to get here," and I made it appear in my hand. "Do you want to see it?!"

Lucia was exasperated and mad to see what I had done. She said, "What have you done?! Don't you understand the consequences of what you've done?! This is taking years off of your life! Did I teach you Nothing?!"

I said, "Well, on the night of your passing, you gave me the book, the Diary. You told me that it was a *magical book* and that I was a witch. I thought you were crazy, of course; however, later that night I sat up studying the book."

"What did you learn?" she asked.

"I was able to master telekinesis, I could move stuff, but mostly break them apart with telekinesis. Flight with telekinesis. Oh, and when I went to sleep, I ended up in *your* dream. You were having a nightmare about the monster. You taught me how to use lightning and teleportation; those are my go-to four spells, probably all the time," I responded.

"Well, I guess that's not nothing," she said.

She summoned the Diary so she could really teach me how to use it. Lucia explained that, "The Diary is like an index for the entire Library; that if we wanted a to see volumes on the subject, it would give you a paraphrased summary, not the whole subject but you can call the actual volume to you," she said then she grabbed a few pages from the Diary and removed an entire book on trans-dimensional teleportation and handed it to me.

"Now, that was impressive! So, does that mean that you're going to allow me to continue studying? I thought I was grounded?" I asked her.

Lucia sighed as she said, "Well, I can't have you going back in time. Doing that is right out of the question! However, you can start reading volumes about it, understand what's been written and you can add to it, what you learn. I've never actually done it. I can obey the warnings, especially when it says it will take something from you as a sacrifice. Most magic involves a sacrifice; something you're giving up, something in exchange for access to power or knowledge. I also can't let you leave the farm. I can't let you out of my sight so if I leave, I'll have to lock you into the study or take you with me. But behave yourself. I don't need you to accidentally do something that may change the course of this reality. Even as a doppelgänger you can still mess with space and time. People may still remember you but as a déjà vu, an impression, a thought, a forgotten memory."

I asked, "Wait, what's a doppelgänger now?"

Lucia said, "That's why you're invisible. That's why you're a shadow, or a figment of peoples' imagination, a phantom."

I said, "That's why I can't teleport or get to use some of my spells?"

Lucia said, "I can only foresee so much. I don't see everything, so I can only plan out what you intend to do. Only what is for me to control; but since you can't go home, I will let you stay here. Yes, I will allow you to study."

I was so excited to get to learn magic with Grandma, I was grinning from ear to ear and I was bouncing.

"I need to show you a better place for practice. "

"What you got a fencing gymnasium up in here?" I wouldn't have been surprised at this point, but I had to ask. "Also, something that would be nice to learn is how to use weapons. Like the focusor, to use swords and stuff," I continued.

"While you are here in the hiding place, things in our world almost stop, time is different."

"I've figured that out, I pretty much live here, in the future," I replied.

"Michael and I are, *were* here most of the time too." I sensed her sadness, but I didn't want her to stop talking. I love to learn from her.

"Go on, I want to hear more," I said.

"Right, dimensional designing creates its own time, its own rules; but it is only as big as we create. Yes, we can make more space if wanted. We could create more but that requires an exchange of physical elements. In this dimension we cannot just create something from nothing; we have to actually bring something in to create more here," she said as she showed me other rooms.

"However, in our dreams we can create something from nothing. Our dreams are where our imaginations are set free. In our dreams, our imagination is its true power. Dreams don't need anything, no offering or sacrifice; all it needs is for us to let go of our inhibitions. Let go of control, just get out of its way, and let it create. Letting go to create our heart's desire, worlds without numbers. All we have to do is get out of its way and that's where I want you to practice your magic. While you're in your dreamscape you'll have full access to your powers, no restrictions. You won't be grounded there. It will feel as real as the real world. You can spend as much time as you want there and you can get a lot more dreaming done being in the hiding place, being in the study," she was fun to learn from.

"OK then, let's do this!" I said excitedly.

"Close your eyes," she put her hands to the side of my head placing her thumbs in the middle of my forehead. She started repeating out loud and in my mind in Latin, *Release the king of dreams;* "Dimittere regem somnia, Dimittere regem somnia, Dimittere regem somnia."

I thought she started snoring, so I snuck a peek by opening one eye. Lucia *was* snoring, she had fallen asleep. *I am not SNORING!* She thought shouted.

"I am not asleep," she said out loud.

"Did it work, or did I ruin it? Do we need to start over?" I asked as I peeked around the room.

"No, we just need to check," she opened the Diary, laughed, and turned it to show me a page full of gibberish.

"I don't get it, Grandma, what's so funny?"

She chuckled, "That's what's so funny. No matter how real the dreams seem, your brain can't read in dreams."

"That's right, you taught me that, in a dream actually," I responded.

"Oh. So, you know this already?" She was getting upset and was getting up to leave.

"Listen, Lucia. Even though I have not done this my entire life; I have studied magic," I replied.

"Fine, figure this part out on your own. I've got other things to do!" She got up out of the interrogation room and closed the door behind her.

"Lu-Lu, wait," I followed her to the door, opened it and began to fall. I quickly threw my arms up to the threshold of the door to have something, anything to hang on to while my legs dangled in the air. I panicked and called out to Lucia, telling her I was sorry. I looked around me, I took a gulp and looked down. She had somehow removed the rest of the real world and had me dangling from a door to nowhere.

"It's not *no-where*, it's called *now-here*. See the difference," she half said this in my head and out loud.

"Lucia, get me down." Poor choice of words.

"As you wish!" she obliged.

Lucia let me fall and of course I was screaming like a banshee. I was panicking not knowing what powers could work or if I even had powers being at the mercy of my vindictive grandmother.

"What do you mean by, vindictive? I'm doing what you want!" Lu-Lu said with a chuckle.

"Lucia, help me! Give me back my powers."

"You still have your powers, you big baby! Just flap your wings or whatever it is you do to fly."

I turned into my murder of crows and we floated up to meet Lucia in the clouds. I gathered myself back together into one massive black form of feathers. I played with my different phases of my therianthrope abilities. As the birds merged together, as I became solid, I turned myself into the harpy for a moment and unleashed my talons of death.

"Truce, truce, I'm not going to harm you! You can put away... the claws," she pleaded.

I shifted one more time into my dark angel form. The way I looked when I battled side-by side with Michael.

"Oh, that's what he meant by angel," Lucia looked surprised. She was examining my wings.

"Tell me, you don't fly around town with big giant black wings, do you?" She asked.

"No, I use telekinesis for flying, mostly. It's only been recently that I adopted the angel wings and they look pretty cool," I boasted.

We stood among the clouds on top of the world of endless possibilities. A world Lu-Lu had created.

"So, this is *Now Here*?" I asked her.

Lucia corrected, "Now Here is anywhere *you* want it to be. This is the dreamscape. This is the part where I explain with a long winded, prepared speech about a bunch of magical nonsense or I just need leave you here to your own devices to figure it out. You seem to be doing a pretty good job so far," she started to leave.

"Look, Lucia. I really could use your help. I don't wanna do this on my own. Can you please, please help me?" I begged her to stay.

"All right since you asked so nicely, I'll give you some pointers. I'll get you started but this is *your* world to play with. You can come here and practice anytime, once you study the spells outside, of course. So, you should memorize them. There's a spell for that too…" She stated as she decided to stay.

"Yes, I saw that spell," I replied.

"But that's the one thing to remember; you can't read in dreams. That's how you know if something is real or not," she continued.

"You keep repeating that, is it important?" I asked sarcastically.

"Pay attention, you can get caught up in your dreams. Our emotional turmoil, our memories can come to life in here. And a daydream can turn into a nightmare in the blink of an eye," As she said this Lucia snapped her fingers and the world around us changed from day to night; from pleasant to chaotic. It was glorious.

"I thought you said that you *didn't* prepare a long-winded explanation?" I asked.

"Your dry wit confirms that you are my family," she said as we watched the chaos in awe.

My lust for power was growing and I was salivating for the chance to play in my new wonderland.

"Oh, no, this is *my* playland. This is my world; you're going to have to create your *own* world from scratch," she clapped her hands three times and the whiteness of the clouds quickly consumed and overpowered the color of everything she has created; forming a blank white canvas, a white void.

She gave me a few lessons, she pointed out some books to read, and left me to my own devices to be again creating my own playland, my dream world where I could keep practicing; exercise my power in safety without fear of destroying the outside world.

I began creating a dream world after studying from the books Lucia brought me out of the library for what seemed like a few days. After a couple trial attempts at creating things from memories, from my imagination.

I was ready to invite Lucia into my dreamscape, my dream world. When she came into my humble room I was studying and the concepts of manipulating matter metaphysically in the dream world and then transferring that power into reality.

She said, "Oh that's a great book that'll teach you a lot of good principles. So, what are you going to show me?" She asked excitedly.

I invited her to sit down, I put my hands on her head and told her to close her eyes. I said, "Now open them!" She chuckled and looked around at my room and said, "Silly girl, that's not how it's done! You're supposed to say the incantation. You're supposed to transport me into your dreams so that we could see what you came up with."

"Oh, I thought that I did! How did I do that wrong?! Here let's look it up, what does it say there?" and I showed Lucia the Diary. As Lucia turned the book to look at it, she had to do a double take.

The words were all jumbled, they weren't even words; the letters were unrecognizable, and they kept moving and shifting. Lucia looked up at me in confusion.

"How did you do that?" She asked.

"I can do anything when we're in *my* dreamscape."

Lucia replied, "Wait, we're already here? I expected something more grandiose. Something a lot more interesting than a dark room where we keep our weapons and torture people."

"Oh, I forgot to turn on the lights!" I turned up the oil lamp in the dark, it turned into daylight like the dawning of a new sun and my bed sat on a cliff side by a tree overlooking the world that I created.

We stood up and looked upon the dreamworld I crafted. There was a great valley and a river that separated the daytime from the night. Beautiful meadows with a lush forest, creatures of my own creation lived on that side. On the night-time side was a more perilous landscape of deadly disease-ridden swaps with black water and dead trees with menacing branches of thorns briers. Mold and fungus with dark creatures living inside the woods. A towering volcano raging and creating smoke and magma. The volcano's ash cloud created a perpetual thunderstorm over the landscape behind it.

Lu-Lu clapped her hands in excitement and exclaimed, "All this is wonderful sweetheart! You did such a good job. I like how you separated the light from the dark," she was admiring my world.

"Yeah, I like to keep things simple; black-and-white and compartmentalize. There is the gray area where the two sides meet in the middle," I said.

"Well, this is a great start, and you've done a great job establishing a world where you can practice and play; but it feels a little cramped. I think it could be bigger. Do you mind?" Lucia said as she was rolling up her sleeves, getting ready to do some magic.

I told her, "Knock yourself out!"

Lucia chanted something in Latin that sounded like 'expand your horizons' and the cliff seemed to stay where it was as the background landscapes appeared to push and expand out. The horizon truly did expand, the river now poured out into an ocean instead of just off into a messed-up blankness. The mountains beyond the volcano created a whole other wilderness vastly more populated with possibilities.

Cities and metropolitan areas; large, spacious buildings strung through the mountainous landscapes of the darker side. Towards the sunny side she was adding some beautiful rolling hills where the sun comes up to the east. Beautiful clouds on the horizon expanded over the forest created great grandiose canyons. She created lakes, fishing villages and small frontier towns. Prairies filled with wildflowers to the south of my dream world.

Lucia created a winter wonderland northeast that transitioned well from a pine forest and then became a frozen tun-

281

dra of misery as it crossed into the borders of the dark and dreary wilderness. She used the Volcano too. She took my hand and said, "Here, let me show you something else."

And we flew across the sky to the south out over the river and across the ocean to the coastline to watch her use the volcanic activity to create islands in the sea and form a tropical paradise. We flew above the world and oversaw our creations. We made our way back to the cliffside and landed on my bed.

Lucia said, "Well, this has been great fun, and this is a good beginning for you. Now you should be able to explore powers; practice your spells, battle whatever you want. Play out scenarios; relive memories, master yourself and your gifts safely."

"What, you don't think I can practice magic safely in the real world?" I asked exasperatedly.

"Always remember that this world is *not* real. Here lies the real danger. I've seen people get lost in fantasies, leaving them to believe it is reality. I suggest when you wake up from your dreams, being in here practicing, that you write it down in *your* Diary," Lucia continued saying.

"Write the things that I've learned for the day, in my Diary?" I asked to clarify.

"Yes, making any notes and references to other volumes of study, or other spells to practice so that others may learn from your notes," Lucia pulled us from the dream by turning myself toward the sun and restoring the darkness to my room making the only light come from the oil lamp.

Lucia continued, "The other thing you'll find when you wake up from dream-scaping and creating is that you'll be extremely famished. I've got food prepared if you come downstairs, and we can talk about the things you've learned."

During lunch we had a good conversation. Lu-Lu encouraged me to write my thoughts in the Diary before I went back into the dreamscape. Her phone rang, it was my mother. It was so nice to hear her voice. She and my father were leaving the old apartment to live in a bigger house. She was wondering if 'Grandma Lu-Lu' wanted to come sit with the baby and visit while they got settled back at their *new* house, I mean, at my old house.

Once she was done with the phone call, I begged her to let me come with her to see the baby even if I was a shadow or a ghost, a doppelgänger, whatever it was.

"I'd love to see Mom and Dad again," I begged.

Lucia stopped me and said, "Well, sweetheart, I know you *want* to see your parents, but *should* you? I just worry about exposing you to them too soon."

"Fine," I pouted. I wasn't happy about it.

"Sometime, maybe after the funeral, then I'll introduce you as a 'distant cousin' who has come for some training. Then it won't be so weird that there's a strange presence in their new house; or some ghostly girl hanging out with me. Maybe since the baby seems to be able to see you, she could be having memories that are invoked by déjà vu? I promise, after the funeral, I will introduce you as a great niece or distant cousin something, and we will go from there," Lucia said.

I agreed but I wasn't happy about it. With that she had left the house and I went back to my room in the study. I returned to the dreamscape to continue to expand my world of dreams and nightmares.

I would lose track of time when I'm playing in my dreamscape. Days, hours, none of that matters. Eating, sleeping and all of that stuff no longer mattered. Not when shear power is surging through my veins. Knowing that everything will be easier having powers. After a while, who knows how long, Lucia came to visit me in my little world.

She had me set up a 'doorway' in my dreamscape that she could access. She had explained, "It's kind of how I break into people's minds."

You use your hypnotic stare to weaken the person; make them more receptible, and then you ask them to open the door. Lu-Lu came through the door and was astonished to see my progress. I was in the middle of designing something new, a creature that would graze in the meadows; but I was having a hard time keeping them from starving to death. She said, "Here, let me take a look, maybe I can help."

Lucia studied my creature like a seasoned veterinarian. "There's your problem, you've made this thing's lower jaw too big! He can't keep enough food in his mouth to stay alive. See, it's not closing here. I'll go find you a couple more books on creature and anatomy. There's a principle in it called 'form follows function.' Everything has a reason, every aspect of our being has a purpose. Everything was engineered by a great designer and architect. Every detail in mind."

"So, you and I; we had this conversation before in the future and I asked you about God. You said that you believed in a supreme being," I said as she was altering my odd creature.

Lucia said, "Well, in all my adventures and everything I've done; I know there's always somebody watching out for me. Somebody that created all of us and has given us all some purpose. I don't believe that people that are born with special powers, gifts like we have; wielding magic, manipulate reality, that we are inherently evil or an abomination. Any tool can be used for good or evil; it's all based on the intent of your heart. I think that we all will be judged when everything's all said and done."

Lu-Lu excused herself from my dream and got me a book to help me correct my anatomical mistakes. Good and evil, had me thinking about the Gor-Nok; what led him to become the way he is?

Lu-Lu returned, "I left a book on your dresser near your desk. Let me see if I can fix this for you." She made the corrections to my small bovine creature and breathed a breath of life into it, then whispered something in its ear.

I asked her, "What did you just do?"

"So, I told it to go graze. You have to tell these things what they're supposed to do. They need to know the measure of their creation. If you're going to make these things to populate your dreamscape in your world, they have to have a purpose. You have to give them something they're supposed to be doing otherwise they will create their own destiny; their own reason for living," she explained.

"Interesting," I said.

I was still busy thinking when she asked me, "So what are we creating next?"

"Well, I've been thinking about creating a copy of the monster," I said not knowing how she would react.

That seemed to distraught Lu-Lu. She said, "No, no, no, no, no! I forbid it! I can't have you creating the thing that killed my husband! I don't want to see it. I don't want it in here, as well. It's bad enough that I'm having nightmares about it already."

"Wait, you're having nightmares about it?! So, what would be the harm in having something that *I* can practice with?" I argued.

She said, "The danger lies in creating an unconscious gateway for this creature to invade your mind and to start gaining control, power, and influence over you. Turning your nightmares against you. No, I forbid it, all right."

"So, what should we do instead?" I asked.

"Have you identified your Nightmare Nix? You can start by fighting it with your Daydream Nix. It can act as a good sparring partner too. Have you identified *either* of them yet?" Lucia asked.

"Wait. What, they're something that I've created? Oh yeah, a part of your subconscious mind is telling you what is in control of your good side and what was in control of your dark side," I recalled from studying the Diary.

"Yes, your Daydream or your Nightmare are part of you. And you've got to name them. Here in your dreamscape and your nightmare land. You figured out the land of their birth but who is running those two places or is it just chaos? Are they still fighting for leadership?" Lucia asked. I had not thought too much about it.

"I don't know, I just started all this," I said.

"You've got to get this sorted out or else it will all become chaos," she told me to go back and read up on some things and leave my dreams where they are at for now and we exited my dreamscape.

Lucia got a call from Harry. He had succeeded in acquiring a 'body' to bury in place of Michael. He had worked his own magic through his profession as a lawyer and performed a miracle of bringing Michael back into the country after being dead. He had used one of the bodies that was found of the victims of the Gor-Nok. It had been burned, charred until it was unrecognizable.

"Embalming practices aren't the same here as there," Harry explained. They burned the bodies to be rid of the demons. The body was a little withered to the point where we decided to do a closed casket. We would have done that anyways because it wasn't Michael. We were telling people that his body was "chewed upon by wild animals before we were able to find it at all."

Harry had said at the funeral that, "Michael would have liked it that way. The idea of giving his life and his body back to the animals that he admired so much. Animals that he hunted because of their beauty and his appreciation of their power. And with that, it is my great honor to announce the future addition of the Metro Natural History Museum. It will be called the Michael Lamia-Great Hunter Exhibit in their Wild Safari Wing. Thank You."

There was an awkward applause to Harry's grandstanding. The Priest had said some kindly words that made me wonder if Michael and Lucia had been attending church like regular people. I didn't really know too much about their beliefs until I got tangled into their world of magic and monsters. It would've been nice to know my grandfather more. I'm grateful for the time that I got to spend with him. I appreciate the opportunities and experiences that I got with him thanks to my adventures through time and our battle together against our enemy the Gor-Nok.

Lu-Lu had allowed me to be at the funeral. I sat amongst the mourners in the row behind the family. I got to see my mom and dad with their new baby. I was making faces at the baby whenever she would sneak a peek at me. Baby Nonabel was definitely curious about who I was and why I was there. She could definitely see me, as me, even if the temporary magical restrictions were removed so I could be there. I was disguised as a family member in the flesh, and as additional security, if the need arises.

Mom and Dad had gotten up to pay their respects, and Lu-Lu was holding baby Nonabel so that my mother could weep and mourn without drizzling tears on the baby. Grandma Lu-Lu had been up now, holding the baby as she was talking to grandpa's coffin. The baby started crying for some reason, I heard the call of a passing raven nearby which made me uneasy. I recalled this memory. My goosebumps went off, maybe it was baby me that was upset about something.

Something wasn't right. Someone who was not supposed to be there was nearby, and I don't think she was worried about me. She was fine with me being there. The raven cawed again its warning. I was beginning to understand their language; being part of them. I think it was Michael's pet Twilight mourning her master. Later I had been looking around the forest near the tree line after Michael's coffin was deposited in its place and the mourners were starting to depart, when someone tapped me on the shoulder.

It was Victoria, I gasped a little. Lucia was scared that I would talk to her and forbade me to do it. *I* was petrified that Victoria would be able to see through my lies. I was scared I would mess up somehow revealing too much of who I was. She had introduced herself. We were giggling about how the baby seemed to like me. She thought it was curious how familiar I seemed.

She doesn't recognize me and asked if I was a family

member. I pretended that I could only speak Italian, forgetting that Mom had spent a semester abroad, when she met Dad. I tried to excuse myself to leave, that's when Lu-Lu stepped in to introduce me as a niece of hers. She said I was a distant cousin of Victoria's and gave me the name of one of her aunts, Lily; the one that taught her magic.

Lucia had handed baby Nonabel to me and was explaining the living conditions and arrangement of my education with Victoria. That I would be staying with her at the farm indefinitely, especially now since Michael's passing.

"Having family around would be nice?!" Victoria said. That would help Lu-Lu a lot since Mom and Dad moved so far away. Baby Nonabel kept trying to touch my face or touch my hands. Luckily, I had worn gloves to keep magical people like my mother and the baby from accidentally touching me and seeing more than they are meant to see.

Mom kept wondering who I was; I could feel her probing me. Being a familiar, yet a new face, she was suspicious enough. The baby thought it was a game. I would push her hand back into her blanket and she giggled. Then she put her hand back up to try to touch my face. She was getting really angry. She reached out to touch me. I moved my hand to push her arm back in; then I saw her eyes flare-up a beautiful purple.

She was using magic; it took me a second to understand what she had done to me. I wouldn't have noticed because I was trying to listen to Mom and Lucia's conversation. I was too caught up in what they were saying to notice that baby Nonabel had frozen my movements. I couldn't move my head, I couldn't feel my hand, the baby giggled at her success at controlling me. She succeeded in touching my face. I was so terrified as I felt her tiny hand touch my face.

I swear that I was sweating out of my eyeballs. I was so worried about what images this baby was going to be able to pull from my mind. Memories I have endured from a life filled with so much pain. I had to block her out, and I blocked out as much as I could; every ounce of effort that I could muster in my paralyze state.

She made the connection from my mind to her mind. The same shock and fear were upon her face that was on mine. I swear I heard her think, "He is here, right now! He is here!" I got a flash in my mind of the Gor-Nok; that flash terrified the baby and she started to cry.

I was released from my paralysis and Lu-Lu grabbed the baby immediately. I sent the nearby raven that was calling to look for something moving.

Victoria asked, "Did something happen?"

"She is OK," I said as I smiled sheepishly.

Something was making my birds afraid. We said our goodbyes and told Victoria that we would see her at the house for the reception. We made our way back to the car.

I told Lu-Lu, "Something's not right. I got a vision; I received an impression he's here. *It* is here!"

She released me from my invisible bonds and told me to go. "Call for help, if you need any, honey," Lucia said as she got into her car. I called up some flowers to my hands from other graves, to pretend like I was someone there to visit a grave as I looked around for any suspicious people.

I have battled the Gor-Nok in the past, in dreams and memories. The impressions could have been déjà vu warnings from the future calling back to my mind. Or me from the future telling myself in the past, the present, wherever I'm at, a warning. Sometime had passed and it was getting late. I wandered off into the trees and turned into my birds to hide away my presence and to increase my ability to see; to keep an eye on the graveyard.

I took Twilight from the flock, my Twilight, and sent her through the shadows, through the vortex, back to the house to pass a warning on to Lucia. This was a way to be able to convey messages without attracting too much attention. I 'cawed' to her, through Twilight, "All clear, all clear. Wait here, all night, not right."

I waited in the woods, knowing something was not right.

Lu-Lu would communicate to me from time to time, stuffing crackers into my cage. We would *think* messages to each other, it was rather convenient. Lu-Lu was telling me it was getting late, and that I was missing the party. Victoria was asking questions about 'Lily' and wanted to know where I would be staying while at the farmhouse. Lucia had told her that I would be staying in *her* old room.

Harry was talking about plans for a new wing to be added to the town's museum, the natural history section. It was Michael's charity foundation. Harry loved talking about that kind of crap. It was kind of fun having a set of eyes and ears at the party and not having to be 'at the party' as a socially awkward, introverted 18-year-old; especially since everyone I knew didn't know me. They had no memory of who I was or any of our experiences together and the life that we've already lived. They would have easily forgotten me as soon as I walked away; thanks to the curse of being a doppelgänger. I was basically déjà vu.

Lu-Lu was asking me questions in her mind.

How are you able to keep track of what's happening at the party and also what's happening at the cemetery?

It's like having multiple monitors or security cameras going at once. I watch for movement. I'm looking for anything out of the ordinary and I've also learned to pass the Seer's Sight to the eyes of my birds; giving each of them the ability to change to different visual spectrums. I pushed the thought to her mind.

"Wow, I see! That's pretty neat! You're going to need to show me how to do that sometime, she thought.

Lucia begged me to come back to the party. "At least to see the baby."

I told her, "It's probably for the best that I minimize my contact with *me* and with my mother." But I assured her that I would be coming home soon after everything calmed down at the house.

Lucia went back to entertaining guests and socializing

and I returned my focus to my vigilante patrol of the cemetery. Fog was rolling in as the sunset and dusk took over. More creatures were scurrying from the woods across the grass looking for things to eat. Flowers, nuts, and berries. Exposing themselves to the open; I could feel their little heartbeats, I could feel the fear, as though someone was watching them. I was watching them. I was causing them to fear.

I could very well *be* the most dangerous thing out here. I couldn't tell if it was the fear that *I* was feeling from the animals or if it was coming from someone else. I couldn't distinguish their fear from my own indulgence of the emotion as my goosebumps flared up, warning me of danger.

The fog wasn't the problem at all. That wasn't what was scaring the animals; it was him. Somehow, the Gor-Nok had arrived. I don't know if we had left a doorway open. A crossing through space and time. I don't know if he had hitched a ride onto the boat that brought the 'remains', could have happened like that. He could have *been* the body. The last blow I delivered to him could have charred his flesh pretty good; but there he was and there was Twilight.

I saw myself shifting forms, trying to do the transformation; but there was not enough of us around to help her. I sent my birds off to meet with her and give her reinforcement. It was the most uncomfortable feeling. I felt half of my soul spilling out of me, pouring into an empty vase, an empty vessel. While the rest of me felt as though I was floating suspended in space and time. I relived the whole battle, feeling just as weak, just as helpless, doing what I could before I blacked out.

When I came to, Lu-Lu was helping me up off the floor. I had unintentionally emerged from my Twilight in the front room of the farmhouse.

"Lucky for you, everyone's gone home," she chuckled as she helped me to stand. I gasped for air as I was solidifying from feathers and claws.

"He's here! He was at the cemetery. I fought him the best I could, but I'm only functioning at half strength, half power. I don't know what happened," I panicked.

"Slow down, let's go to the study, you can tell me over a nice cup of tea. It will calm your nerves," Lucia said as we went upstairs. I spent the rest of the evening describing my fight, my experience; telling her that I have relived this event before.

"It was a dream to me the first time and it seemed like the same problem was happening. I was functioning at half-power, but I think I know what I did wrong this time. I was trying to help a past version of me who wasn't all there to begin with. I should be able to function fully if I don't interact with my past self, or an astral projection of myself," I said between sips of tea.

"Yes," Lu-Lu assured me that would be the safest idea, and everything would be fine. "We will be ready for him if he tries to attack. You won't be alone, not this time."

I began to create greater details in my dreamscape. I even duplicated the town and re-created the street where I grew up. Where my dad taught me how to ride a bike, and where I fell and scraped my knee for the first time. The little pond in the neighborhood where I taught Jesse and Zatie how to hunt toads. I was creating people from memory, names to their faces and faces to the faceless. Lucia had forbidden me to create the murderer, the monster, my enemy. So, I created new ones, other monsters to fight; but nothing as cunning, as devious, as endless, or as inescapable as someone that harnesses the power of fear or nightmares against us.

Lu-Lu had come to visit my dreamworld, making snide comments about how I had spent more of my time here than in reality. She reminded me that, "There is a whole world out there of real people and real experiences."

I reminded her that, "I am not from this time! This is not my world! This dreamscape, this reality, is *my* reality. I'm better off hiding in here than messing things up out there." As I got angry, my world reacted.

The waves crashed harder, the volcano got stronger, the storms and hurricanes became more powerful. The happiness and sunshine seemed to die in my world. Lucia expressed that she just wanted me to be happy and wanted me to have some kind of life. She felt that I should interact with real people more often. So, she told me that I had a playdate.

She invited Harry to spar with me, but I told her that if I wanted to spar with another therianthrope, then I would fight Dominic in the woods at night when she was asleep and didn't know that I would sneak out. I kind of yelled it at her. She felt kind of hurt realizing that I did that.

"Well, it was a thought. Perhaps interacting with some-body that *does* know you exist, even just rarely would be bet-ter than not at all," she continued that if I really wanted to conquer my demons, I needed to conquer the Nix of my night-mares.

"It's the embodiment of everything that you fear," and she asked me if I had figured out what that was yet.

I said, "Oh yeah, I kinda found out what my fears were actually in your future with my past," I activated a small thun-derstorm just above my hand with a tiny bolt of lightning.

Lu-Lu chuckled, "There's no way, there's no way that lit-tle bolt of lightning is your nightmare!"

I said, "So, you believe that it has to be large and out of control? Look, Lu-Lu, I've had lotta time on my hands con-quering this fear. I've been afraid of sudden drastic, cata-strophic changes in my life that could happen in a blink of an eye, and I've come to realize how very small these moments are. I cannot escape it. How they could happen at any time, but I can choose to reduce the magnitude and increase my understanding of life, time, and eternity then focus it into one tiny event."

She said, "Wow, that was deep; but you *do* spend way too much time in here. We need to get you some real people to interact with. I'll come and spar with you from time to time, soon. Sorry, I've just been so busy visiting with Victoria. I'm trying to get her to reconsider letting me teach the kids magic. Then she gets mad, but she has allowed me to get to have them come over during the summer; and I said that would be fine, but I am busy sometimes."

I asked her, "What are you busy with?"

She reluctantly told me that she started seeing someone. "It was so unexpected! Not even *I* could've foreseen it!" She wasn't even thinking about it; to even look forward, to worry about it, to prepare for.

"There's just something about him, reminds me of Michael," she sighed before continuing. "His strength, his masculinity, his bravery, his ability to take control of the situation; being assertive, aggressive, but not too aggressive, but stern. He has always been a friend. He understands our world, he understands me, and he's been there in my life. Wow! A lot of my life."

As she continued swooning, I probed her mind; it didn't take much. I understood that she was avoiding saying Mr. Wonderful's name for a reason. All the things that she was saying reminded me of someone. Resembled someone. A yearning she had, someone to help her to overcome her loss.

"I think I'm gonna be sick, you're in love with Harry?!" I started not really wanting to know the answer.

Lucia blushed and fanned away vapors.

"Oh, God, I'm going to puke. He's half your age?!" I said shocked, trying not to dry-heave.

Lucia corrected me, "He only *looks* half my age. He's actually just as old as Michael, maybe even a little older if you've gone back and read the entries..."

I stopped her right there. "Yeah, yeah, I know who Harry is. I read about when Grandpa saved him. That Harry was bit by a crocodile and that it kind of freezes you in time being a therianthrope."

Lucia's eyes got kind of excited when she realized something, "Hey, maybe that's why you haven't changed over the last few years?! Because you've been a therianthrope, a were-rook."

I sighed and said, "Maybe, but I think it *does* have something to do with being here, because of time travel."

"Not a whole lot of people have done this or lived it to keep notes about it. You should do that," Lu-Lu said.

"Yeah, I have written that down in the entry. Hey, don't change the subject! Do you love Harry?!" I asked.

Lucia admitted it, she was blushing like a schoolgirl.

I told her to get out; "get out of my dream, keep this out of here!" She made birds flutter in and sing, and I was starting to get sick. I ended the dreamscape and brought us back to reality.

Lucia said, "Oh, but that does remind me, Vicki's coming over with the kids."

I sighed in exasperation, and groaned, "UGH, but they're all in diapers!" I knew it was useless to try to change her mind. She knew I didn't want to do this.

"I don't know, it could be fun. Just hear me out. Younger you is almost potty trained; we just have to keep an eye on her. The other two..."

"Yeah, yeah, it's just when one has a diaper problem, you change the other one, it's just déjà vu," I was annoyed.

"Just like raising the same kid, it's not that hard," she said in agreement.

"Why are you telling me all this? Aren't you gonna be around?" I was worried, but I still wanted to know.

"Actually, that brings me back to the topic of Harry. I have a date," Lucia said excitedly.

I growled quietly but I also agreed to babysit the kids. "All right, fine." We were finishing each other's sentences. We were fairly easy roommates to live with. We understood each other's likes and dislikes. I thought it was fine for me to watch the kids. I was, actually, kind of excited for Lucia to be happy again; but still, at the same time, very nauseated that she was dating Harry. Someone that I had kissed in the future and I must never let her know that. I did everything I could to not think that out loud.

Entry #13

Life is a Dream

Life continues; I keep learning and growing as time marches on. I know that I'm becoming increasingly addicted again to magic. I have been locking me up in my dream world for days at a time. Sending parts of my rookery out to forage and hunt while the rest of me was dreaming. Lucia became concerned; mostly when I have ravens serving me as messengers and pizza delivery birds. Lucia expressed that she understands what I'm going through; that I have had some difficult things to process.

I got mad and asked Lucia, "How could you possibly understand?! I haven't felt time pass. I haven't felt myself age physically, but my soul feels older!"

"Yes, it's called maturity; you're maturing. I'm proud of who you are becoming. I feel the future is safe in your hands. Also, I'm looking forward to the day when I can pass my power on to you," Lucia proudly exclaimed as she hugged me warmly.

Knowing the future is sometimes a burden that I feel I only bear. I snuck out, a lot. I got through Lucia's defenses, I got past charms and incantations. I began to know more and understand more than she thought I knew, and I wanted to catch the murderer. But he's cautious now. He knows we're looking for him, he knows there's more of us. He's still out there, he's just hiding; he's afraid. I kept a raven on constant vigil out by the cemetery. It seemed to be where he likes to hunt.

We let Dominic live in the forest. I assured Lu-Lu that he would be safe, and we placed incantations around the borders of our land to keep him in and the unwanted things out. I set watch-ravens everywhere, as an early warning system. I did the math; if I weighed somewhere in a healthy neighborhood of 'just enough' and in between 'none of your business,' then I could afford to let out a couple dozen or so ravens before I became too skinny to function.

It gave me a sense of security, knowing I could be everywhere at once, sort of. I found myself often going to Michael's grave, where we placed the scarecrow as a marker by the pond. It was a good place to come up for air to gain strength and perspective on reality. Plus, I would often need to use some of his hallowed ground to heal from 'Practicing'. I spent the sunsets talking to him and telling him about my life as I wrote in the Diary.

Visiting him became a routine thing for Lucia and me, to enjoy the sunset out there with him.

I asked her once, "Why his soul, why his spirit or his ghost whatever you want to call it, wouldn't come to visit us?" I told her I had been reading about 'familiar spirits' and ancestors watching over us.

"He's around. I sense him and feel him probably more than you do," Lucia pondered.

"Ha, you think so?" I chuckled.

"I see him every time you smile; I see him in your strength. I see him in your arrogance and in your determination. I see him in you when we argue, the way you won't give up. I see him live on through you," Lucia shared her observa-

298

tions with me. We met there every once in a while, just to check in and chat.

I was busy being me and she was busy living. She was happy, she was aging, and Harry didn't care. I tried to avoid them. I think that Lu-Lu had hypnotized him to forget me, or the effects of the Doppelgänger was consistently making him forget that I was someone else from somewhere else, living on borrowed time.

Time passes on and life is a dream. Summers came and went; and with them the grandkids. They grow up so fast! One moment, they're a helpless baby in your arms as fragile as a glass. And would shatter if you dropped them. The next moment they're stubborn little snots, running around the farm casting spells at each other.

In hindsight, maybe I should not have shown them those spells. I would erase their memory before they went home. I became 'Auntie Lily' to Zatie, Jesse, and little me. Nonabel hated to be called by her name. Lucia hardly used it; so, I called her 'Nona' for short. She seemed to like that better.

Five years have passed; five summers come and gone. I adored their visits. I enjoyed the brief catching up moments Victoria felt she needed to have with me whenever she would drop off the kids. Lucia and Harry knew I was uncomfortable with their 'cuddling' so I planted the thought in Victoria's mind via my messenger ravens to 'drop-off the kids.' Mostly because I knew that Lu-Lu hated being called 'Grandma,' especially around Harry. It reminded her of her outward aging as Harry never could age; and she would be ashamed. They would either leave or she would kick him out.

I tried to not engage into prying conversations with Victoria and I would let the doppelgänger power overwhelm her curiosity. Dad, I hardly talked about Dad. He was mostly focused on work and his career. He was friendly and nice enough; but he was kind of quiet and reserved. I think Mom saw him as the shy kid in the back of the class and thought he needed a friend. I knew he had bounced around foster homes growing up. He didn't know much about his own past. He thought it was more important to focus on the future.

That's what drove his ambition to continue schooling and pursue career advancements that took him and Mom away often. Which led them back to Grandma's house as a convenient place not too far away where they can ditch us kids on weekends and summers.

Whenever they felt like they needed to get away from the burdens of being adults and couldn't handle all of us kids. Besides, the farm had much cooler stuff to do for kids. We had animals, forests, ponds, monsters, magic, trap doors, secret passageways, dungeons, and Lu-Lu's library. I shared my dreamscapes and whatever adventures I decided I was going to take them on.

I knew they wouldn't remember it because I didn't remember it; not the way that I did growing up. I know it's fuzzy, hazy, so it must've been magic that was keeping us from remembering these memories; that must've been me erasing their little minds. At first, I felt so sorry for them. Their sad little faces as I took away their happy memories from their brains and stored them into tiny little jars, to save them in my dreamscape.

I planned to give them back to them someday when the time is right or as the need arises. During the rest of the week, I played during my vigilante outings, transitioning between different strategic positions guarded by my watch birds. I was looking for clues of his activities. He thought he was being careful, he thought he could hide it. Hide the monster that he was. But I was on to him; I knew what he was up to. I tried to catch him a couple times.

I relived some of our battles that I had had before from dreams and memories. Waking from dreams not knowing where or when I was, then finding myself at the cemetery again different points in reality fighting different versions of him. I was starting to worry that he was becoming *my nightmare Nix*, my nemesis. I have conquered my fears of lightning, which was my first fear, and I got to relive that memory from that summer again.

Lucia and I had convinced Victor and Victoria to go with us to have a picnic. Lucia socialized and I was being a typical teenager trying to avoid it. Especially with my conditions and predicaments. Harry was talking to Victor about guy stuff, ambitious guy stuff. Like stocks or portfolios and what-not of the financial kind. The kids had been playing hide-and-seek in the woods and lost track of where we were. They did not know what time it was and where they were supposed to be.

I could sense something coming; I can feel the barometric pressure rising, the winds changing, and a storm brewing. I could feel my younger self paralyzing in tears somewhere near. Trying to hide under the tree as a way to stay safe from the storm. I sent some ravens to watch her, to find her for now. All I could see was the memories from her cowardly eyes huddled in her hands. Begging for the storm to go away, praying for help. The adults were gathering up the picnic items and Lucia sent Harry and Victor to look for the kids. Victoria asked Lucia where I had gone; they hadn't noticed me when I slipped away. Part of the advantage of being a doppelgänger I can become invisible, unnoticeable whenever I want.

My birds swept through the forest, in the meadows by the pond, looking by the river, searching, scouring for any evidence of little Nona. We found the other kids and guided them back to their dad, Victor. Victor told Harry to head back to the car with the kids and he kept calling my name. I felt so lost, I felt so alone, cold, weak, helpless, little, and insignificant.

The hairs on my tiny arms stood up on their own. My goosebumps flared, my frizzy hair was released from the bonds of gravity, and floating away from my head, from *her* head. I was feeling everything that she was feeling, trying to help her, so that she didn't have to bear the burden of the trauma alone.

A lone bolt of lightning struck the tree in the meadow with no sound. Just pure, white, tingling light filling my every nerve; it took the breath right out of me. Victor came up behind me in the forest as the sound arrived, startling me. **KKka-rackkk-baba-Ba-DOOM!!**

"Lily, have you seen her?!" I pointed towards the tree. He exclaimed, "Dear God, no!"

I told him, "You might want to... wait. Until the storm passed," but he didn't listen. Bolt after bolt kept striking. Occasionally hitting the lone oak tree where Nonabel hid. This was my most terrifying moment in my life! The lightning was very frightening and fascinating. If you don't understand it, if you don't appreciate its beauty, if you don't know how to keep yourself safe, it can be terrifying. But because it is one of my greatest weapons and my favorite addiction; I have lost all fear of it. Nonabel's powers were increasing, they were blossoming as she got older. Erasing her mind of all the memories and lessons wasn't stopping her. She was unintentionally attracting these beacons of light so that we could find her in the dark storm. This was all her.

Faded memories. After comforting little me after the family reunited, they all had a good laugh at her expense in the car. I remember how mean my little brother was, making fun of me.

He said mockingly, "Nonabel's afraid, she is not able to play she's scared and runs away. Nonabel is afraid, she runs away, and she's not able to face it."

I rode home crying in the back of both vehicles; I was sharing her tears across the years. Little me was still weeping, shaking, terrified; and older me was releasing repressed memories. Lucia reached her hand back to touch me. She asked if I was OK. I nodded, not consoled, as I thought *I could've stopped it*. But I knew I had to relive it.

I buried myself in my anguish by retreating to my dreamscape. Lucia wanted to comfort me. She even sent Harry home for the evening. But I told her I just wanted to be alone.

She found me anyway. Found me in my dreams. Lucia came across the meadow, at the base of the fallen tree. The old oak tree; at least in my mind, it was not like the one from memory. This one was split in two representing: the end of my innocence, and the beginning of my journey to conquer my fears.

Also, for added cool special effects I had a perpetual lightning bolt shooting from the clouds and back up at the sky. I thought it was cool.

"I thought I'd find you here," Lucia said she sat next to me at the base of the tree.

I told her that, "It's where I like to go to brainstorm," she chuckled at my pun. I was still crying but it was hard to cry when she was making me laugh. She looked across the landscape of my mind.

"Wow, honey!" she remarked. "Wow, you've been busy. I mean the detail is remarkable."

"I am in here every day, all day. Also, every night. This is where I live. My body may be out there, but my heart and soul are here. I relive memories here. I use this as a way to keep track of events, so I don't lose my mind waiting for me to catch back up with time."

I took her down to the little neighborhoods, to stroll down Memory Lane. "It's comforting to know the kids now that they're getting older. I know where they are, I know that they're safe for now," I said.

"Your Mother and Father can protect them. They're both quite very skilled for what little they know."

"Yes, so what does my dad know?" I asked.

"Actually, fairly little. Somehow, Victoria has kept him entirely in the dark. She's quite the hypocrite; because she's got to be erasing his mind," Lucia stated.

"There's no way they can have a house full of magical children and I still lived a normal life. I mean you've seen those little terrors, haven't you?!" I asked.

"Yes! When they're here, it's like some curse has been lifted from them and they're free to act on their magical impulses. She must be controlling all of them at home too," she pondered.

"And I lived a normal life," I said vacantly.

"Anyways, since you relived your nightmares today, I wanted to talk to you about your daydream Nix; have you identified *that one* yet?" Lucia asked me.

"Well, that is difficult. I've created all these creatures and I have all these memories and things. I mean, how am I supposed to find it if I'm making all the stuff. If I'm projecting archaic emotions and archetypes from my psyche, into my psyche to entertain me. How am I supposed to know what of all these creatures I've created on my own is the living embodiment of all the things I love?" I responded.

"Well, well, well. Someone has been reading! Here, I'll help. I'm just going to go through the list. What is the thing you love the most?" She prompted.

"Well, I love to fly, it's one of my favorite powers. I love power, but we've already established that lightning was my nightmare nix. So, it can't be more lightning." I said as we went over the list.

"No, no, it can't be that. What's your favorite color? You're always wearing black, it is black, right?" She asked.

"Yeah, that's pretty much my favorite color."

"So, now what is black and flies?" All the answers were right in front of my face and I manifested a raven from my hair and had it land in my hands.

"So, you're Nix is your totem? That's simple enough," she mused.

"I'm keeping with a theme. But what do I do with the Daydream Nix? What was it supposed to help me accomplish?" I asked her.

"Well, you're supposed to help *it* grow; supposed to give it nourishment. Care for it like a baby."

With that thought, my Nix began to grow larger. It became human-like. It was a small fetus, like a baby. It still had feathers, but it had a toddler's head and body; with the round,

304

plump belly and big chubby arms and legs, hands with stubby fingers and arms with long feathers hanging down like cowboy tassels. And it looked up at me and cawed, "Mama."

Lu-Lu and I both, "Ooo-ed" and "Aww-ed." Lucia kissed me on the forehead and said, "Thank you."

I asked her, "Why, what did I do?"

"I am grateful that I get to watch you grow."

I enjoyed the next few years raising my little were-rook, Daydream Nix-totem thingy, or my little man bird 'Dusk.' I figured since I already had a female bird named 'Twilight,' that this little man would be named Dusk. He was definitely a little man; he began to talk more as time passed. He learned more and grew stronger. He had a raspy old codger's voice and somehow found a monocle and a top hat. When I was away for menial, mundane things like showering and eating; Dusk liked to occupy his time with improving his wardrobe. He had matching spats over his talons and liked to carry a cane not because he needed to, just because it was in fashion.

He attended all the high society parties that were held in the nicer part of town of my dreams. These were the strange things that occurred on their own in my dreams; events that I was not aware of but always welcome to attend as an honored guest. It was my world of course and they all worship me as the Goddess that I am. I would send my Daydream Nix on small missions.

Tiny little epic quest to help strengthen the Nix's confidence. I guess he was the embodiment of my masculine side; the aggression and testosterone and he kept it fairly under wraps. He was quite a gentleman and I felt like my little gentleman was always challenging people to duels by slapping them with a glove; or he would duel with pistols at dawn. There were whole towns and villages of creatures like this small midget. Everyone was baby size totems-creatures of different kinds. Having our basic personalities, but animal-like qualities. Just baby were-creatures living little lives in a

little town in my little mind and I got to enjoy it. It was my little hideaway, my way that I could live a life over the last dozen
years.

I was beginning to lose track of the days. What day of the
week it was, what month it was, didn't know what year it was?
I missed holidays, important family moments and memories.
When Lu-Lu was out without me, the kids would ask, "Where
Auntie Lily?"

She would tell them that I came back home to Italy from
time to time to visit distant family. The truth of the matter
was I had issues and problems and addictions and yearnings
that I couldn't satisfy as a doppelgänger. As a creature out of
sync with reality. My boyfriend, in this time period was way
too young for me to date, and the guy I was cheating on him
with, was way too old and dating my elderly grandmother and
my life is kind of messed up; and the only way to deal with
my loneliness was to be alone and hang out with my myself.
Amusing me with my own imaginations.

Being alone is not all that it's cracked up to be. Yeah, I
had got Lu-Lu. I may get to hang out with her and Harry if I
can stomach it. Yeah, I had got the grandkids. They're always
fun but their visits became fewer and even farther between
because of being in school and Mom and Dad are home with
them more often. Lu-Lu pushed that younger me begin formal
magical training. Victoria and Lucia argued and had a pretty
bad falling out. Those regrets, that stress, anxiety, her worries that she didn't have enough time to train and prepare a
younger me to become older me, made her angry and stressed
out. I caught her sneaking out for a smoke. She thought I
didn't notice, I noticed everything.

There are too many of me that just live outside of me as
independent agents. Too many of my ravens out watching the
land in the skies, watching the ground, watching the graves;
constantly watching. I began to worry that the monster had
somehow found a way to escape my attention. I thought for

certain that he had taken up residence underneath my grandfather's coffin; it could've been a memory. Yes, it could have been a dream of symbolic imagery. A dream I could've misunderstood, what I was saying. But I swear that's where he was hiding.

From what I had gathered in my reconnaissance missions, he would return to the cemetery at the same time at dusk so there must be some contractual obligation to return at that time. I had my birds out there watching. I had got birds watching every corner of that cemetery. I had got birds watching Michael's grave, the birds at the church, I had got birds that hang out with Dominic. I had got a bird that keeps an eye on Harry just because. I had got a bird watching Mom and the kids, the kids started feeding it. I had got a bird hanging out with Lu-Lu almost all the time just so that she can communicate with me. I got a bird that acts as an alarm clock and a look-out for me in the study. Like I said, I got a couple dozen or so away from me, which requires a lot of eating. Rarely did I sit and eat with Lucia.

I would have to hang out with her in the real world on mandatory days where she would take me with her as back-up but as a ghost, as an illusion, as a doppelgänger. She was getting older at every passing day and I never changed; I just felt older, colder, distant.

I wondered if time was having less and less of an effect on me as I was coming closer to the end of my journey. Time was starting to pass by me faster here. I was curious as to why it seemed as such. I concluded that there was nothing wrong with the Nevergator; it worked just fine. I actually learned a couple more things; things that don't require sacrifice in exchange for power. Tricks that can be helpful for a momentary rewind or if I needed to pause and collect my thoughts. I shared my notes with Lu-Lu. I thought she would think they were interesting and instead she cautioned me and scorned me for using it saying, "That damn thing again?! It is stealing from your life and your soul of what years you have left."

I told her, "I'll stop my addictions... If you stop yours," as I took her cigarette from her, took a drag and flipped it away; destroying it with my mind.

I knew something was bugging the both of us; I knew it was bugging me. I was tired of waiting for the fateful day to watch Lu-Lu's soul fade away in my hands. Not knowing *why* future me as a doppelgänger could not have saved her. I could've helped her. Couldn't I have done anything more but let younger me watch her die?

Lu-Lu told me, "It's better to mourn, than to dwell on the future. If we didn't do something about it then, it's probably for a good reason."

"Or I could've been busy," I suggested.

Lucia said, "Yeah, you're probably right. Will you be hanging out here in your own head again all night?"

"Probably?!"

"Hey, I want to show you something," Lucia said, "I found a way to give you access to some things. I want you to take care of them until my Bella child is free to use these things," she brought me into her dreamscape, she pulled the skeleton key from around her neck and unlocked the door out of the study from inside. It opened to an entirely different room.

Lucia said, "I want to show you how to use the Lamp. I also want to teach you how to use the focusor sword. You're really good without these things, but I want you to know everything. I want you to know what I can't teach my bella child, little Nona. I want you to learn the things that Victoria would never let me teach her. I want you to learn some things that may be helpful during the end. Things that might help to destroy the monster."

"Lucia, I have doubts that he's out there, it's like he's gone," I said.

"Why, have you been sneaking out to hunt for him?" She asked.

"Not like you would have noticed me."

"I have a confession. I've been sneaking out too," Lucia

said.

"Wait, what Lu-Lu?" I asked.

"Well, yeah I've been causing your birds to dream, to daydream and fall asleep but instantly wake back up in *my dream* or whatever projection I wanted them to see. I even had drugged some of the birds, with you not knowing. I would do anything I could to keep you safe, knowing that my time is almost spent," she said.

"I can't believe that you drugged Twilight."

"Sweetheart, you have your entire life to live."

"Over and over it never ends. Death can come and take as many years as he wants! I've seen how it all plays out!" I exclaimed.

"You've seen the end? You've seen the end of your life?!" Lucia asked.

"Sometimes I... I just want it all to end. Sometimes I want to be done. I get so tired. I feel so alone." I told her.

"But honey, I can spend more time with you. We can spend these days, these last moments together. Would you like that?!" She asked.

"Absolutely! I would love that. There's just so much that I need to be able to accomplish to prepare myself for what is coming. I have to fight this monster. I have to protect my family!" I said.

Lu-Lu said, "But you don't have to do it alone. Let's spend our time together, working together to find an answer to defeat this thing. I'll share my notes."

"I'll add mine."

"I'll add my notes to the Diary of the things I've been doing," Lucia added. "Can you tell me what you've been doing when *you* sneak out at night? I'm still trying to figure out how you do it because your body's here. You snore really loud. I was going into your dreamscape and then no one seems to know where you were. Where do you go, I even blocked you from teleporting?!" Lucia asked.

"Oh, yeah, I re-emerge from any one of my dozens of birds

and I leave a shell of me in my bed. If you hit it hard enough it would probably shatter into a bunch of feathers."

I estimated about a minimum of 35 to 50 pounds should make my main vital organs function. Filling most of my bodily organs with fluids were what was needed to function, but none of the bones. It gets complicated but I had gotten good at it. I do have notes on that, and I practiced a lot in my dream. I died a lot in my dreams, but I come back to life. So, now I can appear as an 80-pound, 85-pound anorexic shell of myself somewhere else, and still have full access to powers and not be bound to the doppelgänger curse.

"You have only bound the outer layers of my skin so there's a few birds that are bound to that curse."

Lu-Lu said, "Well, shoot! I guess you don't really need that any more."

I told her, "No, it's OK. It helps people to forget who I am; and it'll be better for them if they don't remember me. "What have you been doing to sneak out?" I asked. "Well, this may come as a shock, but it's pretty easy to sneak past your birds; they're not security cameras. They're not as sensitive as you think; they're still breathing air," Lucia pointed out.

We continued to compare notes, "I thought it was funny that I was losing weight; and now I know why." Some of my birds were dead. I thought it was the monster. "Thanks, Lu-Lu, thanks for killing my kidneys," I said as I rubbed my abdomen.

Lucia chuckled and said, "You can grow those back. Here, let me show you where I've been keeping some other secrets."

Lucia took the skeleton key then unlocked the door leading out of the study, revealing yet another hiding place. This one is more like a security vault with smaller safety deposit boxes like a card catalog in a library; but each one required a key and password.

Without inserting a key and saying the password, within five seconds with an answer to the riddle found on the index tag, you'll get shocked.

"Lu-Lu, electricity doesn't do much to me. That's not a threat to me any more," I boasted.

"Yeah, but you won't be able to let go of the key and you won't be able to move or do anything until you get the answer right. In the meantime, your body is convulsing uncontrollably and you're foaming at the mouth, spitting pus, and heaving bile from your stomach. Basically, you'll die if you don't get the answer right... eventually," she explained with a grin.

Lucia certainly did like her riddles, passwords, and tortures; and she was especially good at being mean while inflicting pain. I sometimes wondered if Lucia is really a *bad* witch. I mean a lot of the stuff that she has taught me; it is not necessarily defensive, but often to attack people. What she often said was, "The best defense is a good offense."

I argued, "I think that's backwards."

She explained what was in each individual vault. Here were some of her more private secret spells. Her recipes for potions. Entries that she didn't put in the family's magic book.

"This is more for your college education, your mastery of witchcraft. When you are ready, of course. After you receive my powers, your inheritance as heiress that is," Lucia went on.

"Oh, I've already received *my* inheritance. Being the one from the future after *you* in the future died. I've already done sign the contract," I said.

"You have the key?!" she asked.

"Yeah, yeah, yeah," I replied.

"The ceremony where everybody showed up that had our powers, those that had keys to surrender?" She continued to pry.

"Oh, yeah, yeah, everybody... that I can't mention was there," I had to stop her from trying to interrogate me more. I knew where she was going with this.

"Oh, OK," she stopped.

"You're trying really hard to find out, but Grandma, you

really *don't* wanna know," I insisted.

"Just, that's the thing, part of me *does* want to know," Lucia replied.

"Listen, Lu-Lu. Knowledge of the future is a burden that no one should bear. I love the Seer's Sight, from a tactical, strategic point of view. To have an idea what my regular day is like. You know, if I am going to spill my latte, foresight of that cute guy, his smile and all; but knowing things like when someone's going to die because I accidentally touch someone in the lunch line. I don't need to know that crap and I know way too much!"

She agreed, "Fine, I think your Sight works a lot better than mine. I think my Sight is dwindling. I probably don't use it as much as you do."

"Or you can consider my addictions to power and magic. I am constantly using magic. There really was nobody around to tell me *not* to do this all the time. So, going cold turkey now would probably be a very, very, messed up ordeal. Like worse than a crack addict junkie trying to recover at a meth lab. I'd rather go through Death then go through withdrawals of magic. It's, it's really not fun at all," I responded.

Lu-Lu said "Well, maybe someday as you get older, you'll learn to wean yourself off of it."

"Yeah, I am older. I've already cut about 20 years off my life. So, I'm not gonna get too old, I know that for sure." I pondered.

"There are some other things I wanted to share with you, apart from my darker secrets. There's a whole section here on my focusor, the lamp," Lucia continued.

"OK, I figured the lamp was your focusor. I have been trying to keep that safe too. I didn't know that there was a super cool weaponized focusor sword sitting around in the library, either. I didn't even know there was a weapons room to begin with."

She corrected me, "Interrogation room; all those tools are here for the interrogation process, but yeah, if weapons are your thing. OK, you can use those."

"I like the focusor as a sword, instead of a stick."

"Well, they're all priceless family heirlooms on Michael's side. Please be respectful with the weapons, all right?!" Lucia explained.

"Whatever, sure." I said.

Lucia continued, "There's whole book on how to be respectful to swords. Whole books on the art of combat. I was trying to teach your mom this stuff. So, the focusor is yours now; we're going to have to reset that one to answer to whatever password you want to give it. Just so that, you know if... Victoria becomes compromised; nobody can access it."

"That makes sense," I agreed.

"Just probably a good idea not to keep these things laying around, or take them out of the Library," she said.

"Yeah, I read that one part about focusors. If someone else gets a hold of your focusor, and you've channeled your magical energy into it..." I said.

"Forfeited," she corrected me, "but channeling is fine and it's really more of an exchange."

"Yeah, I think it said that it can be used against you or they can control you," I replied.

Lucia added, "They can kill you. If you can destroy someone's focusor. They're dead. Lifeless."

"OK, cool. Noted. Don't let someone break or steal my focusor. But I don't have one. I haven't made one or forfeited my powers into one; and I think I'm going to *not* do that now."

Then she corrected me, "Well, you sort of already have through your birds," she pointed out.

"What do you mean?" I asked her.

"Well, when you did what you did; you split your soul," she explained.

"It was an accident, I mean, I didn't wanna get bit by a dozen birds. But if you need duplicates you can always shed a few pounds of yourself to replace the dead ones, and I get skinnier," I responded.

"The process to create a focusor requires splitting your soul, it is not something to take lightly, my dear. To create your focusor you're putting your life essence into something else; giving them life, your life and if someone got a hold of all of your birds, if they can capture some, capture all your murder of crows. Make it into one..." She continued, but I got the idea.

"OK, so what you're saying is if I have at least one bird that's safe?" I asked.

"Yes, you could, and this is just my theory, because I've never, on purpose... which is what it would this be like if you let a whole bunch of rabid animals bite you. I could possibly try to recreate the experiment with a were-beast..." She explained.

"Oh, and they'd have to be magical at the same time. That's what happened to me," I replied. "But *should* we find out by trying it again?"

"No, you're right, it shouldn't be re-created," she agreed.

"In my defense, Lu-Lu, I wasn't wanting to be bitten by a whole bunch of them. They just kind of attacked. It was actually kind of lucky that Harry was around," I said.

"So that's when he helped you out?" She asked. "Harry got me through the transformation. He is a good friend. I'm glad he is still around. You guys are just not dating, right? I just haven't seen him much. He isn't hurt or anything, right?" I asked.

"Well, you see, the thing is, yeah, we decided to keep it strictly professional. Especially since I'm having him drop off some of the Estate paperwork and place *you* as executor of my will. He didn't like having that conversation. He kept telling me that we have time, we have time..." She trailed out, deep in thought. She spaced out a lot nowadays.

"We got our whole lives together, he said. I tried to help him understand that losing Michael had helped me to realize that life is fragile, but some things are... are fated and meant to be. That some things are going to be, and our relationship is..." She was lost in thought.

I interrupted, "Inappropriate."

"Maybe?" she continued, "I'm just getting older and he doesn't age, I guess it, just now, it looks weird. Anyways, I am leaving these things to you. We're going to give everything to the future you. To the younger you, but *you are* you, already, and you received all the stuff, right?!" Lucia asked.

"Yeah, I have the key; I haven't been in *here* yet. You left me kind of a creepy note. I understand why you did it, your riddles, rituals, and passwords. But now, I know! I know where it is. I didn't even know that this room existed at all." I explained.

"What creepy note?" She asked.

"I got that secret message from you as the 'real will.' It said that the focusor is locked," I explained.

Lu-Lu put the skeleton key into the lamp and the flame grew stronger and brighter.

"OK, cool, yeah. I didn't know that did that!"

We started spending more time together now that I realize that I could stomach being around her and not be worried that Harry was gonna show up and wanted to go smooch on his older girlfriend; inadvertently causing me heartbreak and heartburn.

I modified my security with my birds, now knowing that each of them acted as a focusor for me. We trained on variations of spells and did some experiments with different defensive spells. I mean, yeah, I broke Lucia down and got her to show me some defensive stuff; because someday I may have to teach my siblings how to protect themselves.

"It might be nice to know some things on how to defend others and shield others instead of constantly shooting bolts of lightning at people, crushing their bones with my mind, or liquefy their bones," I explained.

"That's a fun one! It's like turning your blood and your bone marrow into acid from within. It's not really pretty, maybe I won't talk about that; but it's nice to know these things," she said excitedly.

Knowledge is power and I kept increasing, but the thing that kept bugging me was my lack of knowledge on the Gor-Nok. Yeah, I was going to start saying his name. I'm gonna start calling him out, and I was going to start thinking about him more to draw him out.

I need to find him. I'm not afraid of him; not afraid of saying his name any more. What scares me more is not knowing where he is and not knowing what he is doing. Lucia and I were having a conversation about this; she could tell that I was frustrated about something. Her gifts of foresight and intuition were starting to become more simplistic. It was less reading my thoughts and more sensing my emotions. I noted it as perhaps something that happens as the Seer's Sight wears-off and has her powers, her natural powers of invading people's minds weaken.

She expressed, "It's just so much work and I'm so tired. Emotions come easier. You just feel; but invading someone's mind or thoughts takes effort. It takes an exchange, takes requesting permission. It's not so much a cost; nothing is exchanged in an invasion of privacy. It is permission, begging for it, but without them ever even knowing. It's like an unspoken consent."

I told her, "I am frustrated that I haven't seen or heard news of the monster, of the Gor-Nok."

She gasped that I said his name and I said, "Please, you shouldn't be afraid of it. I am open, I want him to come for me. I'd rather know exactly where he was than not know what he was doing."

She said, "Yeah, keep your enemies close in your heart, keep your friends at arm's length and your enemies closer than that. Something like that," she might have been drunk again.

"I've got my birds on patrol, I've got curses and enchantments. I got traps set up, I've got kinds of things, graves laced with poisons. I planted hallucinogens, fungus, and molds. I've got all kinds of natural herbs, and defensive things to work. That's what irks me. Where is that murderous bastard!" I exclaimed.

"Well, maybe we did *too good* of a job and that's why he hasn't attacked us, or desecrated graves, or done anything to us. Maybe you need to look more at the profile, and less at the literal history of what he's done in *your* past. Look at what he could be currently doing in this, your now present. Have you ever thought of it that way?" Lucia explained.

I said, "I thought I was clever. I thought I figured out everything. I'm learning all the spells. I am a God, in my own head; yet I feel so vulnerable. I just keep developing other fears."

Lucia paused me for a moment, she seemed to be deep in thought. I asked her, "Are you OK?"

She said, "I think I know what he's doing! He's playing the long game. Yes, so when you play cards like bridge or something..." She continued.

"OK, I play poker now, in the future. When I get home; I guess. I have," I said.

"Really you should come to bingo tonight, with me at the Civic Center," she said.

"Yeah, I'm not. I'm not going to go hang out with a bunch of old ladies and scream, 'bingo,' and get all excited," I said mockingly.

She looked offended that I was mocking her.

"No thanks, I've got a world to create in my head. Way too much fun going on in there. Dusk is running a haberdashery in there and he's quite the king of fashion."

She looked at me as if I were crazy, "Your imagination is so weird."

"Like look, I just set these things up and they all kind of ran with it!" I replied.

Lucia told me, "You really need to tighten that up. You just can't let your imagination go wild. That's what happens when you don't keep things in check. That's what I wanted to say about the long game; he is probably just waiting to smoke us out. He's waiting till we come out and expose our vulnerabilities. He's got all the time in the world."

"He's a coward!" I exclaimed.

"He's probably terrified. He probably sees our strength, sees the strength in our numbers and what he wants to find is some way to get to us and use that. He can exploit it to kill us, destroy us; do whatever he's here to do," Lucia proposed.

"I know," I agreed.

"Maybe he's here to see the sights. Is he just traveling?" Lucia mused, but I disagreed.

"I'll share this much about the future. He wants us to die! That's basically all I can tell you right now," I wasn't happy sharing this.

"Then I guess they'll be no more taking the Diary out of the study," She said.

I agreed, "Yes, we can try just memorizing stuff, I guess."

"Yes, we can do that. I'll keep it locked in the study. Dominic can stay in the house; the grounds are okay for now. We just need a tighter hold on our defenses," Lucia replied.

I said, "Oh, yeah, I carry a smaller 'journey journal' as I collect thoughts for notes, and I write in that one. I don't write spells or anything, but I just like to write my observations," I shared.

"So, you're journaling now? That's rather elderly of you," Lucia mused.

"I'm becoming *you* in the future. I just like to write my thoughts. Don't laugh at me! Yes, I'm becoming you, but you weren't really around to guide me on how to dress or anything. I had to figure it out on my own," I retorted.

We resolve to take our investigation from a different approach. I began looking at more motives and styles of the things he would do. The types of things he would do if he was running amok. I don't know what he would do instead of attacking us.

Lucia said, "Well, then the next thing I would do would

be to attack our family."

I was just playing with Lucia, I said, "You know, you probably would have been a very thorough serial killer."

"Thanks," she replied.

"That's not a compliment by the way," I said.

She continued with her plans that, "We need to gather newspaper clippings articles. I'll get some string in here, we can start trying to figure out this mystery!"

What he was up to? What was his plan? What was the next move? He was too cautious to really come up on the radar of the Seer's Sight. I recalled events that I had already lived; that I could still see. After some time, who knew how much time passed when I got obsessed with a project. I started gathering clippings and police reports. keeping my ears out for events like unexpected heart attacks, people dying in their sleep, sudden infant death syndrome. Incidents that were similar to the fear induced panic attacks, that his fear toxins cause. After a while of working on this, I let Lucia see the string chart sequence of events.

"Show me the future," she held out her hand as if the vision of the future was just something that I had been carrying around with me in my back pocket.

"Yeah, I guess if it's really something that you want to see," I reached into my back pocket and flashed her an obscene finger gesture.

"I'm not showing you the day you die! Do you understand, No!" I exclaimed.

"Fine, I will agree to not bug you about that day; but I still need to see everything else," she said.

I accepted the compromise, I shared with her my vision of events, the different battles that he and I had; I had in the past. We started, really against my will, dissecting the mind of a stalker-like serial-killer.

The string-theory-graph-chart-thingy we made to track a killer was, admittedly, interesting to study.

"You know, some of these techniques are used in criminal-mind profiling, and forensic investigations. Have you ever considered that as a 'cover-career'?" Lucia asked.

"I never really thought of having a *career*. I was going to just kill this monster, then play life by ear after that." I guess it was the hunter-tracker side of me that thought this was all interesting. Also, Mom's history and anthropology studies with *her* career was coming out as well. Yet much cooler, and I also was trying to avoid being creepy about it.

Reason, anxieties, my life, my concerns, and my fear of not knowing what he's doing; and what he's planning next is feeding him.

"He has to feed off of fear," I explained.

Lu-Lu said, "Maybe we should not worry about him? Maybe what we should do is stop feeding the troll; literally and metaphorically."

"Like literally start thinking 'happy thoughts'? I guess I could be more positive," I responded.

"Instead of giving into despair, give into hope!" she continued, "You know what is the opposite word for 'despair' in Spanish? 'Hope.' It means to wait, but you're waiting for something good to hold on to, a belief in something greater than yourself."

"We can play the long game too," I continued explaining the timeline. Now we have a strategy in the sequence of events leading up to her death. We decided that her death was the central event. We even included the death of Michael, and the beginning was when Lu-Lu gave me the Diary. The sequence of events created a loop, the loop of time in which I am currently living. It was kind of cool to see the loop, see that all these things all focused on one common denominator, Me.

It was a startling revelation I created. There were tons of twine hanging around my interrogation/bedroom. I had pictures, news clipping, details on multiple spells and when I learned them. Also, so I can keep the timeline straight in my head and as an added bonus effect, I had enchanted these samples of evidence so anyone that touched it got a 'flash' of the event. I don't know how long I spent on them.

This weighed low on Lu-Lu's soul. I wanted to finally let Lu-Lu see it. It became my new dark obsession and I was kind of ashamed when I showed it. I brought Lucia to the center, let her take it in one event at a time. She walked around the room under the strange tags looking at different things, letting her see the events, letting her relive my past. Parts of my life when I wasn't my best. She couldn't take too much.

I could see that it was stressing her out and taking its toll upon her body. I was explaining to her my theories of what it is he actually wants.

"Besides just killing people and sucking off their fears; there is an end goal in mind for him that's threefold," I followed one string to the middle. "These are the times that he's mentioned that he wanted the Diary. He wants our knowledge, our power," I went on.

"Next, this timeline is showing that he wants to inflict as much pain as he can. Keeping us living in fear. And the last line coming to the 'time loop.' That's what I called the sequence of events of each and every battle where he could've killed me, but he didn't," I said.

"He's been trying to kill me, but he is saving me for the last," I said as I stood in the middle of the 'Time Loop' and then Lu-Lu understood what I had done.

"For so long, ever since I got here; all the pain, all the suffering, hardship that my family has endured. Ever since I was born when I was brought into this world. When I was brought on to stop this, because I did not, could not stop myself! I became a monster! We really shouldn't bother with him. He's done nothing compared to what *I* have done. The monster that *I am*, the lives that have been lost because of me! And that's why I've come to the decision that this ends now with the one who started it all. If I end the loop now," I explained.

Lucia was crying, "No, not you."

I called the sword to me from off the wall, ignited the blade, making it a brilliant white, surging blade of fire. The power of the sword shielded me from Lucia's attempts to stop me.

"If I end this loop now, I stop me from doing what I *think* I'm going to do! If I just let sleeping dogs lie, we just ignore this guy; we can live normal lives, like Mom has been trying to get us to live. If I give up this pursuit of death, give up my thirst for revenge. If I choose the harder path that I am meant to do, if you can bear mourning one more death and let me go on my way then we'll be free!" I responded.

I activated the Nevergator on my hand. "You can live a longer, happier life. You won't have to give up love, won't have to give a family. Won't have to give up me. You'll get to be with me, me from the present not this future train-wreck version of me. I am the one that caused all this. I am the one that started this loop and if I separate me right now, all the suffering that I've caused, that I've earned, ends with me!" I raised the sword.

Lu-lu tried to stop me; she tried every trick she could. She was so weak from grief, and she was in such pain. I was so full of rage, empowered. I sliced straight through my own arm. There was a brilliant flash of bright white light followed by a small supernova exploding from my forearm, causing Lu-Lu and I to fly back away from the shockwave. I stabbed the sword into the floor to anchor myself in the blast zone.

I was ready to flee from existence. To completely vanish from this time and from life and all eternity. Fully ready to pay recompense for my sins. When the blast was over, and the light receded. Lu-Lu looked up to see my body and severed hand on the floor. My remaining hand still attached to my limp, lifeless body; anchored to the sword in the floor. Lucia began to weep and mourn over my loss. She tried to remove my hand then was shocked by multiple, tiny, electric threads.

I had been fused; small trickles of electricity started pouring off of my hand and arm to the sword. Exchanging power. The severed hand started moving and twitching as the Nevergator activated and the event began to replay itself. Lucia couldn't help but to be pushed back into her original starting position.

She watched a magnificent ballet of a time reversing the shockwave heaving back to the epic epicenter. Brilliant white light of the supernova receding and my hand bonding back together. She helplessly watched me standing there holding the flaming focusor-sword; ready to lop off my hand the moment after I activated the Nevergator.

Lucia cried out, "Stop! No. You won't be able to do this. I just saw it happen. Cutting off your hand, it doesn't sever you from the Nevergator. It doesn't actually work. You're still here. You're stuck! It's actually like the time Michael was in a coma. Stuck between both the living and the dead."

"Let's fix what's wrong then, I'll destroy the Nevergator!" I said as I raised the sword.

"No, Nonabel! Stop!" she commanded me and somehow froze my movements. "I'm afraid that would do something worse. That may scatter your soul across time. You may wake up in the past. In past lives, who knows what would happen?! It's not a risk I'm willing to accept. Nonabel, this ends when we end him. Killing my husband's killer. Fixing my husband's death. It's not in your hands to fix... but in mine!" She separated the Nevergator from my hand and restored it into a trinket of cogs and chains. Lucia called it to herself.

I was in awe by the way that she was able to take it from me. I knew what she was planning. I begged her to see another way.

"No, you can't do this alone! He will crush you! He'll enjoy every moment. Lu-lu, don't give him what he wants! That's what this is all about. We'll end him together. I'll stay. I won't do anything stupid to try to kill myself. I promise!" I used the power of the focusor to call the Nevergator back to myself. "This is my burden to bear. I started this; I will end it." I restored the Nevergator to my hand and I de-activated the sword.

"You're right, let's stay the course. Stick to the plan. This is the safer route. The path I understand," Lucia agreed.

"If you left now, go back farther than I did. Try to stop him, then no one would've ever taught me witchcraft. We wouldn't be talking now, at least not for 18 years, or however so many these past 10, 15 years. Is it 16 years now?" I asked.

"I wouldn't have spent all this time with you, if we do this," Lucia agreed.

"We're gonna lock that damn thing in a vault to keep us safe," I replied as I manifested the Nevergator.

"It too should not be wandering outside the limits of our protection; this is also something that he should never get a chance to put his hands on," Lu-Lu agreed with me and I sur-rendered the Sword and the Nevergator.

We both had the same paranoid delusion that other one was going to do something rash by taking the Nevergator to go to avenge Michael's death. So, we watched each other put it in the Vault box; locked it up and we each applied our own rid-dle-code.

The punishment for not knowing the codes on this box was paralysis. We focused our combined efforts on stopping the beast here and now. We decided that since his defining motivation was to destroy me; that the bait for the trap needs to be me. I called back my birds from their posts; well, most of them. Leaving a few out as anchors and protectors. Guardians over some people I loved. I really wasn't gonna miss a dozen pounds or so.

We did a lot of healing physically, mentally, and emo-tionally. Lucia and I spent more time just enjoying being around each other. We supported each other. We would visit the City Cemetery and make ourselves talk to Michael's fake grave as a way to lure the monster out of hiding. We could feel someone watching, we could tell he was there; salivating over the temptation of weak prey, but he knew we were not afraid.

He knew that we were not weak prey any more. Pain gave us the strength to endure. We gave each other strength.

Soon it was time to take the fight to him. Lucia decided that she was the one that should hang out at the cemetery, as a way to lure him out. She was attending church every week and at funerals as a 'well-wisher.' She got pretty good at giving her condolences to the families of the dearly departed. I gave her the description of the Gor-Nok as a man, we believed that was how he had been hiding. He knew that he couldn't hide his appearance for me, well, not from *future* me. He didn't necessarily know what the future version of me looked like, not exactly. I was very different than what I used to be; more dangerous, more feral. Half monster, half goddess whenever I go out on the prowl at night.

I started chasing down leads with the police scanner that Harry gave us, looking for any similar motives. Seeing the methods of the serial killer, I found a string of sudden infant deaths in the neighboring towns. They started random and scattered, but then started becoming a trend and then it reminded me of the time he tried to kill me pretending to be an orderly, or a nurse, or an intern; whatever. I thought he just wore a disguise and it was one of the first times I had ever seen him as a man. I thought he was just trying to be sneaky but that's him. That was what he looked like. We would both return at the end of each night to compare notes. This gave us something to do that kept us occupied. It felt like a job, felt like a career.

Lu-Lu got really good at being nice to the people in the town. She started inviting herself to more and more town gatherings just so she could make more friends. Then it would be less awkward for her to be at *every* funeral. She started attending church more often too so she could be aware of the latest deaths and when the viewing would be.

I didn't allow her to go out entirely alone. I still had a crow watching her. I had beefed up the security features on my birds. I may have genetically modified them with some spells, giving them the ability to become their own baby were-beasts. Kind of half-bird and half-demons. It was really kind of fun and terrifying at the same time.

Only in Dreams

On rare occasions, I would wake from my dreamscape with an overwhelming urge to satisfy actual hunger. The nearest nuts and berries foraged by my murder of crows scattered across the town could not entirely satisfy. It also helped that Lu-Lu had made her garlic chicken parmigiana and I could smell it even in my dreams.

I had emerged from the Library, chasing the smell with my nose, using my therianthrope heightened senses. I also activated the Sight to find a spectrum that could show me the aura of odors as colors. I chased the smell like I was hunting my prey, down the stairs to the lower level of the house. I could see the casserole dish of chicken parmigiana, fresh out of the oven sitting on the counter. The oven was sitting wide-open, but there was no sign of Grandma Lu-Lu. I couldn't find her; I called my bird that was on duty watching her.

I scanned the floor behind the kitchen island and saw her body lying helpless. I went around the other side to find my bird, Midnight, nuzzling its hard beak against Lu-Lu's face on the floor. I cried out, "Oh dear God, Lu-Lu, wake up! Lu-Lu wake up!" I tried not to let fear and panic take over and went through the steps to check her vitals. She had a pulse, but she had hit her head when she fell to the floor. She didn't seem too good, she was unconscious.

I called for the ambulance and told her regular doctor that we would meet him at the clinic. He asked me if anything changes in her health to give him a call. She had been experiencing some breathing problems but then no one expected the news we got after she had come to. Her doctor got her stable and told me what I already knew. He said he wanted to have her go to the hospital, the main Regional Hospital for observation overnight; to do some tests, but he was certain that she had developed some kind of lung cancer because of her smoking.

I knew she was dying at this point; this was the beginning of the end. I had these dates memorized in my mind. I worried and stressed about these moments, so much bitterness that it caused *me* to take up smoking again and I just didn't notice that Lu-Lu was hiding it too. She had been smoking for years, a lot longer than I knew.

Apparently, addictions run deep in the family. We had transferred her to the other hospital and Lucia said she wanted to see Vicky and the kids. I called them up, talked with them to break the bad news to Mom and Dad. We got Lucia settled at the hospital, in the room for overnight observation. They allowed me to be with her because I convinced everyone I was her caregiver. I saw Mom, Dad, and the kids; I led them to the room. I exchanged a big hug with the much older kids.

Momentarily, it was like waking up from a dream with a happy surprise. "Hello, lovelies, I'm aunt Lilly, do you remember me?!" We had exchanged sad tears and hugs. I let them have their moment with Grandma Lu-Lu. While they were distracted, I teleported to the roof of the hospital. I wanted to scan the area for anything that seemed out of place. Today was a very critical day in the timeline. Since so many events happened that led to death in my family; I wanted to make certain that nobody had tampered with my parent's car.

I quickly turned into my murder of crows and gathered myself together by my parents' vehicle. Everything had checked out. I even topped-off my Dad's fluids while they were all busy visiting. Nothing seemed out of the ordinary. No evidence of foul play. Nothing seemed wrong, it was your typical, normal day. Like any other Thursday. Like any day of the week. I had a couple of birds on lookout outside of on the ledge of the window of her room to let me be able to see what they were doing. Grandma Lu-Lu had assured them all that everything was fine, that she should be able to fight this.

Victoria was especially broken up. The kids seemed to understand what this all meant. I was seventeen-ish, and the twins were fifteen; but they really never fully understood what we meant by saying, "Grandma is dying."

"Yes, I'm *almost* dying, but it isn't going to be happening today," she assured them. I quickly returned to the roof. I was waiting for my family to leave. I mentally called the doctors in to talk with Mom and Dad. The kids had been picking on each other in the hall. The door was left open and I couldn't easily, all of the sudden teleport into the room. I kept a look-out hoping that nothing out of ordinary was going to cause the accident today. I could not accept that it was a drunk driver. It was worth hanging out, seeing it for myself. My younger self, who would be daydreaming during the accident, she wouldn't be paying attention to the right details.

It was late, getting to be dusk soon. I doubted that event had happened already; being nearly sundown, and dusk began. How do you solve a mystery before it happens? By focusing, pay attention to what was happening right now. But I had stopped looking through the eyes of my other feathered friends. The house was vacant, the farm quiet, by the woods; Dominic was sleeping. All the other parts of me, watching everyone else seem to be okay.

Then I saw something. Something grabbed my bird in the forest by the graveyard; and ate it cold. I dropped to the roof, clutching my gut in pain writhing, wrenching. I could feel her little hollow bones crunching in its mouth. My Sight went crazy trying to isolate what just killed one of my birds, a part of me was dying. I sent one of the other birds to investigate what had crushed a part of me. I felt the side of my head being smashed. The other bird brothers flew in from the woods to help make the killer pay for his fluid, stealth assault. Something was taking out my defenses. Something was making it look smooth, too easy.

I slipped through the vortex and appeared in the forest near the cemetery. There was fog forming, and it was getting darker. I felt someone was in the woods, but I could not see them. The Sight wasn't working right. What if my eyes had been damaged?

I noticed I was leaking black fluid from my eyes. It seemed too dark for blood, it was black and putrid. I needed some hallowed ground to recover, to have the strength to kill

329

this annoying beast. A nauseous fog flowed into the cemetery and I needed to find dirt. I had to crawl down in the fog to gather some dirt. I took a breath and began to say the spell. The smell of the fog was rancid, putrid, toxic. Goosebumps shot up, my heart approaching panicky paranoia. Sending all my doubts, worries, anxieties pouring out of my mind, consuming my every thought.

Killing me slowly, tortured thoughts of the death of my parents. Which would be at any moment. My family! What have I done?! I abandoned my post, I let down my guard. I was lulled into a false sense of peace and security. I got distracted; and while I was distracted the Gor-Nok had sprung his trap. He was killing my birds, damaging my actual body, and kept me from actually healing. Caused me to writhe in pain laying in the bed of his fear toxins that had spread all over the cemetery. He rose from the mist to approach me as the Beast, then shifted back into the man. He crouched down by me as I was writhing with seizures.

He pushed his jagged club upon my chest and leaned down upon it, crushing my ribs. I could feel the bones snapping, popping under my flesh. He pulled up on the base of my neck. He said something odd, he began to say some spell to open my eyes so he could laugh at his victories. He relished in the pain he caused me. He used my fears to strengthen him.

The Gor-Nok extracted my memories of tragedy and he said in his thick accent, "Oh, I see. I see your tragedy. Today was a bad day for you, witch. You lost so much today, or should I say... you will," he breathed another lung full of violent toxins into me and vanished.

I knew what was happening. I knew where he had gone. He was going to set up the tragedy because I acted on impulse instead of sticking to the plan. I didn't think before I had rushed off to ruin everything again. I stomached the pain, summoned all my strength to get myself up and out of the fog. Clinging onto tombstones to elevate my lungs above the cloud of fear gas. When I was able to get above the cloud, I held my breath. I dived back in for some dirt then crawled out to the edge of despair. I tried to lean against a tree, and I finished the healing spell, restoring my eyes. I healed, resetting my bones. Healing all that was missing. Reuniting myself with my fallen comrades.

I quickly teleported back to the hospital's roof. I used the Sight to see if I missed the accident; the car was still in the parking lot. Mom and Dad have not yet left the lobby; they were signing paperwork for Grandma Lu-Lu. Lu-Lu was stalling for me. The coast was clear in the room. I swiftly teleported in there to be by her side. I was so filled with fear; panicking because of a sense of urgency for something that *might* not happen.

"Thank you, Lu-Lu. Thanks for stalling them. Wait here, I'm going to make sure they make it home safe tonight," I said as I was about to leave.

She could tell that something was wrong the moment she touched my hand. I unintentionally shared a vision of what had just happened in the cemetery. She seized up on me with all of her strength. She activated her eyes, her hypnotic stare. She commanded me. Forbade me with all her power and authority as the Matriarch that I would not interfere with fate.

I argued with her telling her, "I can stop this!"

She stopped my mouth with her mind, and said, "Honey, I'm so sorry I have to do this. I love you so much. This is for your own good. If we alter anything more, all that we have done to prepare this, is at risk. My gorgeous granddaughter, our time together is at risk and I only have so much time left with you. I cannot allow you to do this!"

"Please?!" I forced out in a moan.

She apologized, laying a finger to my mouth, shushing me. She sealed my mouth completely shut, causing the skin to heal over. No matter how much I tried to break away from her hands, to fight, she got stronger. Her strength was great. She was siphoning the strength from me. I could see my power, my assets, being drained from my being; watched as it entered into her hands. I was panicking; this had to have been a nightmare, this had to have been my enemy.

He had appeared as the form of Lucia before, taking control of her image, pretending to have her powers. This had to be an imposter, she turned me back into a doppelgänger. Binding me to her life, binding me to her side. I tried to separate my birds from within my body, shift them from the outer layers and she suspended them in the air then reversed them back into my helpless body. I was bombarded by the pain within.

Lucia apologized every time she had to counter me. She had been planning this. She knew she had to stop me from changing the past. I tried to retreat to my dreamscape knowing that I could channel myself from there through my other birds. Lucia blocked that way too, a door appeared in my mind, but it was locked. I pried at the lock, I scraped at it. I try to remove it with my fingernails. I returned back to my semi-shaky shell of a form. She was a very strong-willed person.

Lucia was apologizing and crying the whole time. I had been pleading with her in my mind and she shushed me again, turning down the volume of my psychic thoughts. I tried to watch what was happening to my parents in the moment of their impending death.

Flashes kept appearing in my mind. Lucia kept pleading with me, "No, honey, you don't want to see that! Stop trying. No, stop trying to help."

Teleporting wasn't working, there was nothing I could do. I watched helplessly. The Sight was all that I had left, all I could do is see out of my younger eyes. Only pain from my eyes as I was watching a painful memory unfold. The details of every event of the accident. Watching Mom look back, her eyes flashed with colors. She was trying to use every ounce of strength and power that she had. Magic that she had forgotten. She had created a barrier; she protected us, shielded us during the accident.

I never saw what had actually caused it. I didn't get to see the event, apart from watching her eyes. I only got to see the aftermath. I had to remain in the corner of Lucia's room, weeping like some type of phantom. Moaning in the corner. My eyes were bleeding black tears. I was so pain stricken, stripped of all usefulness. I was a hollow shell, filled with torment, and anguish. Lucia had used every ounce of strength she had to battle me and bind me. I hate her.

We later received the notice of the car accident. I was so mad at Lucia. There was nothing I could do about it but hate. I couldn't shout at her; I couldn't blast her with psychic thoughts. I couldn't invade her nightmares. I couldn't fight back; I was stuck in the corner, put on time-out. All I could feel was the emotions that she would let me express.

My misery was everything and she shared it too. They told us that they did everything they could to try to save Mom and Dad. I heard one of the nurses talking to the kids in the hall before they let them in to see Grandma; something about how amazing and special we must be to be so safe. She couldn't believe that they didn't get hurt. It was no consolation, I remembered this. They let the kids see Grandma and the emotion of the tragedy filled them to overflowing. Everyone was crying; even Jesse didn't know what to do, he didn't know how to express his emotions. The girls were sobbing, hugging on Grandma, their faces buried into her arms.

All I could do was moan with them. I wanted it to stop reliving this tragedy. I wanted to attack my enemy. I wanted to be free. I hated Lucia so much for what she had done to me. I didn't talk to her for days, weeks after she unlocked my lips. I retreated to the study, locked myself away in my dreams. It was the only ounce of happiness I could enjoy, to escape from living my nightmares.

Against my will, Lucia had dragged me to Victor and Victoria Venatora's funeral. I felt nothing. I was nothing and there was nothing I could do to fight. I wondered if she did this just to torture me, to punish me. I hated Lucia so much.

The kids had come to live with us. I pretty much lived in the Library, anyways, and was now forced to be a ghost. They hardly, if at all, ever noticed me but thought I was a shadow, a thought. I was a figment of their imagination. They didn't remember their 'Auntie Lily.' Lucia wasn't going to allow me to manifest myself in the flesh enough because she knew I would do something stupid, vengeful, suicidal, like go after the beast myself.

I tried to study as much as I could, but she took the index Diary from me and kept it with her. I had to look through the books in the Library the old fashion way to find the answers, one at a time. I couldn't just ask the Diary for answers. There were a series of spells and curses put upon me to compile the state of being known as the 'doppelgänger.' The biggest curse I couldn't get around was the fact that my inheritance; my powers stemmed from Lucia. While she lived, I was hers, she could do whatever she wanted.

Well, she had to physically touch me to drain me of my power. That's why she wasn't very skilled at stopping me during our regular battles; at least she let me think so. I was certain she could've been playing me the whole time. She could've killed me if she wanted, especially since I had her husband's dead body beneath me when I first arrived in this nightmare.

Days had passed, weeks had passed, months, summer, and calendar pages flying on. School was starting again. The kids, our family were falling into routines and adjusting to their new life. Lucia had begun setting up younger Nonabel to take over the affairs of the Estate. She had begun preparing Nonabel to understand that their time was limited. She was going to become the guardian of the family. The time soon came, sooner than I thought, sooner than I could stop. Time for Lucia to pass the Diary on to me; younger me and share with me our greatest secrets.

I knew everything that was going to happen that night, except for the role that I played as doppelgänger. What was going to happen when the monster came? How did *I* stop it before, sort of? I knew I was there in the past. Somehow, I had my powers; lightning bolts had blasted through the room. It came from *within* the room from near Lucia. So, it must've been me; it wasn't younger me. Lucia must have given me my powers back.

I must've been freed from my bonds. Exercising that kind of curse, it must have weighed on Lucia. It took immense power. She was constantly using her powers; what little she had left to maintain the integrity of my bonds. I wondered what else she was giving up. Where she would have to redirect her focus to pay attention to me. I couldn't speak out loud, I couldn't *think* out loud, I couldn't write anything.

There was no real way to communicate except through sadness. She told me that she was going to give the younger me the book. She's going to tell us. Tell her everything about our family; then she let up on some of my restrictive curses. She told me I could have my powers back, all of them.

However, when I'm in the presence of my younger self, when she could see me, if I'm in close enough range, that I'm within sight of her; I will turn into a shadow. I would become invisible; I would be a phantom again. Still having access to my powers, but Nonabel could not see me. I remained a 'déjà vu' and a figment of her imagination. Lucia kept me from talking out loud for fear that others may hear me. She allowed me to communicate telepathically, so I can talk psychically again. It felt like holding my breath for the longest time and I was coming up from an icy frozen lake gasping for air when I could psychically speak again.

"I want the Gor-Nok to see you, that night is soon. This is when he comes for us. We have to prepare," she told me.

Don't let him come. Please, I'm not ready to lose you, again. I said psychically *We are not ready, what are we doing? We can end this if I can fight him… alone.*

"Sweetheart, no," she started.

Lu-Lu, listen! You can still have a life with these kids. You can still have love. I pushed memories to her.

She said, "I can't lose you!"

She is still here, and she will still have YOU!

"No, Nonabel! It's too late for me. I've already opened the gate. I've set the trap. Please, Honey, Death is coming for me. Let me go," she sobbed.

I touched Lu-Lu, hoping to plead with her, connect with her, begged her to change her mind. She pulled away from me knowing I could see more than what she wanted but it was too late. I had seen what she had done. She had been busy setting up this trap. Opening the gate and exposing me as the bait.

She had removed the rest of my birds, all of my centurion guardians. I had been brought back to the farm, she called them all back using her powers as Matriarch of the family to override my authority and bind them back to the borders of the farm. She allowed herself to be seen with the Diary out at Michael's fake grave. She allowed the Gor-Nok to witness her perform a spell from the Diary by manifesting flowers by Michael's tombstone.

She didn't need the Diary for that spell, but she was trying to lure him to come out. It worked before. She had left the cemetery one day. The Gor-Nok approached her but as a man and inquired about the book. He claimed that he was into antiquities. He used his charisma to try to convince her that he was interested in buying the book. She knew exactly who he was, she knew exactly what he had wanted, and it took every ounce of her self-control to *not* destroy him. She knew that she could not mess with the timeline; she could not mess with fate.

She told him, "Oh, if you like old books, I've got plenty of more books at my house," then she had invited him to come over the next day. The night she was fated to die.

Oh Lu-Lu, you didn't? I can't lose you; not again…

Lucia didn't want me to intervene in the trap. She wanted to lure the Gor-Nok back to the house where he would be on our terms. Where she could get him to expose himself to our defenses. Let down his guard, so she could trap him. She felt that she could bind him with a series of spells and rituals like she had bound me with the doppelgänger spell.

It will not work, I'm afraid. He's too violent. I believe he has too many tools in his arsenal for just you to handle. I begged her to let me help. I begged for her to give me back my powers. She refused to listen. Lucia shut me up psychically again and grounded me to my room. From the dreams I was able to send out my reconnaissance birds. I was not going to hide.

I had a couple of crows that Lu-Lu didn't know of and had set them to watch a couple of things. I have the house being watched, I had the cemetery being watched, then had the Diary being watched. As a way to avoid detection *I might have* sent the birds out as baby-were-demons. My gifts and abilities were limited through these vessels, but I found that controlling them through the power of dreams, a power which she had given back to me so that I could have some happiness, actually gave me all the power I needed.

I was not going to leave Lucia helpless without proper protection. The time was closely coming for the alleged book salesman to arrive. I don't trust the guy even to let him fall into a trap. The motto: "You should keep your friends close and your enemies closer," doesn't work with this guy. You keep this guy as far away from you, your friends, anybody you might be 'friending on social media' or your pen-pal. Just keep this guy away from everyone and anything that you love.

If I thought it were possible to truly be able to trap someone like him, someone like me with the curses and enchantments that she had done to make me or this guy into a doppelgänger, a ghost and have him be forgotten; then I would be all for it. I would agree with her plan but since I already had figured out how to get around the defenses and he could find a way to destroy his jailer.

I knew I had to get some help, something, or someone that Lucia would listen to. She wasn't going listen to me. I tried to think of ways that wouldn't mess with the timeline, and this was an event that I did not know of in the past; and there had to have been a reason the kids all stayed in their rooms. Zatie was in her room which made it difficult for me to physically leave the study to begin with, and Lucia had set up the 'no teleporting into the study rule' so I had to sneak in and out as a ghost. Jessie was always on the couch and younger Nonabel was either on dates with her boyfriend or hiding in her room half the time.

Tonight, Nonabel had happened to be out on a date. In hindsight, I think I distinctly remember Lucia *encouraging* me to go out and have some fun, enjoy myself. She was trying to get rid of me, even younger me! Maybe it was because I have been able to manipulate younger me, make her do things through hypnosis and Lu-Lu caught on that I was doing this. She thought of almost everything, she seemed to forget that I'm a were-creature and that I can become *any* one of my birds. I'm glad she didn't know of all of them.

The one at the cemetery didn't see anything out of the ordinary. I didn't believe the Gor-Nok was living there but he's frequently there. Must be something that tethers him to the fake Michael's grave. I know that there's some secret chamber underneath, but I haven't figured out how to open it. I wondered if it was only something in my dreams, something from a memory that wasn't real in reality. I sent *that* bird on a separate side mission. I needed him to find help because I could hear someone knocking at the door of the house through the ears of my other bird 'Shadow.'

I didn't have much time. I needed to get someone else here, quick, someone quick. I could get Dominic if things got really hairy, that's it! Harry, he could show up unexpectedly to do the whole lawyer bit with paperwork, the same way we had done it before.

That's what we'll do, I send my little soldier as a messenger bird. I just needed him to get close enough to Harry that I could relay a psychic message. Harry only knew younger Nonabel now, having completely forgotten who *I* was; not that he really knew the future me to begin with. It was too painful to try to rekindle that flame and gross especially now, knowing that his mouth had been on my grandmother. Yuck.

I found him out at his usual spot. Harry liked to have a nightcap at a local bar almost every night. I couldn't get in without being noticed but I was close enough to *think* a thought to him. I called his name and thought for him to check his car. His alarm sounded in his mind like it's going off. That was all I needed. Harry shot-up, paid for his drink, stepped out and walked to the lot listening intently for his car alarm.

Upon finding nothing to be wrong, I had my bird land on the car, it startled Harry. He tried to shoo me away after he chuckled a little realizing it was just a bird. I cawed in my bird voice, "Lucia, Lucia. Help! Help!" Then I flew away. Harry knew what that meant, he hopped into his car, and made his way quickly to the house. I flew overhead to make certain he was on his way. While we were on route, I returned my focus back to the man at the door.

Lucia had let him in, she sent Jesse to his bedroom. I don't know how the Gor-Nok was doing this, but he seemed to have acquired some manners, some etiquette, education. He knew exactly what he was talking about when it came to antiquity. He introduced himself rather properly as a distinguished gentleman would to a respected woman of the community. He had style, he had class. He was sophisticated, he was charming, almost seductive. He must've been using some kind of 'glamour magic' of some sort to try to convince Lucia that he wasn't a murderous, vile, evil, monster.

I could still tell he was my grandfather's killer, quite possibly my parents' murder; somehow, he had to have been involved. Somehow, he did it. It took every ounce of me to *not* kill him dead then and there. If Lucia truly had a trap, I wanted her to have enough back-up. Harry was on the way. I could summon Dominic in an instant, teleport him there. I could teleport, I could be in multiple places at once in the form of tiny were-rook-demons. Sure, we are small little midget versions of were-beasts, but we are scary as hell.

The Gor-Nok seemed mostly interested in books but knew enough about other antiquities. This guy was a lot older than he let on. The therian side seems to do that to us; he could very well be older than any of us. Lucia and the 'antique collector' talked about items in the house, but I know he's after mostly one thing, the Diary. Lucia brought him into the parlor and had the Diary at the coffee table so they could examine it.

He immediately produced a pair of museum quality inspector gloves as he looked through the pages. Lucia had done something to the Diary, it didn't seem to contain any magical spells from what I could see from my vantage point hiding in the shadows. It seemed like a family Bible, like an *actual* Diary. He praised the book, the quality of the craftsmanship; he flourished about the rarity. He laid it on real thick, I think he even made Lu-Lu blush once or twice. He inquired if there were any other books like this in the house. Lu-Lu was beginning to say that she had others when Harry finally arrived at the door. It took him long enough.

Lu-Lu excused herself to let Harry in and then right back out again. They had a brief conversation on the doorstep. Lu-Lu seemed annoyed.

Harry said, "A little bird told me I should stop by today." I was *literally* on the front porch as Midnight. Harry said, "See?! Selfsame little bird," he pointed at me. Lucia was super annoyed and shooed me away, teleporting my bird back into the study within me. It was rather uncomfortable to have the bird teleport back into my body without my control, or consent.

She allowed Harry to enter under his guise of having

paperwork to sign. Lucia was hoping to spring the trap, but she decided to continue this some other time. She sent the antique salesman on his way since it didn't work out how she had planned. I had my other little bird in the parlor watching out the window as the Gor-Nok got to his very nice vehicle in the driveway. Before he got in his vehicle, he looked around at the house.

He produced something from his hand, lighting a cigar. He chuckled to hear Lucia and Harry arguing within the parlor. She was mad that Harry had showed up unannounced. He was confused as to why he was summoned. That some little bird literally told him that Lucia needed help. Lucia was so mad at what I did, she screamed at me in her mind.

The Gor-Nok seemed content at the discord, smoking a cigar he took another puff, igniting it more. The ember was glowing bright orange in his dark silhouette against the light of the setting sun. He looked at the embers and extinguished it in his hand, smashing the cigar. Producing some kind of dust, with both his hands he took the burning embers, the crushed herbs and blew them out with the smoke in his mouth. He had done some kind of hex, an enchantment; he did something to us because we all got quiet at the same time.

He seemed content with it, dusted his nice suit coat, got into his car, and left. I gasped when I saw him perform the spell. I was worried that we might be in danger. Lucia already knew I was out and about, so I cawed, "Danger! Danger!"

Lucia got mad at me and screamed, "There you are!" and captured me with her mind, then pulled me out from behind the curtains; right to her grip. I transformed into my little weird demon and she barked orders at me.

"Back to where you belong, you little rat with wings!" and she teleported my little weird demon back into me. Again, not very comfortable. I could hear Harry and her arguing; I was listening with my remaining bird in the kitchen. I needed to be more careful and avoid detection. She needs to not know about this last bird. It was hiding in the cookie jar. I needed to maintain a way to escape and protect her.

I heard a knock at the door of the study, later that night. Lucia came in to scold me, "What the hell was that?!"

"You invite 'the devil' into our home!" I scolded her back.

Lucia said, "I set a trap and he fell for it. He came. I now know how to catch him. He doesn't necessarily want our power, but he wants our knowledge."

"Lu-Lu, he can already take whatever he wants. Did you know that he can pull thoughts from your mind? Fears, worries, doubts, anxieties? He lives off of that stuff! We cannot let him have the book! We cannot let him in the house! How are you planning on catching him? What is your *actual plan?* Sleeping with him?! Because you seem to be flirting with the guy! Harry also noticed a little, he was threatened by how friendly you were getting with this guy. I know you're lonely but you're *literally flirting* with 'the devil'!! If I were to die for my sins today, that's who I expect to be on the other side, waiting for me with a pitchfork in hand, leading me to my eternal damnation, that guy! And you let him inside! I thought you would've killed him as soon as he got to the house. I didn't know you're going to *actually* show him the Diary," I screamed.

"You know that wasn't the Diary, right?! You were spying on me," she replied.

"Yeah, what was that thing? There weren't any spells on those pages. I saw actual journal entries from an actual diary," I replied.

"It's actually a trap. I was hoping that he would touch it with his bare hands. I had placed some curses, poisons on the pages that would literally suck his memories from his mind," Lu-Lu explained.

"Oh, I know that spell! I've done that one," I said.

"Yeah, but this one would've removed *all* of his knowledge, giving him complete amnesia. Putting him in a comatose state of mind. Then I would've bound him physically and performed any other missing enchantments from the doppelgänger protocol."

"So, the book was laced with all doppelgänger traps?" I asked.

"I would've made him a phantom, a ghost. He would not have been able to talk, like you. Not mentally or even psychically. I would've made his brain a vegetable and then once he was pretty much powerless; I would teleport him under a rock, or a mountain somewhere and let him spend all of eternity in darkness," she declared.

"Oh! So, you *do* have a plan," I mused.

"But he was too careful. I think he was as afraid of us as we are of him and he prepared. He was cautious. Those damn gloves, the long sleeves! My next step would've been to try to make skin to skin contact," she said as she pondered.

"Lucia! You were going to kiss the guy?!" I said.

"If needs be? Yeah, we got to stop him."

"You can't!" I exclaimed.

"You and Michael couldn't have killed him and you both fought valiantly. I think this thing is much worse than a man or a witch or anything else. He may be a devil, a demon," Lucia said.

"There's no telling what this guy is! I really think that you and I are not equipped to stop him," I said.

"But trapping him, yes. If my plan had worked. I could've done it, but you *had* to call Harry! Ruined all of my fun," she declared.

"I was worried, you seemed out of your mind! I had to help," I responded.

"How did you even do that? I bound you and every one of your birds," She replied.

I chuckled a little, "Not all of us. Just let me help. Unbind me? Release my bonds, let me have *all* of my powers back?! I promise I'll behave, just release me, release me," I was trying to hypnotize her.

She chuckled, "Now, I know you better than you think. You and I both know you're lying through your teeth! You're a bad liar, my dear! I can't trust you. You don't even trust yourself, that's why you lock yourself in here. What, do you mean to tell me you can't be outside? You can be in the yard. You don't have to be hiding in here all the time," Lucia continued.

"There's no point in me being out if I can't destroy this guy. There's no future for me until he is dead. Until he dies, there's no life to live. There's nothing but death for everyone. Everything I ever loved, dead. Until I conquer that thing, until I find a way to be stronger than death. There's no point in living," I said before I departed into my dreamworld.

To see it happened from outside of my body is weird. My eyes kind of 'twitch' and it looks like my brain got severed from my spine internally. I drop to the floor and have a little seizure 'twitch' and become lifeless. At that point, I was at a deep level of 'R.E.M.' sleep; dreaming away and playing in my dream world and no amount of slapping, cold water, or shot of adrenaline will wake me up unless I want to.

That's how I ended most arguments with Lucia. I disconnect my brain from my body, then sleep in my dream world. I locked her out. It seemed kind of childish, like a toddler throwing a tantrum, but it was effective. She would later apologize, she always did. Then she feels compelled to give me back a power or let me have an ability back or share with me a new spell that she happens to be hiding from me until now. It wasn't a very healthy way for us to resolve our differences and arguments, but it was effective. I was still mad at her. I thought her plan sucked. I disagreed with her plan; and I knew there had to be a way to kill this guy.

Later that night, the night of Lucia's death, she told me that she wanted to give younger me the Diary.

"Yeah, I know. I know everything," I told her.

She laughed mockingly. She continued, "No, seriously I'm giving her the Diary tonight."

I said, "No, seriously. I know, I was there, and I also think that *I* was there, too. You know what I mean." I tried to plead with her one more time. "Please just let me be there?! Let me at least witness it. I don't need to be able to talk. I don't need to be seen. I'll just stand in the corner, being on the lookout for a strangely good looking tall dark and handsome gentleman."

"Handsome guys that spontaneously turn into evil killing death monsters?" She asked mockingly.

"Yeah, that kind of stuff!" I exclaimed.

She agreed to let me be there only in spirit.

I said, "Fine, but the moment my younger self leaves the room, I get my powers back, right?!"

"Yes, when she is out of sight, that's how it works with doppelgängers," Lu-Lu agreed.

"That's one hell of a curse! That's good to know."

She looked at me with a stern stare, "What are you planning, my dear?"

"Not one of *your* elaborate plans and schemes. I just drive by the seat of my pants!" I replied.

We waited in Lucia's room for younger Nonabel to show up; come back from a date. I remember that night. I was extra clingy and needy. I needed Derik to comfort me and he's such an awesome boyfriend; I was such a terrible girlfriend.

Younger me tried sneaking up the stairs. She had no stealth powers, no cat like reflexes yet, really no abilities. Every stair creaked like an ancient coffin with rusted hinges, making the nastiest noises. I think *a cat falling down the stairs* would've made less noise that night. Lu-Lu was trying not to chuckle at my thoughts. She was trying to pretend to read the Diary. When she heard the younger me walking past her door, she called for me.

Nonabel reluctantly entered. She was already rolling her eyes behind her closed eyelids. She politely asked Grandma Lu-Lu how she could help, "Did you need a glass of water, or something? Have you forgotten to take your pill?" *Chill pill,* younger me thought.

I thought back to Lu-Lu, *Wow, was I really that sassy?* But Lu-Lu shushed me; *Shh, don't make me regret giving you your powers back.* I thought, *fine.*

I quite literally watched the events of the night of her death unfold, getting to see the memory of when Grandma ruined my life by sharing with me the family secret. I was critically analyzing my own behavior. I was such a brat, a *spoiled rotten brat.* I really didn't appreciate what she was trying to do and what little time we had together. I was glad I got to spend these last 18 years making up for my mistakes; especially the mistake of not appreciating my family and spending more quality time with them.

I appreciated how patient Lu-Lu was with me, with younger me and me now. *I'm still a spoiled rotten brat.* Younger Nonabel had left the room. Lu-Lu was sobbing, she was worried that I didn't believe her.

I approached Grandma and the doppelgänger curse was wearing off. The curse was losing its strength as younger me got farther away. I was solidifying as she arrived in her bedroom. I sat next to Lucia on the bed. I held her hand as she cried, and I gave her a kiss on her cheek. I gave her the memories of what I did that night.

I showed her everything that younger me was going to do and I thought to her, *thank you.*

For what, my dear? She thought.

Thank you for sharing the truth, thank you for helping me to become who I am. I shared with her.

She was weeping now, we hugged for the longest time. After a while I laid her down and tucked her in.

I asked her, "Should I turn off the lamp?"

She said, "Usually, I leave it on as a night light. It scares off evil; for tonight, let them come."

I found myself a cozy corner where I could stand watch while she slept. I looked out the window of the house; the window that got destroyed that night, seemingly by me. Right about this time, younger me has learned how to move objects with her mind and learned how to fly, well, float. I know this because things in *this* room started to levitate and I had the weirdest sensation in my stomach as if gravity was falling out of my butt. I heard a 'thud' from down the hall. Yes, she just learned to fly.

It was getting late. I was getting tired and there was no sign of the Gor-Nok. Maybe Lucia's plan caused an alternate time-line, maybe I have somehow altered time. I thought we were careful. She had put up so many safeguards to keep me from messing with my own future. Maybe with all the changes in time he wasn't going to come at all, who knew; *I* should have known.

Before I had even noticed, I had fallen asleep. Even ghosts need to sleep like the dead. I heard Lu-Lu moan in her sleep, it woke me, and I gasped for air. I looked around the room, it was still intact; the monster had not arrived yet. I thought he was going to show himself physically, but Lu-Lu seemed to be struggling in her dreams. Did the lamp keep him out? There was still so much I didn't know, but she seemed to be in trouble.

I let myself slip into the dreamscape as I touched her hand; I saw that she was sharing her dream with younger me. The first dream where she taught me so much. She was trying to bind the monster, not try to kill him, but she was trying to bind the Gor-Nok instead. She still thought he was a demon and was doing a series of curses and rune circles trying to trap him. I had seen this before; I knew this wasn't going to work. I tried to let her know as clearly as I could, but it seemed like I wasn't able to use very much power in this state of being.

I told her with my mind, *he's going to kill us! Get us out of here! Get Nonabel out of here!* She teleported my younger self out of the dream. And it was just him and I left in the dream-scape. I took the lamp in the dream and tossed it on the floor at his feet, igniting him as it burned brighter. I could feel the light growing in the actual room and I woke up. I inadvert-ently turned on the lamp revealing the Gor-Nok standing in the room as a man. He had been chanting some type of curse that was keeping Lu-lu asleep. His eyes were glowing green and he was shaking that weird voodoo doll thing around his neck. Whatever he was doing, he was killing her!

He hadn't seen me yet; I was still a ghost. I psychically called out to younger Nonabel to wake her up. I drew the focusor-sword from a tiny vortex in my hand. I took a breath before I stabbed the sword towards his heart. He slapped the blade of the sword between the palms of his massive hands.

He chuckled as he woke from his trance, his body shifting from man to boar-beast. We fought over the sword a bit in the room making quite the mess and the monster demanded to have the Diary in exchange for the life of Lu-lu. Saying, "The power there in will make me unstoppable!"

Lu-lu screamed for me to not listen to him, "it's not worth it!" The commotion had woken her. The monster began to strangle her more with its mind connection with her. I ignited Lu-lu's sword, giving me access to her powers and I stabbed the beast in the stomach. He laughed and continued to strangle Lu-lu psychically.

With all of my rage, I shot the biggest blast of lightning I could ever remember and blew a hole straight through his chest crushing him through the wall and out into the yard. The beast laughed as he hobbled into the forest. Lu-lu was dying, she couldn't breathe. The Gor-Nok had taken something from her. The light of the oil lamp was flickering weaker. I knew it meant she didn't have much time. Nonabel and her family were coming, and I had blocked the door. I said my good-bye, I told her sorry and left the room through the hole in the house.

The Gor-Nok was getting away, he had stolen something from her, he had stolen her soul; and I needed to get it back. The beast was laughing at me. I was raining thunder down from the sky. I sent lightning bolts to block his retreat. I was flying and riding the lightning down missing, him almost every time. He wasn't trying to stop me or fight me; he was trying to get away. He was trying to evade me. He was trying to get somewhere in a hurry. We battled throughout the town, matching blow for blow against one another until we got to the cemetery.

I lost him somewhere in the dense fog. I was worried that he tried to do the same trick of spreading his toxic, fear gas all over the place; make it look like fog. I held my breath; the tombstones seemed to be getting taller, rising up out of the fog, taking on the head and shoulder silhouettes of dead men. The silhouettes started to enclose around me, getting closer; moaning, whispering.

He had gotten to me already; he had infected me with his gas. I fell for the trap. I need to be more careful. This guy was smarter than I am. He was way better at this game of cat and mouse. But why is he running? He could easily come back and destroy me; end my madness with one blow.

I have no idea what I'm *actually* doing, in reality I could be swatting at gravestones with my bare hands, busting them or my hands. Breaking all my bones against stones. I could be in the middle of a grocery store, freaking out at local town people not knowing what I was doing because of the madness; because of the toxins in my mind.

I teleported myself back to the forest, hoping I was still somewhere nearby, hoping I had imagined all this; and this wasn't some kind of nightmare. I circled the cemetery staying in the forest, staying away from the fog. I tried to keep myself as stealth and invisible as I could. I was learning how to manipulate the powers of the doppelgänger, how to turn it off and on. I became a shadow, so I could sneak to the other end of the cemetery, the older end.

The Gor-Nok had changed back into a man and was trying to catch his breath. He looked around to see if the coast was clear before he opened his one hand, revealing a small flickering flame. He used his necklace again; his weird voodoo doll thingy, and was shaking it, chanting some weird words. I listened to the whispers in the wind in hopes of translating the spell; he was calling for Death.

I was ready to oblige! I activated my talons of death but that wasn't the death he was calling for. Some of these older statues in the cemetery were symbolic images of angels and saints, of demons, or even Death. There was a statue of a Pale Horse with a Pale Rider. The Gor-Nok was standing by the statue chanting, calling for Death. Everything living, every plant around us fell to the earth, and wilted as though dead. The air became electrified, my goosebumps stood on end; the hairs had stood up.

My Sight activated involuntarily enraging in my eyes, cold, icy liquid pulsating through the veins in my sockets, surging through my brain. I had not seen this many ghosts before, but I could see the souls of the dead lingering around their graves. The statue wasn't made of stone but was a spirit, a shadow of pestilence, the Grim Reaper himself. "Who has summoned me?"

The Gor-Nok bowed down before him and held up the tiny flame in his hands. "It is thy humble servant. I have promised thee 100 souls and here is the 99th."

My heart gave out and my strength completely left me. He was the Devil and he made a deal with Death to end my family, to end it with me! He was seeking revenge for what I did to him by coming back in time. They heard me gasp.

Death was outraged, "You are not alone! Bring me that 100th soul and then I will give you back yours."

I knew I couldn't fight them both. I had a hard-enough time beating the Gor-Nok in small battles. No matter how much I had learned, no matter how much more experience I gained. All the new tools I had acquired, new powers I have, he seemed to get stronger.

I think I knew why I was not able to beat him. Because his ally was Death. I was not about to fight him now. I wouldn't even begin to know how that fight would go down. I quickly excused myself and vanished in the vortex. I retreated back to the house and began the work of setting up the enchantments, the hexes, the curses, poisons, the traps, and snares; everything that Lucia had done before to protect us. Every nasty curse I could imagine I set around the borders of our land.

I commanded Great-Grandfather Dominic to patrol to keep us safe. I scattered out my army of birds from within me around the perimeter of the property and to other strategic places in the town. I commanded them to be quiet, to be alert; to be my eyes, and ears. I resolved to keep watch over the family. I allowed my younger self to go through the motions of the events in my memories as they were meant to play out.

I guided her as much as I could as still, small voice, a whisper, influencing her to fulfill her birthright. There were times I had to be forceful. There were times I had to pretend to *be* her. There were things I needed to teach her, and I could only teach her in dreams. I begin to understand and accept that I was always meant to go back in time. I was always meant to get to know my grandfather and see him in action. Meant to battle alongside him, to fight the devil. Meant to bring him back to Lucia so she could say goodbye. I knew I was always meant to come back to this time and learn everything I could from a woman I thought I hardly knew. I knew I was meant to make up for all that lost time and she somehow knew it to the day, when time was fast approaching, another momentous day when younger me and only slightly less experienced, from a certain point of view, was about to take her trip across the world and across space and time.

It was a scary thing being on the threshold of the future, not really knowing what was going to come next. I had used up all of my memories and I had an entire other Diary to add to the index of my time I spent in the past training and learning and loving my family. I heard someone talking in the library, I got excited to hear her voice. Zatie had come in to do as I had asked. I could hear my own voice telling her what to do psychically. When their conversation ended, Nonabel had kicked her out of the study; I followed them down the stairs.

Nonabel had slammed the door shut after leading Zatie back to the other side of the door. Zatie had been weeping; she was losing her mind, trying to come to grips with what she just learned. Zatie worried for me, worried I was about to do something stupid. I had just asked my younger sister to tell me how to make a 'time travel device.' I opened the door to find Zatie crying on the floor. Her tear-soaked eyes were sore and red. Somehow, she could make sad tears flow, in an instant and turn them into happy tears the moment she smiled. She smiled just like Mom. Zatie was a lot like Mom in so many ways. I was so glad to see my Zatie again.

She couldn't believe that she was seeing me there. I know there are so many questions going through her mind. I picked her up and hugged her and thought to her again: *I know, I was stupid. It was so stupid of me to not share this part of my life with you; but I'm glad I'm back.*

"Back? I was just talking to you. Well, in my brain, some-how? Are you tricking me again?!" Zatie asked hysterically. I smiled and nodded 'no.'

I opened the door to the library telekinetically and shook my head, "No more lies, no more tricks. Come Zatie, let me teach you all about our magical family.

Entry #15

Daydreams

After bringing Zatie into the Library, I turned up all the lamp lights so she could see everything. I no longer wanted to hide, and I needed a confidant. I needed someone to share this part of my life with. Someone I can trust. Someone I knew could keep a secret and help me protect it. Zatie had so many questions.

I felt like I was being interrogated again just not as torturous as with Lu-lu. I gave Zatie the full tour of the Library. She ate it up like a kid in a candy store. We were playing like little children on Christmas morning. For her, heaven was an enormous library. Zatie was always reading, she loves books! She rattled off questions that I ignored as I gave my tour.

Then she had asked me, "If I could actually have gone back in time, I would've saved Mom and Dad. Where, when did you go when you had asked me for the time travel device? Did you go to save them?! Did it work?" I took her to see the Nevergator in the Vault. I activated the Nevergator with my mind, then showed it to her. I let her see the cogs spinning, the dials moving then I turned it off. I caused it to shut-off in its glass vault box. She reached for the box, and I instantly swatted her hand, then wagged a finger at her.

"You *don't* want to touch that," I told her.

She asked me, "How did you learn all this? When did you have the time, Nona?"

I knew she wanted me to answer *all* of these questions. I just wanted her to calm down.

I asked her, "I know you have questions about all of this. What would you like to know first?"

Zatie said, "Is this where you go all the time? Where did all this come from? How did you learn about all this? When did you have the time to learn this and go to school? You're sick half of the time? Why are you so sick half the time?"

I summoned the Diary to me; I knew I needed to update some things. I opened it to a blank section. I summoned my journey journal from my little room. I opened the journey journal to its middle and laid it on top of the Diary, our family Diary and melted the journal pages into Diary as Lu-lu had done before.

Then I called the book on Time-travel from the book self, the volume with the torn pages on the Nevergator and restored them.

I explained to Zatie, "The Diary acts as an index to the entire Library. Whatever book we bring in here to the Library, if you want to be able to access it through the Diary, you have to insert it information into the Diary. It acts as a gateway to all the knowledge."

"All of this stuff was written by people like us," Zatie had asked, presumptuously including herself to that list of authors.

"Yes, Seers and Sorcerers from a time before time. Earth worshipers and Sun Gods followers all have added their secrets to these pages. These refugees hidden from the rest of humanity. Who are the dreamers, thinking up dreams?" I mused with a profound respect for my ancestors that had come before.

"Honey, are you all right, you're talking like you have a concussion?" Zatie asked me.

"I might need a vacation, or a nap," I replied.

Zatie said, "Well, you're not due to be back for a day or two and the only people expecting you to be home are myself and Jesse."

"Oh, I would *love* to take an actual nap."

"I'll hold down the fort alone, just sitting here reading books," Zatie said hopefully. That sounds like a welcoming temptation, but I could not leave Zatie unattended, tempted with all these powers.

I told her, "First things first. I need to establish some ground rules. I am the Matriarch of the coven, the Priestess of the covenant power; all our family inheritance of magic flows through me. If you or Jesse were to receive an inheritance it would be by my authority. If you were to do magic and I didn't like what you did I literally have the power to reverse it; to undo what you've done. I can take the power away, even take your normal human abilities away."

I caused the air around Zatie to vanish creating a void. She started to gasp for air. I snapped my fingers and restored the air.

"I can take your very will from you and trap you in a cell of helplessness. That's what you need to understand first and foremost. There's always someone who has more power than you and I can take your will even while I am sleeping. So, please don't burn down the house, just read, just catch up on what I've gone through the last eighteen years."

Zatie mouthed questioningly, '18 years?'

"That's how long I was trapped back in time, I think if you read the journey journal first, that section of the Diary, then you should be caught up to where I'm at now," I said as I pulled the journal from the Diary.

"Let me take a nap. Recharge my batteries. I'll set an alarm." A flutter of feathers appeared from my chest; my bird, Twilight, landed on my wrist. I sent her to the cage, then shut it with my mind.

"Whoa, is that real?!" Zatie asked about Twilight.

"Yes, she is my alarm-crow clock-thingy. When you're caught up then we'll talk," I half-yawned.

"Ok, night, night!" Zatie was trying to get me out of the Library as soon as she could.

"Get caught up, then I'll start teaching. Until then, as Matriarch, I forbid you from doing magic the moment I leave this room. In fact, I have placed some bonds upon these books, this room, nothing from this room is to leave without my permission," I replied.

Feeling that I had safeguarded the Library, and its knowledge from Zatie causing *too much* trouble while I have a nap; I felt a great weight of stress relieved from my body and I laid myself down in my bed in the study. I allowed Zatie to catch up on my adventures while I caught up on sleep.

I entered the dreamworld and I was greeted by my little man Dusk, my Daydream Nix. He bowed courteously and said, "My Queen, it is an honor to see thee! Welcome home."

He escorted me to a black horse-drawn carriage that was pulled by six miniature black Pegasus ponies and he took the reins after helping me mount into the carriage.

"Where to today, M'lady?" He politely asked.

I told him as I yawned, "Somewhere to sleep. I want to be alone."

"Right away, M'lady," he said, and the carriage took flight. He escorted me to my mansion in my dreamscape. I went to my large comfy bed in my safe room. Having unloaded my mind into the Diary, and having confided in Zatie, given her charge to understand who I am and what's going on; I felt such a relief, a burden that I felt that I alone had to carry.

The release of all the worries was so nice. Zatie was so sweet and so welcoming as an ally. I quickly drifted off to my peaceful dreams within my dream world, knowing that everything was going to be different; everything was going to get better, that everything was safe.

The morning air felt crisp when I woke from my bed to the sound of sweet songbirds chirping outside of my window. I sat up in my soft white bed and stretched out a huge yawn. I was yawning for the longest time, it felt so good to recharge and refresh! I lounged for a while in my mansion, like I did on Saturday mornings when I was nine years old.

I enjoyed a nice, relaxing bubble bath being serenaded by invisible musicians with floating instruments nearby. I enjoyed a beauty routine. My own mental day spa to recoup and recover. When I emerged from my mansion ready to face the woes of this world, and I had Dusk take me back to the door to the threshold between dreams and reality.

I woke in my room in the study to find that Zatie had put a blanket on me. I didn't need one, I was a hollow shell made of feathers and beaks; but she doesn't know that, yet. She had brought me breakfast in bed and had set it on my nightstand. The sweet smell of fresh French-toast, cinnamon-maple syrup, melted butter, and a side of bacon was surreal and intoxicating. I can't remember the last time I ate *real* food. I had been on my diet of birdseed for so long that I had forgotten what it was like to be human, to be loved.

As I ate my breakfast in the privacy of my little room, I was curious as to how Zatie was accepting all of this, all of the family lies and truth, read between the lines, blurred, faded, in foggy memories. The holes in her own mind being refilled. My role as 'Aunt Lily'.

I had activated the Seer's Sight and used it to rewind the last few hours. Zatie had let me sleep through an *entire day* and it was now Sunday morning. That's why she brought me breakfast; I must've really been tired. Even though this has been my home for eighteen or more years, more than I can remember now, it didn't feel like I was back home until the curse of time, the curse of the doppelgänger had been lifted from me. I knew I had my powers back every ounce of it. I knew there was nothing binding me, trapping me anymore, forcing me to watch my family die.

Now I have the power to change my future and save what's left of my family. I fast forwarded our next conversation to see how long it would take for me to answer her questions verbally. She has so many questions. Zatie started her own journal of notes. I don't even know where she found another empty notebook to do that with, but she had done it.

I decided that the best way to go about this was to show her, teach her. I had done enough talking. Time to start doing! Lucia has already given me a gift by giving me a place where we can practice, a place where we can train. I know how to bring people into my dreamscape because Lucia had shown me how to do these things.

I opened the door of my little interrogation room out to the main area of the lobby of the Library. The Library appeared much larger when you have all the lights on. Zatie was hard at work studying from multiple books, taking notes in her own journal. I let out the biggest yawn of relief and as she began to speak, I psychically pinched her mouth shut then I shushed her.

"Coffee first, then I'll answer all your questions," she happily went to go get me coffee. When she came back, before she began to speak, I reminded her, "I already know what you're going to think before you think it. I know what you're gonna say before you say it. This is not me being arrogant, this is a gift. It's a spell that I have already performed, a spell that you might need to learn. Actually, it's more of a potion but there are spells involved; there's a process to the whole thing, as you can tell from your studies. The things I'm about to show you, I do not grant you permission to share this information, this knowledge, share this location or anything that I teach you to any other entity living or dead, do you understand?"

Zatie was so excited, she was on the edge of her seat ready to burst. Ready to explode with her questions. I took a giant sigh to relieve possible anxieties. I released her lips from my mental block.

"Let us start from the beginning. Zatie, the very first thing that I feel that you should know is that we are in a dream," I explained.

Zatie raised her hand, "Um, are you talking philosophically or metaphorically?"

I began to change the familiar landscape of the Library by pushing the bookcases back with my mind, expanding the size of the room. Cleaning up the clutter on the floor, the stacks discarded notes, pages. Making desks melted into the floor, creating a much larger room, more suited for fencing and fighting.

"Welcome to *my* dream and *your* worst nightmare," I declared as Zatie started clapping.

"Don't do that," I said. I was starting to regret this. I remembered my first lessons from Lu-Lu. Fear. Zatie needs to know her fears.

"Ho-fu!" I whispered. I called plants from the corners of the room, causing them to grow like ivy, like giant plant-snakes to bite and hiss at Zatie's heels. For her benefit, I was saying spells out loud at first. I used the Fear spell, taking advantage of the fact that she doesn't like what she doesn't understand. She's afraid of the unknown, like most people. That's a good place to start. As a sneak attack I floated off the ground, so that my sightless snake vines would only try to go after Zatie solely based off her body heat. Zatie started to scream, kick, and dance in place to avoid the snake-vines.

"The second thing you need to understand is your fears. What are *you* afraid of? What causes you to lose control, lose your sense of security, and confidence? Confidence is the key to overcoming your fears."

Zatie ran away from the snakes and hid behind me. She started pulling me to the ground. I gave her my hand and lifted her up above the ground. Then I made the floor fall out from beneath us. She clung to me and screeched a little. I let us fall and I narrowed the chasm so that we could use the snake-vines to save us. I tried to get her to no longer be afraid of the snake-vines.

"You'll want to use them to save yourself from falling forever!" I yelled as we fell.

She had let go of me to get hold of the snake-vines and they held onto her. I stopped falling, stood there in the air.

"What are you gonna do, hang there all day? Tell them what you want to do," I said.

"You mean the snake-vines?" She asked.

"Tell them what to do, they belong to you."

"Belong to me?!" Zatie questioned my commands.

"They are *your* nightmares, *your* fear made manifest in this place. It is the pure essence of fear, it is embodied in a lack of control. You show that by how you prune your garden and take care of your plants. You try to keep weeds from uncontrollably growing and choking out your plants. Correct me if I'm wrong. It's just the fear that you let me see." Now she has other fears I thought.

"No, that seems about right. Can we get out of here now?" The vines quickly pulled her up from her hole, that wasn't that deep. She was lifted up into the bosom of a giant plant-monster. I rose out of the hole and was on the grassy meadows of my dreamscape with her in the dark side before the dawn.

Zatie shrieked a little, realizing that the vines were an extension of this tree monster that had a giant head that looked like a rose with petals as lips. I reacted a little to her fear and I chuckled.

"Are you sure that everything's OK? See your fears obey your commands, that's why she pulled you up. This is your creation. Fear can create all kinds of imaginary elements in our mind. It, well, *you* can create obstacles, walls." As I was saying these things, we were coming back into reality. We watched the walls of the Library close in around us.

"How do you feel?" I asked.

"I'm shaking, I'm terrified!" she replied.

"Come here," I gave her a hug as she cried, I tried to calm her mind.

"Now, by touching me, you've given me access to your mind. Involuntarily giving me access through tactile-telepathy, to know things, secret things. Emotions. Remember that touching someone is an exchange. You have to block out messages to people when you are touched," I said as I ended the hug and looked into her sore eyes.

"Zatie, you're so good at empathetically feeling what other people feel! That's a natural gift. Your gift! Feeling the emotions of others without having to touch them. Without having to siphon it from them. Like I have to, like Lucia. You need to learn to perfect it, that way it can be a shield and protection for you. Sensing the emotions that others are unintentionally broadcasting because they have not embraced their fears. They have not learned to control what they're feeling."

"Broadcasting? Don't you mean thinking?"

"I mean broadcasting, we can have feelings, we just don't need to broadcast them." *Sure, you keep it inside your mind.* I echoed in her head. Zatie raised her hand after rubbing her head.

"Honey, you don't need to raise your hand."

"So, it's not real, none of this is real?" she asked.

"Zatie, this world is as real as your mind wants to make it. In fact, this is as real as *my mind* wants to make it," I made the room behind us fade back into the meadows of my dreamscape. She was startled to see the outside world, the daylight, as dawn approached with the rising of the sun in my world.

"Zatie, I want you to understand, now that you're part of my world, now that you can walk into the world of witches and mystery, of monsters and mayhem, that fear can stop us; we can get in our own way. The things we think, the feelings we have, the illusions we create in our mind. Whether in our mind or in reality, fear can stop us from living, from being happy," I explained.

We spent the next few days hiding there in the Library, whenever we could. We occupied our free time with studying but pretending to be doing girl stuff in Zatie's room. In the next few days and well, every night we were sharing our dreams. Zatie was a fast learner, a very quick study. She had an amazing memory for the slightest details. She could catch on to subtle changes in emotion, moods, connotations, and things that people said or thought. She was very sensitive. She had more energy and a boundless passion for learning than I have ever been able to obtain unless I was addicted to studying magic.

Zatie understands, at her young age, the dangers of addiction and what happens when we give into carnal, physical desires. She knows what it does to our minds. She understands how the brain works better than I ever have. She was learning her lessons very well. I had to recharge my batteries more often and take a break to keep up with her.

I was still dealing with a lot of leftover emotional baggage; I'm having to relive all the trauma of my past. The younger kids were fairly sheltered, they didn't see as much as I did my first run. I definitely got to see a lot more my second run. I know that I feel old or more worn out in my soul, I feel that it's been 20 years but for Zatie it had been 20 seconds when I had gone back to the past.

While I rested, Zatie was not only conquering and mastering spells, she was writing new ones! Zatie had such an intuitive way of thinking. Every new idea was so exciting that you wanted to do it as well. She had such a scientific mind; she had a great understanding of how everything works and how everything is interconnected.

We had greater freedom to explore these new powers in the privacy of the Library and in our dreamscapes. Jesse hardly cared that we were gone *all the time.* He kept himself busy with watching his shows and barely doing homework. I might've hypnotized him to leave us alone. I didn't always work though.

Once in a while I would give Zatie real world, practical lessons with less safeguards and more opportunities for chance and failure by being outside of the Library. It was mostly practicing in the barn or in the woods against me as a dark angel. Once or twice, I might've hurt her with our real-world battles.

"Debris and broken glass flying at you from different angles is harder to anticipate in a world where your brain doesn't control everything; in a world where you didn't make up the rules. You just showed up as a new player at the table and have no idea what the rules are until after a few rounds of losing," I told her as I pulled glass fragments from her cuts.

"Wait here while I get some dirt," I said.

"Oh, Nona, I hate the dirt-method, there's gotta be a healthier way?!" She was taking care of her wound in the kitchen while I was getting some hollowed earth from Michael's grave.

Jesse had caught her cleaning her wounds and asked what had happened. She said that she was all right. She has a slight stubborn will about fixing her problems by herself. It's a good trait, we have to realize it, then later how capable we are or not, that things are better if you have help. Jesse noticed she was struggling, getting a Band-Aid on the cut and came to help her.

He wasn't buying her on-the-spot excuses for how she had got cut. She claimed to be working in our garden. Jesse had a pretty good bull-crap detector; having told a few lies himself. Despite our efforts to hide our practical real-world training; Jesse was growing suspicious. All the lies, erasing his memory; I was getting the nagging feeling that he was onto us. He knew we were up to something.

Jesse always seemed like a relationship I could fix later over a bottle of beer. I always felt like I had more time with him; that I'd have a hard time kicking him out of the house later when it was time for him to go off to college.

We were getting into a new routine of life. We were using magic to solve almost everything. It was fun having someone to help me protect my secrets. Protect my family. We got really good at dream manipulation. We got really good at trapping people in a daydream or a nightmare of our choosing, without them even ever being aware it. It was like letting them believe slowly until their mind boiled in the madness of the fantasy.

I believe this was the key to trapping that murderer, the Gor-Nok. We would lure him to believe that everything is okay; getting him to trust in *our* illusions. We tested our illusions on each other, also on Jesse; messing with him was fun. We even messed with Harry from time to time. I started bringing people into *waking dreams* during school.

Unless I was with Derik; the rest of the time I was practicing breaking up with him. I didn't feel right having feelings for other people. If not for his cousin or my lawyer; I might try to make it work. But it wasn't any more, not for me. So, I worked out my therapy through real world scenarios. Practice daydreams using the actual people and then resetting them, rewinding their minds, getting them to forget. It was fun, it was somewhat therapeutic; I was building more and more confidence in the hopes that I would someday figure a way to let Derik down easy. I might have to do it before I go off to college.

My real life was just *too* much to explain, especially to someone who doesn't understand my world, and someone who hasn't really *been* in my world for a long time. I might be better off with someone *more* like me, with someone like Harry. Harry already expressed that our relationship would be inappropriate and for some reason that makes me want to be with him even more.

I needed to distract myself from my feelings, I needed to stop indulging in emotions I wasn't really ready to follow through with by actually doing something in the real world to fix it. I buried myself in the books and schoolwork, witchcraft and dream-scaping, combat training. I got better at isolating myself from those who wouldn't understand.

I might have used my gifts to convince Derik to spend more time with his cousin. I spent a lot of time teaching and training Zatie. Teaching each other spells. Perfecting, mastery and the execution of spells. Zatie had an academic approach to everything. Everything became a lesson plan, or a lecture. She had especially loved the concept of conquering your daydreams and your nightmares. Her nightmare of her life getting out-of-control was easy for her to figure out. I did it by giving her a place where she could, with 100% confidence, manipulate and organize.

She got over her fears by understanding what she had not understood. The conjuring of fears. They are greater than any powers we have seen, and I had ever mastered. Zatie realized that embracing our fears, losing our fears of the unknown was the key to conquering them, gaining their confidence, their trust. She was actually quite the perfect individual; well rounded, well educated, kept her passions and appetites in check. She held herself with confidence. She spoke with authority. She delivered with expert execution.

I was creating new doubts and new fears; doubt I would never be able to stop her if she had somehow become my enemy. Fears. I would avoid answering questions about the Gor-Nok. I have been telling Zatie that he comes and goes. Sometimes he acts like he's interested in coming around for a fight. Then he'll scare off due to what we have done to protect us.

We had enough defenses in place and I'm not trying to let him walk in our kitchen, like Lucia. I needed to be certain that we can for sure end him for real this time before I let down my guard. Our defenses were good enough that we had set into place. They exceeded in keeping him out. We had become pretty good at spotting his disguises, and his decoys. Pretty good at recognizing his attempts to 'hack' into our nightmares.

I spent most nights on the prowl, after we had set up our security defenses and my watch birds. I would spend my nights patrolling the town as a ghost-phantom. Shifting locations between birds in different places. Teleporting through each different crow as though they were a gateway with greater ease. The doppelgänger state of being a ghost requires less physical, tangible elements. So, I could more easily operate as one bird at a given time.

I told Zatie she should try something like this, becoming a whole nest of rats or spiders; it's a good way to be in multiple places at once. She argued that I'm too spread out, "your defenses are thin. but after reading the process it took for you to accidentally discover this," she politely said, "thanks, but no thanks; I don't feel like splitting up my soul," she argued that dividing her attention would diminish your focus.

I respected her decision. Sadly, though, we discovered that she did not carry the therian gene. It wouldn't necessarily work the same way, but it was fun watching her get bit by different animals.

We began actively planning on how to kill that murderer. It was time to let Zatie meet Grandpa Dominic and Harry; not Harold Anderson, the lawyer, but Harry the werecrock. Zatie said that she had caught up on my 18 year-long journey journal, but I knew there were things that she still wanted me to show her. Things like Michael's final resting spot, for instance.

I found her out at the spot by the pond. It was starting to become sunset. "So, this is where he *really* is?" Zatie asked, pointing to the base of the scarecrow.

I shared with her some of the memories, conjuring it around us, images of the private service that Lucia, Harry, and I had with Michael. I opened up the memories but Zatie had to pull herself out, she was too overwhelmed with emotion. She was feeling so many things, mostly she felt pity for the tragedy.

I said, "Do you understand now why I had to leave before? I had to try to save him. Save Michael. I couldn't beat the monster then and I am having a hard time beating it still."

Zatie noted, "On the bright-side, Grandma got to see Grandpa one last time."

I told her, "That's true, I guess I *did* do something good. Speaking of something good, I have a gift for you. I'd like to give you the chance to meet your great-grandfather, Dominic!" I whistled for Dominic who was somewhere in the woods, I could hear his footfalls, he was coming in fast.

He bounded out of the woods; dark, sleek, and hairless. Blazing, glowing red eyes, his sharp, spindle black teeth smiling. Zatie cowered behind me. I activated my were-rook abilities to give me increased strength and power in my arms, exposing my talons. My feathers were emerging from parts of my arm and hair.

Zatie was startled by this impromptu display of my powers. I guess I haven't shown her what my therian powers looks like.

"I can't wait to hear how loud you squeal when I go full-harpy!" I said to Zatie as I grabbed Dominic by his collar and leash chain.

"Harry had to help me put this on Dominic so I can take him on walks when I go out on my patrols in the woods," I said as I pet Dominic's head.

"Wait, Harry knows about *all this*?!!" Zatie asked.

"Yeah, you didn't read about Harry in the Diary?"

"I read that he and Lucia were dating, and I got grossed-out; but I didn't know that you and he are, were..," she was fidgeting with the words.

"Bite your tongue Zatherine." I tried not to think of too many times about Harry.

"No, I didn't know that Harry is a were-thingy." "Were-croc, did somebody say my name?" Harry walked casually out of the woods like he just got out of a board meeting, still wearing a suit and tie, looking dashing and debonair. I might have pushed the thought into his mind, a little.

"You've been waiting for me, haven't you? You don't write, you don't call. If it wasn't for your sister, I wouldn't have known that you come back at all! It's almost as if you're... avoiding me. Are you avoiding me?" Harry asked.

"No, no! I'm just a bit busy with the other magical things in my life," I replied.

"It was magical, wasn't it?" Harry responded.

Zatie, being way too intuitive, having too many gifts that came natural to her, was catching onto our subtle banter.

She gasped, "Wait! You two kissed, didn't you?!" I immediately tried to shut this down, "Oh no, no, no, no, no! I would never, especially now!"

"Oh, but you wanted to," Harry reminded me.

"Lucia dated you, eww!" I exclaimed to clarify.

"What's stopping you now?" Harry asked.

"I have a boyfriend," I replied.

"That didn't stop us before. Have you been talking to him or have you been avoiding your boyfriend as well?" Harry asked.

"Wait, you're avoiding Derik?!" Zatie asked. "SILENCE!!" Everyone and everything got quiet.

"Harry, I summoned you here to help my sister understand were-creatures." I said through gritted teeth.

"I don't see why you called *me*. You're the expert by now," he said as he turned his back to me.

I know that you are mad at me. Harry, you and I need to talk, yes, but we're not gonna have this discussion NOW. I thought to him.

"Please, give her a small demonstration," I asked.

"Well, why don't you?" Harry replied.

"I'm about ready to show *you* a thing or two!"

"As you wish M'lady," Harry said as he took off his jacket, then slowly unbuttoned his shirt a little, then rolled-up one of the sleeves. Zatie was getting a little *too* excited. She was blushing.

"Harry, could you please just perform the transformation?!" I said abruptly.

"Well, Zatherine, is it? Sometimes when the therianthropy trait exhibits for the first time..." "Zatherine's gene is canceled or dormant..." I said.

"Zatie, it's just Zatie please," she stated.

"When someone like me has been bitten by a rabid animal, we are subjected to the first level of the were-beast curse. Your grandfather was there to help me with a potion he had that makes the transition easier. A potion which you used to a whole other level of therianthropy," he said pointing to me.

"A poly-therianthrope. Poly-therian," I said.

"Yes, Michael could become multiple animals at will without having to go through the initial pain of the transformation," Harry started changing his hands and arms; he was increasing in size. He tried not to bust the seams of his shirt.

"Oh, don't worry, I'll fix the shirt if it breaks, tears or rips," Zatie sheepishly mumbled mostly to herself.

Harry said, "But I like this shirt. So, I'm only going to go so far. It takes many years to get to where you can use the powers on different incremental levels. There are unfortunate souls that don't have someone like your grandmother and your grandfather, or your sister now to help them with these painful transitions. And educate them, they have no control over it, when or how intensely the transformation will be, but I'll tell you this; the pain is like nothing you'll ever feel, trust me."

"Well, she'll have to trust you, sadly. I think that gene skipped Zatie. However, we discovered she has a different trick! Zatie, show him!"

She picked up my flowers from Grandpa's grave. She smelled it and was mentally preparing herself for what was about to happen.

"All right, are you ready? Are you sure about this?!" She hesitated.

I said, "Yeah, it's freaking awesome!"

Harry was a little cautious of what was going to happen as well. *Nonabel, what is she doing?*

"Just watch, Harry, this is so cool! It's a new level, a whole new level of therianthropy for you."

"OK, this should be interesting," he sighed.

Zatie smiled with her lips, bit her tongue, and then bit into the Rose, thorns and all letting her lips bleed. She looked as though she was a Vegan-vampire, sucking the life from the rose, draining the petals of colors and it wilted to the ground as she dropped the stem.

Harry gulped and said, "Wow, that was, that was, um..." *Disgusting,* he thought.

"Disgusting. I know, just wait," I said pointing excitedly at the ground.

The Rose started twitching, the leaves, the petals, the stem all started to swell and grow then expand; contracting as her genes and DNA were intermixing with that of the plant. It was her blood that carried the venom of transformation. Zatie was the 'rabid animal' that bit into the helpless creature, causing it to turn into a Were-plant. Mind you, it was a small, weird demon thingy, but vicious, nonetheless.

"This is your ability?! You're right, this is a new level. You Lamia-Venatora women never cease to amaze me!" Harry was slowly clapping in surprise.

Zatie wiped her lips and said, "Thank you."

The small Were-plant bowed to her, she curtsied. Zatie called it up to her, patting her thighs below her pleated skirt like she would call a dog. The plant jumped up into her arms and she held it on her shoulders like a pet parrot.

We discussed the other levels of therianthrope. Harry noted that I had taken being poly-therianthrope to an entirely unique level of not becoming a separate animal of different species, but separate individual animals in the same species, like a whole flock of crows.

I gave Zatie a little demonstration by causing several

birds to exit from my body as though I had them hidden under my jacket. At the end of the evening, Harry said goodbye as he gave Zatie a business card and instructed her to call if ever she needed anything.

I walked him to the driveway and said, "Here let me walk you to your car."

Harry replied, "But I ran here."

I made his car appear here again in the driveway. "Yeah, I don't miss that. But I do miss you," he said. "Yeah, okay, Harry. We will talk later. I'm just not ready right now. All right?!" I replied.

"But you owe me a story. I want to know what happened in Borneo!" He said as he ducked into his car.

I waved goodbye. I was dreading having that conversation, like discussing my feelings with him or my feelings with Derik. I was enjoying my escape from reality. Doing magic with Zatie was so much fun! Everything was exciting, everything was new. I wasn't being punished or tortured, I wasn't being pushed harder than I wanted to be. It was relaxing, it was enjoyable. I was grateful that I got to have this opportunity to share this, to share this part of my life with her.

I stood there on the front porch thinking about the lives that I had ruined, letting out a sigh of regret. Jesse was sitting in the porch swing whittling a rabbit out of a piece of wood with a pocketknife. Just minding his own business, not thinking about a thing, just being a typical, invisible, middle child. I hardly noticed he was there until he spoke. I was so caught up in my own thoughts I barely heard him speak at all.

"What was that?" I asked him.

"What, d'you find Grandpa's killer in Borneo?"

I felt my heart fall out of my stomach! My anxiety was taking over. How could he have possibly known that I was gone hunting down our grandfather's killer?

"Excuse me?" I asked, incredulously.

"What was the lawyer asking about Borneo for? Did you go on vacation without us?" Jesse clarified.

"Oh, that! I was having him investigate some assets. Apparently, Grandpa owned a timeshare out there." I forced an awkward laugh.

"Right, timeshare. Good one," he walked away.

I need to get better at lying to him. He's kind of like Dad in that respect. He can read your face like a treasure map. He was always better at card games. He could study people without really having to look at them. Jesse should become a cop or at least an undercover narcotics officer. He looks like one, not a cop, but like a future druggie. I'll erase his mind later, erase the memories of this awkward conversation. It was growing more and more difficult to make up excuses as to why Harry was just showing up.

I told Harry when we needed him for sparring practice to just run here like any other animal or let me teleport him. He respectfully declined to being teleported. Zatie and I had to pretend like we were exercising out in the barn. We even made a pretty decent rustic workout room, if you didn't mind the hay or the dust. Jessie somewhat bought the idea; he liked the punching bag, the bow-staffs, and swords. Didn't even wonder why we had swords; it just seems like something we would do. I told him they were Grandpa's and I found them an old trunk. I think that piqued his curiosity more. Now I have to keep an eye out for him rummaging through the barn and the sheds, looking for old antiques to sell at pawn shops.

"Well, if any other old crap is found just laying around, let me know. I know a guy that's into buying Antiques. I can make us some money without waiting till we graduate and get our trust funds."

"You're still bitter about Grandma doing that to you, huh?" I asked him.

"Yeah, just seems kind of unfair. You know? I don't even know what I'm going to school for. Now I feel obligated, just so I can earn my inheritance. I'll probably end up at a party school," he stated.

"Yeah, that's what I thought." like I said, I'd probably

have to fix my relationship with my younger brother Jesse over a bottle of beer. I'd let him know what was going on with our family, someday. He may be useful. I'm just not ready to bring somebody else into the group and I've already got Zatie to focus on.

A lot of this may be way too much for Jesse to handle responsibly; it's bad enough that he bugs me for money all the time, knowing that I'm stinking rich. But I give it to him, as a way to get him out of my hair. In hindsight, I probably shouldn't have.

When he mentioned knowing a guy that was into Antiques, it made me wonder if the Gor-Nok was up to his old tricks again. Posing as an antique salesman. I had Harry look into it, to be subtle about it.

"Just search around to see if the guy has set up shop somewhere nearby."

"Oh, that guy. Yeah, I know him. He was sniffing around your grandma. I heard that's what the Gor-Nok looks like as a *human*. Yeah, we've got a lot to talk about," he reminded me that I had avoided it still.

"Fine, name the place and time. I'll tell you what happened in Borneo," I replied. I could feel his excitement over the phone, getting to hear about this adventure. The intrigue of the mystery, understanding more about this monster. I just didn't know if I was ready to tell him that I had traveled back in time. That Harry has known me for over two lifetimes.

It was a Friday night when Harry had arranged for our conversation about Borneo. I had to make up excuses to practically everyone of what I was doing or where I was going. It was especially painful to break Derik's little heart, not be able to hang out with him and his cousin, to drink some beers while they work on their cars and motorcycles. That would be fun, more fun than being interrogated by Harry. I told everybody that there was some type of estate charity thing downtown, that I had to take care of with the lawyer. Even

Zatie seems suspicious of my activities.

"Is it really out of the ordinary for me to wear a nice dress?" I said before he could speak.

"Who died?!" Jesse asked as he passed me in the hallway. I guess I don't wear a dress every day.

Zatie stopped me at the bottom of the stairs, "No, seriously. Who died?! You look all dressed up for a fancy ball, but your face says funeral."

"I don't seem happy about this?" I mused.

"Is there some *other* aunt or uncle we don't know about that just suddenly passed?!" Jesse asked as he passed me again on his way to the couch.

"I have to do this annoying estate thing. It's a charity dinner thing in honor of Grandpa's downtown Museum Wing. Just annoying adult things, I have to do with the Lawyer from time to time," I lied as I smiled.

Zatie pulled me aside. She made bare skin contact with my skin. I automatically flared my hypnotic stare and began telling her, forcing her to not ask.

She released me. I could tell by the smirk on her face that she already knew.

"Look, I'm late already. I'll talk to you later. Yes, I'll tell you every juicy detail," I said to her. Harry had sent a limo, trying to keep up with the charade of the charity ball. He helped me to get into the limo.

I asked him, "Where are we going, *really*?"

"I thought I'd take you to a charity ball and I'm not really that good at lying. Not as good as you think I am."

We went downtown to one of those big fancy hotels with a giant ornate ballroom and everyone was dressed up in big fancy outfits. Harry looked rather dashing in his tux. We danced and dined the night away and I avoided contact, skin to skin contact. Not wanting to let my heart feel again; not wanting to have it broken.

Harry *was* someone better suited for me, much better than Derik is, or could ever be. In all honesty, I *did* need to be with someone like Harry. Someone more like me, someone that understood what I was going through. Someone who understood my world.

"I just have lost so much, Harry. I just can't let somebody else back in," I said to him as we embraced after a dance. He understood the queue, we sat down, and he asked me to tell him about Borneo.

"What did you find?" He asked.

I tried to keep the story pretty vague; avoided going into details about time travel or about having already fought this guy a dozen times. Having inadvertently attracted this guy's attention and put us on his radar. I didn't know, but I think Harry could tell when I was lying. I just didn't want to go into the whole conversations of who I was back then in the past. A Jane Doe that was living with Lucia all these years. That he did not even remember I went by the name of 'Auntie Lily.' We erased his mind so many times I doubt he remembered that he and I had kissed.

"Oh, I remember that," he said.

Dang it! He had heard that.

You forgot I could read your thoughts when they're about me. I had let down my guard.

"Harry, it's late. I'd like to go home," I felt uneasy, it felt awkward being there. I really didn't want to discuss parts of my life that I regret. I just didn't feel right being with him even though I should. Maybe after I'm done with college, maybe a few years down the road when neither of us have aged everyone around us is older.

"Why wait, the night is young and so are we. Come let's have *one* more dance," he was still listening.

"Fine," he had drug me out to the floor one more time. I was lost in thoughts of a life with Harry when a man asked if he could cut in to dance with me. At the charity ball, everyone is wearing masks of course. Harry had got me a mask like a crow and Harry was wearing a snake like reptilian crocodile mask. Of course, Harry would let this man cut in.

He was a tall, darker gentleman, wearing an all-white suit, gold jewelry, very nice shoes and he had on odd looking pig mask. I knew as soon as he touched my naked hand who the devil it was! The Gor-Nok in the flesh! Human and charming as ever. He's almost more dangerous in this form than as a wild savage Were-beast. At least when he's the monster I know what to expect. When he's like this, I have no idea what he's up to.

"Why are *you* here?" I asked "No bull crap! Is it not enough that you killed my Grandfather?! *That, my lovely friend was your fault.* He projected the memory of Michael's death into my mind.

"My Grandmother?!" *Also, it's your doing, by breaking the rules to tamper with time.* He showed her dying moments to my thoughts.

"My Mother and Father?!"

"Ha, you forgot that I offered you a chance to save them?! You can end all the suffering by giving in, give me the book," he reminded me.

I wondered where Harry had gone off to, I needed him. I didn't think he was going to let me dance with someone like the Gor-Nok, but he stepped aside rather easily. The Gor-Nok asked me politely, "Please, try not to worry about your friend? He is being otherwise entertained," he smiled devilishly.

The Gor-Nok somehow orchestrated this conversation. He knew I was going to be here.

"You are not the only one able to predict what other people will do. I've been doing this for many years, my dear little witch," he boasted.

I asked, "Why are you ruining people's lives?"

"Of course, that is what you think. Listen, Nonabel. is it? You and I are not too different. We are both headstrong, arrogant, overconfident, power-hungry, ambitious, dangerous in a corner when up against our enemies; and we can ruin the lives of everyone around us with our stubborn rage just by existing.

I don't have to do much but stand back and wait you out. You will bring that book to me, or it will ruin you and your family. And you will ruin them on your own. You will bring the book to me," his chocolate smooth voice was filling my heart.

Before I knew it, I had been hypnotized by his eyes. They turned that hideous shade of green. He had got to me. He made me doubt and worry, he knew my fears, he knew I blamed myself for all the lives I had lost.
Harry came back from this phone call and the Gor-Nok bent down to kiss my helpless hand, smiled wickedly, then politely excused himself.

Harry didn't recognize him at all and asked, "Do you know him?"

I replied, "A lifetime ago, we might've met in a dream."

When we left the dance; I made certain the Gor-Nok was watching us, I was thinking about him, trying to get him to hear my thoughts, trying to lure him into a trap of my own. He was watching; he enjoyed toying with me, taunting me. We drove part ways away from the event. I used *my* hypnotic stare on Harry.

I told him to enjoy his evening at the bar and told the driver to get him home safely. I gave him a kiss good night and teleported from the limo. I appeared up in the sky as my giant wings expanded, becoming my dark angel form and flew through the night in the full moon.

I patrolled around the area; I circled a few blocks until I spotted the Gor-Nok getting into a White Rolls-Royce driven by a small withered older man. I had him. I could finally fig-ure-out where he had been hiding; what he had been doing, who he is as a person, and how to get into his head. He got back to a building downtown; it was a rather nice apartment com-plex. I watched him for a minute as he entered the building. I sent out a couple crows to spy on all sides and on all exits. I had him.

I could take this whole building down if I wanted to, I

could make it disappear, vanishing into a vortex. I could collapse whole floors, crushing him. There are so many things I wanted to do to this murderer. The elderly man helped him immensely, he brought him into his apartment. He seemed to be having problems, struggling. The elderly man brought him some type of tonic, a drink, I couldn't tell from here.

I needed to get closer to hear what they were talking about. I got a couple of my birds closer so we could triangulate what was being said. The Gor-Nok took his tonic out onto the patio of the sky-rise penthouse apartment. He watched his skin in the moonlight, his face was shifting back-and-forth in the Therianthropy phases and back to the human form.

He got mad and said, "This isn't working as well as it needs to! I need you to try harder!"

The old man asked, "Maybe if I had access to the book, I would know how they're doing it? Are you sure they are like you?"

"They're more than me! More than I ever could be! Especially the girl. The old man I fought; he could be more than one animal, at will! More than one host, where I'm stuck with my host! But the girl, she can be a whole herd of animals! Separate herself at will! Live forever. She will be hardest to stop. Won't you, witch?!"

My goosebumps had flared, he looked right at me across the street, his eyes glowed in the dark as he saw me. He activated his host the boar-beast and the old man collapsed to the ground as a pile of bones. The were-beast launched from the patio to the next building, stampeding towards me. I scattered into my cloud of birds to avoid him. He threw his sawblades of fear-demons into the sky after me as I turned my birds into baby were-demons-crows to fight back. All of them had the power to electrocute and we killed all of his little ghost monsters. It mocked him.

I teleported back to the farm, turned my feathers back to my Ballroom gown. I made my way up the stairs, trying to keep quiet. Zatie was in my room. "Spill it!" she said.

Entry #16

Nightmares

After a couple of days, I decided it was time to do some additional were-beast training with Zatie. Harry came by hoping to finally have an awkward conversation about our date the other night.

"So, what happened to you the other night?" He said in his rough, coarse Were-croc voice as we were sparring with each other in the barn.

"I had other things to do, other people to see."

"Is that what we were doing? Seeing other people?"

"Dude, I have a boyfriend!" I said while punching.

"Do you? When was the last time you actually went out with old what's his face?"

"That's none of your business!"

"Tell you what, let's make a wager! Whomever can beat the other person using only Therianthropy abilities gets to either avoid talking about the subject or gets their questions finally answered," he offered.

"Fine!" I said begrudgingly. "So, you mean I can't use any of my other powers?!"

"Yeah, let's imagine if you would, that the enemy somehow figures out how to rob you of your powers. So, let's say that they knew one secret about Witches," he said in between blocking my punches.

"Oh yeah, which is what?!" I asked as I swung.

"Oh, I don't know, like how an iron nail, when stabbed into the shadow of a witch, can stop her where she stands; robbing her of her powers!" He lectured.

With that Harry grabbed a loose board from the barn with a protruding nail and did just that. He stabbed it into my shadow, freezing me in place! There was an icy chill coursing up my spine and into my brain, locking my neural pathways. Keeping me from accessing my powers. I couldn't use the Sight, I couldn't move things psychically, I couldn't shock him. I was stuck, I couldn't teleport, nothing! I could do nothing! The board was too far for me to reach and my foot was frozen in the ground.

"Pretty neat trick there," I admitted.

"You'd be well to remember that trick and to be mindful of not stepping on nails," Harry's no-fair trick was working too well.

"What can I do to fight?!" I whined.

"You are a were-beast, use those powers! Feel them out! See what works. Lucia taught me this trick to protect me from your kind," Harry responded.

I reached out with my other senses to find an answer. I could make my claws grow longer. My birds could pop out of me and turn into tiny were-demons, that startled Harry. He did his best to fight off the demons.

He protested a little, "Hey, how is that still fair?!"

"It is for a poly-therian! I don't make up the rules, I'm just writing them down as I break them!" I could create my angel wings and left one bird on the ground stuck in his place frozen in my shadow.

It was weird that my shadow was still stuck to the ground. It reminded me of old fairy-tales Lucia read to us. I turned myself into my harpy form and sent some more of my were-demons at Harry. He finished his full transformation with a tail and all.

Zatie was having a fun time training with Dominic, using him more like a dog and not as a sparring partner.

I yelled at her, "Zatie! You know you're supposed to fight with him, not play with him, right?!"

She said, "Oh, I forgot!" Zatie took the twig that she had been tossing at him, then bit it like a vampire, sucking some of its essence, swapping her venom, then continued tossing it towards Dominic. It transformed in his mouth into a small plant demon and fought back. Dominic, growling, tore it to shreds. Zatie got kind of mad. She created more summoning them out of the ground by sheer will, not needing to bite, not needing to spread her venom. Just by magic and will.

"Zatie, don't kill him! He's the only Grandpa left!" I called her and chuckled.

Zatie was having too much fun with her new pet, Dominic; playing fetch and teaching him games and having him fight her baby were-plants. She needed to fight someone who is more human than animal, more cunning than primal, more conniving then instinctual. I told Harry that I appreciated learning the new trick about the nail and told him that he should try that with Zatie.

We switched sparring partners. I was still all business and Dominic still wanted to play, but I projected a thought for him that it was *time to hunt*, that he was *hungry*. His manner- isms changed. His tongue wasn't hanging out and he wasn't panting any more. A vicious snarl formed on his face and his eyes seem to glow a brighter red.

Zatie on the other hand had distracted Harry by admir- ing his crocodile muscles on his forearms. Harry of course, loves the attention. And thought it was funny to use my 16-year-old sister to try to make me jealous, a 36-year-old trapped in an 18-year-old's body. I projected a thought to Harry's head so loud that it came across more like microphone feedback and ringing in his ears than an actual thought.

I thought that he *should focus on training and avoid flirting with a minor.* His attitude changed and he got into perfect professional fighting mode. They worked on improving Za- tie's strength and stamina by getting her to rely less on her intelligence but more with the strength that comes from our powers.

Zatie argued with him, that she didn't have therian powers like the rest of us. Where was she pulling her unnat- ural strength from? Her non-existent host totem? She and Harry had to think for a bit, that was true.

Meanwhile I let loose one of my birds and had Dominic 'Stay' for a second and then sent the bird off to fly into the woods. I told him go get it. I gave him a 20 second head-start then I transformed into a Harpy and took off after them. I let my bird just fly free, let it act on instinct. I didn't influence its thoughts and I didn't cheat by influencing Dominic's thoughts either.

This was purely about the hunt; purely about using our regular senses. Normal senses, not the magical senses. I was looking for clues; broken branches, discarded feathers, claw marks, saliva, bird guano, things like that. Listening for the sounds of his foot falls, but then they stopped.

I thought that he caught the bird, but was stuck, cutting through some branches, cawing for help. Dominic had gone off after it up into the tree, scratching, and breaking branches. I arrived at the scene, called for Dominic and my bird. I praised them both for a good hunt and patted Dominic on the head before we teleported back to the barn.

When we emerged from the vortex a giant battle was taking place between Harry as a full were-croc and what seemed to be a living tree suit with Zatie inside.

She had figured out how to form a suit of were-plants. The armor was made up of several different types of plants. She had vines that she could activate at her command, poison darts and spines, clouds of petals, leaves, branches, roots; you name it she had it all. The rough texture gave her a good advantage against Harry's tough, scaly, leather skin. She had logs for arm covers made it difficult for him to bite or harm her. They were fairly evenly matched with Zatie in this plant suit. She could somehow combine her brains and brawn.

Every night before bed we would perform spells and incantations to protect ourselves from the monster invading our dreams. I got tired of doing this every night and made plans to sneak out, to go on vigilante patrols, to try to catch the monster because it had been killing people in their sleep. My birds and I went out to scour the city, searching for the Gor-Nok. The Seer's Sight could only show *intentions* and possible futures; I think the Gor-Nok has figured that out. He had talked about having the gift of foresight, I wonder if his deal with Death gave him extra powers.

I hated to admit how much more he was like me than Harry. I have to know for sure if he was still operating from that apartment, I wanted to know where he slept so I might enter his dreams to end him. I sent a bird to keep an eye out at the penthouse while I patrolled the rest of the city with my other birds. I went back to my standard regimen of shedding 50 pounds of birds, about two or three dozen, and scattered them strategically across the town. It was a long boring night, seemingly nothing happening.

I stopped a couple of the robberies and muggings. I did my best to leave no trace and to erase memories, so I could continue to be on the lookout without attracting attention from local authorities. That was the last thing I needed was someone like Derik's Dad snooping around in my life. It was really boring though tonight. It wasn't too quiet that I felt something odd, or suspicious was happening; there was enough activity. It was just not what *I* wanted. I started to wonder what my friends were doing. Most should be asleep. Derik, on occasion, would go hang out with his cousin Johnny, who was the king of partying.

I guess I thought his name too many times because Derik called my phone. I was bored enough so I decided to answer.

"Hey you, my boyfriend! How's it going?" I said doing my best to pretend like we were still actually dating. It was nice to hear from him.

"Hey, Bel, I just wanted to give you a call. You know, see if you were still awake. Are you doing anything?" He seemed hopeful.

"Nope, not doing a dang thing! Why, you got something in mind?" Derik always had great date ideas.

"Yeah, we got a party. We're delivering this keg for Johnston's Bar. We'll probably hang out there for a little bit after. They should be like the last delivery we're doing for the night." He had been hanging out with Johnny more now that I have been busier.

"Oh, it's that kind of a delivery job. Yeah, yeah. Can you come pick me up?" I asked.

"Sure thing, baby!" Derik exclaimed excitedly.

"Let me know when you guys get by the road so that we don't wake up the kids, okay," I requested.

"Yeah, okay, we'll call you when we are getting close, later sweetie," he must be with Johnny. He kept saying 'we' the whole time.

I did a scan through all the different security-birds, taking in all of their locations like looking through security cameras. Because my attention was so spread thin, I was only worried about motion detecting. I had them all set on night vision. I projected my image to Dusk's location; he was startled by my ghostly, sudden appearance. He immediately transformed into his top hat-wearing-midget-version of himself and bowed to me on the roof of the police station.

"Caw, My Queen! How may I serve you this fine evening?" He said as he bowed.

"Dusk, you don't have to bow, but thank you. There's not a whole lot of activity going on. So, I'm going out! You are in charge of security; please follow procedures and protocols. Continue monitoring the enemy," I responded.

"As you wish my Queen!" he replied.

It was nice to be able to go out, to let my hair down. I saw through the Sight that Johnny and Derik were rolling up the road by the house soon, so, I teleported by the barn, then I teleported some clothes from my closet. I did a quick-change spell which is basically teleporting clothes from my body back onto my body. The teleportation spell, apart from lightning and flying, was probably one of my favorite spells.

As I was adjusting my clothes, I could hear the roar of a muscle car down the road. The Camaro's noises and the thumping of Johnny's engine could be heard from miles away as I met them half a block from street to the house. I waved at Johnny and flashed him a friendly smile as I got in the car with Derik.

"Hey babe, give me some sugar." Yes, it felt nice, and it had been so long since we just had fun; since I let myself have fun. I kept an eye on my birds from time to time while we were partying. I just scanned through the different locations. When I needed to get a new perspective, I went to the bathroom and looked in the mirror like a video monitor.

It was a typical party. I'm not sure of what we are celebrating; just a Thursday, I think. We had nothing going on Friday for school, so that was just good as any excuse to party. There was plenty of drinking and I think some other illicit activities were happening. Derik was having some problems at home with his dad, he really didn't like him hanging out with his cousin, Johnny. With him being an obvious bad influence, and all. Derik returning to his choir-boy ways come Sundays, but during the week he likes to have fun just like anybody else. He loved working on his car, and he did that a lot with Johnny at their uncle's garage.

Uncle Mike also owned the bar where Johnny worked as a delivery guy and as a bouncer from time to time. Johnny was older, I think he had already had to take this grade over again. He tried, but not too hard; just enough to keep a social life. I can't help myself; I keep looking at him from time to time. It's a shame I didn't meet him before I met Derik.

Derik came to talk to me and give me updates from his conversation with his dad. His dad had been harassing him all night. Interrogating him trying to figure out what he was doing, where he was going, and trying to get him to come home. I told him to finish delivering the kegs and go talk to his dad.

"If you need to go home, I'll find a ride," I said. Johnny offered, "Yeah, cousin. I'll take her home."
Derik was annoyed with his dad and he really just needs to work this out. It was my turn to be the supportive girlfriend. He had been so supportive of me and gave me so much space and time.

"Yeah, it's OK, honey. I can take care of myself, I'm a big girl. I can find my way home," I assured him.

"OK, he's just being so annoying tonight. He's upset about some vigilante person stirring up trouble."

"Yeah, doing his job for him," Johnny said.

Derik continued, "Yeah, some eyewitnesses were saying it's some kind of dark winged angel chick."

I spewed out my beer and Derik slowly continued.

"So, now there's some chick that can fly that's been beating on bad guys downtown."

"You don't say," I said as I wiped my chin.

"Yeah, my dad just wants me to be careful and try to get me to come home for stupid curfew or stuff. I got to deal with this, thanks hon," he kissed my cheek.

"Yeah, I'll get her home. I'll take care of her," Johnny yelled as Derik left the Party.

I don't know what was in this drink and I don't know if I really care. It was just nice to be out with my friends, with all my beautiful people. Johnny and I were having a great time just hanging out and *finally* getting to talk to each other. We really started to connect, to communicate our feelings on the mutual loss of our parents and being orphans.

Like I had said before, we had a lot in common. Johnny carries a similar weight on his shoulders of the pain he bears as I do. Yet, he deals with his loss by drowning his pain in liquor or spends his time working on cars and motorcycles.

He told me that, "It's good to have a creative outlet, it helps with the pain," he asked me, "what do you do to cope; to get through the dark nights and painful memories?" He said, "I know it's not drinking! I haven't seen you at these things too often. You haven't been around Derik in the last while," he finally paused.

"Oh, I keep busy with schoolwork and studies and all. I do needlepoint, some gardening, charity events, travel. I don't know, the usual thing," I replied. We had a good time talking.

I might have fallen asleep a couple times in his arms while dancing. He smelled so good. I was just so intoxicated, so ready for a vacation from my regular life that I wanted this. I wanted this little moment to escape and explore what it was like to be held in someone else's arms. Don't get me wrong, Derik was amazing! Almost unreal how nice and supportive he was; but ultimately, I'm damaged goods. He wouldn't understand that and wouldn't be able to comfort me and support me with the trauma, the pain I deal with daily. The darkness and negativity that bloomed in my soul, without having to go through a similar loss like Johnny had.

I doubted Derik would understand my sadness and pain, he tried to counteract it with over-positivity which I found annoying, smothering. Johnny didn't force himself, didn't force his way of thinking on people. It was like the difference between a cat person and a dog person, and not the people that take care of cats and dogs. I'm talking about people that act like cats and dogs. It was like a dog or a little puppy that needs attention and wants you to pet it, play with it, take it on walks, hold its hand and tell it that it was pretty. A person that acts like a cat didn't really need you to cuddle it, touch it even, unless it wanted to be touched; but it was nice to know that you were there at arm's length. I think that I was a cat person and Johnny was as well.

"Are we really doing this?" I asked as I was nuzzling Johnny's neck.

"Doing what? You can do whatever you want; I'm just here," he replied. I gave him a little kiss on the neck, just to see how it felt, knowing this was wrong, knowing how selfish this was, forbidden. The intoxication of desire is more enticing than the nagging moral annoying warnings from my conscience. I ignored that inner voice compelling me to do something good and chose to do something that felt good, knowing full well I was going to regret this, but accepting that this little lapse in judgment may be the offense and trigger I would need to finally end what wasn't going to survive my darkness.

I was giving into the forbidden fantasies, falling in love with the feeling of falling in love. The feeling of acceptance, in wanting someone, and being wanted. The hunger consumed us, then we found our way into one of the other rooms in the house; assuming it was safe for us to explore our passions in the dark. Abruptly a knock at the door and a sudden burst of light as an unexpected visitor came bursting through, calling out our names.

"Yo Johnny, Bel. Where you at?! Someone said they saw you guys..." Derik was at a loss for words, we were both terrified, getting caught in a moment of weakness. Johnny immediately started making excuses,

"Dude, Bro! She just was all over me and just started kissing on me and everything. She is wild, man. Please, can you take your lady out of here?"

Derik didn't want to hear it and went straight from nice guy to a beat-down without a moment's hesitation. He was pounding his cousin's face into the floor. I was scared, mortified; screaming for them to stop but no one was listening.

"NO MORE LIES!!!" It happened without me even acknowledging that I wanted it, but I screamed so loudly that the banshee in me came crying out sending them both through the walls into the other rooms, disrupting the party.

Having attracted attention, I began screaming for everyone to leave, still in banshee-mode. I knew my eyes were all a flame with a brilliant purple rage; lightning pouring from my hands destroying anything I came across. I was so overwhelmed with adrenaline and anger at them both for fighting over me. I was not worth it! I was angry at myself for doing something so stupid. I was in full banshee-mode still, screaming at people, knocking them through walls and furniture. I was making a way out, clearing a path when I remembered I could just teleport and be done with this.

I cleared the crowd out of the middle of the room with a thunderclap, then I teleported magnificently from the middle of the open room with a large vortex in front of all of them. I no longer cared who knew what I was. My secret was out. My life was over. The cat was out of the bag and this cat has claws.

When I went through the vortex I blacked out. I don't care where I went, I just needed to get out of there. I woke up the next morning on the front porch. It was cold, I didn't have a jacket. I started to get up and lost my balance, then face planted on the front porch. Zatie heard me, she opened the front door and gave me a Mom glare. "Well look what the cat drug in?!" She said with her arms across her chest and tapping her toes impatiently.

My head was throbbing, and I couldn't think straight. "What time is it?" I regretted asking.

"It's 6:30 in the morning, we're about ready to leave to go to school. I didn't know what your plans were for the day," she replied.

"School? I thought it was a holiday! That's why everybody was partying so hard!" I exclaimed.

"No, that's next week! Who told you that, Derik? Johnny? Like those guys keep track of what day of the week it is?!" She responded.

"What day is it then?" I asked her.

"Friday. Do you think that you're sobered up enough to make it to school or is Derik coming to get you?" She asked me.

"Um, I don't think Derik's gonna be talking to me for a while," I began to sob.

"Do you want to talk about it?" she asked.

"No, actually no," I didn't want to be scolded again by my self-righteous baby sister.

"Well, don't forget that test today," she said.

"The crap?" I already forgot it.

"Far as I know, it was today. Well, you are going to be no good today. You'll still need a ride, cuz I'm taking your keys. Safety first!" Zatie said as she left. Zatie was doing her best Mom impression. She was right, though, my head was still throbbing.

"I'll just take the bus like you mere mortals." I quickly gathered my stuff and ran out the door. Zatie had an iced latte to help wake me up; then continued to scold me. Zatie was mad at me for leaving the confines of our protection. She didn't say a word out loud, she just started as she knew I could hear her thoughts.

Everyone stares today, especially when they know I was

hung over. I continued that way throughout the day. There was an agonizing headache pounding at the walls of my head mostly because I am dehydrated but I just hammered down so much alcohol last night that I was out of it before everything went bad.

Having powers can be just horrible, I could hear everyone's whispering thoughts. People were whispering, pointing at me, thinking of me as a weirdo, the freak. But I couldn't leave school yet, I had to get these tests done and out of my way. I was almost done with school, almost done with this place. I'm so much more than any of them. I was no longer bound by laws of man or the routines we put ourselves through. The hoops we jump through to prove we were better than ourselves. Here in reality, I am subject to my weaknesses, my body is suffering a hangover from having too good of a time giving into selfishness.

My teachers kept harassing me to pay attention. They kept asking me for missing assignments. I did my best to hypnotize them, tell them that they, "didn't need to see my assignments," that everything was fine and that they were going to pass my grades. Yeah, I might've cheated a few times to fix things. I need to stop focusing on what everyone else was thinking, but their self-righteous judgements were so loud. I was trying to just get through the day without more interactions.

I couldn't pay attention in class. My eyes wouldn't stay open. I couldn't focus. I couldn't read along, it's just jumbled. I was too hung over to function. My teachers were getting mad at me for wearing dark glasses inside, I don't even remember putting these on.

My eyes were probably still glowing purple from all the power still surging through me. To top it all off, Derik was avoiding me. He wasn't talking to me, he wasn't thinking about me, he was just looking at me. I could feel the hate pouring from him. He wasn't even talking with his cousin. I don't think Johnny even showed up today.

Derik was still mad at me for kissing Johnny. I tried to stop Derik at his locker to talk this out, but he brushed me off. He wouldn't let me touch him and told me to get away from him.

"Don't... touch me. I don't wanna have anything to do with a freak!" He said it with such hate.

There it is. What I'm always worried about. Derik hating me because I was different, he was no longer understanding or compassionate. He's quite the opposite. Bitter, dark, hurting physically, and emotionally. Mostly because I broke his heart, with or without magic, because *I* am weak.

I was sent into the Principal's office; someone had said that I smelled of alcohol and one of the teachers complained that I was trying to manipulate them. I laughed at the Principal when I heard this.

"How am I supposed to be manipulating?"

"Well, one of the students said they saw you, you... use magic?" They asked.

"Light came out of you?! Is that true?" They said.

"Actually lightning, yes," I corrected him.

"Came out of your hands, last night? And everyone is terrified of you, my dear. I'm gonna have to ask you to leave the school. Your boyfriend, he said something's wrong with you and that you should be locked up. Now, I know you don't have any parents and it's unfortunate for the passing of your grandmother. Is there anyone you can turn to?" They asked.

"I'll call my lawyer; he can settle this. He can straighten this up with a phone call and I'll be owning this school by the end of the day!" I was getting hostile.

The Assistant Principal was trying to calm me down with her best Mom-voice, "Now, now, honey, you don't need to act all hostile and fussy."

I glared at her; I think. The color of my bright purple eyes mesmerizing her. Shutting her mouth with my thoughts, thinking for her to sit down.

"All right. We'll call him. What, what's your lawyer's

name?" they asked.

"I'll write it down," the assistant said, "I'll give him a call; we can talk about this on Monday when everyone has calmed down a bit."

I told her, "It's Harry Anderson or Harold Anderson. Here let me write it," I grabbed the paper and pencil and gave it right back to him; I had the hardest time reading what he had scribbled.

"Wait a second! Give me something else to read!" I looked around the room at the Principal's diplomas and the school motto; it was all gibberish. Was it because I was drunk? I should've sobered up by now. I couldn't read the words.

"This is wrong!" I exclaimed. Something wasn't right. I don't remember falling asleep, so maybe I was still asleep. Maybe this was all a dream. Somehow, I slipped into a dream not knowing; but who's dream? I don't have dreams like this. My dreams are awesome. I control everything, but this one. I'm somehow out of control.

My fears were coming to haunt me. My friends are turning against me. My weaknesses have taken control, ruined my life, have ruined me. I told them something was not right, and I left the room. They tried to stop me, but I pushed them with my powers back into their office and slammed the door. I made my way out of the school's office and down the halls. More and more kids were shooting thoughts of me being a freak, a witch and I pushed them out of my way as well. They wanted to see a freak?! I'd show them a freak, they just needed to get the freak out of my way. I wanted something from my locker, I needed to be certain. I needed to look at my books in my locker. Something I was familiar with, something I knew.

I needed something to prove that this was a dream. I made my way through the halls, getting hit and pushed and shoved by the meanest people. I shot back psychically. Finally, I made it to my locker. Everyone was thinking, whispering, and saying things. I just needed to find a book. I needed to find something I knew. A journal, a yearbook, a textbook, something. Everyone kept making noises and talking. The kids staring, thinking, talking about me.

I thought for all of them to be silent. I heard their bodies fall to the floor and made them fall asleep. I made them pass out, at least everyone within 100 feet of me. I found the books, but I couldn't read any of them. I knew the one should've said mathematics, but it said a bunch of gobbledygook, just gibberish. I threw it back in the locker, slammed a lot of them shut when I shut my door and flew out of the school, right out of the glass ceiling like a superhero.

I needed to wake myself up; I thought that if I tried falling that might work to wake me up. I flew to the nearest bridge and hoped that the impact on the water would wake me up. Zatie and I had tested it, so I knew that falling in our dreams was one of the fastest ways to wake up. I crashed landed hard on the bridge and it startled the spectating towns people out in the streets. They all started talking about me and calling me freak; and a mob started to form. People wanted to run me out of town. They weren't going to put up with a witch.

The mob started to become the whole town. My so-called friends were turning against me. My family were against me, Zatie and Jesse were screaming, 'WITCH!' with the other people. I knew this was all a nightmare, this couldn't have been real. People started trying to attack me, throwing rocks and then I deflected them. I just wanted everyone to leave me alone. I lashed out at everyone with a thunderclap, knocking people to the ground. I imagined the bridge breaking apart as a way to keep them from getting to me. And the bridge obeyed, buckling from beneath them all.

I wanted to jump from the bridge but not be pushed. I finally jumped off the bridge and fell to my death. The water was as hard as concrete, and not very shallow. I felt my bones smash against the surface. I fumbled my way to the shore, with busted broken bones. The fall should have woken me, I knew this was all a dream, but I should wake up if I had died, or that fall should have killed me. Or at least now I wish I was dead.

Derik pulled up in his Camaro and called for me to get in. I crawled to his car. He scooped me up like I was nothing and put my broken body in the passenger seat, and then he walked around to get in the driver's seat and slammed the door shut. I woke up in his car just as we arrived at the party where I had gotten drunk. I was startled and relieved that the vivid nightmare was over, and I asked him if we could just go home.

"I just don't feel right about tonight."

"It's cool, babe. Might as well call it a night, my dad's been buggin' me to get home already."

"Why is that?" I asked him.

"Some weird chick is takin' the law into her own hands and being a super-hero or some junk," Derik said.

"That's not too bad, right?!" I responded.

"Yeah, he's all by-the-books and all..."

I don't remember falling asleep, or saying good-bye to Derik, but I was home again. Zatie opened the front door before I could. "Well look..."

"...what the cat drug in?!" I interrupted her as I pushed passed her and entered the house.

"Yeah, how did you know what I was? Never-mind, just get to bed," Zatie said as she sent me to bed.

I spent the night in the Library trying to understand what went wrong. Who did this to me? If it was him, how did *he* do this to me? It had to have been him, but I couldn't figure it out. Zatie came into study with me, I told her of my current conundrum. I told her my nightmares.

I thought that I had been careful outside. I set out watch-birds; there wasn't any activity last night. It seemed like it was safe, and that was probably when he had set the trap and I fell for it. Just what had happened to me, I was not sure I understood.

"What was the last thing that you remember being real? Zatie had asked me.

"I asked Dusk to watch out for me, if he could keep a look-out," I told her.

"When were you aware of what was happening?"

"Knee deep in a nightmare that resembled my life falling apart; that's when!" I exclaimed.

"Where are your birds now?" She asked.

I said, "Out doing their job, but something feels odd with Dusk."

"And that's probably what's going on. Isn't he your day-dream Nix?" Zatie asked.

"Yeah. He's smarter than the rest of them. So, I let him out into reality," I said.

Zatie questioned, "Does that sound like a good idea? Isn't that like allowing your subconscious to be exposed? Isn't it ike leaving the back door open? That's probably why, he probably got to Dusk somehow."

"Lu-lu had done it before. She was able to catch on to my security birds and how to knock them out or make them fall asleep. He could've done something like that. He could've made Dusk fall asleep," I said.

"The only way to find out is to examine him. Bring him in for questioning; at least scan him with the Seer's Sight," she said.

I agreed with Zatie and called for Dusk to come home. I brought him back to the Library through a vortex, but he seemed oddly not wanting to go back into the iron cage for some reason. We caused a deep sleep to come on Dusk and used the Seer's Sight and a new spell I learned. Zatie had found it, I told her to go ahead and let her perform the spell. Zatie excitedly exclaimed, "Alah-ka-zam!"

That's all she said, and something had changed about my bird; Dusk metamorphosed into his half-dwarf half-were-crow self with an extra set of demon eyes being held over his regular eyes. One of the Gor-Nok's demon-servant-transparent-ghost-thingies had been strangling him, wrapping itself around Dusk's neck. It was like a scarf with two little arms holding up a new set of spectacles made from its fingers, clouding his decisions; making him see what they were wanting him to see. Making him think it was OK and normal and that was how he got in. That was how he was able to see what I saw and manipulated what I was experiencing last night.

I was about to destroy the demon and kill Dusk temporarily in the process. I would bring him back but be rid of the demon. I was about to do it, but Zatie had stopped me. She touched my hand and shared the thought, *Wait, this may be the advantage we need.*

What do you mean? I thought.

We let him continue to believe that he has a spy, that he at least has a set of eyes on the inside. So, let's give them an eyeful, Zatie smiled as she thought.

What do you want to do, give the guy a peep show?!

Gross! No! Let him see the Library, didn't you say that he was interested in antique books?

He wants to get his hands on the Diary, I thought back.

Let's allow him to see the spells we can do! Let's show off the Library and entice him to want to actually attack us on our ground!

All right, but the moment this thing tries to do something that I don't like then I'll fry them both!

That's fine, it's your daydream, your subconscious you'll fry, Zatie thought.

It's a risk I'm willing to take, I thought.

I kept Dusk locked in the cage in bird form and put him on sick leave in my dreams. I put him in an endless loop, reliving a DeJa'Vu of one of his high society parties, and locked the whole room at the bottom of the oceans of my mind. Dusk was innocent and didn't understand what was going on, I'd have to deal with that event later but for now we just continued studying magic a little bit more openly in the library than in our dreams. The last thing we need is this guy messing with her our minds while we sleep.

We had a conversation about Zatie's future once. One night, we were in the library studying and Zatie decided to break the silence of our private quiet time by sharing some random useful facts. This one seemed interesting. She said, "Do you know what I find interesting about all of this about magic, about the Diary?"

"What's that honey?" I said trying my best to not seem annoyed.

"I'm studying a section on runes and writing spells, symbology etc. And it made me think about the psychology and neuroscience of it all. The chemistry of what's happening in our brain as we read a combination of pictogram, symbols that are etched onto a blank paper," she was lecturing.

Too late, I was annoyed, "What's your point, Zatie? Is this going to be a *whole* lecture or is this gonna be quick? I don't have time for your doctorate dissertation on penmanship. So, what's your point?!"

I know she likes being an academic and philosophizing about how much she loves learning. I went back to studying, I was learning some complicated spells and sometimes you just have to keep her on track.

"Well, what I was saying, before you interrupted, that we have collectively agreed that these scribbles and lines and circles and symbols represent a sound; and combined them with other symbols, sounds read represents a word that you can recognize in different fonts and yell in different languages. Sets of symbols, that series and sequence of pictograms in your head causes chemical reactions and neurons set things to fire off in your brain; creating an emotional connection to that image, that phrase, that symbol," she continued.

"Z, all that was eloquent, beautiful; still Zatie, get to the freakin' point!" I exclaimed.

"I'm saying, writing is one of the last forms of... Well, it's, how do I say this exactly?"

"Zatherine!" I yelled.

"Writing is one of the most ancient and one of the last widely used forms of magic; and people don't appreciate it," she finally finished.

"Oh honey, does it hurt to be in your brain?!"

"Oh no, not at all! I love it! I keep myself thoroughly entertained all the time!" She responded.

"I know honey, I know. I'm glad you're learning this stuff. I knew you were gonna be good at this."

"How did you know?" She asked.

"What now?" I replied not really paying attention.

"How did you know that this was gonna be something I'd accept and be good at? How did you know that, honestly?" She demanded.

"I was scared and alone. Desperate and needed help and I know that you're always willing. And I needed a friend, I needed an ally in this. I can't do this alone," I told her.

Zatie was starting to blush, "Oh, that's so sweet, Nonabel! You're sharing feelings!"

"Quiet you!" We went back to studying and we were quiet for about fifteen seconds before Zatie broke the silence again.

"But seriously, how did you know?"

"I actually can see the future," I knew that I shouldn't have said that.

"You can do what now?!" She asked.

"Yeah, that was one of the first potions I ever did was the Seer's Sight. It's complicated, but essentially with it you can see the future. Actually, it's more like I can see intentions and once I made the decision to, in essence, alter *your* future by intending to share the secret of magic with you. It led us down a different path."

She closed her book and stared at me incredulously. "So, you mean to tell me that you can see the actual future?!"

"I now regret sharing this with you, forget everything I said," I replied, and I tried to go back to reading, or at least pretend to read.

"No, no, no. Don't try any of your weird voodoo hypnosis on me! I can't un-remember that! What was I going to do if you didn't show me magic?! What would I do, you know, do for a job, a career?!" She demanded.

"Oh, honey, you're still going to college and you're still getting a career, there's no question about that! Otherwise I get all the estate money, so, if you want any of the bling you got to go fill that thing with knowledge and crap. You get a job and then you get the money. While I live here. But I'm kicking Jesse out as soon as I can figure out how to teleport him to some cabin up in the woods with a bunch of food that randomly gets dropped off every once in a while. I'm still trying to figure out something with Harry, legally. Don't judge me; it's just a back-up plan. Seriously? I just might have to someday if he never leaves. Look, with the ability to see possible futures, that's how I roll now. I prepare for worst case scenarios such as my deadbeat brother never getting a job because the conditions of the estate say that I will have to provide for him; just as long as he's maintaining a certain GPA," I rambled.

"So, he could be going to school online for decades!" She stated.

"I'm not ready for that! I shall sooner fake his death than put up with Jesse living here for the rest of my life, no thank you," I said.

"Oh, he'll be fine, we'll get him through school."

"Yeah, kicking and screaming!" she said.

"Or we could just start planning seeds in his brain while he is sleeping, encouraging that academic side of his brain to wake up from dormancy," she said.

"Good luck with that!" I replied.

"I would, seriously. Now, what was I gonna do for my career, can you tell me?" Zatie asked.

"I love you sister. I answered your question."

"You *avoided* answering my question," Zatie said.

"That, my dear, is called misdirection. It's one of the first tricks that any good magician learns to perform a trick of tricking people. Jesse can tell you that. Talk to Jesse about up-close magic tricks; that's one of the first basic parts. That's why you have an assistant and all, and some magicians will straight up label her name 'Ms. Direction.' She's there to distract," I rambled again.

"Interesting, I do see what you did there and what you're still trying to do. Why are you avoiding answering my question?!" Zatie responded.

"What was the question?" I asked.

"What am I going to do in the future?!" She said.

"Darn-it, you remembered. Here's the thing about the future, Zatie; they're fragile, they're delicate. It's like trying to catch a bubble; they're pretty and they're colorful and you can't help but chase them and become a little kid again and get excited about the possibilities of catching this bubble," I told her.

"You're evading again, stop it!" She ordered.

"Zatie, I don't want you to chase that bubble. You'll be better off leaving it alone and letting it become what it's going to become. I'm not gonna tell you what your future is. If you know; you'll change it. You'll affect it. I've already messed with time enough; I've already ruined too many lives," I replied.

"So, where was this Seer's Sight spell?"

"Zatie, don't! It's way too complicated and it's... a burden. A responsibility I just don't want you to have to bear. Maybe after I'm done being the Matriarch of the Coven and you take over you can do it and become an Oracle or whatever and then you can be responsible for the things you see. I'd rather you maybe know what's going to happen right before it happens like a momentary bit of foresight. Less intense, less sacrifice involved version of the Seer's Sight and that will help you with fighting. It's kind of, you know like the Goosebumps thing; don't you notice me do that?" I asked her.

"Yeah, when your goosebumps flare up and you look at it like you're telling time, or you have an invisible watch," she responded.

"Yeah, that's a form of sensing the future; but it's not the full Seer's Sight. I might have to use the binding spell to lock that spell up in the vault."

"Wait, we have a vault?!" Zatie exclaimed.

"Seriously, Zatie?! Did you *not* read my entire Diary? I've written that stuff down, and everything that I've learned, it's in the Diary; in one of my indexes or my, I guess, 18 years of volumes or whatever, but it's in there. Here you, go you should go back and study that; but yeah, there is a vault. I didn't say how to get in there and I am on purpose gonna start omitting things from the indexes from my journals. I don't think you're ready for some of this stuff; just give it time," I said.

"You're not much older than me!" She stated.

I took a moment aside, took a breath, thought about the irony of that statement. "You really want to say that as your final answer?! You? Your whole argument to try to convince me to teach you what I know, all the terrible secrets I know, based off of *you* believing that *I* am not that much older than you?"

"Yeah, you're only two years older than me." "Zatie, we just got done talking about *time travel* and seeing future events! That stuff ages a person, that ages your soul. My physical body as a therianthrope and the constant healing therapy I do every time I hurt myself or when the neighbors' cat attacked my crows; that's the part of me that I can heal; so my body may not age but my soul, my spirit, my consciousness and understanding is well over 40 years old by now!" I replied.

"You do seem more mature; you have less of an urge to do stupid things with your boyfriend in front of everyone. Thank you for that," she said.

"You're welcome," I replied.

"How is everything, in the boyfriend department, may I ask?" She asked.

"No, you may not! It's not going that great. I might break up with him," I said.

"What?! But he's so great?!" she replied.

"Yeah, *he* may be so great, but I am horrible, and he deserves better than that. It's not fair for me to keep a claim on someone so wonderful when I'm literally a monster. I'm no better than this murder that we're trying to destroy; I should be destroyed," I said.

"Oh, Nona, don't. Don't talk like that. You're a good person," Zatie tried to comfort me.

"Am I?! I constantly lie, I avoid answering questions, did you see what I did there?!" I said.

"You did, you got me distracted," she realized.

"Yeah, I'm not a good person. I'm not able to maintain healthy relationships," I said.

"What about Harry, that's a working relationship? Right?" Zatie knew I understood her implications. I glared at her incredulously.

"Oh, you're kidding me, you guys *are* having an affair, right?" she exclaimed, as her eyes widened.

"Quiet Zatie. We're done talking," I snapped my fingers and took her voice from her throat just like somebody pressing mute on a TV remote control. She wasn't happy about it, but it did the job, and we went back to studying in silence.

Entry #17

My first Haunt

I thought that she had forgotten, but Zatie had scolded me for not letting her help me hunt down the Gor-Nok. We were patrolling the perimeter of the farm when she brought it up. I told her it was too dangerous.

She told me, "I could help! You shouldn't do these things on your own. And now he's found a way into our minds and into our privacy. He can peek in whenever he wants by taking over your daydream Nix!" She said.

"Zatie, I know. I know what I have to do, I just don't have the stomach for it," I replied.

"What very bad idea are you planning to do now?!" Zatie asked me.

"I need to just kill my daydream and recreate it."

"Kill Dusk?! You can't just... wait, can you? Can you do that and not cause irreparable damage to yourself?!" She asked.

"Ha, trust me, I'm damaged enough as it is. Not that I like hurting myself. I have lost birds before and had to regrow them. Then we will just exercise the demon after that. No more spy!" Ultimately, Zatie disagreed with my bad idea.

Dusk had been placed in the cage to impede him with

404

extra magic spells and we took additional precautions leaving another bird in the library to watch the one in the cage. I removed his vocal cords so that it would not make a sound; we called him 'Peep.' Yeah, we're having fun with the names.

We discussed possible ideas for trapping the Gor-Nok. Zatie had agreed to let me go out and do my vigilante patrol if I would let her be my dispatch back up at the house. Also, if She got to design my Butt-kicking outfit. I reluctantly agreed to her demands and let her get the equipment. She wanted to go for a combination of modern technology and witchcraft. I just want to project my thoughts to her head, but we agreed that would be a bad idea; and it took a lot of energy to do so.

The alternative was to designate a bird to communicate to her. It was just funny for me because when I would talk, the bird would say what I thought. We called him 'Mockingbird.' The next thing we needed to do was set up Dusk so that he was only looking at some parts of the library and not allowed to get out of the cage. We found that in bird form and trapped in the iron cage, it would prevent the Gor-Nok from using magic through Dusk. We had to set up yet another bird, Peep, to keep an eye on dusk in the cage so that Zatie could focus on what she was doing. The rest of me went out on patrol while Zatie stood watch at the house and listened to the police radio scanners.

It was a typical boring Saturday night, not a whole lot of crimes. "Most everybody is terrified because of the urban legend of the Dark Angel! Half bird, half angry teenage girl who can't figure out how to maintain a healthy relationship, so she is taking her aggression out on the criminals of town," Zatie declared.

"I'm cool with just 'Dark Angel,'" I said. Zatie was trying to relay the different police codes to me through Mockingbird. Using the numbers was easier to cut down on the chatter.

A number had come across the radio scanner.

"What was that one?!" she had asked.

"Look it up, that's why I gave you all the books. That's why you're in the Library. That's why you've got the computers. So, you can look these things up," I said.

"I know, give me a second," she replied.

"I'm here to stop the crimes, not do your job too."

"Oh, that one is a mugging!" She declared.

"Is there a robbery in progress?" I asked.

"Yes, somebody saw a guy right now, um fighting a girl over purse and the guy ran-off!" Zatie said.

"OK, are the police on route and in which direction?" I responded.

"The assailant went eastbound on 13th. Officers inbound, so hurry!" Zatie said.

"I'm on it, going dark!" I took off running at full speed to the edge and leapt off the roof. I burst into the full swarm of birds and scattered them across the city in that direction. I veered off here and there, all the while using the Sight to scan through multiple possibilities. One of me found the perpetrator trying to get away; I caught the guy trying to go through the contents of the stolen purse.

By the time one of my birds landed I started calling out to him. I was waiting for the rest of me, convening on that location. He wasn't listening to me and was trying to shoo me away, so I spoke.

"Not yours!"

"Shoo bird!" He said.

"Not yours!" I repeated.

"What did you say to me?!" He stopped to ask.

"I said, **NOT YOURS!**" I growled as I had appeared behind him in my Dark Angel form, barely human, mostly harpy. Usually all I have to do is bear my talons and people scatter; but this guy decided to pull a knife. Knives are usually easy to handle. I lifted off with my wings and kicked him in the throat with my foot; then grabbed him by the neck with my claws. The police were coming, all I had to do was leave this guy unconscious nearby. So, I strangled him until he passed out. I let him go 15 feet off ground, he might have lanced off the dumpster before face-planting.

I went back to my usual perch up near the courthouse by some gargoyles. "I'm waiting for further instructions. Zatie, do you have anything else besides muggings?" I asked through Mockingbird.

"Oh, hey you're back! Nope, nothing else. That seems to be all that's on the menu right now. What are you looking for?" Zatie asked.

"Homicides," I stated.

"Excuse me?!" She replied.

"You heard me, the Gor-Nok likes to torture people before he kills them. So, kidnappings or homicide. I'll show up and work my magic and get some information." I stated.

"Sorry, hon, nothing like that," Zatie said.

"Not even a car accident, anything?" I asked.

"Well, unfortunately, no one died, yet. But you got a complaint about a dispute, a couple people fighting outside of a bar," Zatie responded.

"I'm on it," I said.

"That's over on Eighth and Winchester."

"Copy that!" We were getting good at the cop dispatch thing translated through the crows. There's still no sign of the Gor-Nok tonight.

I jumped off the building away from the gargoyles and pulled my wings in tight so that I could dive faster. Before I hit the ground, I opened the vortex. I popped out on the other side above the corner of Eighth and Winchester and perched on the building nearby.

I scattered out a couple century birds to be my eyes and ears. The group of on-lookers seem to be dying down outside of the bar. The bouncers were taken care of it. One of my birds picked up a signal, a woman crying for distress around the corner, but it was muffled.

It was dark in the alley. I activated the Sight on my

407

birds so they can see in night-vision. There was a woman struggling on the ground with a dark hooded figure crouching over top of her carrying a knife. The birds seem to like shiny things. I adequately used the bird as an exit-point and tele-ported through them into the alley. I swooped in quickly to snatch the assailant before he began to use the knife to cut the women's clothes. At least that's what I saw through the Sight; that was what they intended.

I need to stop this; I dug my talons deep into their back and shoulders, ripping them from being on top of the woman and carried the assailant up into the night sky. They screamed in pain, begging for me to let them go. I made them stab them-selves in the leg psychically; forcing the knife to tear through the flesh to the bone and telling them to break it and toss the handle.

The assailant struggled to follow my commands, I pushed it harder. He was whimpering, he was crying as the blade plunge deep into his thigh and stabbed his bone. He screamed for me to let him go, so I complied.

"As you wish!" I enjoyed this part of the job too much, dropping criminals from the sky. Gravity made a good weapon. Plus, it helped that he was already injured. He did a weird flip in the air and he spun back around.

I didn't know if he was trying to see me or trying to reach for something to hold onto. It was kind of hilarious watch-ing them try to stop themselves from falling. OK, I loved this part. As their body spun around, the hood had fallen off their head revealing their face in the moonlight.

I had only seen tears in those eyes like that once before; only one other time, that was the night our parents died in the car accident. I remembered that face well; the face of my brother Jesse was screaming, falling backwards to his death. Why was he about to die not knowing that I had just let him? In the blink of an eye I plunged down to try to catch him, but I wasn't quick enough Jesse was nearly to the ground.

I had to make a snap decision. This was all happening

much faster than I was ready for. It was more real now that I was fighting someone I loved. I opened the vortex and teleported with him. I was in shock, I was in pain, I was so angry, I was out-raged. I should've let him fall; I should've let him die.

Nothing he could say could stop me from doing the job now. I landed on his chest and arms with my claws full out as we exited the vortex. I know I had crushed some of his bones and ribs; I heard the crunching against the floor of the barn.

Zatie had appeared instantly coming through her pink vortex. She tried in vain to stop me, but unfortunately, she had no power over me. She screamed for me to stop! She used the banshee cry; it was like trying to swim through water where you are all dressed up; everything got heavy, but I could still move. She was trying psychically and sonically to stop me. She had succeeded in pushing me off of Jesse and he crawled backwards to cower in fear behind her.

I snapped my fingers; removing Zatie's powers and slapped my hands together, causing a thunderclap shockwave throwing them both across the room. I had calmed my form down a little bit more from full blown harpy to winged Dark Angel. Somewhat more humanoid, but still fierce and violent as the gale force winds in a hurricane with bright purple, flaming eyes.

Zatie begged me to stop. Jesse was crying trying to find reason in all this. He was asking, "What, what the heck is that?! What's going on?!" I restored my form more to my human self but kept the crow talons on my hands and the flaming purple eyes.

"Please, Nona?! How are you doin...?" he cried.

"Never mind how I can do this! Why were you doing what you did to that poor girl?!" I screamed.

"I didn't do anything; we were just messing around!" He responded as he cowered with Zatie.

"You had a knife! You were going to use it! You were going to cut her clothes!" With each word I was getting angrier. Lightning was coursing through my veins, erupting to

409

the surface of my skin.

Zatie was pleading with me, she was grabbing plants from out of the ground. I knew what she was going to do, I made the weeds wither and die in her hands. Jesse was pleading with me as well.

"But I didn't, I might've thought about it."

"Why would you do that?! Would you do that? Are you going to rape that poor girl, Jesse?! I asked.

Zatie asked through her tears, "What were you doing?" She had pulled herself away from him.

"I don't know, she's kind of a tease. She flirts with everybody, and she's gone out with everyone. I just wanted to take my shot with her, have my chance. I'm just sick of people taking stuff from me. I wanted someone to give me something, even if I had to take it from them," he was sobbing.

I was forcing him to tell the truth; I knew he was prone to lying. Zatie hadn't seen the hypnosis spell; she was helpless and powerless as she was besides herself in shock of the situation.

"I think I'm gonna be sick," Zatie whimpered.

"Jesse, still that doesn't justify what you were doing! With all the things that have been taken from us, that doesn't give us the right to do evil just to make us feel good!!" I flared my eyes, and coursed lightning through my claws. I made my claws grow sharper and expanded my wings.

"I'll stop, I'll change!" Jesse pleaded with me.

"Please, Nona, I beg you. Have mercy," he cried.

"Mercy?! Were you showing *her* mercy?! Did you listen to *her* when she was saying to stop?! Why should I listen to you? No, I'm done with this right now. I end this now," I created a feather sword, the crow's blade from my wings.

Zatie was begging me now, trying to stop me. I cast her aside with some lightning; just enough to scare her back. She cowered on the floor; Jesse was trying to shield her. I took the sword and plunged deep, as far as I could until I had to stop.

They both opened their eyes to see the crow's blade

stuck between them and into the barn post. They looked up to see me shaking in my rage, so full of power and adrenaline. So full of shame and hate, hate at myself, hate at what had just happened; hate for wanting to end him. I only felt blinding hatred.

"Nonabel, I'm so sorry. I promise I'll change. I'll do my best. I just felt so weak. I'm just sick of weak people getting stomped on. I just wanted to feel power."

"I... know how you feel. I'm sorry for being weak too," I responded. Zatie was crying, so I motioned for her to hug me. Especially since she thought she could solve everything with a hug, even if I didn't want to be touched before.

I knew that Jesse was hugging us too, I could feel the sincerity in his embrace. He was sorry, not the kind of sorry because you were caught, but sorry because he was weak and couldn't stop himself. I told him if we lose ourselves to our weaknesses then we're no better than the people we tried to stop; the monsters we're trying to fight. Then Zatie asked me, "Who is gonna stop you when you become a monster? How do we protect ourselves from you?" I didn't have an answer.

"Zatie, I don't know how to stop me, I don't have all the answers. I'm too powerful as it is. But with all my power, I don't know how to teach you guys how to be good people. I don't know how to *be* a good person on my own. I am not ready to be Mom. I'm not ready to be Dad. I'm not ready to be Lulu. I'm not ready to be what everyone needs me to be. I just get out of my own way. I stop giving into the weaknesses of self-doubt and self-loathing. I stop whining about what I have to do because I don't have all day to sit around and mope. I've got sweet seconds to stop myself from killing my brother. I am the Devil!" I continued weeping as we hugged.

"Nonabel, how in the devil did you do all that?! Did you sell your soul to the devil or that dark angel thing?" Jesse was still in shock.

I let out a sigh, "This is *not* how I imagined sharing this with you, Jesse. I'm sorry I lied to you your entire life," I was sobbing again.

"Am I adopted?!" Jesse asked.

"No! No, you're just an idiot. Zatie, can you deal with him?" I laughed as I asked.

"Do I get to train him?!" Zatie asked.

I sighed again, "Yeah, I guess."

"Sweet, I'll get the training montage music going!"
"Please, don't! Please, please, stop. Just call Harry up, Harry will teach him," I regretted letting her get excited.

"Oh, but I want to train him," she said.

"You can't beat me though, but Harry knows how to stop me. He has a few tricks up his sleeves," I said.

With that I teleported out of the barn and locked myself in my interrogation room for a week. I was disgusted at what I had done; sick of myself.

On the bright side, Jesse was taking the whole 'magic thing' pretty well. When I finally emerged from my interrogation cell in the Library, Jesse was actually reading a book. I lost the feeling in my knees and had to catch myself on the nearest chair because I was about to cry. Zatie looked at me from across the room and mouthed, "I know right?!"

Later that day Harry and Dominic showed up to the Barn for training. Zatie excitedly filled me in on the things that Jesse was apparently a natural at; she had made a list. I watched my brute of a brother get schooled by Harry in hand-to-hand techniques, while Zatie rattled off the list.

I was only half listening, because I was putting thoughts into Harry's head to *not hold back*. He obeyed and landed an open palm slap straight through Jesse's face that should have made his head spin. But he barely moved, he smiled even, as though this was fun. I got a flash of Dad wrestling with us as kids in that instant before Jesse plowed through Harry the were-croc and into the barn door.

"Oh, yeah Jesse is a therian," Zatie said.

"Wait, he just did that without a tot... Totem?"

"Yeah, Harry can't believe it either," she said.

"He's strong?!" I exclaimed.

"And fast too," Zatie added.

"More like slippery!" Harry said as he tried to grab Jesse but fell short of succeeding.

"Harry, how is this possible?!" I asked.

"You?! You can question me about the possibilities?! All of you have different traits from Michael, just manifesting differently," Harry replied.

As I was distracting him, Jesse took advantage and struck with lightning speed.

"Yikes, but shouldn't he need a totem animal to have these powers," I asked Harry.

"It's not an exact science, therianthropy; however, what rules we have, albeit limited rules, can always be broken. As you, yourself have exhibited. It must have something to do with the two species mixing bloodlines," Harry was lecturing in-between receiving and delivering blows.

"Okay, switch partners, Zatie coached him as he fights with Dominic," I ordered.

"Who's Dominic?!" Jesse asked.

"Oh, right we haven't shown you Dominic. Come with me," Zatie left me with Harry in the barn.

"Do you want to spar it's been a while?" He asked.

"No. What do you think about him?" I asked.

"I think that he's doing just fine. We should've brought him into the group long ago. What made you change your mind?" Harry asked me.

"I almost killed him," I was still ashamed.

"I had asked, but nobody wanted to tell me about what happened. Zatie called me and said I needed to help. Thanks to your brother, I thought it was going to be your typical 'father son time' discussions about becoming a man and body odors and stuff like that," Harry joked.

"No, Harry, my brother is kind of a criminal. I stopped him from almost date raping some chick. Yeah, I guess she was a floozy, but nobody deserves that."

"Did he deserve it?" He asked.

"He needs to be scared straight! but I don't have time to, you know, to be a father figure. I can never be that for him. I've got a hard-enough time just keeping myself from killing everyone when I'm mad at life."

"I can do that for you. I'll always be there for you. And your family," Harry said.

"I know. Here Harry, this is what I want from you. Now if he doesn't need an animal, a totem, then what are his limits?" I inquired of him.

"His limits?" he asked to clarify.

"Let's test his strength, his agility and speed. His senses, run through everything you could think of, push his limits," I responded.

"He heals quickly. Today he showed me where he got stabbed by your claws; it's barely a bruise!" he said.

"It's only been a few days hasn't it? How long was I in my dreamscape, moping?" I asked.

"You were gone for about a week," he said.

"I'm sorry, I just, I was just so ready to kill everyone! I almost, almost hurt Zatie." I sobbed.

"Neither one of them can stop you." he stated.

"That's the other thing, Harry. I need you to teach them how to stop... a witch. I need you to show them how to stop me. They need to be able to protect themselves from me." I responded.

As we were discussing Jesse's possible strength training, Jessie came running through the barn scared out of his mind screaming, "It's trying to eat me!"

He cowered behind were-croc Harry and I as we instinctively got into fight-mode. Dominic came bounding through the barn doors with his tongue wagging. Zatie teleported next to him, "Oh, Jesse, you big baby! Dominic is just a puppy, he wouldn't hurt family." Zatie calmed him down and was teaching him how to play her version of fetch with her baby were-plants and Dominic while I continued discussing training with Harry.

"What about magic? Is he exhibiting anything? Are you running him through the therian-think-talking thing, right?" I rattled off excitedly.

"Oh, he's definitely strong on the therian side there, a were-creature. However, it's almost as if he has been in a daze and just doesn't know it," he pondered.

"What do you mean?" I asked.

"He has these gifts without a trigger point or an initiation like being bitten, it's very odd. And he has all of our daytime strength without the moonlight side effects. It's very odd. I think it is kind of cool though. I almost think he doesn't really need a totem. But on that note, it could become a future problem, you know, getting bit by a spider or a rabid dog," Harry rambled.

"How do we know he didn't get bit by anything?"

"I tested him in the moonlight with a device Michael and Lucia invented, the Moon-Gazer," Harry said. "Michael's idea, it's silly looking, but it's helpful."

"Well, we should still initiate the trigger event."

"Let some poor animal bite your brother?!" Harry laughed at my idea. *I wasn't joking.* "Oh, you want to!"

"I mean, we got to at least test it out, see if he's got Michael's genes or if he's just got a whole different set of DNA going on," I responded.

"What's the worst that could happen, we pick the wrong animal and it turns him into something stupid, like a flightless bird or a starfish," Harry replied.

"Wait, that would be great, re-growing your limbs would be so cool!" I exclaimed.

I let Zatie be in charge of teaching Jesse magic and I had Harry in charge of helping him figure out his Therianthrope powers. When I felt like he was ready, I would bring him into my dreams and teach him the nature of true power.

I gave Harry and Zatie instructions individually on how to train Jesse. I was impressed with how quickly he was learning but I was still hesitant to teach him *too* quickly. I wanted to see how well he understood.

I reached out to his mind and spoke my voice through his thoughts. Projecting a thought into his head. I told him to meet me in the Library when he was done training for his next lesson. He looked at me and nodded before getting punched in the face by Harry. I chuckled and teleported back to the house.

I remembered that we had a prisoner in the Library. My poor baby bird Dusk had been possessed by the that murder's demons and now he had a new pair of eyes to spy for the monster. I had to pretend like everything was normal so that we could use this tragedy for a trap.

I discussed my day with the bird and asked the bird how it was today as I changed its water and food in the cage. I told Dusk I was thinking I may go out later tonight to hunt down bad guys and asked if he wanted to come with me. The bird cawed in excitement; he bought the bait. I told him I think I have an idea on how to catch the Gor-Nok, but I just need to set the right trap. I went to my private room and took a nap as I waited for Jesse to finish his training.

In my dreamscape, I had prepared some things for Jesse's first introductory crash-course on shared daydreaming and manipulating the dreamscape. After a while of altering my reality, I heard a knock at the door.

I opened the door to welcome Jesse into my room.

"Wow, Nonabel, this is where you've been living?"

"How do you know I've been in here; have you been sneaking into my room at night?!" I asked him.

"Yeah, scrounging to see if you have any spare change laying out. So, what are we gonna learn?"

"Consider these lessons the 'master course' on magic," I responded and was about to continue.

"Zatie's already teaching me magic," he stated.

"Correct, I will teach you the advanced lessons. What kind of things is she teaching?" I asked him.

Jesse was casually strolling through my holding cell, possibly casing the place. I kept my eye on him.

"I am trying to move stuff with my mind and also trying to stop stuff from hitting me when they throw it at me. I'm getting better. I know I have a lot to learn."

"Good, humility is a good way to start. Do you know what this room is used for?" I responded

"For prisoners? It's not much of a bed and are those swords? Is this what you wanted to show me; Grandpa's stash of antiques?!" he asked excitedly.

"No, not exactly. And some of these are off-limits, but weapons training is on the list of things you need to learn if you're going to be a part of this," I replied.

"So, what is all this? Was this where all their money came from? How did Grandma hide this room, this entire Library in the attic of the house?!" he asked.

"Oh, yeah. We're not in the house anymore."

"Wait, what?!" he asked as he looked around.

"Yeah, once you went through the door, you entered into an entirely different dimension, in another, world not even in the house. And if we would open up the door, we would be floating where the house used to be; but the doorway would still be here, waiting," I said.

"How?" he asked.

"Magic," I said.

"That's gonna be your answer for everything, isn't it?" Jesse asked me, annoyed. I walked him around the Library as I pointed out important items in our new life.

"Listen, Jesse, the answer to anything that you don't understand is, repeat after me, 'magic!' Got it?!"

"Got it. So, what is this stuff for, is that what we do with it, magic? Do we torture people in here?"

"Well, we do a lot of studying, actually. A lot of reading,

I'm glad you're doing that, by the way. I didn't even know you could," I replied.

"I just don't let you guys see it," he stated.

"That's cool," I said.

"Don't judge a book by its cover and all. So, reading; why?" he responded.

"Learning our family history, our inheritance and our true nature," I said.

"How long have *you* known about this?" he asked.

"I? Um, it's been going on for a long time, but mostly we protect this Library. We protect the Diary which is an index to all the knowledge in this room. Plus, the Library has books on all kinds of topics, not just magic. Basically, anything that Grandpa Michael and Grandma Lucia wanted to read about. They had a lot of time on their hands," I replied.

"So, yeah, Harry was telling me Grandpa was like super old but because he was a were-thingy..."

"Yeah, we don't age; not like other people, but that's not why I brought you here. I'm going to teach you the first lesson that Lucia taught me the night she trusted me with the Diary. So, take my hands and I want you to look at the light in the lamp. Watch the flame flicker, watch it pulse, getting brighter and darker. Light and dark, day and night. Your eyes are getting heavier, your soul is getting lighter," I was trying to hypnotize him.

"Are you trying to hypnotize me? Because it's totally working," he laughed.

"And we're here!" I declared.

"Where?!" he asked as he opened one eye.

"Look around the room, Jesse," I told him. He realized we were no longer in my bedroom in the Library, but we were in Lucia's room. Lucia had just died, and the lamp was just about to go out. It was flickering in front of us as lightning was striking outside; giving the younger me, panicking by her grandmother's bed, the idea to use lightning for CPR.

"Whoa, wait! Is that what you did?! You were trying to

bring her back to life?!" Jesse exclaimed.

"While we were sleeping, she was fighting for her life, fighting a monster. While she lay here dying, younger me, well, *I* was trying to save her," I pointed outside; the future me was trying to kill the monster.

Jesse could see out in the yard; I was fighting the Gor-Nok with lightning. It startled him to see the lightning strike outside, to see the monster for the first time in the light.

"Oh, dear god! What is that hideous thing?! Is that an elephant, what is that?!" Jesse was disgusted.

"From what we know..." I made time stop in the room around us. I faded everything to white and then pulled the image of the Gor-Nok towards us so we could study it closer.

"...he is an ancient evil Grandpa was hunting in Borneo," I responded.

"Is that why you went there?!" Jesse asked.

"Yeah, I was trying to find some answers. It didn't seem right. Lu-lu thought that it was a demon," I manifested the vision of Lu-lu trying to capture the Gor-Nok. "She had tried to trap it, but the spell went terribly wrong and the monster broke free, striking Lu-lu. After it was free, it tried to kill me. That's how I learned to teleport. I learned all of these things through dreams; like I'm teaching you right now," I stated.

"Wait! We're dreaming?!" Jesse asked.

"Yeah, you're asleep dude!" I said.

"I don't remember even falling asleep," he said.

"Yeah, when I was hypnotizing you, I put you to sleep; that was lesson one," I responded.

"Are you sure we're dreaming?" He asked.

"Yes," I said, getting annoyed.

"So, you're in my head?" he asked to clarify.

"Exactly!" I continued, "You have all your powers in here, and I have my power because I know how to control them while in someone's dreamscape. But ultimately you have all-power; you are God in this world of your dreams. You can be every bit as powerful as I am in the real world, here in your dreams and eventually you'll take that power from your dreams into the real world," I stated.

"Anyways, we thought that maybe the Gor-Nok was a nightmare or a demon apparition, a Nix of the nightmare. Apparitions here are called Nixes, there's one for your accessing the power of your nightmares and there's one for your daydreams," I said as I made different miniature totems appear.

"Do you remember when I was caught out in that storm, *the* thunderstorm?" I manifested a tiny storm cloud above my hand.

"Oh, that thing is so cute! But why is it so small?"

"Because I've conquered my nightmares. I'm no longer afraid of it, but it represents my control over the things I'm afraid of or the darker side of me. It can become much worse if I let it, but I choose to manifest it as a small storm in my hands." Rain fell in the room.

"If you want to go, we can go," I told him.

"No, I'm good. I needed a wet dream," he smiled.

"That's gross!" I said.

"So, that's your nightmare? What is your daydream?" he asked me.

"Oh, any one of my little baby crows in my dreams. They're like little people," I called Twilight to me and she came out from a white door. She had a cute little dress and bonnet.

"Oh, that's cute too! Is she small because you conquered your daydreams here by dressing up your birds?" he asked mockingly.

"No, the birds, they become like little people and they still have their own personalities. I can show you the whole world, but right now I wanted to discuss the dark-side. There's both good and evil in the dark and the light, but also hope. I want you understand what we're up against. Lu-lu died protecting me from this thing," I restored the vision of the beast.

"As far as we understand he's like us, a therianthrope.

He becomes this half were-beast, were-boar; whatever and his culture feared him as a god or monster, but they hired Michael to kill it. So, I went there to see what happened and well, let me rewind it."

I caused the illusion around us to reenact some of our battles and had Jesse and I stand a little way off as we watched Michael and I fight against the monster.

"I got to fight by Grandpa Michael against one of the greatest evils I've ever met! I am grateful for the experience, but I regret it because I brought this evil upon our family. He has somehow followed me back!"

"But Nona, that was like 20 years ago?!" he said. "The other thing is I've traveled back in time," I replied.

"Dude, you've been busy!" Jesse exclaimed.

"Yeah, every time you guys thought I was sick, or I slept in or something, I was busy fighting this guy. I nearly died or fell 10,000 feet my death, drowned, but going back in time does have advantages. Do you remember this day?!"

I opened a vision to his mind of when he was really young. Lu-lu had stepped out of the room to answer the phone and the kids were scared of the storm outside. A young lady had one of the kids by the hallway door and younger me had said, "Lily, auntie Lily! Is that you?"

"Wait, I remember! Yeah, yeah, there was some girl that was living with Grandma. She's like a cousin or some crap," Jesse strained to remember.

"Yeah, look closely, not through your little kid eyes and all that crap," I stated.

"You? Is that you?!" Jesse asked with tears welling up in his eyes. he was finally remembering.

"Yeah, that's what happened to me, I got stuck back in time. Grandma wouldn't let me travel back, so, I had to live an entirely new life pretending to be your cousin or aunt or whatever and I read you guys stories and junk. I often enjoyed playing out visions in your minds or just in front of you as I read fairy-tales."

"Oh yeah, Zatie and I love this one. *Alice in Wonderland* is the best!" He pointed to the memory.

"Yes, Zatie always thought she was Alice and you loved the white rabbit for some reason," I stated.

"Well, it's true. I love rabbits! When I wanted to be a magician like, you know, for school. Grandma said she had those ones in the back still. I take care of them OK. And then I hate being late to things like the white rabbit; even though it seems like I don't care. I mean it's embarrassing to show up late to class now. I'd rather be early so I could be the guy that makes fun of people that are late," Jesse was really opening up.

"Well, it makes sense. So, I think we found your daydream and your nightmare," I laughed.

"I'm not afraid of rabbits, no threat there," he said.

"That's gonna be your strength, your daydream. But you're afraid of missing out or being late, that's your fears. Oh, and I'm sorry that you were late to this party. I'm sorry that we've left you out, but if you want, I'm willing to let you in, to be a part of our crew. I don't know what we are, but we're trying to stop this evil. Protect the weak like you said, and this guy preys on the weak through fear. Fear becomes his strength."

As I was teaching him about the Gor-Nok, Jesse had frozen an image of the monster.

"So, you told me this thing killed Grandpa and Grandma?" He asked.

"Oh, it gets worse!" I said.

"How can it get worse?!" He asked.

"I'm pretty sure he killed Mom and Dad too."

"Oh, this guy is dead meat. Could point me in the right direction?!" Jesse exclaimed.

"You wanna take him out?! That's what we're trying to figure out. We're trying to figure out where he hides, smoke him out! We know there's something he wants from us," I responded.

"What does he want?" Jesse asked.

"To kill us, for one, and he wants to take our power; mostly he wants the Diary," I explained.

Jesse asked, "So, does this thing have weaknesses? What can we use against it?"

"Well, as far as I can tell, it feels pain, it can be hurt. I've hurt it with lightning, he doesn't like being teleported; it's kind of chokes on the dark water of the vortex," I said as I listed his weaknesses.

"Oh, couldn't we just shove his head into the vortex and then close it?!" Jesse asked.

"Yeah, it's kind of doesn't work like that; it's all or nothing. You really can't be tangible until you're out because you're going through a wormhole that transfers matter from one plane of existence into it a limbo and then re-creates you on the other side just as you were; but you are the smoke that you see, like Zatie still has," I explained.

"You don't have any," he stated.

"You don't necessarily see my smoke anymore."

"So, that's your matter coming back together, your cells. OK, so we could separate his head from his body." He responded.

"Yeah, I don't think it will work," I said.

"It was worth a try," Jesse said.

"I've electrocuted him, fire could hurt him, it was typical things that can hurt him; he is still mortal but just hard to kill. Oh, and he's made some deal with Death!" I explained.

"Like the actual Grim Reaper?!" Jesse exclaimed.

"Yeah, that guy," I said as I shared that memory.

"Oh, that's, that's terrifying!" he said.

"Yeah, you sure you want to continue with this?! I've been living in a waking nightmare ever since Mom and Dad's car accident; but mostly I was aware it was a nightmare and not the real world since Lu-lu's death."

"Well, I mean does this guy have any addictions? Things like any habits or hobbies?" he asked.

"What, like basket weaving or gambling? I don't know a

whole lot about his regular life as a person."

"Wait, this thing is a normal person?" Jesse asked.

"Yeah, he's a therianthrope like Harry. Well, he's kind of like me where he can do both witch-thought and were-beast communication," I explained.

"And he does magic?!" Jesse exclaimed.

"So, he's more like me not Harry. Here, I'll show you what it looks like as a man," I said.

I changed the Gor-Nok's image from the monster into the man. He looked like an indigenous tribesman from Borneo with his skirt of pelts and his weird voodoo necklace. He had his body paint, his body scars, and tattoos as well.

Jesse said, "Weird, I know that dude. Oh, he's the antique collector!" I snapped my fingers and put him in a white suit and had him stand upright with gold chains and rings and bling.

"Yeah, yeah, I know that guy! His name is 'Wha go no.' No, his name is Rob Bono or something like that. Yeah, he's got an antique shop kinda like a fancy pawnshop downtown. I, um sell, I mean he buys stuff. OK, yeah, he buys stuff I have stolen," Jesse replied.

"OK, this is helpful! Do you know where this antique shop is located?" I inquired.

"Well, it is kind of private. It's by appointment only," Jesse stated.

"But you do know the location, or you can point me in the right direction?" I asked.

"Yeah, I can show you where it is, but why do you want to know that? Don't we want to catch him?"

"I don't just want to catch him, I wanna end him! I want to destroy him and make him hurt while I do it! I want vengeance for what he's taken from me!" I said.

Having Jesse as an ally and his unfortunate knowledge of the criminal underworld had proven to be valuable. I brought him with me on one of my nightly patrols to confirm the location of the Gor-Nok, and his antique shop. We watched the location; I sent some birds out to scout around. I'm waiting, hoping for confirmation that this is where he lived. Jesse, of course, asked really quickly how long it has been since we started watching.

"Well, I think it's been all of 13 minutes," I said.

"Are you kidding me?! It feels like forever!"

"Well, it's what you gotta do; it's part of the job."

"This job sucks, we don't even get paid for this!" He was frustrated with having to wait. "Listen, Bel, we could be using our powers to make it, that money! You know what I mean?" He said.

"No, Jesse, I don't know. How would I go about getting paid for sneaking in the shadows and creeping on people, right after that maybe occasionally beating up people? How do I get paid?!" I asked sarcastically.

"Oh dude, I got connections! I can hook us up with all kinds of 'bosses' that need like people, you know what I mean, taken out. You can do that kind of stuff; teleport with them to the bottom of the ocean or something, make them disappear," he continued.

I was aside in disbelief of this conversation.

"I can't believe that I even had asked 'how?' You do know I was joking, right?! I don't really wanna know," I said exasperated.

"Aw, come on Bel, we could be making some serious money on some hits. Taking out bad guys left and right! Getting rid of the competition," he said.

"Who's competition?" I asked.

"Taking out drug dealers for other drug dealers." "Clearly you are high. How do we get paid by taking out a drug dealer unless somebody put a hit out on them?" "Yup, we become bounty-hunters!" he exclaimed.

"No! Ha, I will do it for free!" I stated.

"Listen, Bel, I just, like say to them that I'll do it, they show me a picture or whatever and you and your Birds, you swoop in and take them down like you did me in high heels!" He reminded me. "And I'll take the credit for the hit," he continued.

"OK, yeah, I, I'm feeling bad about that," I said.

"Don't, I don't even feel it!" he stated.

"Yeah, how is it that you're healing so fast?! You haven't been bit by any animal," I asked.

"Yeah, I haven't picked one out yet but I'm thinking about it. I think maybe a rabbit," he said.

"A rabbit would be cool!" I said.

"Yeah, I think I will stick to a theme like you got. Make my daydreaming-baby-thing, you know, the white rabbit from *Alice in Wonderland*. And I'll work on my punctuality as I worry about time," he continued, and I just listened as I was doing my surveillance.

"I don't know, it comes from how Mom and Dad's life got cut short. Grandma and Grandpa were like a million years old. It didn't seem like they had much time either. I take too much time in life and I got stuff, I got things I want to get done, things to do, places to be. It just always feels like I'm late! Teach me that time travel spell!" he demanded.

"Absolutely not! It's not just a spell anyway. It's a tool," I responded to him and I activated the Nevergator in my hand. He was mesmerized.

"It becomes a part of you," I said.

"What happens if you take that thing off?" He asked me as he eye-balled it.

"I don't know if I'll fade out of existence or if I end up with a massive déjà vu headache. But when I tried to remove it once; well, I tried to cut it off and it exploded! It was, it wasn't pretty, but I was stuck in a time loop and besides, it's an ability that we really should not be messing with without doing some careful thought," I lectured as I deactivated it and remembered why I removed it from the vault. The night I had attacked Jesse, I wanted to rewind and repent. I still might if he keeps making me regret letting him into my world.

"That's cool, so speaking of Time. How long has it been?" He was getting impatient again.

"Since work started?" I asked to clarify.

"Yeah, working if that's what we're calling this now," he asked again.

"We're at 20 minutes now," I chuckled knowing how he was going to react. He got frustrated again.

"Are you kidding me, this is gonna take forever?!"

"Do you want to go home? I got this," I said.

"Yes, please!" He hugged me.

"Oh, hold your breath, and plug your nose," I said.

"It just feels like the stuff gets down my throat, don't you? I hate it," he responded.

"I don't choke. No. I don't even notice it," I said.

"How far is it to swim every time when you do the spell? Just, I don't like the stuff in my throat," he said.

"Then plug your nose, and swim to the light on the other side!" I said as I made him fall through his vortex and he landed on the couch back at the house.

I remained throughout the night watching the antique shop and I had my other birds on lookout at the Gor-Nok's apartment. I was willing to wait all night but Zatie reached out to me psychically, calling me with her voice in my head, she seemed anxious. I could feel the fear in her voice, something was wrong.

Nonabel, we need you home, we need help! Jesse got bit by something! Jesse got bit by something!

I told her to call Harry, *I'm on my way!*
I teleported back to the house. Jesse was laid out on the floor convulsing, foaming at the mouth.

"What bit him?!" I asked.

"He said he was feeding his rabbits!" Zatie said.

"Get a wooden spoon from the kitchen!" I told her.

"What's that for?!" she responded.

"Gonna keep him from biting his own tongue!" I lifted him up off the ground and suspended him in air so he would not hurt himself. Moments later Harry arrived, immediately removed his jacket, and started rolling up his sleeves. He grabbed Jesse to restrict his arms.

"Oh good, you already started! Did you identify the animal?" Harry asked.

"Yeah, Zatie said it was one of his rabbits, right?!"

"You know what to do. Go! Get the rabid animal!" I vanished at Harry's command.

"Zatie, do you know how to brew the potion, the Weremen's Whiskey?" Harry asked her.

"I believe so?" she said timidly.

"Hurry!" Harry ordered her and she ran upstairs.

I appeared at the rabbit cages, one of them was squealing pretty badly, blood on his mouth. I got a flash of the past, it was a white rabbit, the white rabbit that Jesse used for his magic act. I lifted his cage rather than grab the rabbit and we all teleported back to the dining room. I set the cage near the table, then I teleported upstairs to check on Zatie. We went through the instructions one more time.

I conjured the tiny sun for her to activate the potion. Then we went back down. Jesse was getting worse, he starting to phase.

"Harry, his feet!" Rabbit feet were starting to tear through his shoes, his legs were starting to rip apart his pants below his knees. His legs were growing longer with massive feet. His feet look like they could kick a truck. His legs were racked with lean muscles. His hand started to twitch and convulse worse.

Harry woke me up from my lack of focus, "and Nonabel, now!"

I told Zatie to step back, "You might wanna close your eyes, honey."

"I can watch, I'm a big girl," she was sobbing.

"Yeah, you say that now," I declared.

I separated the cage psychically, removing the metal, and floated the rabbit in the air. I pulled apart the rabbit into the several pieces that we needed; bones tissue, sinews, marrow, organs, blood, spinal fluid, and anything else that I needed. I tried to shield Zatie from seeing it and she tried to brave the whole thing once everything was removed. I put it all into the potion and handed it to Harry at the same time the half torn apart dying rabbit was floating in the air, squealing.

"Zatie, help Harry with Jesse! I've got to heal this rabbit," I teleported by Michael's grave and got some hallowed ground to heal the rabbit. We teleported back to the house, and I restored the cage.

Jesse was phasing back into a person; Harry was helping him nurse the rest of the potion.

"I've got you," Harry reassured him.

"You got to drink it all honey!" Zatie was saying. Jesse was trying not to puke out the potion. When he calmed down, I brought him his bunny to comfort him. "Look who's all better!" Zatie said.

"Are you still jealous you're not a were-creature?"

"No, I'm good," she awkwardly smiled.

We watched Jesse through the night, taking turns as he slept with his rabbit; it seemed to comfort him. Harry and I were talking on the front porch in the seat-swing while Zatie watched Jesse on the cot in the study.

"Well, I guess he found his totem," Harry said.

"Yeah, Jesse and I kind of discussed the idea of what animal he wanted. I was training him on dreams and nightmares and daydream guides and the Nix as they are called. This is a concept Lucia was teaching me; you probably haven't heard of it," I shared.

"She tried to teach me of shared dreams. It's a little odd," Harry responded.

"So, yeah he pretty much picked out the rabbit as his totem," I told Harry.

"Hopefully, he has that trait and not all of them. The next thing to do is determine if he can transform like Michael into different animals," Harry pondered.

"Yeah, but Harry, give him some time," I said.

"I'll try him in another month or so. Let him go through the lunar cycle first," he assured me.

"OK, thanks Harry," I said.

"Hey, any time," he smiled then sprinted home.

I went inside to relieve Zatie for the night. We talked a little bit in the study as we watched Jesse.

"You know what? Earlier, he was showing me where the Gor-Nok lives. Well, where he works. An antique shop. I've got a bird still scouting it right now."

"Why do you wanna know where the guy lives and all that?" Zatie asked me. "If you get a chance to sniper him then you better shoot him," she continued.

"And if I have a chance to burn down the building, then I'll burn it! He's taken everything from me, I want to do the same to him!" I declared.

"This is about revenge?!" Zatie asked.

"Maybe if you had watched him kill everyone you've ever loved, you would understand!" I stated.

"Understand what?! Your hate?! Honey, I understand these things! I just don't know why you want to carry these things through to closure. I understand closure, ridding the world of this murderer, absolutely! I'm on board, but don't let this take *you* down too. Don't let this turn you into a murderer as well," she warned.

The room was quiet for a moment, until we heard the wannabe Dusk moving in its cage, eavesdropping. Zatie's eyes widened, I winked at her when she realized the *point* of this conversation. She continued talking.

"How are we going to trap him? Even if you do find where he lives or works and let's say we set a trap. What's your plan? How are we killing this guy?"

"I think I want to bring him into a dream or a nightmare," I responded.

"A shared dream?!" she asked to clarify.

430

"Yup, and have you, Jesse, and Harry and I take him on!" I explained to her.

"By God, are you nuts?!" she laid it on thick.

"Yes, and you guys will have all your powers and abilities. Plus, some extra abilities because you'll understand that it's a dream, but he won't. He'll still think rules like gravity and oxygen, space, and time, that kind of stuff still applies to him and not us," I declared.

"So, when we start doing some pretty crazy stuff and messing with him on our ground..." she said.

"On our playing-field, with our rules; we will have the home-court advantage! Sorry for using sports references," I responded to her.

"But once we have him, how do we actually kill him?" Zatie asked.

"We don't! We have to physically destroy his body, yes. But I want to destroy his vessel that carries his totem. He has some type of amulet, it's like a voodoo-doll. I think it's what tethers him into this world. I saw him using it on several occasions. I think it's his focusor and I believe, even in the dream, it will kill him."

"But how does it hurt him in reality?" She asked.

"If it's done in a dream, his subconscious will project it out into reality," I said.

"Hopefully, his subconscious mind will destroy it in reality," Zatie said.

"Trust me, Zatie, I've done some weird stuff in reality when I was dreaming. I am hopeful, like I said, and I don't know all the rules, but I know how to break some of them; but I think this is what will give us the advantage we need," I stated.

"So, now let's just set the trap!" she exclaimed.

"Yeah, when Jesse's feeling better, I'll get him to tempt the guy with a couple of antique books; because as far as he knows, Jesse is just a normal kid," I said.

"Well, he's a weirdo but he doesn't know what Jesse can

do yet," Zatie said.

"There are some other things we can do to kind of mask him from being detected as well," I said.

"We just need him to get a book to him, so he'll fall for the bait, then we'll have him," Zatie stated.

We continued to thicken the plot for our eavesdropper to pass on to his master as we watched over our recovering brother and newest partner in crime.

Entry #18

My first Hunt:

We decided that our best course of action was to send in Jesse to set the trap by bringing bait for the monster. We gave Jesse a book from our Library, an ancient book with an ancient

432

language. Written in one of seven ancient dialects, and even fewer understood it. To do so required having done the Seer's Sight and the gift of tongues spell. It was in an ancient dialect older than the druids. It was older than any known records, so I figured the age of the book would be enticing enough to lure him into our trap.

We placed some hexes on it; nasty hexes and curses to keep him from reading it but to make him desire to come and get the Diary to unravel its mysteries. We even discussed our plan of setting a trap for him here at the house that we would lure him into the Library. Get him to step into a circle of enchantments we had drawn in the ground and banish him to another dimension. Granted, we said all this in front of my compromised poor bird Dusk who still had demon-eyes.

Jesse did well with his transition; he seemed like his usual cracked out junkie-self. Thanks to needing some quick cash, or the idea that he did caused him to hang out all day waiting for this RoGono guy, his human form and it paid off. The white car pulled into the parking garage.

Jesse approached him like he was going to beg for money and asked him, "Are you still looking for a rare old stuff?" The Gor-Nok laughed, "May I help you?!"

"I think it's the other way around, I can help you. I got another place they don't think I know about it, but I know! I've got a whole library full of books just like this one!" Jesse flashed the book and got caught up with his excitement. The Gor-Nok seemed suspicious and eyed him side-ways; but then he spoke after a pause, "Come, let's discuss this in my shop." Jesse got to go inside.

He's been there before; he may have stolen some jewelry of grandma and has sold it to the Gor-Nok. He scolded him for touching the book with his bare hands.

"They touch the books all the time," Jesse said, "they're always using them at the house."

"You'll defile it!" he said as he put on his examiner's

gloves and a little pair of glasses. He carefully opened the pages; he sniffed the pages and examined the words.

"It looks old enough, I'll give you a thousand. But I'll make it ten thousand if you can get me into their Library," his eyes flashed green with greed.

"Are you kidding me?! It's gonna be impossible, they're always in there!" Jesse declared.

"How did *you* get this?!" The Gor-Nok asked.

"They left it on the coffee table." Jesse said.

"You *will* find me a way into that Library. I must have that Diary!" His eyes flashed green again.

"You... must... have... the... Diary," Jesse was repeating his hypnotic request.

"You will find a way!" he was hypnotizing Jesse.

"I... will... find... a... way," Jesse stated.

"Do it tonight!" The Gor-Nok commanded.

"I will do it tonight." Jesse repeated.

"Here you go, young man!" he said to Jesse.

"Here you go young man." Jesse vacantly repeated as the Gor-Nok gave him a thousand in cash, then walked him out the door. Whispering in his ears, "You will find a way to let me in," he continued hypnotizing him.

"Let him in tonight," Jesse didn't remember how he ended up back at the farm; it was all blurry.

We asked him to tell us everything, after we got him to stop being hypnotized. We did this in front of Dusk because we knew *he* would be watching. Zatie was a good actress; she really was panicking.

"We can't let him in here! This is ours! I love these books; these are my *favorite* books! No, I'm not selling these books! No, we don't need the money!" Zatie said, and Jesse continued, "You may not need the money, but I need the money. You guys can get rid of *some* of these books. You can't possibly read all of them?!" Zatie was surprised that he would even say that.

"She could read all the books; we've read all these books,"

I responded.

"I'm getting there," Zatie said as Jesse looked at her and I incredulously.

"Yeah, I like reading, I've had a lotta time on my hands, so I read. But we're not selling the books."

"Aw, Bel, C'mon!" Jesse replied.

"You can't be trusted, Jesse! I must ask you to leave the Library. You are not allowed in here," I said.

"It's too late, he's coming to buy more books?" Jesse warned us of the pending incident.

"More, you stole books and sold them to him?!" Zatie said in a rage, a nerdy-librarian rage.

"Wait. Jesse, you did what?!" I asked him.

"All right, so I might have sold him one, no biggie?!" Jesse confessed.

"I can't believe you stole from us!" I exclaimed.

"You don't even know what was in that book, do you?!" Zatie responded.

"I dunno, just old junk. What's the big deal?!"

"Zatie, it's fine. We will just set up some traps and keep an eye out for him. If he shows up, will be ready, right?" I assured her.

Zatie huffed as she stormed out of the Library. I began to chase her but then I realized that Jesse was left alone to salivate over the monetary value of the books.

"Nope, no you don't! Don't touch my books!"

"Now you're starting to sound like Zatie!" he said and I slapped him in the back of his head, assuming that his comment was meant to be an insult. As we left the Library, Dusk seemed especially anxious that we were leaving. I teleported us to the barn and as soon as we left the room. I kept my other lookout, Peep, in there to watch what Dusk might do once we left.

"Right, now we need to discuss the *real* plan. When we bring him into a daydream, we basically make him sleepwalk," I explained to them.

"He won't be able to control what's happening around him?" Jesse asked.

"Not in the way he can when he's awake; and by the time he realizes it's a dream, it will be too late. I'll already have control over him he'll be my prisoner."

We spent the rest of the day preparing for the night's imminent dangers. Zatie set up her were-trees all over the grounds, everywhere. Any plant that she could find, she altered it and set them out strategically around the grounds. We put our hexes and curses on every single doorknob and metal surface that could be charmed.

We had Dominic on constant patrol; unfortunately, we didn't test Jesse's therian-powers enough to see if he could change into other animals besides the were-rabbit or were-hare. However, he sure seemed to be happy with the rabbit as his totem and that he was pretty certain he could do some damage. My worry was we have not had enough time to train with their Daydreams and their Nightmares Nixes.

Jesse had only dealt with projecting the powers of his Daydream Nix but hadn't quite figured out how to tap into his Nightmares, yet, or his fear of time.

Zatie was the opposite, she figured out how to tap into her Nightmares but hasn't quite figured out what her Daydreams were. I found her later that afternoon meditating, she was in her dreamscape.

I went into Zatie's room to discuss things in private, more details of our plan to trap the Gor-Nok. Sitting in the Library, I could feel Dusk staring at me trying to probe my mind. I had stacked books with the labels facing towards him, so he had something to read; something to tempt him to make a move. I didn't like being watched so that's when I got up to talk to Zatie. When I got down to her room; she was asleep, she seemed to be dreaming about something exciting, she was kind of giggling.

I did a shared dream spell and passed out on the floor near her. It's been a while since I had been in her dreamscape. She kind of likes the billowy clouds and Greek and Romanesque style architecture. She created a 'Mount Olympus' type of paradise for her daydream and her fantasies. And a dark, dreary wilderness below where her mere mortals roamed that were being tortured by the Titans. Her Titans were giant god-monsters that she created from the earth and plants.

Her fears and worries were more chaotic, but her daydreams, the manifestations of her dreams were of hope, charity, and love. Filled with faith, happiness, and positivity. These are what she called Cherubim. The Nixes start off as a baby, a fetus form of pure creation and then manifest whatever your daydream desires. To come from your unconscious mind as a projection of your subconscious and I had shown her what it was like when I gave birth to a brainchild.

Basically, the same but most of mine are all crows. She on the other hand kept them as babies; as small cherubic cupids, each possessing a different bow and arrow imbued with power and magic that she could use in command at her request. You had to remove or hide certain emotions when around the Cherubs; they were kind of annoying because they were attracted to emotions or the void of emotions. They can feel if you were heartbroken or scared or needed comforting and they would just hover around you; it was kind of annoying.

I had to swipe a few of them away as I approached her. I walked up the palace stairs to her slumber chamber. She had a balcony that overlooks her kingdom as she would sit eating grapes and drinking wine. I was ushered in by some cherubs and announced by some of them as, "The dark queen of the land of oh snap!"

"Land of Oh Snap?!" Zatie was embarrassed that I was there and that I had heard that.

"Oh, hey, Bel! I didn't hear you come in. I didn't even *feel* you enter. Shouldn't I feel that?" she asked.

"Not if you have practiced like me. You really wouldn't notice unless you can feel the change in the weather. It feels like the barometric pressure or seeing the sea tides, and a change in the wind," I was shifting the weather around us. "Then that may indicate that someone had entered; but if I pay attention and squash the emotions that I project then you won't be alerted."

"You didn't, did you kill some of my cupids because I set some to guard?" Zatie said anxiously.

"No, now they are otherwise detained by a couple of my warrior birds. I wanted to discuss, in private, some more ideas to trap this guy. How are you doing with your Nixes? Your nightmares are strong enough for battle," I said pointing out the tree titan.

"Oh, yeah, we're getting good in the Nightmare department. I think just naturally being afraid of this guy and monsters in general will make them more intense."

"Hopefully, how about your Daydreams, what can these little guys do?" I said as I pointed at the half-naked flying toddlers floating around my head.

"Here, I'll show ya. I learned a couple tricks," she called one of the Cupids over.

"Here baby, let me borrow that." The little flying baby floated near and handed her his baby-size bow and a golden arrow.

When Zatie held it in her hands, the bow expanded in size to be appropriate for her to use. She aimed at a nightmare plant monster on the world below. A Titan made of rocks and trees that enjoyed destroying the city.

"Watch this!" She said as she pulled back on the bow. Golden lightning bolts ignited in the place of the arrow as she let it loose. I watched the arrow strike the monster in the heart, causing it to moan and wail in agony. It drowned in its own tears until it died and fell to the earth. I was both terrified and amazed.

"Wow, Z! You, you amaze me sometimes! Can you manifest this in the real world? Can you manifest one of your little daydream cherubs?"

"I think so," Zatie responded.

"This could be very useful!" I replied.

"I'll work on it. Though, I don't think we have much time for experimental weapons?!" Zatie said.

"If you can do it in the dreams, you should be able to do it in reality by willing it. I've done it, I'll show you when we are awake. Jesse has already set the bait, so anytime here, any minute, that monster can come knocking on our door. We need to be ready. We need every weapon in our arsenal," I replied.

"Do you really think this trap is gonna work?" "Well, we can do what needs to be done, or we can die trying. Let's try creating your Daydream nix in reality. Wake up and meet me in the library, and I'll take you into one of my dreams and will see if I can fool you into believing it is reality," I teleported out of her dream.

Zatie woke up to find me on the floor not moving; she thought something was wrong and she tried to get me to wake up. She checked my vitals; I had a pulse and I was breathing. It just didn't seem like I was waking up, so she slapped me. She was thinking about slapping me again, but I stopped her with my mind, open my eyes, and yawned then I asked her what time it was.

"How long was I out?" I asked.

"I don't know how long you were out," she said.

"Well, what time is it, now?" I asked her. She tried to look at the clock on her desk, but the numbers got all blurry, and the hands were melting, then the clock was melting.

She gasped and asked, "Oh my gosh! What's going on?!" *Yeah, it's hard to tell what's real and what isn't.* I had said in her mind and echoed in the room. Zatie looked around to see I was gone from that space. I had removed the doors and started turning the room around causing all her furniture to spin and fly across to other walls leaving her tethered to the floor.

"Nonabel, stop, stop!" Zatie screamed. I slapped her across the face waking her up to her room in reality.

"Now, do you think the trap is going to work?"

"How do you make it look and feel, so real?! Everything I create is too bright and colorful and I can't get those muted subtleties. How do you create a false reality with such bland details?" Zatie said to me as a back-handed compliment.

"How? You spend way too much time here, at the house and here between worlds. That was part of my training with Lucia, was pulling each other into illusions of reality and try-ing to make it as real as possible. That's how I think we can trap him," I replied.

"We need to, somehow get him to fall asleep by touching one of us or we need to catch him when he's asleep at his house and…" she proposed.

"No, I've never caught him asleep. He's too aware of when I'm nearby. I'm hoping he'll pass out when he reads that book that we gave him," I said to her.

I felt impressed to have a shared dream lesson with Zatie and Jesse both to teach them how to project, manifest their daydreams or their nightmares into the real world. We also worked on having to bring someone into a waking dream or into a daydream as they slept. Jesse was mostly caught off guard not knowing reality and dream, but Zatie keeping con-trol of her sanity by asking questions.

"Bel, but how do make them real?!"

"I just project that aspect of the dream into the real world through one of my birds," I said.

"But those are part of you? I don't have other creature fly-ing out of my body!" Zatie stated.

"Well, your venom is in the veins of the were-plant, right?" I asked her.

"And?!" Zatie asked but did not understand me.

"There's a Transfiguration Spell in the Diary for that! You can metaphysically change the tree babies into you cupid babies," I explained to her.

"Of course, there is! Why didn't I think of that?!" She said sarcastically as I manifested the Diary in front of her in the air. She scanned it quickly.

"But does granting the manifestations powers, give them access to the powers that the daydream or nightmare Nixes controls?" Zatie asked.

"I have, and yes, it does."

"I swear, Nonabel, I'm going to puke if we keep messing with my head," Jesse said as he was trying to create his nix. I was training with my new daydream nix, Twilight, that has already been manifested into the real world. Dusk was still on extended time-out.

"I need to show you how to manifest it, here project your dreams into the room. It seems to be a correlation between dreams and teleportation," I said.

"It becomes an astral plane projection. You are using teleportation to create in reality?!" Zatie asked.

"Yes, you get it!" I declared.

I have done this where I had teleported from a dream Raven, and then teleported back into reality or I had somehow woken up in a different location not knowing if it's a dream or if it's reality and I teleported myself back.

"So, the astral projection will be a form of teleporting an object from your dream into reality."

"Yes, the stronger the connection and the stronger the manifestation is in the dream, the stronger it will be in the really real world." Once we understood the concept, we were manifesting all sorts of things into reality from the dream world.

Jesse snapped his fingers and pulled a rabbit from thin air. The rabbit got bigger as it transformed into the half-toddler size bunny-Nix. Jesse's rabbit was too fast for him to catch; mostly because it moves at a different rate of speed. It could move at a different rate of time than we do. His Nix could self-manifest and then disappear, phasing in and out of time. Jesse lost him back into the dream.

"Jesse, maybe that's something that we have to work on," I assured him. Zatie had been manifesting hers through the were-creatures, were-plants and then turning them from carved wooden dolls to eventually real cherubs.

The bait was set and now we waited for the Gor-Nok to fall for the trap. A couple of days went by since we sent Jesse to give the Gor-Nok a book from the Library to tempt him. He kept us waiting. We practiced binding circles in the Library in front of my compromised bird, Dusk, knowing that *he* was watching us. We found it awkward to be in there, we could feel him watching us, waiting for us to make a mistake and we tried to act normal, as normal as we could.

I stopped going out at night and helped Zatie and Jesse master dreaming. We called it 'meditation or naps,' but it was mostly daytime naps. Jesse was starting to understand the principles of Time, palpable time. He was manipulating time as if it were matter to mold. While he was in his dreamscape, he had his Daydream Nix create a pocket watch as a way to help focus his power. I warned him against the use of focusors; that they can seem like an easy, quick fix. I encouraged him to take the time to learn to do these things without the need of an amulet or other imbued objects. I was extremely impressed with both of my siblings.

I sent my birds out at night instead of going on patrol so I could continue practicing dreaming with my brother and sister. I helped them to quickly slip into others' dreamscapes and recognize if they were dreaming or not. The quickest clues, I would give them was to try to read something. Sometimes it's difficult if the dreamscape looks like the outside of the farm or outside of the barn with the exterior of the house.

"Not a whole lot of things written to read?"

"Nope, I could tag some stuff on the side of the barn?" Jesse responded as he manifested a can of paint.

"Jess, no that can't always be the answer," he was thinking of something, I probed his mind.

"Jesse, show me!" I said.

"Whatever do you mean?" he asked me.

"The Tattoo? Show me!" I ordered.

"How? Fine!" He lifted his sleeve to reveal a small hand-made tattoo of the white rabbit saying, 'I'm Late!' on his forearm.

"That's cheating!" Zatie was furious.

"No, it's actually a clever idea. Good work. Now watch this!" I touched his tattoo and made his Nix appear from his arm. It was dressed in his jacket and all.

"Nice! Now who's cheating," Jesse said. I was showing off, but it was fun to teach them and play make-believe like I had done as Aunt Lily in the past.

"Wait Bel, just now, were you thinking about when we were little kids?!" Jesse inquired.

"Yes, I was thinking about…"

"The past, time! I can see your memories when you thought of the past! Normally, I can't see your thoughts," Jesse exclaimed excitedly.

"That's trippy, bro; but cool! We'll practice time manipulation more, but later. Now it's time to wake-up!" *Wake-up, Wake-up, wake-up…*

We were practicing the ability to put someone to sleep by talking to them through hypnosis or by tactile telepathy, skin to skin contact. Zatie was also working on a potion powder that we could blow into the Gor-Nok's face to knock him out.

One afternoon during our meditation sessions Zatie had put me under with the powder and the vision that played out in my mind was overwhelming. I believe it was intensified by the Seer's Sight, a foreboding premonition of the future; a future where the Gor-Nok defeats us all and wins.

I saw a victorious procession, a parade of many people marching up my driveway towards my house. A vast group of the townsfolk led by our Daydream Nixes; bound and chained, beaten, and hurt, injured, and driven by their taskmasters, the fear demons, and the Monster that they worship, the Gor-Nok.

In the middle of the parade procession was a pedestal, a throne that carried the Gor-Nok upon it, hoisted up by four people, four creatures. Harry as the were-croc, Jesse as his were-hare and two other were-creatures I didn't recognize but I had a feeling that they were people I knew. I just didn't know that they were also meant to be Therianthropist. They were various other creatures, zombies, monsters, and an army of fear demons. Saw blades of fear were tearing up the landscape around us.

Hordes of people enslaved. I was terrified to keep the dream flowing. The cloud of fear was palpable like a fog around the parade. They stopped in front of our house, then they lowered the Gor-Nok to the ground and the four footmen were bound to him by fear-demons attached to their heads. The same way that my poor bird Dusk had been infected. The crowd had parted in front of him and the Gor-Nok stood before me. I was out in my black feathered ballgown with my angel wings.

The Gor-Nok announced, "My dark angel! The time has come for us to end this. Join me or all that you love, everyone that still lives, that is, will be my slaves! You will be my queen."

"And if I refuse?!" I responded stubbornly.

He clapped his hands three times, the fear-demons attacked everyone causing them all to die from heart attacks and nightmares. I watched as they collapsed to the floor. I teleported from the dream gasping for air.

"He's coming!" My eyes were still inflamed with the

Seer's Sight.

"Where is he coming from?!" Zatie asked.

"The front porch! I saw them from the front porch," I was trying to catch my breath; it was like I was underwater. I was still traumatized from watching everyone die. I began to sob.

When the Gor-Nok had arrived in my actual driveway, not with a procession as elaborate as I had envisioned, but something more terrifying; something I never expected. Harry had got out of the passenger side of the white Rolls-Royce and Jesse got out of the driver seat. Jesse had opened the door for the back-passenger seat and out stepped the Gor-Nok as a person in a white suit. I scanned everything really quick with the Seer's Sight. Someone else was in the back of the car with him but he had shrouded them with fear.

A cloud of terror was shielding me from seeing who he had with him. He told them to wait there. I told Zatie in her mind, *stay away from the windows, stay away from the doors, lock yourself in the Library, and begin the Spell to bring us into the dreamscape.*

"I'll try to stall him," I said as I went for the door. Harry came up to the porch, Jesse stayed with the Gor-Nok by the car. I had answered the door before Harry could knock.

"Hey, Harry! What's this about?"

"What's this all about, Nonabel? I'm here to serve you with a cease and desist order. I'm sorry Nonabel, it's official," Harry explained.

"Harry, this is horse-crap!" I declared.

"We just came from the courthouse. He's putting out a restraining order against you. Apparently, you put a death threat inside a book?"

"This is a bunch of bull crap, Harry!"

"I read the court order. I have been trying to talk the judge into reassessing this, but this guy has got a lot of power and influence. A lot more than I have apparently, and the judge was pretty convinced. If we're not careful, they could take away your brother and sister. They could take away your guardianship rights for delusional tendencies. He said that he had evidence that you were *The Dark Angel vigilante*! If they can make it stick, Detective Bradbury wants your blood!"

"Derik's dad?!" I scoffed.

"Supposedly, you've been impeding investigations. Just back-off the guy for now! Nonabel, you can live a normal life; just leave him alone," Harry tried to calm me down by placing his comforting large hands on my shoulders, but I pulled away from him.

"Harry, he killed Lucia! He killed my grandfather! He murdered my parents!"

"You don't have evidence of that. You don't know that one for sure, but I know we screwed this up. We just can't stop this guy, Nonabel. You need to give this up!"

I was trying to read the legal documents, but my eyes were still phased in three different spectrums of the Seer's Sights. I looked up at Jesse and the Gor-Nok. Harry was still talking to me while they were pointing at me. It looked like something was on Jesse's head, grabbing his eyes. I could barely see it, but it was one of those invisible fear-demons. It somehow had taken over my brother and I looked at Harry and he smiled at me as his eyes glowed green. His body trembled as he began to transform into the were-croc in front of me. He pushed his way through the front door as I tried to stop him. I cowered back, crawling backwards on the floor through the front room.

Harry was tearing up the house, he had gotten a hold of Harry as well. The Gor-Nok had taken control of them. He sent Jesse in after us and he told them to bring him the book. I heard Zatie screaming from upstairs. I did a thunderclap to knock Harry back and pushed the furniture towards the front door to block the stairs. I teleported out of the way, up to Zatie, to see what the matter was, why she was screaming.

"Zatie are you OK?! Are you all right?! We got to go! He got Harry, he got Jesse!" I said as I exited the vortex. Zatie was screaming and pointing at the cage. Dusk had transformed into a fear-demon, were-rook and was trying to break the cage.

I grabbed Zatie and the Diary. I could hear Harry and them tearing up the room outside. I needed to find the door, I got us out of the Library and was able to keep the door shut before Harry popped into the room. Jesse as the were-hare and the Gor-Nok came in up the stairs laughing entering Zatie's bedroom. Harry had picked me up by my throat, Jesse had Zatie by the hair. She was screaming. I begged and pleaded with the Gor-Nok.

"Please, it doesn't have to be this way!" I said.

"You're absolutely right! No one *has to* get hurt. No one else will have to lose their life, because of *your* bad choices," The Gor-Nok tapped on Zatie's door. "Is this it?" He asked and Jesse nodded his head. "Show me!" The Gor-Nok demanded.

Zatie cried, "No! Nona, don't do it!"

"Show you what?!" I replied indignantly.

"Show me the other books," he said.

"There's no other books," I responded.

"You barricaded the door. You are hiding more!" "It just goes downstairs!" I screamed back.

"Do not lie to me! You are not good at it! I would ask this one, but apparently, he does not know how to open the door. And that one does not know how to open the door. Yet they both have seen the room full of magic books. So, one of you two is going to open that door. Let me in to the Library," The Gor-Nok was growing impatient.

"What Library?!" I screamed in frustration.

"I have seen it with my own eyes!" he stated.

"Oh, so you were spying on me!" I replied.

"And my spy cannot get out! He is trapped in there! Now open the Door!" He demanded.

"I don't know what to tell you, but if there was a door, I'd rather die than show it to you!" I responded.

"That can be arranged!" the Gor-Nok replied.

He had Jesse pick up Zatie by her hair.

"When I am done with her, you will be begging for her death," The Gor-Nok said before he blew some fear gas into Zatie's face. She was coughing and choking. Her eyes went bloodshot, and she trembled in fear. She was screaming as though every ounce of her nerves were on fire. She clawed at the floor, convulsing screaming, and kicking. Finding no relief, clawing at her own skin.

He was right. I wanted this all to end, even if it meant ending her life than to watch her suffer. I surged with bolts of lightning within and the storm was brewing as my anger grew. I struct me and Harry, electrocuting the fear-demon that was attached to his face.

I was about to electrocute Jesse's demon. But the Gor-Nok raised a hand, "I wouldn't do that. I could kill your sister with a thought! Kill your brother with a snap of my fingers. I could have your brother kill your sister right in front of you. Just say the word, and if those words are not: 'I give up. Here's the book,' or anything else I don't like; your family dies."

He added a fear demon back onto Harry, by blowing out fear gas and molding it into a little demon. I begged for him to release Zatie.

"Please wait. If I open the door...?" he released Zatie immediately. She crawled to me whimpering.

"You open the door and I will let her go; she can leave here," he said. I opened the door and my demonized rook had come out when the door opened; and the Gor-Nok told him to stop.

Dusk tried to attack me but the Gor-Nok stopped him, "No!! I need her, for now. Bring them!" he said to Jesse and Harry. They dragged us into the Library, and up the stairs. The Gor-Nok took in a giant breath of relief and victory. He had succeeded. He had succeeded to step into my trap.

The Circle of Runes lit up around him on the floor. Harry and Jesse clinched their heads as if they were fighting invisible helmets of fire. The Gor-Nok was being torn from his human form as Lucia had done the night, she had taught me this spell by mistake. She made the mistake of believing he was a nightmare; and now I know he is just like me. He was just a person who happen to be at the wrong place, and at the wrong time.

I electrocuted Harry, Jesse, and Dusk, freeing them up to fight on my side again. The were-demons of fear were dying on the floor. The Gor-Nok was using every ounce of his power and everything he could think of to fight against the power of the Runes.

He was smashing into the floor with his bare hands; it was starting to break. He was sending whirlwinds and saw blade of fear demons to try to break the circle. It was starting to wane; the Circle was getting weaker. I told Jesse and Zatie to get on the other side and repeat the chant with me. It seemed as though we were winning against him, we were strengthening the binds; fiery chains were emerging from the runes. As the runes were spinning and solidifying to form his new prison, a flaming chain of molten metal latched onto him.

The chains grew like vines sneaking towards his hands and wrists, his ankles, and feet and around his throat. He grasped at the one around his throat, it burned his hands and his neck. He screamed, spouting spells of fear, conjuring images in our minds. Forcing us to relive our worst memories, fears, and nightmares. Zatie was crying, Jesse was losing strength. I begged for them to hold on, to stay strong. I looked at Harry, there was such a panic in his eyes. I knew his fear reflected my fear and pushed in his mind to get them out.

Harry... get them out. Keep them safe.

The Gor-Nok began to change the monster, he screamed with his rage, destroying the circle of runes. The binding curse had failed and exploded in a magnificent flaming supernova with him at the center the flames. The molten metal and fire spewed across the Library, igniting the books, igniting the papers, and the walls.

When the Gor-Nok caught his breath, he looked around at what he had done. Fear and panic filled his eyes.

"No, nO, **no!!!**" he screamed out in his rage.

Harry had grabbed Zatie and Jesse and they hobbled out of the Library to escape the fire. The Gor-Nok manifested his club and was about to swing the shock wave of fear, but I blocked him with my sword.

I ignited it with power like Lucia had done before. We fought viciously as the Library was turned into burning ash all around us. A raging inferno that was quickly consuming every page, every secret, every spell. Everything I fought to protect and everything he tried to take was being destroyed in front of us both.

We were fighting, trying desperately to kill one another; pounding and slashing, cutting, and scraping, the fire and ash, the smoke, and anarchy surrounding us. All was chaos, all was destruction. All around us, every book seemed destroyed except for the Diary. It remained on the ground in between us.

He tried to reach for it. I sliced his hands with my talons as I held his staff, his mangled club back with my sword. I left the sword there with my mind and dove for the book. I pushed the Diary into the vortex with me. The Gor-Nok tried to slip into the abyss to escape the fire and come after the book.

Something caught me, kept me from crossing the threshold completely. My foot was still sticking up out of the ice. The Gor-Nok had seized me with his free hand. I tried to fight, still with the sword suspended in the air. He crushed my foot in his hand, and I could feel the bones breaking in his grip as though it was a thousand miles away. It still felt real, I released the sword psychically and used it to sever my foot and pulled the sword through the vortex with me. I emerged together on the other side, climbing out of the vortex.

Zatie and the others were outside of the house. Smoke and fire were billowing out the windows of the upstairs bedrooms. I climbed out of the hole of the vortex pushing the Diary out in front of me, telling Zatie to take it. I wasn't completely out of the hole and the Gor-Nok started pulling me back through the vortex by my missing foot. He had some type of puppet spell that kept me tethered to my other body part. I screamed as he pulled me back through the hole. I emerged out of the vortex being dragged by my foot by an invisible force. He hauled me down through the house as he busted through rooms and beams that were on fire. He burst through the walls of Zatie's room and out of the house to the yard, dragging me with him.

Zatie had zapped him with the sword and I was freed to regroup with the others while the Gor-Nok was recovering. "Zatie, please tell me you were able to initiate the dream?!" I asked her.

"Everything happened so quickly, your bird was freaking out. It turned into a monster in front of me, it tore the cage apart. I don't think I had time to finish!"

"Do you have the powder," I replied.

"No, the potion got burned up in the fire in the Library!" She responded.

"It's gone?!" I asked in exasperation.

"Do you want to bind him again?" Zatie asked.

"What we do?!" Jesse was panicked.

"We fight is what we do!" Harry said as he got into were-croc mode. Jesse followed suit and turned into his were-rabbit. Zatie activated her were-plants and created her suit of plant-based armor. I set up the Runes to protect the Diary, to keep it safe; while they went off to defend me. I looked up from creating the Runes to encircle the Diary and saw that the Gor-Nok had beaten Harry and was grabbing Jesse by the bunny ears. He was using him to beat on Zatie's tree-armor. She was being trapped under her dying were-trees. Zatie was being smothered in the ground with every blow.

I teleported over there quickly and began screaming for him to stop. "Give me the book! That's when I'll stop," he kept beating on them. I couldn't teleport them away without hurting them. He had pulled me through a vortex. That wasn't going to stop him, and if I shot him with lightning it may hurt Jesse, it may hurt Zatie. Her voice was in my head, *do it!* Jesse thought it as well, *do it Bel, he's killing us!*

I summoned the sword, caught it in my hands, and channeled the bolt of lightning through me, through it and towards them. It knocked them all away from the blast crater. It fried Zatie's were-trees and had reverted both Jesse and the Gor-Nok to people again. He hobbled off into the woods clinching at his wounds. I sent bolts after bolts, striking the ground and his path, scaring him back away from us. When the dust settled, the Gor-Nok was getting back to his feet.

I had called for help mentally from Dominic. It seemed that everything I threw out the Gor-Nok just made him stronger. He was much better at fighting multiple people than one on one. It's like he used our abilities against each other, he could invade our minds and anticipate our moves like Lu-Lu could.

I called upon storms and he tried to silence me and strangle me psychically to keep me from muttering the spells. I scattered myself into a hundred birds as Dominic arrived. I projected to Dominic the idea that the Gor-Nok was dinner and he attacked. I turned into my harpy-self to aid Dominic. Zatie, Jesse and I with Dominic and Harry were in full were-beast-mode, beating on the Gor-Nok.

One of his favorite moves was grabbing us as we punched him or claw at him; but mostly we overshot our attacks and he would take our limbs and throw us into the next person. Or he would send spinning sawblades of fear demons tearing through the landscape and we have to evade or get destroyed.

We tried coordinating our attack psychically. Harry told me to call out his weaknesses. I mentally told Harry, *'We need to disarm him! If he can't hit us with the club, then he can't direct the fear-blades!'* Zatie and Jesse focused on that while Harry and I attacked the Gor-Nok from the land and the sky.

I rained down thunder and lightning from above, trying not to hit Harry. The Gor-Nok could hear my fears and would use Harry as a shield from time to time; making him take the blow. The Gor-Nok seemed to enjoy a fair fight; to finally have people who are like him, just as powerful as him. The Gor-Nok was vastly outnumbered, but he had years of experience.

The farm was getting completely destroyed, the house was still burning. The yard and the fields were being torn up by the fear-blades and bolts of lightning. Zatie told me to lure him towards the forest and we'll let the trees help in the fight. Harry was telling me to lure him to the lake and we can drown him.

"OK, these are both good ideas, but we got to pick one!" I shouted to them. We lured the Gor-Nok to the lake to drown and electrocute him at the same time if I wanted. I did my best to not think of it, I thought of him fighting me in the past. I tried to use everyone's names when I gave them directions to confuse him.

We were having better success at coordinated our attacks, bombarding him from all sides; keeping him confused. Jesse had been knocked down on his back, but he immediately leapt up from a handstand. He launched his rabbit feet right into the Gor-Nok's chest, knocking him into the lake. Harry went to work in his natural environment being able to stay underwater for a longer amount of time then the boar-beast.

Harry wrestled with him, spun-strangled him, pushed him down into the mud at the bottom of the water face first. The Gor-Nok was helpless, his fear demons were incased in gases and came out as bubbles underwater, easily avoidable. I knew he didn't like the water because of how he would choke in the vortex.

I told Harry to get clear and I teleported him out of the water and on the ground as I fried the lake completely with about a thousand bolts. The water began to boil the fish as they were popping up from the borders of the lake. The shore was completely seared and fried; the sand turned into glass. Trees in the nearby forest were on fire. Zatie was putting out the fire, having her trees put themselves out in part of the water.

I lifted the Gor-Nok from the mud; they were burns and sores all over his body. He seemed to be unconscious. I suspended him in the air and began to strangle him. Jesse and Zatie began to question, "Isn't he dead?" "Is he?"

"If he *was* dead, he would change back into a man. It's a natural reflex. He's *not* dead," Harry said.

"Shouldn't someone check him, you know, see if he's got a pulse?" Jesse asked in a hush.

"I can feel it in my hands," I squeezed tighter, just in case. The Gor-Nok woke, his eyes were blazing green as he muttered something in Swahili. The ground began to shake. I could only catch a word or two; something about, 'raising the dead.'

Immediately I was horrified and turned to face Harry. I whispered in a shuddered breath, 'Michael'. "He's raising Michael?!" I shouted to the others.

"Oh crap, I can't let go!" I was frozen trying to psychically strangle the beast, "You guys will have to keep him at bay." Michael's corpse was rising from the ground. I tried not to think of it. I tried not to think to remind the Gor-Nok of the fact that Michael can turn into different monsters. That's what he wanted.

He raised Michael up as a corpse, and forced his body to contort and twist, changing him into a were-elephant; it was horrifying. The were-elephant corpse came charging towards me as I floated trapped in the air. Everyone did their best, but they were grossly undersized compared to Michael and his massive elephant form. I was finally able to turn into several different birds, but it wasn't fast enough to get out of the way. I exploded in a cloud of feathers and smoke as the Gor-Nok attacked.

The Gor-Nok was free and sent a shock wave of fear out towards the rest of them; they were all paralyzed, quaking in agony and going into shock on the ground. I begged him, "Stop, please!" He pointed to the Diary. Michael charged towards the book on the ground. Before Michael got there, I teleported in and dropped Michael on top of the Gor-Nok. Michael turned back into a corpse after the Gor-Nok muttered his counter-spell, then threw the bones off of him. This battle was relentless, it was never ending. I needed to defeat this guy. I need to figure out how to kill him.

He shook his amulet, his weird necklace and poured out the fear-fog all around the yard. His necklace! I needed to destroy it. It was his focusor! I summoned a baby tornado from my hand to blow the fog away. I wasn't going to get trapped in that mess again, but my fallen comrades had. I found them and I teleported them to be by me, to be safe. I watched carefully around me, the Gor-Nok had retreated into the fog, using it to shield his attacks. I summoned the Dragon's breath, not knowing if his fog was flammable, but I knew he was breathing oxygen.

At least I could suffocate him. I manifested the dragon's breath as large as I possibly could. With the fullest amount of the ragon's breath, a ghostly serpent emerged triumphantly from my lungs the size of a truck. My mouth spewed out a fireball across the yard, igniting the smoke snake. It sneaked in and out of the fog. It didn't do too much damage though, so I summoned it back. I commanded it to swirl around me in a circle. It kept him at bay as I did what I could to save my family.

Zatie was coming out of the haze of the fog, and began to heal herself, then healed Jesse. As I was working to heal Harry, but the Gor-Nok seized upon his crocodile tail and pulled him into the fog with him. I used the thunderclap to part the clouds of fog and fear, but it was too dense and too late for Harry; they had vanished into the fog and forest.

I summoned some dirt from Michael's grave nearby and begin to heal my wounds.

"What do we do?!" Zatie had asked while she worked on healing Dominic.

"We wait. They're still out there, I feel them."

We watched for the Gor-Nok, and before I was finished with the spell to heal myself, Harry's clawed hand covered over my face and picked me up from behind. He was pulling me by my face towards the driveway in the front of the house. I cracked my head on the ground, I could feel blood from my hairline pouring into my eyes. I zapped him with a bolt from behind and ran away. I rubbed what dirt I had left onto my face and healed myself as quickly as I could. Before Harry could catch up to me, I called to Zatie and Jesse across the field of fog, telling them to *hide and protect the book.*

I could hear the Gor-Nok laughing, He made Harry laugh. He appeared from his vehicle as a man in his more tribal outfit holding a voodoo doll, a Gollum he had made for controlling Harry like a toy, like a puppet. Using Harry as a shield and a weapon against me.

Harry and I had fought for a small moment, I was pissed that he was using my loved ones against me. Harry punched his way through my onslaught of pitiful power as my pain overcame me and Harry's blows pummeled me to the ground. He dragged me by my hair across the gravel on the driveway, scraping my knees and legs. He picked me up by my hair and set me on my knees with his claws in my forehead, gouging, applying pressure to my skull.

The Gor-Nok knelt down and breathed fear-smoke into my I nose. I couldn't think straight.

"It scares you, doesn't it? Losing. Is it defeat? Is that what scares you? Losing time and time again. It's not losing your family; you seem to enjoy hurting them yourself."

"Shut-up!" I was crying, being tortured by painfilled memories of their deaths.

"You are a hard one to crack. Your fears keep changing," he responded.

"I do fear losing to you." I cried.

"No, you fear losing loved ones, but not family. Lovers, that is what you fear! Ha! You fear living alone! A life without love; but you do not love one person, your heart yearns for more. You want to be worshiped! Adored! You cannot be pinned down by one person."

"Stop!" I shouted but he continued.

"I thought it was the lawyer, but you have broken his heart and he broke yours. So, I did some digging. You can come out now!"

The other car door opened, a fear-demon was attached to the head of my boyfriend, Derik. He looked deranged, like he had been starved for days. He was possessed, foaming at the mouth, blood-shot eyes, pupils dilated, straining, restricted in his walk as though he was a puppet. He had him stand by Harry so I could watch.

"Go on, choose! Use your foresight! See which one dies first?!" He had me trapped; he was waiting for me to pick. He knew I loved them both; to him, it didn't matter. I knew he would kill them both. I knew I had to choose; but I didn't know how to make this decision.

"Let me make the choice for you!" He took the voodoo doll and snapped its neck, Harry the were-croc dropped immediately to the ground as I screamed out in pain.

The Gor-Nok laughed while I held Harry's dying body in my arms. Death was draining him of his Therian-lifeforce, restoring him to his human form.

"Harry, No! Not you, Harry, not now, no!"

Bel, there's no time for tears, no time... Harry thought as his heart stopped. *Time?!* I activated the Nevergator in my hand without a second thought. I only needed to go back a few seconds, a minute before. I could take the choice from him and not be clouded by my decision. Plus, he would have to deal with two of me in that instant, for a split second as another one of me emerged. I could choose to emerge from the vortex of time right on top of him and break his neck.

"Wait, what are you doing?!" he seized upon my hands before I could engage the Nevergator. He looked at the Nevergator with excitement.

"This is how you entered my life the first time? When we met, you were a time traveler. You *were* a time traveler because now *this* and the Diary will belong to me!" He pulled out a knife to sever my hand, I called my sword to me, hoping to beat him.

It was instantaneous as the tip of my sword began to shatter the Nevergator, he had slit open my arm, severing it from me, exploding the time vortex, and trapping us in an endless loop. When the explosion subsided, and we reverted back to the split-second before my decision. I activated the Nevergator instead of calling the sword allowing him to cut my other arm and sent us both back to whatever random date and place I had put in. Anywhere away from there was safer, away from the Diary, away from my family. Perhaps I could save Harry. We landed in a parking lot on top of some cars startling some people as the time-lightning had struck the ground.

I bounced off of a car, then landed on the ground. The Gor-Nok had landed face first into a truck, crushing the vehicle. The Nevergator was still fused to my hand, I looked at the date. It was the day my parents had died. The sword was a few inches from me, it made it through the time vortex. Apparently, I made my decision after the loop was already set in motion to call the sword and it was already on its way to save me. I was glad to have it, I needed it to focus my power, to make precise, split-second, lightning fast decisions that have not yet happened.

I had minutes, mere seconds before the event. I must end

this, stop the Gor-Nok from hurting anyone else. I raised more cars and crushed them upon the one he was stuck in before he could wake. I began the binding curse and fuse the cars to him. I could hear him squeal like a pig on fire. He busted through the cars causing the cars to explode with a shockwave of fear. The fear demon saw blade hit me; they were tearing apart my mind. I was reliving the car accident; they had deactivated my Sight to see what he was doing. I was reliving it over and over again from different angles. I tried to shake the vision but the Gor-Nok was breathing in fear into my tear stained face.

"Thank you," he said, "for bringing me to this very special moment. I remember it well. If we are truly time traveling, another one of me, younger, stronger, right now is setting these events in motion like a ripple in a pond. Do you want to see it?" he asked me.

"Go to Hell!" I shouted.

"Shall we go there together?!" he replied.

He called me up to him with his mind. I tried to use the sword against him, and he knocked it away with his fear demons. They had a hold of it and carried it off. He dragged me to the nearby street and held me up so I could see. He picked me up by my hair.

"You haven't seen it from this angle, have you? It's quite spectacular. See, that's me getting out of that car and that man there is about to crash into your family. Well, you know the rest," he held my eyes open with his fear demons and forced me to witness their death. I was sobbing uncontrollably.

"Here, let's go watch it again!" he said as he tried to activate the Nevergator again.

I called the sword to me, with demons and all. It was coming at him and he couldn't stop it. I decided to end the loop, I activated the Nevergator. I didn't care if he got stuck there, I'd be ready for him on the other side. I switched it back to a few seconds before Harry had died.

I exited the vortex as I caught the sword and struck him with a bolt of lightning across the void, not caring if I left him back in time. I appeared from the time-vortex just seconds before I first made the decision to use the Nevergator. I was just about to stop me, but Jesse was quicker and intervened. *Bel, I got this!* I heard his voice say as Jesse had shot the Nevergator, guiding Zatie to see me and the Gor-Nok as we were stuck in the time loop.

As everyone was waking up with the worst DeJa'Vu headache, I was the only one that knew what had just happened. The blast of the time shockwave had knocked them out. Jesse woke up first, quickly he checked on Zatie as she awoke. I told him to go fight the monster with Dominic. Zatie started setting up were-plants to guard the Diary. She put Baby cherubs close by with arrows. Meanwhile, I went to check on Derik and Harry as Jesse and Dom were fighting the beast. They both were in full-on were-beast mode.

Beast-mode Jesse was doing pretty good, he had been working his agility. He was strong, not very big, but a good fighter. He had a natural sense of déjà vu because of his Nightmares of time. He has a different kind of foresight because of this power. He was briefly reliving moments of the fight, seeing what could happen and living it too.

When I arrived, I found the crushed golem of the poor Harry. I told Zatie to go help Jesse while I repaired the golem and repaired Harry. I left them momentarily so I could get some hallowed ground by Michael's grave to heal them both. Harry wasn't waking I tried to resuscitate him same way I had done to Lu-Lu.

Every jolt of lightning was turning him more human. Derik was waking, but the fear-demon was attached to him still. I electrocuted the fear-demon, Derik woke momentarily. I continued to work on Harry. Derik was shellshocked trying to figure out what was going on. It was unnerving to watch my sister and brother fighting a monster and then look over to me beating on Harry's lifeless body. I was resuscitating him and was waiting for my hands to charge up, crying the entire time, begging him to live.

"Nonabel, what, what the hell is going on?!" I looked up at Derik with shock in my eyes. They were enraged with the Seer's Sight still.

"This is all a dream!" I said as I tried to hypnotize him. He fell and I caught him. I kissed him on the forehead, then teleported him out of there to his home, knocking him out with the good-bye kiss. As I returned, I noticed the sound of fighting had stopped. I saw that the Gor-Nok had succeeded in taking over Zatie and Jesse, by attaching fear-demons to them.

They began charging at me. I couldn't finish working on Harry. I teleported him out there and to the hospital. The Gor-Nok and the others were following me through the open vortex. I tried to get someone to help Harry. I grabbed the first nurse and pushed the thought that Harry was in a car accident. I had to leave poor Harry there as I tried to get the Gor-Nok to follow me back to the farm. Zatie and Jesse were chasing me through the halls too. I did what I could to fight them without hurting them. I teleported them back to the house, one by one and when I found the Gor-Nok, I hauled him through the vortex. I know he hated it, we fought in there at the snail's pace.

Magic moves slower in the vortex and he didn't know that. He also didn't know that the Abyss was full of monsters. At any rate, if I pushed him down to the bottom; they will try to drown him. The monsters of the Abyss tried to hold him as I pushed my way back up to the exit-point of the farm. I could save Jesse and Zatie, I do not know about Harry. I got back to the farm and they were fighting each other. I separated them with a thunderclap, and they turned on me.

While Zatie and I were fighting, Jesse was trying to go for the Diary. Jesse started fighting me when I teleported to stop him from touching the Diary. I had let them divide my attention, and Zatie's Plant-Beasts were destroying my barrier to get to the Diary. Zatie was opening a vortex for the Gor-Nok just as Jesse came at me. I electrocuted the demon on Jesse I went after the Gor-Nok as they were trying to get to the Diary.

The cherubim warriors were shooting arrows at them as

Zatie used trees to try to kill me. I took flight with my angel wings and called lightning down upon all of them trying to avoid the little cherubs. The cherubs, I teleported them back to where Jessie was now fighting Zatie. The Gor-Nok was trying to free the Diary from the Runes with spells and his club.

Jesse could see the fear-demon possessing Zatie. He moved quickly to evade her, but she shot tree roots from the ground, finally catching him. He found an arrow on the ground and stabbed it into the roots, freeing himself. She grew vines from her plants to trap him, but Jesse flicked the arrow at the demon, freeing her.

I blasted the Gor-Nok with a thunderclap and began to restore the Circle before he could recover. Dominic joined Jesse and Zatie as they hammered down on the beast. They were succeeding in defending me, while dodging, and destroying his attempts to attack.

Zatie summoned her angels to let loose a volley of arrows down upon the Gor-Nok. The arrows hit their mark, overwhelming him with emotional pain, crippling him. Zatie was enraged and caused the roots to come up to capture him. They began to pull him underground.

Before he was completely pulled underground, he reverted back into a man. The vines constricted tighter, and tighter. She did it, Zatie had buried him!

"You did it, Z!" I exclaimed.

"I know, right?!" She clapped and bounced. The ground swelled and grew where she had buried him.

"Stay back!" I ordered as we readied ourselves. The Gor-Nok used his full size as the were-boar to bust free of the vines. He used individual fear demons with claws and teeth, spinning them like smaller sawblades to cut Zatie's tree limbs. He blew fear gas from his mouth and claps two stones together to ignite the toxic gas. It created a fiery breath to burn the plants and Zatie's mental connections with them. Causing Zatie to collapse on the ground under the strain. He placed a fear demon on her head and charged toward Jesse.

I told Jesse to keep the Gor-Nok away from Zatie. I landed by Zatie and blasted her with the bold lightning killing the fear demon. While I was distracted with healing Zatie, the Gor-Nok had thrown Jesse flying at me, knocking me to the ground. When I got up, he had Zatie and Jesse under his control, again.

"Let's try this again!" he said. "How many more people need to die before you'll give in and give me the book?!"

Entry #19

The Price of Power

"Give me the book!" He squealed again in anger. I held the Diary closer. He tightened his psychic strangle hold on my struggling siblings. Their cries of fear and agony echoing through my soul. My mind was racing for an answer, another trick to save the day. I was out of ideas, everything else had failed.

"Don't give it to him!" Zatie screamed in defiance. She was gaining control of herself and summoned were-trees to her aide. They came to save her, and the Gor-Nok ignored their approach. They grabbed Zatie and slammed her to the ground. The roots began to crush her, burying her mouth and part of her body into the ground. Jesse was mad, crying now, seeing his twin sister in pain and being powerless. They were dying, he was going to kill them to get what he wants. I cannot stop him.

The Gor-Nok had exerted what remaining power of mind control over me and caused me to take a step forward. Fear was consuming my will to fight. He was winning, and he knew it. I was moving too slow for his liking, so he activated more control by using my powers against me. His demon-filled fear-fog was all around me, infecting me.

The Gor-Nok had his fear demons poke and prod me to edge closer. They actual stung me with lightning to move me. As I got shocked, the Diary fell to the ground and me with it. The Diary flopped open to a page of when the twins were born. Their pain and cries were mingling with mine as I laid on the ground. I glanced up at the Diary. I saw the passage, not really reading, just looking at their faces in the photo.

They were so innocent, so pure, and naive. I looked back up at them by the Gor-Nok. He was screaming his orders for me to get up. I looked back at the Diary passage, the words were smudged, blurry, it was just hard to read. Or was this only a dream?!

I tried not to think about it, but I needed to know, I had to test my theory. I decided to test it by causing a storm to brew nearby. I closed the Diary and limped my way closer. The storm got closer and the monster rejoiced in the fear he sensed in me. I tried to help Zatie by loosening the roots, lessening the pain. All the while whispering to her the thought to *keep up the act, you are in pain.* I did the same with Jesse, he reacted so amateurly, it was almost laughable. It was hard to keep up with the pain if it wasn't for the actual pain. The beast suspected nothing.

Realizing it was a dream, I amplified my powers to thwart his efforts, robbing him of his powers. He was growing impatient as I slowly limped toward him with the Diary. He wanted to rain down lightning, to scare me into moving faster. I knew his thoughts. He slammed his club on the ground as he thought it. I let the storm obey, my storm. I flinched with each bolt like I was worried about the Diary, but not entirely concerned for myself.

I was standing there with the Diary, He held out his hand.

"Good witch, now give it to me!" he demanded.

"Over my cold, dead body! Run!!" I screamed. "Rrraghc-ckKK!!!" he squealed in rage as he swung his club into my spot, missing me as I vanished.

The Gor-Nok fell into the mud as he over compensated to crush me. He got up from being in the mud on his face. He was scared as he witnessed me restoring everything that was destroyed. I reverted everything back to reality. Waking all of them up when I was done at the end. It only confused them to fight this battle again. The Gor-Nok woke up still having possession of Derik's and Harry's minds at this point. I was re-lieved that Harry was still alive but regretted that he was still under the monster's control.

The Gor-Nok was in human form, definitely uncertain of reality. I knew I had screwed up by giving up my best trick, we had showed all our cards too soon. Everyone was confused and in shock. The Gor-Nok was waking Harry and Derik before I appeared out of a vortex with the Diary, Jesse, Zatie and Dom-inic behind me. The twins were ready in all-out battle mode, fully displaying their powers in front of Derik.

"Bel, what is happening?!" Derik was asking before the Gor-Nok sealed his mouth shut. He still controlled them, and we were back to square one.

"Let's try this yet again!" The Gor-Nok was holding them

both by the throats, "I want you to choose, between love and fear! Who will live knowing that you don't love them, who will watch you cry over the death of another?!"

My storms of rage were looming around us. I thought to Zatie and Jesse to *Run* when I attack.

Harry told me, "Don't give him the satisfaction! Take it from him," he strangled Harry tighter.

"Quiet! I will make her watch as you breathe your last breath, snake!" The Gor-Nok shouted in his face.

"We can take him, Nona!" Jesse assured me.

Be ready you two! "We can do it, and he knows it!" I said as I extended my talons.

"Choose, the boyfriend or the Lover?" he said.

"She won't do it!" Harry hissed. "But I will," Harry stabbed himself in the heart with my clawed hand. And the Gor-Nok chuckled, as I fell to the ground with Harry's writhing body, my claws still in his chest.

Run! Jesse held Zatie back from attacking. *Run!* I thought to them again. My storm raged with the fury of my emotions. As the storm crashed around us, they barely made it away with the Diary as Dominic attacked the Gor-Nok. I had to break my talons off to free myself, leaving broken shards in Harry's heart.

Derik was muzzled, his flesh sealed across his mouth. He was terrified, crying and hyperventilating. I had no time to act, I had to choose who to save. The twins, Derik, or Harry? I needed to try to save Harry, but Derik could forget this whole nightmare if he was gone. I freed him from his binds and kissed him good-bye as I put him to sleep. I teleported Derik's sleeping body to his front yard.

When I returned, I tried to heal Harry. But just like Michael, he had fragments of my claws infecting him. I pulled my fragments painfully from him and hopefully the venom with it. We teleported to the hospital; I hypnotically commanded the healthcare workers to save him, knowing he was probably going to die. I kissed him one last time before returning to the battle at the farm. *Good-bye Harry.*

The Gor-Nok had chased the twins and the Diary into the forest. He tried to use the trees to terrify them, to turn them against the twins. He filled the forest with a dense fog of fear. We got separated and we got infected by the gas. Either way it was difficult to trust your own eyes, your own thoughts. I told my siblings in their mind, spoke to their hearts, to close their eyes, to not trust what they see. They should only see darkness, anything they see with their eyes closed is a lie. I told them to trust your other instincts, your other feelings, other senses, to stay where there were.

I told them to stay, that I would come to them. I would only speak to their mind. They should not trust anything that they see; even if it's me. Unless I'm speaking to their mind *like I am now.*

I tried to calm them, I tried to give them confidence that we could succeed. I told them to try to feel their way around them. *Try to find someplace safe, like a tree or a rock and stay there.* I told them that they are going to act out of fear, the toxins the Gor-Nok creates, *his fear toxins infect our minds.*

After few minutes of exposure, you just can't trust what you see or hear. But if you block it out of your mind, find a nice quiet place in your thoughts, trusting only what you can feel, the other senses. *You'll want to see, view what is going on, but don't!*

It seemed to only affect your hearing and your visual, which will get your heart rate up. Boost your adrenaline. *The way to overcome him is to be calm. Be confident. Trust in me, trust in your training.* I could hear them screaming for me to help them.

I asked Zatie in my mind, *did you just scream?*

She thought back to me, *Nonabel, no. I'm not screaming. That's not me!*

OK so that means he's to the north of me. Jesse, what about you, are you making any noise? I hear you shouting, 'don't hurt her' is that you Jesse?

No, I'm not saying that!

Jesse, you have to say my name first for you to think it ONLY to me. I could hear a commotion in the forest but couldn't pinpoint it. *Keep quiet!*

Nonabel, he's coming! I can hear him.

Think about Dominic, call for Dominic to come to you. Dominic, while he lives in the forest, his mission is to protect the family.

Dominic knows he's your family. Call to Dominic. I could hear Jesse's thoughts; he was trying his best to call Dominic. I could feel Dominic coming closer. I projected that he should find Jesse. Dominic obeyed.

Zatie, can you feel your trees? Can you feel the plants around you? Reach into the ground and feel the trees, that's your power! I thought to my sister.

Nonabel, what am I feeling for?

*Zatie, feel for their life, their pulse, their energy. Zatie, project to them the thought to Stay still, to hold against the wind, to not make a sound. That should help you to hear the **Gor-Nok** walking around.*

Got it boss! Nonabel, shouldn't we also avoid saying or thinking his name? Zatie asked

Yup! Think something else.

*Ok, then why are **you** thinking his name?*

I want him to hear me, the Gor-Nok to find me. I'll give him something to fear.

I transformed into my murder of crows and rose up above the cloud of fear. I 'cawed' wildly to distract him.

Zatie, do you hear my birds?

Nonabel, yeah, I can hear you.

Let me know when you hear one close to you. I don't know if I can trust what I see yet, I thought to her.

Nonabel, aren't you scared?!

I am, Zatie baby, I'm absolutely terrified but I don't have time

to worry about that anymore. I've got to get you guys to safety. I've got to end this as soon as I can. Zatie I see trees moving. Is that you?

Nonabel, none of the trees should be moving. They should all be still.

I think I see him; I think I see the Gor-Nok.

When I thought his name, a saw blade of fear came by, missing me a few inches from my face. It had come from among the trees towards my cloud of birds. We teleported back down towards the ground and appeared as the Harpy; fanning the fog with my wings before I landed. I manifested swords from my feathers and kept my eyes closed; trying to not trust what my birds' eyes could see, but only what I could feel.

Why don't we just use lightning?

Lightning, my dear Zatie? Lightning may ignite the trees, it might ignite the fog, which I know is flammable or it may hit one of you.

Wait I hear one?!

Zatie, remember to say my name. Don't give up your location. Nonabel, I hear a crow. Zatie, are you by a rock? Zatie, raise your hand up, if that's you.

I gathered some birds together and became part of a harpy at least a pair of wings. I had wrapped myself around her and lifted her out of the fog and teleported her to safety. Zatie, concentrate on Jesse; give him instructions. Don't break protocol, always use his name. I'm going back in!

I teleported my crows to the forest and kept circling for Jesse. I heard him screaming, "Oh God, no! Nonabel, he's found me!"

There were trees being torn apart, rocks being tossed, boulders being thrown, smashed. Jesse was that you? Jesse answer! Zatie can you feel him?

Nonabel, I can't feel him! Zatie, I'm gonna have to trust this vision of what I'm seeing is true. I'm going in! As I hovered closer, trees were scattered, the fog parted, revealing Jesse's crumpled body. *Zatie, your trees and Dominic are defending him against the Gor-Nok.* Dominic and I fought the Gor-Nok back.

I was using my sword feathers against the Gor-Nok's club. He shattered the swords into glass. I had activated my talons of death and clawed away at him. Dominic was relentless biting and clawing at the Gor-Nok's tough hide, inflicting pain with every blow.

While Dominic was distracting the Gor-Nok, I went to check on Jesse. I woke him up, he was terrified.

"Bel, what are you saying," he asked me if this was real. He covered his eyes still.

I said, "Oh yeah, this is real. I'm gonna send you back to Zatie. Hold your breath!" I opened the vortex.

With terror in his eyes, he screamed, "No, watch out!" He moved me out of the way as Dominic's body slammed him into the tree behind us. Dominic woke up and lunged at the Gor-Nok.

I told Jesse, "Quick, get into the vortex! I'll be right behind you." He slipped through, and the Gor-Nok hit Dominic in the face, then he swung at me.

With his other hand holding the club, bashing into the tree behind us, he grabbed me, by the hair and shoved Dominic's head into the vortex, trying to drown him in the black water. I pulled Dominic's body through by creating a larger vortex underneath him.

The soul-sucking black hole was pulling in the ground and the trees in around us. We came out the other side of the threshold in the vortex; fighting each other, struggling for dominance, fighting to get out of the exit-point. I thought to Dominic to, *swim towards it. Go protect the grandbabies!* He tried to swim away toward the exit. I dodged a blow from the Gor-Nok, all our movements were severely slow in the dark-water.

The Gor-Nok caught Dominic by the tail and pulled him back. I blew Dragon's breath at the Gor-Nok's arms and he backhanded me in the face. I fell off the floating island of the dirt and rocks and trees that I pulled into the vortex and started drifting down to the abyss. I was fully unaware of what he was doing to Dominic or what Dominic was doing to him. I woke still in the vortex gasping for air instinctively, forgetting that you're not drowning or breathing; it's just uncomfortable.

I started to pull away from the abyss, but the dark monsters were grasping at my ankles. I created my talons and clawed my way through, and rose up towards the exit-point, hoping that Dominic had gotten away. I didn't see him. I didn't see the island. They must have disappeared. I swam to the exit-point, coming out on the other side as the rocks and trees just settled seconds before me, the trees were falling over nearby.

Zatie and Jesse were screaming, crying over Dominic's crumpled body a few feet in front of them; but not being able to reach him. The Gor-Nok had smashed Dominic with a rock the size of a car. He held Zatie and Jesse at bay with fear demons in front of them. All they could do is cry in terror, watching yet another love one die in front of them.

I raged in my anguish and released the twins with precision bolts of lightning, frying the fear demons that had stopped them. We all released hell on earth upon this monster. Full powered hatred fueled our blind fury.

Jesse had turn back into the were-rabbit and was quicker, faster; more agile, stronger than he would be as a man. He pommeled the beast with precision until the Gor-Nok released a whirlwind of fear, paralyzing Jesse again. Zatie and I were fighting off the fear demons that had taken possession of Zatie were-plants who were attacking the Diary. They were pounding on the Runes and the protective barrier that Zatie had set up. They were trying to grow roots underneath. Zatie and I fought them back, as she tried to cause them to revert back to plants form from monsters, but she no longer had control over them. Were-demons were controlling them, we tried to use other magic, other offensive means to stop them.

Zatie had called upon her cherubic-angels-babies with those arrows to help her. She bowed, they gave her a bow and arrow for her to use. They began firing upon the fear demons with Zatie. I flanked the other side and sent my were-rooks out, each with the capacity to electrocute the demons. An army of fear demons were encircling the runes, all trying to work their way through the barrier. It was a strange battle of Nixes versus Nixes.

Jesse was physically holding his own very well with the Gor-Nok and learning all the while as well. He had tied his shirt around his eyes to blind his vision. The Gor-Nok kept taking hold of his rabbit ears from time to time and would use that against him. Flinging him back and forth, beating him into the ground or nearby trees. Jesse learned quickly how to phase back into a human to get out of harm's way, out of the Gor-Nok's death grip.

Every once in a while; Jesse got in a few good blows; he got in a couple rabbit kicks to the face of the Gor-Nok. I could communicate with him as they fought.

Jesse, try magic against him! He only had a few tricks! He will use his fear breath, which he knows now that we know it is flammable. I told Jesse to use the dragon's breath spell to fight against the fear gas. His version of the banshee cry is his pig squeal, which conjured insanity, conjured physical pain and emotional anguish. Which had more effect on Jesse because of his large rabbit ears. I told him to teleport to avoid it. I was coaching Jesse, trying to keep an eye on him while helping Zatie fight the fear demons to protect the Diary.

Jesse tried to avoid the Gor-Nok, but he was outsmarted when he teleported, and was caught by his foot before he could vanish. The Gor-Nok slammed him against a tree trunk then pulled him down to the ground. He crushed Jesse's rabbit leg against the rocks. Jesse's screams were so loud both audibly and psychically.

Zatie and I were floored and crippled by Jesse's outcry of agony. The Gor-Nok was loving this, he gained strength from our pain. I could visibly see him absorbing our fear with the Seer's Sight. I fought through the pain to come to Jesse's aid. I teleported to his last location, but he was gone.

The Gor-Nok was hiding him in the fear fog.

"Where is he, give me my brother!?" I gasped and coughed sucking in a lung full of bile.

"Give me the book!" he whispered.

"You know I won't!" I scanned through the dense fog with the Sight.

"When will you? Who else needs to die?" he said.

I couldn't see them; I couldn't *feel* Jesse anymore.

"No, no you didn't?! Jesse..." I was crying miserably on my knees, no longer feeling my brother's presence in my heart.

"You can't feel him, hmm? What about your sister, can you feel her?" I freaked out at his question because I *could not* feel Zatie either. I appeared at the Circle of Runes, at the Diary, to find trees swatting cherubs to the ground by Zatie's crumpled body.

I collapsed in a pile just short of her and cried out the last ounce of my soul. Zatie was the last remaining shred of happiness in my life. She was my heart, the only thing left of my life that was good. The Gor-Nok was somewhere laughing over his victory, gloating over my defeat.

My descent into darkness was complete, I drowned in my sorrows, to a lower level of a living hell. I was almost certain of my failure. I could not lose her, I had to try, or give my life trying. I reached out to her broken body, hoping I could still save her. I was fearful of finally touching her because the cold truth of feeling her lifeless body would be revealed. I would lose my faith in the power to save her completely. I hesitated and pulled back my hand.

I remembered a Spell, probably the last one that Zatie

had shared with me. It was a Spell to help us reveal the truth as a way for her to have a form of the Seer's Sight, called 'Alakazam.' I whispered out the word still worried to actually know the truth, know if she was dead.

As I spoke the spell, it revealed that her broken body was an illusion of fear. I gasped at the truth; it filled my soul again with panic not knowing where she was or if she was alive.

The Gor-Nok laughed and mockingly clapped as he exited the forest as a man. I brandished my claws and screamed my demands for my family.

"Give them back to me!"

"Oh, my dear little witch. They are fine, they are alive," he manifested them at his side, holding Jesse and Zatie as hostages. They were on their knees with fear demons restraining them with pain. "No other life needs to be taken because of your selfishness."

Dominic gave his life protecting me and protecting the family; just as Harry gave his life, I cannot allow someone else to die for my mistakes. My family was at stake. I removed the protective runes from around the Diary. I unconsciously caused the storm that was looming above it all, to churn, reflecting my pain, my rage. All that was left were Zatie's tree guardians and some cherubs. I motioned for them to stand-down.

The Gor-Nok demanded the book again, "Just give it to me girl, then you and your family can leave."

"How can I trust you?" I picked up the Diary and dusted it off. Uncertain of what was real anymore.

"Just leave me the book, leave me the Diary, leave me the Library, leave me all the power, the knowledge that you possess; and our quarrel will be over. Our fight throughout time will have ended," he assured me.

"You promise?" I asked hesitantly.

Zatie screamed at me, "No, Nonabel! Don't listen to him!" He squeezed on her head, he pulled up on her hair causing her to scream in pain.

"Oh, she will listen to me, as should you. She will give it up and I can see it. She has already decided."

"No, Bel! Don't do this! He's lying!" Jesse said, before the Gor-Nok could covered his mouth with his massive hands and breathed fear into his face; causing him to be tortured by his fears. He knew I would save them if I could, but I have lost enough.

"Which one will you save? Which will you choose? Will you watch your family die and we continue fighting until you die; or will you give it up?! Give up this pointless conflict! Give up your hate! Give up your vengeance; and come with me! All of you, and we can rule this world! With your power, your knowledge; Our powers, we can be unstoppable! Or you can leave it all here. Let me have it all and leave here to live normal lives. Death isn't the answer."

Death, I might be able to make a deal with Death; I thought as I slowly crossed the field to my family.

"Death?! Ha! You think that they are on your side. Ha. He has gladly accepted every soul you gave me because of your failures. You might be able to convince him to spare the life of your loved ones, or maybe bring back your lover; but I need to give him a gift, the exchange your powers. Join me and we may entice him to make a *new* deal. Without me, he will not reveal his presence to you as you die," he stated.

"What can I give Death that he hasn't already taken from me?!" I shouted back as pondered the idea.

"Your servitude. As his slave, it may give him what he needs to bring back your family, all of your family," the Gor-Nok explained.

"Isn't that what *you* want? All of us as slaves!" I replied.

"Is it not what *you* want, to have your family alive and well; free of all of this, this curse, of this conflict?!" He asked me. He had me, he had me convinced. He was right.

"That may be what I want. We could make this work, maybe we could make this deal," I said.

Zatie knew he was in my mind, none of these ideas were real suggestions. She tried to stop me.

"No, don't listen to him, Nonabel! No, don't listen, he lies. You can't bring back the dead!" he yanked on her hair to quiet her.

"Fine, fine, if you will not join me by choice; then I'll make the choice for you!" he said as he tightened his psychic grip upon my family. Jesse was writhing on the ground; he was trembling in fear and pain.

"They will continue to suffer but your sister is ready to die for this cause. Your brother is in so much pain that he just wants to die, he welcomes it!"

He summoned my sword psychically and had it pointed at Zatie's chest. "Your sister will not come back from this. If I do this, there is no coming back! Do you understand, witch?! No power on earth can undo this."

I saw his thoughts, he intended to kill her.

"Wait, please wait," I responded.

"No, Nona, don't!" Zatie coughed out. She wasn't ready to lose. I looked at her tear-soaked face.

"Listen, Zatie, I have to do this deal with Death."

I activated the storm above us, the Gor-Nok eyed my dark clouds. He suspected my lack of trust and decided to strike first. He used his club to summon lightning from my cloud, literally stealing my thunder and used it on Zatie. She collapsed to the ground crying, convulsing with the pain of the electricity. I opened the Diary to find something new to help, he was stealing my powers to use against me. I was frantically opening to different sections, stopping at a section of the genealogy, commemorating the day of the birth of the twins. I could read the passage; this was not a dream, but I had hoped that it was.

He read my thoughts, "No, this is not a dream. It is real! The pain is real. What your family is feeling is very real. Now make your choice! They will die unless I make it stop," he slowly started psychically plunging the sword into Zatie's chest. She was screaming for me.

There was nothing I could do to save her. The monster got stronger through fear, his curse towards Jesse increased. He transformed into the beast once more. Releasing fear demons as they began to tear out Jesse's flesh and soul. I screamed for him to stop, to beg him, "Please set them free?! I'll do anything!"

He beckoned for me to come, "Give me the book and I will set them free," he said. I got closer; I held the Diary out in front of me, I was shaking with fear and pain. I was hurting more because of my psychic connection with my siblings. It felt like a good idea making this deal with Death. He reached for the book.

"I'll make my own deal with Death!" I slammed the book shut and I dropped it to the ground. I called the sword, ripping it from his grip and plunged it into the Diary. The Gor-Nok screamed in rage as a giant bolt of lightning came crashing from the sky between us, burning the book. He shielded himself from the blast, still holding onto Zatie by the hair. The power of the lightning bolt burnt the book into the ground, causing Jesse, myself, the Gor-Nok and Zatie to be blown back from the depths of the epicenter.

"Why, why did you do that?! Your family has given their life to protect these secrets, to keep them from people like me. You will continue to give their lives to protect it!" The Gor-Nok called the sword then plunged it into Zatie's chest. Even though I could foresee this, I could still not bear to watch or hear her screams.

I channeled her pain in a bolt of lightning through me towards the Gor-Nok. The blast of the bolt separated him from my sister. I crawled over to Zatie's lifeless body. Pouring tears from my eyes over her face as I remove the sword from her chest. I felt her soul leave her body. There was no coming back from a blow like this. I looked at Jesse, the fear-demons had finished him off. He laid lifeless as well, torn to shreds, there was nothing left, nothing left to save. Nothing left to stop me from tearing the beast to shreds.

I activated my talons, I sent dozens of crows out of me, turning them into my own version of were-crow fear-demons and I waged full on war against my enemy.

The Gor-Nok was laughing at me as he blocked me blow after blow. Pitting demons against were-rooks. He battled tirelessly against me, his rage and hate fighting against me. I used the magnetic powers of the sword to magnify my electricity, creating combinations of vortex, lightning, and electromagnetic energy; manifesting baby black holes, sucking in anything in its way.

As we waged full on war against one another using magic and fear; I conjured more fear-demons of my own by mutating the corpses of the dead cherubim angels, transforming them into vicious little monsters. Their bows and arrows were producing the opposing power they once had of positive emotions to reflect my own deep darkness and despair.

I was in full dark-angel mode again, and I shot glass feathered knives from my wings into the beast. He overpowered me with the aid of our mental connection through my fears of losing this war. The Gor-Nok tried to frighten me by summoning lightning to strike me.

I chuckled as I brushed off the slightly ticklish bolts. I laughed as I informed the beast that this was my Nightmare Nix, not just a force of nature but a part of me, my soul. "I am no longer afraid of what I am!"

The Gor-Nok tried to run away but I reappeared through a barrage of lightning bolts inches in front of him as I grabbed him by the throat. I breathed out a lung full of fear, using his own fear spell against him to sense *his* nightmares. I could see his victims coming for him and I made the zombie remains of the farm animals rise from the ground to pull him down into a black chasm of pain.

I used the Alakazam spell to separate him for the evil that was the Gor-Nok. He was in pain now being torn apart from his power, his totem. As I sealed up the hole with my mind, the Gor-Nok and his host, the man, both pleaded with me to have mercy.

He summoned Zatie and Jesse's zombie bodies and said that he can restore them. "I can bring them back! Your Family. Your parents, I can bring them back too like you saved your grandfather. Wait! Please, You and I can end this war."

"How?!" I asked. He restored Zatie and Jesse to normal with his illusions, thinking that I was deceived.

"No, Nonabel! Listen to his cries, he's telling the truth!" I ignored his fake Zatie

"Tell me!" I screamed at him.

"If we go back through time to our battle in the jungle, where we first met. If we were to show ourselves that we can choose peace, appearing together, hand-in-hand, then we can end this," the Gor-Nok proposed.

"And you'll leave my family alone?" I asked.

"Yes, take my hand and I will leave you alone, forever. Here, as I a gift I will give back the souls of these two," he snapped his fingers, fully restoring the twins to life. He could tell that I didn't trust him still.

The Gor-Nok showed me his deal with Death, the moment when he had died. The moment when I had killed him and the deal he had made.

"I will end this deal with Death to bring him your souls. I will serve you as a pupil, as a student, as your disciple. To learn your powers and I will change my deal with Death and give him less worthy souls," he showed me that he would take the souls of drug dealers, pedophiles and criminals. He showed me and him working side-by-side to fight evil and crime in the world.

"Ruling at my side, worshiping you as my Queen."

"Nona, STOP!! It's a trap!" Zatie was pleading with me hysterically as Jesse was holding her back.

Now that the Gor-Nok was sharing his dream and that we could share control of it we were both manipulating the world around us. Zatie kept pleading with me to not listen. I studied the vision, there with the Gor-Nok was Death collecting the souls of my loved ones. The Gor-Nok was given a shrunken-shriveled corpse by Death as his focuser, his amulet that he wore around his neck.

The chain around the necklace was a 'witch's ladder', a triple knot cord of string with a feather in each knot used for a magical charm to bring to past nightmares, misfortune, illness, or death to their enemies. I remember reading about it in the Diary, and now I know how it tethers him to this world.

I came out of the vision with a greater understanding of how to kill him. I was deeply tempted by his idea, thinking about this new deal with Death.

Zatie reminded me, "This is not who you are!" *He doesn't love you and he's not willing to die for you. That is what Mom and Dad did, that is what Grandpa did, that's what Lu-Lu did, and that's what we are willing to do to protect evil from gaining this power.*

"Nonabel, are you willing to die for love?" she asked me as she sobbed.

"Yes, my queen, will you die for our love?"

I was so torn between thoughts of love and power, trying to focus on what I wanted. Lost in a world of dreams and nightmares, knowing I had lost everything and not knowing who to trust, or if I could trust myself. *Focus.*

The Gor-Nok had no power over me, there was nothing he could do, not in this place, not in my world. I could take everything from him starting with the things he wanted most, my power. I called for my sword and envisioned plunging it into his necklace and through the Gor-Nok's throat without a second thought.

He tried to stop me, to take the sword to attack me with

it, but I caused his hand to burn at the touch. He went for his necklace for strength and most likely about to activate a spell. I lunged at him, knocking him to the ground and pushing against the sword in my hands; hoping to drive it through his necklace. Hoping to really destroy his tether to this world. *I hope this works*. Hope was all I had left.

I drove the sword through the necklace and into his throat. I summoned a bolt of lightning from the clouds then channeled it through me and into the sword, magnifying my power. The Gor-Nok's molecules and cells tried desperately to stay tethered to this world as the electricity and magic fought against each other.

I pushed the sword further, each of us pushing power through the other. I pushed my powers through the focusor, channeling all of my energy to banish him from this world; separating his totem and his will to live. Exerting every ounce of pain I could inflict upon his mind. Giving him a vision of this moment, of his death. It exploded in his mind and in reality, with a magnificent green fireball as fear demons tried desperately to escape from being burned as well; only to fizzle out in green flames on the ground.

The air around my lifeless body grew cold and still as though time and life itself had stopped. I worried that I had failed, that I had stopped time again, but then I felt him. All happiness was gone from the world, and only Death remained; somewhere clapping, mockingly.

I found my strength returning as I also found myself by the broken bodies of my siblings. In vain, I tried to revive them through resuscitation, yet nothing happened. I was most powerless in his world. I heard him chuckle as I tried to heal them. I cried and Death laughed.

I found the remains of the Diary, I attempted restore the Diary from the ashes with magic, it was slow and most painful. Death laughed. I finished it draining my energy again and called it to me. The pages were blank, I panicked, turning page after blank page, crying. Death laughed. I screamed in rage as he mocked me, and I said a few spells at once. I slammed the blank pages with my palms and poured out the depths of my souls. The words were flowing from my palms to the pages. Death was still, he wasn't laughing any more.

The Diary opened to the section on *death* and at that moment I could feel the cold breath of Death breathing down my neck. My goosebumps reacted to protect my fragile frame. I knew he was no longer hiding, my attempts to use power in his world got his attention. I screamed and flinched when I realized that Death himself was actually breathing down my neck and reading over my shoulder. He laughed and applauded at my success.

"My dearest Dark Angel, well done. I am most impressed. I was beginning to think *he* was never going to die," his voice had an eerie echo to it.

"But *you* gave him life, made a deal to bring him back," I responded.

"And you ended him, twice! Congratulations my dear! Well, it is a pity that our deal could not be completed, because *you* survived," Death said.

"That was your deal?" I asked.

"Yes, for *you*, your soul. I gave him life so that he could end yours, have his revenge against *you*," Death stated while conjuring a ghostly vision of the past, to play out in front of us.

"This was all about getting to me, then what about...?" I started to ask, but he interrupted.

"The others? Collateral damage as they say, wrong place at the wrong time."

"You mean that they didn't *need* to die?!"

"No, Heavens no! He just wanted you."

"Then take me!" I held my hand out to him.

"What?!" His voice was much more than an echo now. He seemed more solid.

"Yes, my life for theirs, take me and bring back my family," I offered myself to Death.

"What, why?! You defeated him, you won!" "Won?! I lost everything I loved! No, I made all of these mistakes; my family shouldn't pay the price for my sins!" I responded.

"Sins, eh? Are you sure this is how you want your journey to end?! There are countless possibilities for how your journey shall end!" He slammed his scythe against the ground casting vision after vision of the different ways for my life to end. Too many to count, but it was too late. I had made my choice.

"If you won't fix this, then I'll do it myself!" I painfully activated the Nevergator in my hand. It took a few attempts, but I got it to work. Death chuckled.

"Oh, shinny! What's that going to do, my dear?" Death wondered as he studied the device in my palm. He looked as though he wanted it.

"Help me fix past mistakes!" I stated.

"Or make more," he argued.

"You have a better idea?!" I continued dialing back the years, looking for a point that would change everything, fix my mistakes.

"I can only give you one," Death stated.

"What?! One idea?!" I asked.

"One soul. A life for a life. Your life for one of them," he manifested the ghosts of my dearly departed, all of them; even... no. *Not Harry?!*

"I am sorry about that one, my dear. They did their best and he fought the good fight, but some things are even beyond my power," Death explained.

"You monster! *You* took everything from me!!" It was agonizing to produce, but I managed to manifest my talons to use against him.

"LIES!! You know that it was you! You took everything

from yourself. All you!" Death screamed.

I felt like dying, I cried so much that I was out of tears. "Are you done yet?! Are you satisfied?! What more do you want of me?!" I asked him.

"Oh, my dear, Dark Angel. I want you! I want you to bring me more souls. The lost, the tortured, tormented devils like *this one* that dealt with me poorly. I want you to work for me. Tell you what, as a sign of good faith, I give thee back thy sister, Zatherine!" Death said as he waved his hand over Zatie's corpse.

Zatie wakes up gasping for air next to me.

"Consider her life as a signing bonus!" he said.
Zatie and I hugged together in disbelief, not knowing what was going to happen next, being at the mercy of Death.

"If my sister is a gift, then what is the deal that will get them all back?" I pleaded.

"Tsk, tsk my dear. Too greedy! Officially, I can only give you one life as part of my deal," he stated.

"Just one then," I clarified.

"One. Choose with caution," he warned me.

"Why, what is the caution?!" I asked.

"Nonabel, don't trust this guy. We can find a different solution. We can save them all," Zatie said.

"Not all can be saved, Zatherine. That is my caution. Choose the soul that *can* be saved," Death manifested a contract in the air that appear to be written in blood on dried skin, it reminded me of Lu-lu's will.

He plucked a black feather from my half-harpy arms and dipped it into my open wound for me to use to sign the deal and handed it to me.

"Wait, run this by me again," I said.

"Sign here, and add the person's name here, and when it is your turn to die, i.e. the end of your natural life-span; that you will gladly go with me in exchange for One soul," Death declared the terms and conditions.

"So, how do I 'work for you' then? How do I bring you more souls like the Gor-Nok? If I come looking for you, how do I contact you?" I replied.

"I will contact you, my Dark Angel. There's no need to look for me, I am always near," Death smiled.

I took the pen, knowing full-well that I would regret this. I looked to Zatie for her disapproving look.

"Don't look at me. You already made the choice. Just pick a good one, I support your decision." I quickly signed my name then wrote his name without a second thought. Death snapped his boney fingers and brought breath back to my brother, Jesse.

Death gave me a parting vision of my future by kissing me on the forehead. He vanished before Jesse could realize what had happened. We watched in awe as life returned to the farm. We combined our powers to return all that we had destroyed, back to normal.

We hosted a funeral for Harry for the public, he being as important as he was, to not just me and my family, but to countless others. His assistant, Charity, a paralegal form his law firm gave me a note as she left.

"You can call me anytime, Ms. Venatora," she half-hugged me around the shoulder as she walked away. I did not want to read the note, seeing that it was written by him, by Harry.

I just wanted to cry, to be alone in my misery. I was talking to Lucia's grave, Harry had a plot near her so that they could be together, even in death. It was gross, but cute at the same time. I spied the note, a little hoping it was a last confession of love and hope. Nope! The bastard left me everything, even his law firm.

"What a Jerk!" I muttered to myself.

"Who is a Jerk, Bel?" I let out a tiny screech when I heard a voice. I turned to see if he was standing there alive and well. It was wishful thinking.

"Oh, hi." Derik looked *so good* in a suit.

"Yeah, my dad made me wear it, he had a lot of respect for... Harry," Derik stated.

"Right, thanks for coming," I said.

"That's not why I came, Bel," Derik corrected me.

"Oh? Why?" I was worried about the answer.

"I woke up from the strangest dream the other day. Well, my dad had found me in my yard, shaking. Bel, please tell me it was a dream!" he pleaded.

I couldn't lie to him anymore, the hurt in his eyes was surreal. Fear was all over his once happy face.

He knows! "Yeah, I know. I can hear you in my head still. I relive it in my sleep, that beast. All of you! What are you?! Why did you hide this from me?"

"Everyone I love, dies, Derik," I was sobbing pathetically; I couldn't bear to hurt anymore; now this.

"Is that why you don't love *me*? Is that why you chose *him*? Why you chose to love him over me? Was it to...?" *Protect.* "Protect me. Right. Well, stop. Just Stop! Get outta my head and stay outta my life! I don't need your protection, or your friendship," Derik responded.

"Derik, please, let me explain. It's all a huge misunderstanding?" I was hoping to hypnotize him.

"Lies, all lies! We are done, Nonabel!"

I didn't even see him walk away, all I could see were tears and rain. I wanted to teleport away, but I came there for one other thing. I came to Lucia's grave not for comfort but to bring her home, to be with the real grave of her husband, Michael. I used my fresh pain to help me heal my broken life. I teleported Lucia with a snap of my fingers as I stood by her grave. The ground beneath the grave seemed to collapse as the coffin disappeared to be by Grandpa's grave by the pond at the house. I appeared by their graves and cried quietly to myself. I went back to my room when it got late. I found the Diary waiting on my bed. I read about Lucia's fears, and her nightmares. I opened to the last page of the Diary and I poured out my soul, my pain, as I began to write about *my* nightmares.

Entry #1

Revolver

What goes around, comes around: My worst nightmares had come true. No, the Gor-Nok hadn't returned. If he did, I would bind him to my servitude so that I can conquer my fears with his powers. Derik finding out my secret became my *new* nightmare as soon as I learned about my destiny to be a witch.

Well, it broke my heart at how ignorant Derik and his parents were, so I guess I'm single again. I wondered if Johnny was as closed minded as his dunce of a cousin. Derik started drinking more with Johnny than studying and they eventually had to repeat their senior year of high school. Derik's parents were furious, but Johnny's parents were dead, just like mine.

Except for them it wasn't a drunk driver; or a monster, it was something much worse…

Acknowledgement

The Author would like to also thank those who inspired him to dream. To his teachers that did not let him quit. To his parents that taught him how to make his dreams a reality. To the wise Sages, Prophets, Professors, Partners, and Pals who pushed him to pursue his dreams.

...and thanks be given to the dreamers.

About The Author

Luke R. Harris

What I learned from 20 years of procrastinating.

Thanks for taking the time to learn more about me as an author, & creator. I have created all of my life. I began my life creating works of art; paintings and drawings mostly. Sometimes I'll fall down a rabbit hole of creativity, the later be stuck at the bottom of a dried-up well of creativity.

I love telling stories, I do this to pass the time and to entertain others. I always have a movie idea playing out in my head. Often I want to unload the images in my mind through painting and writing. At a young age I would start sharing my stories with others. Some of my friends encouraged me to make these stories into movies. So I do what every self-respecting writer does; move to Hollywood.

Mostly I worked as a Carpenter but it was still Hollywood. I met some actors, read some scripts and started writing in that style. I let some friends read my first script, one was a professional editor for a production company. I know what you are thinking, "Did you get discovered? Did you sell your story?" No. I was rejected, criticized, even had my ideas stolen. But I didn't let that totally crush my hopes and dreams. I took their words under advisement. One suggestion was that I should rewrite my story as a Novel instead of a script. I was too visual.

It makes sense, I like art. When I write, I see the scene playing like a movie in my head. So I wrote.

20 years later, Life happened. Wife, kids and all, but never quit thinking about my stories. I almost gave up on art as well. Every now and then I would re-light the fire under my butt and finish my ideas. That's when I discovered a life lesson, give yourself a Dead-line. Have an End in Mind.

The Dead-line gives us a sense of obligation and urgency, even if it is a fictitious date, you are compelled to beat the clock. So do this first, create a count-down, a Dead-line to finish.

Getting out of your own way. As life happens, don't let it distract you from finishing your goals. You just need to control the one thing, the one person you have power over, YOU. Now tell them to get out of your way, or wait, stand-down, stand-aside while you finish your dreams.

Excuses kill creativity; STOP making them and start making your dreams a reality!

Books In This Series

The Dream Diaries

After the tragic death of her parents, a young girl named Nonabel is forced to live with their dying grandmother Lucia. Nonabel is gifted a mysterious family diary by Lucia on the night of her death. Before her foretold demise, Lucia reveals that it is a magic diary and that she is a witch. Skeptical, and curious, Nonabel explores the mysterious diary and gets hooked on the power of magic.

Through this power she discovers a world from her dreams and nightmares. Nonabel learns secrets from beyond the grave as she tries to unravel the mystery of her grandmother's suspicious death at the hands of an unknown killer.

Nonabel finds that this killer uses his victims fears and nightmares as weapons against them. She tries to battle this murderous monster across space and time using magic learned through a homeschool process of trail, and error. She realizes that she cannot fight this monster on her own and enlist the help of family and friends to stop it and avenge the death of her parents.

The tragedies and mysteries will unfold as Nonabel and her family fight the evils that plague our world. Evils that hide under our beds or lurk in the corners of our mind. Join her through the on-going journey that will cross the borders of time and reality.

The Dream Diaries will take you on a journey that bends the rules of your imagination and may haunt your nightmares.

Nightmares

Take a magical adventure with Nonabel the Witch and her band of Dreamers as they fight Nightmare Monsters.

Join her through the on-going journey that will cross the borders of time and reality.

The Dream Diaries will take you on a journey that bends the rules of your imagination and may haunt your nightmares.

Revolver

What goes around comes around...

Continuing adventures of Nonabel the Witch and her band of Dreamers as they fight Nightmare Monsters.

The Dream Diaries will take you on a journey that bends the rules of your imagination and may haunt your nightmares.

No Fate

We all have demons that we hide from the ones we love, sometimes it is hard to tell the difference...

Continuing adventures of Nonabel the Witch and her band of Dreamers as they fight Nightmare Monsters.

The Dream Diaries will take you on a journey that bends the rules of your imagination and may haunt your nightmares.

Hunter

The line between Hunter and prey becomes blurry when vengence clouds your sight...

Continuing adventures of Nonabel the Witch and her band of

Dreamers as they fight Nightmare Monsters.

The Dream Diaries will take you on a journey that bends the rules of your imagination and may haunt your nightmares.

Nevermore

Never start a fight you can't finish...

Continuing adventures of Nonabel the Witch and her band of Dreamers as they fight Nightmare Monsters.

The Dream Diaries will take you on a journey that bends the rules of your imagination and may haunt your nightmares.

Victims

SPOILER ALERT!! Everyone dies in the end!

Continuing adventures of Nonabel the Witch and her band of Dreamers as they fight Nightmare Monsters.

The Dream Diaries will take you on a journey that bends the rules of your imagination and may haunt your nightmares.

Redemption

The Final entry of the epic Dream Diaries Series...

Continuing adventures of Nonabel the Witch and her band of Dreamers as they fight Nightmare Monsters.

The Dream Diaries will take you on a journey that bends the rules of your imagination and may haunt your nightmares.

Made in the USA
Columbia, SC
13 February 2023

11931062R00295